IN THE DARK HOURS
BEFORE DAWN
TERESA'S DREAM BEGAN.

She could hear the squeak of wagon wheels on hard gravel and the sound of his voice as he spoke to Yves. But still she could not make her senses awaken enough to rise and greet him. Then she felt his presence filling the room. She felt the weight of his body tilt the mattress as he sat on its edge, then spring back as he crawled beneath the sheets and molded himself to her form. . . .

She moaned and rolled to greet him then. His hands became rough and demanding. Instantly she awakened, alarmed. Frantically she began to push away the man who had been so familiar in her dream world but was so utterly foreign to her in the world of reality. . . . He was the one man she could never have. The one man who would never let her go!

ROSE
of fury,
ROSE
of flame

Jeanne Sommers

A DELL/BRYANS BOOK

Published by
Dell Publishing Co., Inc.
1 Dag Hammarskjold Plaza
New York, New York 10017

Dell ® TM 681510, Dell Publishing Co., Inc.

ISBN: 0-440-17589-5

Printed in the United States of America

1991 EDITION
LEISURE ENTERTAINMENT SERVICE CO., INC.

ROSE
of fury,
ROSE
of flame

PROLOGUE

The small, darkly handsome man stretched contentedly in the cooling shade of the wide oak tree and drifted into a relaxing slumber. He dreamed of the ravishing beauty who was preparing herself for him in the nearby carpeted tent. His desire for her had been so consuming that it had caused him to do many foolish things. Too often circumstances and fate had thwarted him from possessing her entirely. This time there was nothing to stand in his way. Doña Teresa Maria de Alarcon Rosa was his prisoner. She would never escape him again, and he—General Antonio López de Santa Anna—would taste the bittersweet fruit of revenge. He would crush her patrician will in the same manner as he would crush the ragtag, puny Texan rebel army he had cornered here on the banks of the San Jacinto River. And once victorious—in love and war—he would not only be the president of the Republic of Mexico but be within reach of his ultimate dream: the emperor of a land mass that was only exceeded by the tsar's dominion over all the Russias. He was the conquistador ready to thrust these arrogant American frontiersmen from centuries-old Spanish and Mexican land.

But as he dreamed of the lovely Teresa and his glorious future in the world of monarchs, lowly men who had come to fight for new pioneering land were silently poking their way through the tall prairie grass and crouching down within twenty yards of a barricade of Mexican packsaddles and camp impedimenta, lying inert in the oblique rays of the April afternoon sun.

Almost too late they were seen. Behind the Mexican line a bugle shrilled. Soldiers groggily came awake from their

7

siestas. General Cos, Santa Anna's brother-in-law, slept on. Caro, the president's secretary, came scurrying to the oak tree.

Above the bright meadow of shimmering grass a powerful man astride a white stallion waved his hat in signal. A blast of horseshoes from twin cannons laid flat a section of the fragile barricade. The hidden infantrymen rose, loosed a volley of shot at the breastwork, and lunged forward, drawing their hunting knives and opening their throats with a vengeful chorus:

"Remember the Alamo! Remember the Alamo!"

Now there was no need for Caro to arouse the president. The cries and shooting brought Santa Anna to his feet in a single movement. A half-dozen strides brought him under the striped marquee and into the tent. Within two women sat elegantly gowned and bejeweled, although strangely serene and unabashedly unconcerned with the noise and confusion growing constantly outside the tent.

He glowered at them, turning his full intensity upon the taller of the two.

"You whore!" he bellowed. "I should have listened to the report of my spies."

Emilia Rosa Hoffman Morillo rose from the carved chair until her stature was equal to his. Her entire golden bronze face was accented by the Mona Lisa smirk playing at her mouth, while her Aztec black eyes danced with her mother's Mexican-Indian mischief and her German father's cool arrogance.

"If that is all they learned, señor," she said with gentle mockery, "then they are quite correct. I have never claimed to be anything other than a whore."

"You know of what I speak," he roared. "Can you deny that you know the Escovarro men?"

Emilia raised her fan and moved it back and forth slowly. The longer she kept Santa Anna from his troops, the better chance the Escovarro brothers had to help General Sam Houston defeat the man. "Really," she said with a light laugh, "you are aware that I have known many men."

"Bah!" he fumed, tearing off his uniform tunic and rummaging through his luggage. "I should have known something was amiss when you so readily agreed to come with me from San Antonio. I was warned, but that damn brother-in-law of mine put my fears to rest. Why would you open your bed to that dull, unattractive fool and not to me?"

His entire army was being devastated, and the man's only concern was his personal ego. It delighted Emilia, although she kept her face devoid of emotion. She looked at the man and thought of the one that was opposing him. Once she had done what she had vowed she would never do in life—she had fallen in love. It had been with the wrong man—Sam Houston—and he had spurned her. In her eyes they were one and the same, Houston and Santa Anna—power-hungry men who were capable only of self-love. She had not agreed to delay Santa Anna to give the winning edge to Sam Houston. Her concern was centered solely on three people: one whom she dearly loved with all her heart and soul, one whom she wanted to dearly love with all her heart and soul, and one whom she would rather disregard but was forced to accept because of the love of another for him.

They were, of course, in the order of her mind: Teresa, who in spite of her breeding and patrician Spanish background accepted Emilia for what she was. Miguel Escovarro de Sanchez was second, or perhaps first, as far as this battle was concerned.

Of pure Spanish ancestry, he had gone against tradition by giving his time and effort to support the rebels, become an aide to Sam Houston, and encourage other Spanish-Texans to do the same. On two separate occasions they had saved each other's lives. Now Emilia was unsure if it were love or admiration that she held for Miguel Escovarro. Her mind was a solid font of information on his younger brother, Felix. She positively did not like the man but was forced to abide him because of Teresa's passionate love for him. She felt that as long as she lived, she could never forgive him for impregnating Teresa with a child and then turning his back. Only a miscarriage had saved him from scandal. Emilia had been incensed when he was so quickly accepted back into Teresa's arms, but she was loath to speak out. No, on this day, she had to protect all three of these people.

"Is the question too embarrassing to answer?" Santa Anna demanded, putting on a simple jacket and forgetting that he was still in bedroom slippers.

A raucous laugh was her only reply.

Santa Anna spat at her in contempt and wheeled on the other woman. She sat calmly, no emotion showing on her beautiful face. Her hands, her gown, her posture, even the flow of her mantilla were as though she were sitting for her portrait. But when her velvet brown eyes came up to lock on his own, he seemed to shrivel and shrink back.

Damn those eyes, he thought. Why must they be so like her grandmother's haunting, accusing eyes; and when will I stop being haunted by the fact that I brought about the woman's death.

"You may think that your moment of rescue is at hand, Doña Teresa," he warned. "But I will have done with Houston in no time, and then we will settle our differences."

He ran from the tent and directly into a wave of panic-stricken soldiers.

"Idiots!" he screamed. "Don't stand in their line of fire. Lie down on the ground until they must reload."

He turned in every direction, aghast at the sudden carnage. Wherever his officers were falling, their men were scattering in sheer terror. Down the bank of the river a hundred of General Cos's best cavalry went charging madly. Inextricably the horses and men were swept away in the current, and within moments every man had perished. The Texans were pursuing, clubbing, knifing, shooting the Mexicans wherever they were found.

In the midst of the carnage Santa Anna vaulted on a black horse and disappeared.

It was all over in eighteen incredible minutes. General Cos's cavalry . . . the silver chamber pot . . . the striped marquee . . . the brightly decked dragoons . . . Caro's portable escritoire . . . the whole Mexican infantry of 1,150 men—gone forever.

The Escovarro brothers, looking like golden gods out of

a Norse myth, had slashed their way to the collapsed tent and defended it until the last musket was fired, the last knife flashed.

Out of his fear for her life, Felix Escovarro was grim-lipped and stern with Teresa.

"You damn little fool," he barked. "I thought I'd left you safely in San Felipe."

She smiled sheepishly. "I don't seem to be one who can stay out of harm's way."

"That is quite apparent," he said thinly. "Although I'm still at a loss to know how you got here."

"Foolishly," she laughed. "I didn't like you asking Emilia to decoy Santa Anna on her own, and so I got on board the riverboat to catch up with them." She shuddered. "I got caught. The Mexicans were trying to lasso the smokestacks, and I got roped and hauled into the water instead."

This really angered Felix. "And put yourself right back into that madman's hands. I'm amazed it didn't give away our whole scheme, and he didn't have you both shot right on the spot."

Emilia bristled. "He was unaware we knew each other, señor. As a matter of fact Teresa's misfortune did more to delay him than you are aware. He had believed the rumors of her death and thought he was pulling a ghost out of the water."

Miguel Escovarro chuckled. "She certainly doesn't look like a ghost now. Why all of this finery when he knew he was going to be doing battle this afternoon?"

Teresa blushed. It was left to Emilia to answer.

"In spite of my charms and abilities he hardly looked at me again after Teresa was captured. We determined you still needed time, so we convinced him that she was ready to forgive and forget. He was told to take a siesta until I had her properly dressed."

Felix scowled. "And what if we hadn't been ready to attack by then?"

Teresa flared. "I would have handled him, Felix Escovarro, in the same way I handled him in Saltillo until you came along in your make-believe priest's robe and falsely married me to the man. Do give me some credit for knowing how to take care of myself."

"Señorita, I, for one, give you more than credit," a booming voice said behind them. "I give you my deepest gratitude."

General Houston had been riding among the wreckage of the Mexican camp. He was on his third horse of the battle, and his right boot was full of blood that trickled down from his shattered knee.

Miguel was quick to act. "General, let me present Doña Teresa de Alarcon and, of course—"

"And of course," Houston cut him short, "you are well aware, Miguel, that I am already well acquainted with Amarilla Rosa." He swept off his hat and saluted her grandly. "Emilia, a hundred steady men could have wiped us out. How in the world did you ever hold him within the tent for so long?"

Emilia had not as yet looked up at the man, and when she did, it was like looking upon a total stranger. The rugged masculine face she had so desperately loved four years before had changed. His face was fuller, the cheeks beginning to sag, and the hair gray and thin. She had feared this moment ever since Felix had stolen into Santa Anna's camp at San Felipe and begged her to stay with the general and delay him on his march. She knew that would mean an eventual meeting with Sam Houston. She did not know how her heart would react. But she felt nothing, no emotion whatsoever. She even wondered now why she had fallen in love with him in the first place.

"I was unaware," she finally said, "that time was passing."

Houston roared. "Well, I was aware. Goddamn good job. How can I ever repay you?"

At last Emilia smiled, openly and genuinely. "I was already in your debt, señor, for having saved my life four years ago. We are now even."

Houston studied her intently, musing. "Four years? That long. Goddamn, woman, you are even more beautiful now than then. At this rate I would love to see what you will be like at forty."

Emilia only nodded at the compliment. She knew now that she didn't care whether she ever saw the man again.

Felix was growing concerned. "General, that leg looks bad. You'd better get off the horse and let us take a look at it."

Houston ignored him for a moment, his attention drawn away by some fierce screaming on the far side of the camp.

"Goddamn those bastards," he roared. "They've started to kill the prisoners. Miguel, spread the word that I want everyone captured alive now. Santa Anna has to be among them." Then he quickly raised his field glasses and told Miguel to stand fast.

Across the prairie a gray-clad column, marching with the style of veterans, headed toward the scene of the recent battle. After a long look he lowered the glasses with a thankful sigh.

"It's General Almonte. He's surrendering his entire four-hundred-man force in a body. There is no one else to fight."

And as he slid down from the horse, he fainted in Felix's arms. They put him by the oak tree that Santa Anna had slept beneath and slit open his pants leg. It wasn't his knee, it was worse. His right leg was shattered above the ankle. Miguel went to carry out his orders, and Felix hurried to find Dr. Ewing.

The sun was beginning to set, and the campfires were rekindled. Before it was fully dark, over seven hundred Mexicans sat huddled within the circle of flames, and more were being brought in. Each was checked to see if he was Santa Anna. The Texans were growing angry at not finding him.

"Goddamn, where is he?

"Goddamn if I know."

"Goddamn, if we don't find him, we'll pick ourselves one and tell Houston he's goddamn Santa Anna."

The Mexican officers who understood English began to pull off their shoulder straps against such a thing happening and spread the word.

"Goddamn" was also the first word Houston uttered

coming awake while Surgeon Ewing probed fragments of bone from the mangled flesh.

"Here," Ewing demanded, producing an ear of corn from his pack. "Bite down on this."

"Goddamn the pain in my leg," Houston growled. "I'll nibble on it to ease the hunger pain in my belly."

A kernel fell to the ground, and a soldier stooped to scoop it up.

"You that hungry, lad?" Houston demanded.

"Naw, jest thought I'd take it home and plant it. Somethin' growin' might make me remember if we don't get to execute that goddamn Santa Anna."

"Is that how the mood is running?"

The soldier nodded. "Soon as he's found, he's as good as hung."

Houston began to break off more kernels from the cob and pass them out to every soldier who came to check on his health. "My brave fellows," he told them, giving them kernels. "Take this along with you to your own fields, where I hope you may long cultivate the arts of peace as you have so ably mastered the art of war. We have seen the last of bloodshed in this war."

"We'll call it Houston corn," a genius suggested.

"Not Houston corn," he said gravely, "but San Jacinto corn."

"Goddamn good name," they agreed.

Then they all seemed to agree upon their next course of action. "Goddamn time we started getting drunk. Hell, we won!"

The Texans roistered all night to the terror of the prisoners who designated their captors by the only English words that were repeated enough for their bewildered senses to grasp. The Texans had been warned to make a wide berth around the two grand Spanish ladies, but no one had said a word about the forty-odd camp-following Mexican women and girls. One young girl was so fearful that she threw herself at the feet of a drunken Texan soldier.

"Señor, goddamn, do not rape me for the love of God and the life of my mother."

The tent and marquee were reraised within a few yards

of the tree under which Houston lay sleeping. His sleep finally came from a drug slyly given him by Dr. Ewing.

There was no sleep for the Escovarro brothers that night. As the only interpreters available to the Texan officers, they were hard pressed to be everywhere at once.

Emilia, who had been born and raised in a noisy brothel, had no trouble sleeping through the din of the carousing soldiers. It was not so for Teresa. It had been an extremely hot April day, and the evening produced no breeze. The humidity from the swamps was kept locked close to the ground, and the tent became suffocating. At last she could stand it no longer and went to sit outside in the shadow of the tent so that she would not be seen by the soldiers.

At first she paid no attention to the patrol of five men who rode into the camp with a prisoner. Mounted behind Joel Robison was a bedraggled little figure in a blue cotton smock and red felt slippers. The patrol had found him near the ruined Vince's Bayou bridge seated on a stump, the living picture of dejection. He had said he had found his ridiculous clothes in a deserted house. He looked hardly worth bothering to take the five miles to camp and would have been dispatched on the spot but for Robison, who was a good-hearted boy and spoke Spanish. Robison and his prisoner chatted on the ride.

"Am I one of many prisoners?"

"Less than eight hundred."

"Then tomorrow brings another battle?"

"I don't see how. About six hundred are dead and over two hundred wounded."

The man was sullenly silent.

"Do you have a family?"

"*Sí*, señor."

"Do you expect to see them again?"

The little Mexican shrugged his shoulders.

"Why did you come and fight us?" Robison wished to know.

"A private soldier, señor, has little choice in such matters."

Robison came into the camp nearest the tent and its line of campfires. A stout Christian man, he was violently opposed to the whoring and drinking that was going on. As a family man he thought the Mexican would feel the same.

"Stay up at this end of the camp, señor," he said as he let the man dismount from behind him. "It is quieter and will keep you out of harm. Tomorrow I shall look you up and see if we can't get you an early release to return to your family."

"God will bless you, my son," the Mexican said humbly.

Joel Robison saluted and took his patrol back out of the camp.

Teresa rose from the shadows and chuckled. "Whose god do you speak of, señor?" she asked.

Santa Anna peered into the darkness and blanched.

"Well," he said sourly, "from a moment of hope to a return of despair."

An expression of quiet triumph glowed on her face.

"Aren't you going to call the soldiers?"

She didn't answer. Her mind was a whirl of emotions. She sat back down on the padded gilt chair that had been until that night the exclusive property of the president of Mexico. Not knowing what else to do, Santa Anna pulled away the matching footstool and sat down facing her.

"It's odd," he said quietly. "I have become Napoleon to Houston's Wellington, but how shall we account for you? Are you held here as prisoner? Do you hope to expose my identity to secure your release?"

Teresa's eyes, looking down at him, were cool and remote. "Let someone else have your blood on their hands by exposing you."

He sighed. "I hardly think they would spill my blood."

Teresa didn't answer. Instead she sat there, daintily creasing the pleats of her dress, smiling softly and secretly to herself. Finally Santa Anna could stand it no longer.

"Well," he said hoarsely, "they wouldn't dare kill the president of another country. The whole world would rise up against them."

"Then you'd best prepare for the world rising up. That's all they can talk about: finding and executing you."

She saw his face darken.

"Then you must protect me," he gasped.

16

Teresa was incredulous. "Me, protect you! Even if I wanted to, which I don't, it would be out of my hands. At dawn you will be instantly recognized."

"By whom?" he demanded indignantly. "My officers and men will not betray me, ever. Besides you and Emilia Hoffman Morillo, no one knows my face. I may still be safe."

"I doubt it."

"Why is that?" he said grimly.

"There is another here who knows you very well."

"Who?" he snapped.

"Felix Escovarro."

He cursed and pounded on his knees. "I knew he didn't die in the Alamo, even though I had him trapped there. I would give anything to know how he escaped me."

Teresa laughed. "You have to give nothing, señor, I will gladly give you the information free, because you were responsible for it."

"Responsible?"

"Responsible," she echoed amusedly. "If a man can pose as a priest in Saltillo, why can't a man pose as a priest in San Antonio. I was one of the women who took food into the Alamo, and under my dress, to make me appear pregnant, was hidden priest's garb. You gave him enough time in Mexico to perfect his masquerade."

"You're in love with him," he said sharply and with total disbelief.

"Yes," she snapped. "If you had not been such a damn greedy fool, I never would have learned he was a false priest and our marriage a mockery. I would have gone with you to Veracruz and forced myself to love you. But, no, you had to take that little slut with you and palm her off as your wife. You forced me to fall in love with a priest, which I still thought he was until I returned to Texas. Now that I know he is free to love me, I shall never love another."

"Well," he laughed, "I think I begin to see the role you played, my dear. I was duped and set up for this defeat. My genuine congratulations."

Teresa shook her head. "My part was really all by accident. Emilia should be given the full credit."

17

Santa Anna's eyes flared. "More worms crawling out of the woodwork."

She saw no reason not to let him know all the truth.

"She was supposed to stall your march until Houston could prepare his army."

"I hardly understand," he muttered. "What would she hope to gain? She was more than a help to General Cos during his occupation of San Antonio and a perfect hostess to me."

"Did she have any other choice, in either case?"

"I still do not understand."

"Oh, Santa Anna," she exclaimed, "you are so blind at times. Miguel Escovarro is in love with her, and I think the feeling is mutual."

"So," he said sharply, "I was surrounded by traitors from the very first. Do you know how bitter that makes me feel? To have enemies, I can understand, but to have people that you loved and trusted and respected turn on you . . . bah!"

"That you loved," she repeated softly. "I think you are totally incapable of the feeling. You only know how to take and bully and command. To you, all women are whores, is that not so?"

He sat up straight and stared at her.

"Except for one!" he growled. "I wanted you so badly that I resorted to trickery and then I became afraid of you. Do you know what it is like to desire someone so much and not be able to have her?"

"Yes, because you taught me that feeling by turning Felix into a false priest."

He was silent for a long moment. "I will never let you go, Teresa. I can still get a divorce from my wife. I can still make you the wife of the president of Mexico. Let me make up to you for everything I've done in the past."

"You had best see what your future is before you start making rash promises. These Texans are not exactly happy with anyone of Spanish origin after what happened at the Alamo."

He did not want to think of that ugly massacre and how it might affect him. "There will always be a Santa Anna," he boasted. "And to prove it, I wish to give you something."

"I want nothing from you, señor," she said coldly.

"It is of no value," he said, digging into his pants pocket. "It is a part of me since a little boy. My mother presented it to me before I went to school in Spain. It was to remind me to come home again. I wish you to have it to remind you of this land after the Texans have pushed us all out and it is ours no longer."

She tried to resist, but he firmly opened her hand and laid the object on her hand.

The rough little reddish stone had a velvety warmth that amazed her. "What is it?"

"Nothing more than a piece of gypsum crystal that is quite commonly found in our southwestern regions. Just a piece of home."

"It looks just like a rose."

"Aha, it is! A desert rose! A piece of rock that has been naturally sculpted by the elements to resemble a perfect rose blossom."

Before she could refuse again, he quickly got up and stalked away. To call out to him would immediately expose him. She had a thousand good reasons to seek revenge against the man, but that was not in the nature of her character. She was sure that he couldn't go unmasked for long. She closed her eyes and felt the desert rose. She was not as superstitious as her grandmother had been but was well aware of the ancient Spanish adage that a gift from an enemy, honestly given, would eventually bring good luck and fortune.

Robison kept his word the next morning and was taking the polite little fellow to a place where he might be released when the other captives began to raise their hats and shout: *El Presidente! El Presidente!*

Teresa had been quite correct.

But Santa Anna was even more correct in his appraisal of the Texans. In spite of the fact they had fought the same battles, the Escovarro brothers were bitterly surprised to learn that the new constitution would do away with all former land grants from Spain and Mexico. What had been theirs for three hundred years seemed suddenly doomed. They left the camp with Teresa and Emilia as though they were the defeated.

"We would have done better siding with Santa Anna," Felix growled. "Then, at least, we would have stood a chance for new land grants in California or New Mexico. Houston has won everything."

"Oh, has he now," Teresa flared, sounding so much like his Tía Patricia that he blanched. "It's going to take months for these political idiots to even find a proper way to let Santa Anna return gracefully to Mexico. Months longer for them to decide if they want a republic or statehood under the United States. In the meantime there are a lot of men waiting to learn what you and your brother are going to do about running the *ranchero*. To hell with these damn Anglos! Let them come and force us off the Escovarro land. It's time you stopped being such a goody-goody priest and started being the man that . . ."

She never finished. He leaned from his saddle, his mouth buried on hers, crushing her to him.

Miguel chuckled. "Looks like there really is going to be a wedding in the family."

Emilia didn't answer. She was wondering if she were really woman enough to make it two marriages.

CHAPTER ONE

The refusal by Father Montclava to marry Emilia Rosa Hoffman Morillo in the church of San Antonio de Valero riled the Irish anger of Doña Patricia Escovarro. It was to have been a double ceremony, the old woman's two nephews, Miguel and Felix Escovarro de Sanchez, marrying Emilia and Doña Teresa Maria de Alarcon Rosa. The quartet had shared many adventures in their young lives and refused to be separated for this special occasion, although Emilia secretly tried to persuade Teresa to go ahead with a church service for herself and Felix.

Doña Patricia, the daughter of an Irish potato farmer who had married well after emigrating to the Mexican *Tejas* area via America, was not about to give in to her old friend. Having become more Spanish than the priest himself, she browbeat him into a compromise: he would perform the double ceremony but not within the church.

Doña Patricia's puckish nature than came to the forefront. The service and reception would be held in the fashionable hacienda and garden of Emilia Hoffman on the Calle de los Pantalones.

The patrician families of Santa Fe, having filtered back to their homes following the defeat of the Mexican army at San Jacinto, were aghast at Doña Patricia's temerity but still clamored for invitations. For different reasons the men and women wanted to see the interior of the Villa Amarilla Rosa. The house of the "yellow rose" was almost as legendary as was its owner. It had nightly been the place of recreation for General Martin Cos and his officers during the siege of the city, and no less a person than the president of Mexico, General Antonio López de Santa Anna, had used it as his private residence while preparing for the battle of the Alamo. It was also the owner they wished to gaze upon, as well as her finery.

A month before, they would have averted their eyes from her proud, golden face, spitting in the dust after her carriage and muttering "whore." Now she was somewhat of a celebrity, having delayed Santa Anna so that General Sam Houston and his Texans could meet and defeat the Mexican. Now she was about to marry the scion of the Escovarro family, one of the largest landholders in the republic. Now they would have to have quite different thoughts about the "half-breed" woman they had snickeringly called "the yellow rose of passion."

There were just as many people curious to see the other bride-to-be. Although many of them had known Teresa de Alarcon for all of her twenty-two years, they had believed her to be the bride of General Santa Anna for the past three years. They were still unsure of how he could have faked such a marriage for such a length of time, but the nickname given to Teresa by the Mexican soldiers, "blanca rosa," led the wiser women to nod and comment that a "white rose" had to be an unsullied rose from an unconsummated marriage.

There were those, also, who would attend out of respect to the de Alarcon name. Teresa was now an orphan, and they would try to be family to her, although she had been less than cordial on her return to San Antonio after the war. They suspected that the suicide of Doña Helena de Alarcon still upset her. It did, but not in the way they suspected. Teresa fully blamed her mother for the death of Carlos Juarez and the baby she had been carrying in her womb—Felix's baby—the one she had not wanted before the miscarriage but so desperately wanted now. Had her mother not been so weak and fearful of the Texas rabble, Felix's eighteen-year-old aide and possibly Felix's child would be alive. But Doña Patricia had advised her not to look back, to walk away and begin anew.

Teresa had tried but failed. At first she had thought she could sell the de Alarcon villa without returning to it, but the house was haunted far more by the memory of her father and her late grandmother than her mother. Two ghosts did assail her when she entered: she could almost smell the rancid breath of the Mexican who had tried to frighten her into confessing she was Señora Santa Anna, the same Mexican who had then frightened Doña Helena into revealing that Emilia was hiding Teresa. The other ghost lurked at the spot where her mother had hung herself. Teresa had shivered, not out of grief but pity.

Like a robot she selected a few pieces of furniture she would store at Doña Patricia's: her father's massive oak desk, his portrait, a reading chair and stand from his study; the four-poster bed and bureau which had been in Doña Clara's family for two hundred years, and that woman's portrait as well. Nothing of her mother's. Then she walked away forever. Once she was an Escovarro, there would be no more de Alarcons; the family name was dead.

The wedding, held in the beautiful and ornate music room of Emilia's mansion, was a magnificent affair. There were only eighty guests. Doña Patricia, acting as Teresa's mother, spent her money lavishly. A dozen servants busily polished the house from attic to cellar; gardeners trimmed and pruned the trees and shrubs, setting out new beds of early summer blooms.

The house was a garden quite on its own, the massive curve of the grand staircase festooned in a garland of yellow and white roses and fern, its steps covered by a runner of white silk. Potted plants and ferns, precisely placed, created an aisle down the center of the music room. Unable to find eighty matching chairs in all of San Antonio, Doña Patricia borrowed those that most closely matched and had a battery of women sew up white slipcovers for each; and upon them she had embroidered intertwining yellow and white roses, never once thinking upon the symbolism of how intertwined the two women's lives already were.

But something that had started as a tweaking of Father Montclava's nose became the sensation of the day. A carpenter had fashioned for her a large wooden frame, placing it at the end of the music room and crisscrossing it with twine. From that moment on the music room was off limits to all but those working on the project. Next a long, narrow table was constructed to sit before the structure and was covered in white silk. A foot high, solid gold crucifix was placed in its center, banked by matching gold twelve-stick candelabras.

A great bustle descended on the villa the day of the wedding. Teresa and Emilia were confined to their upstairs rooms until the ceremony. Miguel and Felix remained in seclusion at their aunt's house next door. A dozen Mexican women worked in the kitchens of both houses to prepare a repast that would make people wonder how Doña Patricia had been able to secure such foods in a city that had been under siege just a little over a month before.

Big John, who had become a servant for both Emilia and Doña Patricia, had been badgering people for a week to open their wine cellars and give bottles of champagne in lieu of wedding gifts. Now, his black face beaming, he carefully placed his twenty prizes in oaken buckets of spring water to cool throughout the day. In the cool, dank cellar he was thankful it was to be an evening affair. It promised to be an extremely hot, humid June day, with no hint of a breeze until evening.

Throughout the afternoon delivery wagons rolled up the calle, and men bustled into the mansion with covered buckets and tubs. Once they had completed their errands, they were shooed away, and the music room doors closed again, leaving Doña Patricia and three gardeners to their task.

A half hour before dusk a calm settled over the lower floor of the mansion; a calm brought about by the sudden transformation in Doña Patricia. Throughout the day she had bullied, threatened, and cursed. She had cursed the heat, the lazy cooks, the maid's stupidity, the gardener's ineptness, Big John's calm smiles, her own madness for having taken on such a burdensome task. No one had seen her depart the music room and slip next door to her own villa, and she seemed to be back as suddenly as she left, resplendent in a soft green dress and matching mantilla. Moments later the musicians arrived, and she ushered them into the music room without a single word of instruction.

The same was the case with Father Montclava, but a devilish twinkle came to her eye after she had closed the door behind him.

After personally seeing to the lighting of the lamps and wall sconces in the salon, living room, dining room, foyer, and study, Big John stationed himself at the front door to receive the early arriving guests. Maids would see to the illumination of the music room on a given signal from Doña Patricia.

Soon the rooms were filled with brightly colored gowns, flowing mantillas, carefully shaved and powdered faces, laughter, and wonderment. Although the majority of the guests were quite accustomed to wealth and splendor, they were not fully prepared for what awaited them. Those who had expected a garrish brothel atmosphere were greatly disappointed but were still enraptured by the elegance and artful simplicity surrounding them. Hesitantly at first they accepted the crystal goblets of chilled Madeira, while awaiting the opening of the music room for their seating.

The calm that Doña Patricia was creating on the lower floor had been present throughout the day on the upper levels. At first Teresa had vetoed the idea of wearing white, until Doña Patricia took a hand in the matter.

"This is what you shall wear," the old woman demanded a couple of weeks before the wedding.

Teresa looked apprehensively at the cedar casket Big John had placed on the floor and then quickly departed. Teresa knew she had no choice but to open its lid, but the contents were alien to her eyes.

"Please, no," she begged, "it doesn't seem right. Whose was this? Yours?"

Doña Patricia laughed. "Good heavens, child, the Escovarro family cut Eduardo off without a cent when they learned he was going to marry me. I was married in a simple cotton dress with a garland of forget-me-nots in my hair. Maybe that's why I want your wedding to be so special. You're going to be more like a daughter than a niece to me. Besides, it's tradition. Years ago, when you were a child, Doña Clara showed me this chest. It was her wedding dress. I think she was saving it for you."

A lump rose in Teresa's throat but with it also a tremor of doubt.

"Did my mother wear it, as well?"

Doña Patricia snorted. "With her figure? More than likely she wore her own mother's gown. I'm sorry if this has upset you, child. I thought I was doing right by getting it out of the attic of the house before you had it sold."

Teresa sprang forward and gathered the woman into her arms. "I love you for going to the trouble," she began to sob. "I'll wear it with honor."

Now Teresa was elated with the choice. The wedding dress was an old-world masterpiece of Spanish lace and ivory silk, lavishly bustled and draped. The ancient lace mantilla billowed about Teresa like a diaphanous cloud. Later, as she would float down the aisle toward him, Felix would recall that she looked exactly the same as the first day he had met her in the sala of the Casa del Sol, awaiting his greeting. Eyes like crushed velvet which seemed to melt into the whiteness of her skin—a skin so smooth and white that it was difficult to distinguish between it and the creamy white of her lace mantilla. And, as on that earlier night, she had chosen to wear no jewelry save a single diamond necklace that sparkled at her throat and seemed to accent her round swelling breasts.

While Teresa was a quiet beauty in white, Emilia was flamboyantly beautiful in her wedding dress of tea-rose yellow and slightly darker-hued mantilla. She was obliged to coat her face with talc to subdue her natural high golden brown complexion from clashing with the outfit. But she was pleased by her appearance, for she was tall and lavish of figure, and her thick black hair curled entrancingly.

Only one thing displeased her about the entire day. Because Teresa had once stood up for the orphaned soldier Pedro Perez's marriage to the "reformed" *puta* Anna-Maria Morales, he had been asked in turn to give away the now orphaned Teresa. Anna-Maria had pouted until it was decided she could be the matron of honor. Anna-Maria was florid and dumpy in a green gown that was unable to hide her pregnancy, her brown face stained with sentimental tears. She embraced the two women frequently, thanking them, not initimidated by Emilia's thrustings off. Having been born a lower-class whore, raising herself up out of the gutter on her own, Emilia could not now stand her former equals. But as the first strains of violin music reached them, she chided herself for being uncivil. Then she smiled inwardly, for she had a secret of her own that might make some of the old biddies downstairs sit up and take notice.

As the three violins and cello began their first selection, Doña Patricia opened the doors of the music room and waved the guests to please enter the brightly lit room. The first group stopped short, staring in benumbed surprise.

To one side of the makeshift altar stood Father Montclava in vestments of black and white. Towering over him were Miguel and Felix, in matching fawn-colored evening suits with velvet lapels, the hue making their curly golden hair seem radiant in the candle glow. Each brother, in his turn, would act as best man for the other. It was hard to tell which of the three men was the more nervous: Felix, who loathed all this pomp; Miguel, who had desired Emilia for so long that he was now beginning to doubt his own desires; or the priest, who was wondering what these parishioners were going to say about this "church," knowing full well his private feelings about one of these marriages.

And towering over them was what made him quake. Doña Patricia and her gardeners had created the effect of a stained-glass backdrop, that made a gentle arc from one end of the silken altar to the other, out of flowers. Rising to within a foot of the twelve-foot ceiling, it not only added fragrance and color to the room but an overpowering majesty. In the years to come other grande dames would try to outdo this wedding for their daughters, but none would ever achieve the success of Doña Patricia's "cathedral."

Now the strains of the wedding march sounded from the corner of the music room. Pedro, uncomfortable in the most elegant suit of clothing he had ever worn, knocked timidly on the bedroom door. Pride swelled his heart when Anna-Maria came out after Teresa and Emilia; then he took Teresa's arm and descended the garland-covered stair-

way. Emilia and Anna-Maria followed. It had been decided
that Teresa would go down the aisle first, as Emilia had not
wished to be escorted. She had never known her father and
seriously doubted that her mother would have the courage
to make an appearance, although an invitation had been
extended to her at Teresa's insistence.

Teresa stopped at the door, tears welling into her eyes.
She reached out and caught Doña Patricia's hand and drew
her close.

"Where did you find so many candles," she whispered.
"I thought Santa Anna had confiscated every last one in
San Antonio?"

"Some of them may not be made of the very best
tallow," she chuckled, "but we found them, here and
there."

"Oh, I love you! Thank you for this day . . . and for
your nephew!"

The music swelled triumphantly. Teresa floated until
handed over to the strong arm of Felix Escovarro. She
heard nor saw anything else except the all-encompassing
love that emanated from his chocolate-brown eyes.

Emilia stepped to the door and paused, as regal as any
queen ever born. She hesitated for a moment, to let every
one of the eighty pairs of eyes encompass her from head to
toe, and then she slowly raised her right arm and held it
expectantly. Big John stepped from the foyer and gently
put his arm beneath hers.

Amarillo Rosa was making her final appearance in public, and she made her entrance as though it were a command performance.

Anna-Maria, who had always envied the woman, now
loathed her with a dark passion. No one was paying her the
least bit of attention as she came down the aisle, not even
her own husband. Every eye in the place was riveted on the
"yellow rose." And one set brimmed with tears of utter
pride. Doña Patricia would have started a round of applause if her churchly setting had not made it seem so inap-
propriate.

The rest of the evening passed like a gala of old—too
brilliant, too festive, too noisy. By the time the couples had

been joined in matrimony and slipped away to their respective bedrooms, no one was paying them any mind. For nearly two years a soirée, such as this had been an impossibility in old San Antonio. The Anglo takeover of the new republic created a strong doubt that the old ways would ever return. The eighty guests, by unspoken bond, determined to make this celebration last them a lifetime, if need be.

Teresa came from the dressing room to find Felix lying across the bed, still fully clothed. She said nothing. But she slipped about the room softly, lowering the window sash against the din from the garden. Felix seemed unaware of her presence.

She finally returned to him and silently helped him undress. He submitted to her ministrations, just as he had done in Saltillo. She asked no questions. This time there could be no remorse, and their dreams could become a reality. She assisted him under the cool sheets and let the nightgown fall from her body.

He reached up for her hand, smiling shyly, as if ashamed. Teresa climbed into the comfort of strong male arms without reservation. She closed her eyes and ears to the sights and sounds of the past, nestling close to his chest and its promise for the future. Arms that had always longed to hold her passionate body encircled her protectively.

Felix Escovarro was shaking with far more nervousness than the first time. She was now totally his, and he still could not quite believe it. No ghosts now stood between them. He no longer was the false priest who had married her to Santa Anna and then had made love to her like a child playing at a game without knowledge of its rules. This was only the fourth time in his twenty-eight years that he had lain with a woman, and the thought of it still benumbed him with wonderment.

Again it was Teresa who curled her hands into the tight ringlets of his golden hair, caressing his eyes, cheeks, and lips with her lips. And again an intense, delicious capriciousness overcame her as she marveled at the furry softness of his chest and stomach hair and the fiery heat that emanated from the muscular torso it rested upon. But this time the heat growing in her loins did not stun her. This time she knew its reason and would make the most of it. This time she stiffened only momentarily at the massiveness of his manly assault, then was swept away as the union became a wild, passionate meshing of bliss. They were now one, a husband and wife.

There were tears on Teresa's face . . . tears of unmeasurable happiness.

CHAPTER TWO

In addition to everything else she had done, the honeymoon trip was a present from Doña Patricia. Big John would take them by carriage to Galveston Bay, and from there they would take a paddle-wheeler to New Orleans.

It was a nostalgic journey for the quartet, retracing the same route they had traveled in April to help bring the war to an end. They had begun that journey with great fear and trepidation, with Santa Anna's army close upon their heels. Although the side for which they'd fought had been totally victorious, they had come away with the bitter ashes of defeat in their mouths. The new republic was not going to honor the ancient Spanish land grants. The vast Escovarro holdings on the Rio Frío stood in jeopardy of being taken away from them.

In spite of this Felix saw the New Orleans trip as a great boon. The old French-settled city had become the gateway and supply center for the new republic. There he hoped to recoup some of the equipment losses they had suffered at the hands of Santa Anna's army.

"You might have consulted me," said Miguel surlily. "I believe I *am* the head of the family now."

Felix beamed with his old sunniness. "That's it, Miguel, that's it. You're going to have enough to worry about. Sam Houston owes you a debt, and you can collect by saving the ranch."

Miguel scowled darkly. "What is to save? Didn't you listen to Pedro and Anna-Maria's account of the attack?" His eyes became fierce pools of hatred. "They barricaded them in the hacienda, Felix. Shut up our mother and father in their own house and set it to blaze. Adobe doesn't burn, so they say," he scoffed. "But it did, dear brother. Pedro said the fire from the roof and furniture became so fierce that the adobe bricks cracked, turned to dust and the ancient straw within it ignited like tinder. And the soldiers stood and laughed."

"Don't dwell on it, Miguel," his brother soothed. "We can't bring them back. We do, however, owe an obligation to the other people on the ranch. They're poor people and need us now that Father is gone."

Miguel sniffed contemptuously. "Gone? How can you be so sure that they, too, are not gone. God, Felix, they massacred everyone in the village of Escovarro and then razed it to the ground. They were mostly relatives of our workers. Would you stay around with so much hatred directed at the Escovarro name, for that is the only reason that bloodsucking madman ordered its destruction."

Felix drew a deep breath. "Why don't you say what's really on your mind?" he said very quietly.

As quiet as the words had been, they were like an electric charge to Miguel's senses. He had never been able to hide his true feelings from his younger brother, even having accused him once of having the power to read his innermost thoughts. He was now almost afraid to answer Felix.

"They would be alive today," he said meekly, "if you had not brought *her* back from Saltillo."

"I thought as much," he said with a note of derision in his voice. "You didn't listen to Father that day in the library, did you? It was his decision, Miguel. I told Steve Austin the whole story of the fake marriage when I brought him back from his imprisonment in Mexico. He and Father discussed it and determined it would be proper to get her back to San Antonio."

"And like a good soldier," he sneered, "you obeyed."

There was a coolness and narrowness in Felix which had made him a remarkable Texas spy on the staff of General Santa Anna. That was never more apparent than at this moment.

"If you were not my brother, I could easily kill you. I disregarded their orders, but circumstances made it necessary for me to bring her along. Now we know that she overheard our conversation in the library and learned that the divorce papers and marriage were a fraud."

Miguel's face turned livid. "It wouldn't have mattered if they had not been. You and Father were determined to lure Santa Anna into a full-scale war by using her as bait, and all you have to show for it is the ruination of three centuries of Escovarro work."

Felix clenched his teeth. His eyes did not leave his brother's.

"And it will be Escovarro money and labor which rebuilds it. We don't know where we stand, Miguel, because no one knows if Father's money perished in the blaze or not. Doña Patricia was willing to loan me some of her Escovarro money so that we could make equipment purchases in New Orleans. Pedro is taking word back to Rodriguez to see to the herds and for Guido Herrera to see to the ranch and its people. We are Escovarros, Miguel. We are now family men. We must begin to prepare for our children as our father did for us."

That, perhaps, was Miguel Escovarro de Sanchez's biggest problem. He had never had any affection for the ranching and farming business of his father, showing no aptitude for its demands of time and patience and business acumen. As an officer, under General Sam Houston, he had shown a flair for the politics that arises in every army. He had secretly hoped that Houston would retain him, after the war, to make use of that same political sense when the man became the president of the republic and needed a strong Spanish voice on his side. Instead he had been pushed aside, just like every other Spaniard or Mexican who had helped the Texans. But Miguel took it personally, for two reasons: his brother's involvement with Teresa de Alarcon and Houston's one-time involvement with Emilia Hoffman. Houston, as Miguel saw it, did not want the embarrassment of either woman—which might hinder his quest to become a "king."

Another uncertainty was troubling Miguel, eating into his soul like an unseen cancer. Their carriage, and attire, for the hot, humid, east Texas summer days, was a repugnant sight to the countless wagons of poor Tennessee and

Kentucky farmers streaming down from the northeast. It was a show of riches they really no longer had, and he was sensitive to the resentment on the faces, even though the others tended to ignore the shouted insults and rude gestures. He instinctively knew that these people, who had not even fought in the war, were someday, somehow, going to steal his land. Thus he was virtually resigned to giving up the battle before it was even fought.

But he was only fooling himself by considering that his real uncertainty. Outwardly, during the days between quick sunrise and sudden sunset which seemed interminable, he appeared to be the essence of a young man on his honeymoon.

But, when they were at last aboard the paddle-wheeler headed for Louisiana, cramped into their steamy staterooms, his dark brow would furrow, and his hands would clench with concern over his foolishness at having gone ahead with this marriage. He began to doubt his love for Emilia, because it was a love based on a sexual dream.

He could still close his eyes and see her in the Cantina del Monte. She was a goddess when she danced, making every man present aware that he would give up all his worldly wealth to possess her for a single night. But Amarillo Rosa was an artist off the dance floor as well, an expert at passion without a trace of love. And when she had whispered to him, "Love me," it had begun as little more than a purely professional command.

In time, out of mutual need, they melted into an unspoken union of equal giving. She was the teacher he the novice. Avenues of sexual pleasure were opened to his pristine mind that stunned and shocked and then titillated him. He became, after a while, a connoisseur of the unusual.

Had Doña Patricia not learned that Emilia was a *puta,* when Miguel had first brought her back to San Antonio, their lives might have been quite different. Spurned by the Escovarro family, Emilia might not have become rich and famous as the most illustrious *puta* in San Antonio, more prone, however, to entertain in her music room than in her bedroom. Because it was the fashionable thing, men paid dearly just to be included in her social evenings, and only a few, who were more wealthy than wise, ever saw the lush interior of her third-floor bedroom. Emilia had allowed herself to fall in love only twice, both ending in disappointment. And when Miguel had become a military aide to Sam Houston, her other love, she cast them both from her mind.

But fate kept placing Miguel Escovarro in her path of progress. Finally, she knew, he would be the last man she would ever allow to crawl into her bed.

"Damn!" Miguel cried, hitting his head on the upper bunk while trying to reach her lower bunk in the dark. "This is asinine."

Emilia giggled. "I think it's rather fun. These narrow bunks are going to make it more intimate."

Miguel growled. "I much prefer your spacious bed back in San Antonio."

"Hush," she warned in mock alarm. "We don't want anyone to know that we were jumping the wedding ceremony by a full month."

"I doubt the knowledge would ruin your reputation," he said snidely.

She knew the argument that was coming and sidestepped it with silence. It was a breach that had started between them on their wedding night, and she didn't want it to go further.

Miguel, knowing when to leave well enough alone, crawled into the narrow bunk and found her nude and waiting. His hand snaked over her belly and fondled what he sought until her breathing grew rapid. He muttered into her ear and then let his mouth go down to close around a swollen nipple.

"No," she whispered, knowing his actions were trying to carry her into a lenghty bout of foreplay.

Miguel ignored the warning, rubbing his aroused manhood against her leg while attempting to roll her onto her side. Emilia stiffened and spread her legs to absorb every last inch of the narrow bunk.

Miguel was furious, rolling the full weight of his frame atop her and crushing down upon her heaving breasts. Always before he had been gentle in his advances, letting her passion fully arouse him and spread nuances of delight through his body.

Emilia fought to keep from crying out against the delicious agony that his brute massiveness was causing her. She knew that she was right and wrong, all at the same time. He had been untrained and almost untried at their first meeting. She, alone, had introduced him to the exotic variations in their couplings. But then she had been a *puta*, although she had never accepted money from Miguel. Now her desire for him was not simply carnal, but sensual and loving. She wished only to be a real woman, a real wife. Because of Miguel's constant demands for the unusual, she had grown to fear the ghost of her past rising between them.

But she was still woman enough to relax and make them melt into an unspoken union of equal giving.

Miguel shuddered. His body stiffened, and the climb of her own desire reached a swift, nerve-shattering peak of sensation. As had happened many times during the past three years, and especially the last month, she felt the gouting of his maleness as stormy waves of release curled through her loins, complete, intense, fulfilling.

Miguel rolled away and sat for a long silent moment on the edge of the bunk. The foghorn on the paddle-wheeler sounded, making him feel even more forlorn.

"No children yet, Em," he said darkly. "We've got enough problems ahead, without that."

Emilia smoothed a velvet hand down his muscular back. "It's never happened yet in all my twenty-seven years."

He grunted and climbed up to the other bunk. Within seconds she could hear his heavy breathing and a slight snore. She wrapped her arms around her full breasts and hugged herself deliciously. "But then again," she thought, "I was always very careful in those days."

CHAPTER THREE

During the night the soft Gulf wind ceased. Like a slowly revolving top a tropical storm had built itself to gale force. By morning the *Yellow Stone,* hove to, wallowed in the Gulf of Mexico like an old candle box. The wind blew hour after hour: it blew with spite, without interval, without mercy. The passengers huddled in their cabins, not even daring to think of food, least of all trying to make it to the galley on the slippery, heaving decks.

Miguel took it upon himself to learn the true nature of their condition. He was thoroughly drenched by the time he reached the pilothouse. It was lightless and dank; he had to blink water from his eyes to keep the shadowy figures in focus.

"Captain?"

"I am here," a voice came serenely from the gloom. "What do you wish of me?" The quiet manner in which the question was asked infuriated Miguel. He could now see that it was taking three sailors just to keep the wheel steady.

"Turn back!" he shouted, realizing the stupidity of his demand even as it was uttered. "You're going to sink us," he hurriedly mumbled to hide his previous words.

The laugh unnerved him. It was the sound of a man not fully comprehending his own internal fears.

"What am I supposed to do, señor, stop it?"

"Steam out of it!"

Captain Sprainero looked at him sympathetically. "I can't use the paddle wheels, son. I've got to let them spin free with the force of the waves or else they'd just shatter and break. All we can do is ride it out and pray."

"For how long?" Miguel asked dumbfounded.

"She's a hurricane, Señor Escovarro. Only God knows her size and strength." Then as though to soothe him, he added: "We're but about a hundred miles from the delta of the Mississippi. Once there it'll be different."

Their world became nothing but an immense foaming wave, rushing at them under a sky low enough to touch with the hand and dirty like a smoked ceiling. In the stormy space surrounding the *Yellow Stone* there was as much flying spray as air. Hour after hour and on into the night there was nothing round the boat but the howl of the wind, the tumult of the Gulf waters, the noise of breakers pouring over the deck, the cries of children.

Near midnight the howl of the wind seemed to fade away like a dying echo. The Gulf still churned, but the relative quiet was instantly comforting. The captain and crew, knowing they had as much as an hour to right their course and steam closer to land while within the eye of the storm, paid little heed to the passengers who came cautiously on deck to gain a breath of fresh air. Time enough, they thought, to get them back inside before the other arc of the hurricane hit them.

Except for the pitching and bucking, it was a phenomenal night. A full moon cast everything in a silvery glow. St. Elmo's fire lights danced up and down the guy wires of the twin smokestacks as though to celebrate the end of their fears.

Felix had to cajole Teresa into leaving their cabin. She was ashen and her stomach devoid of all but bitter yellow bile. They found Emilia and Miguel already topside, clinging to the railing and gulping in the warm salt-tinged air. Teresa took one look at the rolling waves and clung desperately to the companionway doorjamb.

"Let's go to the galley and see if we can get something hot for them," Felix suggested to Miguel.

"I don't want anything; don't go!" Teresa pleaded.

Emilia came and put an arm about her waist. "Even if it's warm water," she soothed. "You've got to get something in your stomach. Here come with me. We can sit behind that air stack."

Teresa sank down and pressed her back firmly against

38

the protrusion. It kept her away from the railing and created a sense of security. She had kept her fears from Felix but knew they would overwhelm her unless released.

"I don't seem to have much luck with this boat, do I?" she asked lamely.

Emilia didn't understand. "Why is that?"

"This is the *Yellow Stone.*"

"Oh, my God! It never crossed my mind, because I never really knew its name that first time." She started to comment on Teresa's fear and then thought better of it. She would try to keep it light. "I'll never forget that comic-opera scene. Those poor Mexican soldiers who had never seen a riverboat before and then this monster comes belching and tooting down upon their flatboats."

Teresa smiled weakly. "I suppose it must have been comical."

Emilia put back her head and laughed. "Not as funny as Santa Anna. We were among the first put across at Thompson's Ferry. All he could do when this thing ran down the flatboat was to scream at the troops to kill the beast with their muskets. What he really wanted was to capture it. The orders got so confused it turned into a circus."

Teresa had thought it a circus at the time, as well. The soldiers who drove the supply train cattle began to use the only weapons available to them—their riatas—swirling them into great circling arcs and attempting to lasso the smokestacks. The other soldiers had ceased to fire and filled the air with olés and catcalls, according to the attempt. Even the crew and passengers of the *Yellow Stone* were drawn into the rodeo spirit and crowded the rail to crane their necks up to the smokestack. Among them was Teresa de Alarcon.

"You never did fully tell me why you left San Felipe," Emilia said, wishing to avoid what had happened next.

"I think, now, I was just trying to spite Felix for letting you go with Santa Anna when we could have saved you in San Felipe. It was stupid of me to think that I could protect you and save you. All it got me was a close call with death."

She shuddered at the memory. Forever she would feel the backlash of the rope which made her lose her balance and tumble over the railing. She had tried to put the nightmare of the icy water out of her mind. But it would never fade, and this storm had only revived it. Her fear of drowning now unnerved her like nothing before in life.

Emilia would hear none of it. "You've been through much worse."

Teresa shook her head. "No, Em, no. The other nightmares of the past three years I could do something about. There I was helpless. I couldn't swim and my waterlogged dress weighed me down like a rock. That was just a river. Can you imagine going overboard into something like this."

Emilia stood and held out her hands. "I think we've had enough fresh air. With the storm over, we still might get some sleep tonight."

But even before Felix and Miguel had returned with mugs of hot broth, the wind had begun to intensify again. Nature had cut the captain's hour in half and increased the wind velocity to over ninety miles an hour. The riverboat was a toy against such might.

She tossed, she pitched, she stood on her head, she sat on her tail, she rolled, she groaned, and the sailors had to hold on while on deck and cling to their bunks when below, in a constant effort of body and worry of mind.

The *Yellow Stone* was dying. The boat was going back to the sea, piecemeal: the bulwarks went, the stanchions were torn out, the ventilators smashed, the smokestacks twisted and bent, the cabin doors burst in. She was being gutted bit by bit. The malice of the hurricane changed the lifeboats into matchwood. And there was no break in the storm. It had stalled in the Gulf and was not moving. They were a handful of humans caught up by an infuriated sea.

One of the smokestacks blew away. She lay broadside with the paddle-house superstructure completely out of the water, and Teresa did not care. She had forgotten what it felt like to be dry, to be safe, to be upon firm land. She fought her nausea until she was too weak to fight any longer.

When the calmness overtook her, she would never be able to recall. All that came to her over the howling storm was the sense that she had traveled this road before and could not travel it again. At first she thought it just another of the fanciful dreams brought on by her weakness, but this dream had meaning which intensified in her mind.

"What in the hell are you doing?" Felix gasped from his bunk.

Teresa was lurching across the narrow cabin to where the door hung by a single hinge.

"Too much water!" she screamed over the storm. "Got to keep it out and get it out."

"Really now, Teresa, there's nothing we can do."

"Be still!" she screamed. "It's going to sink if we don't do something. All the cabins on this side must be the same. Open the porthole and find something to bail with."

"You're not being rational. She's a wooden boat and wood floats. Just keep calm."

That was the problem. Teresa was calm, too calm. From somewhere, perhaps the remembrance of how her saturated dress had pulled her body down so quickly, she knew that the boat, overweighted in the same manner, would sink just as fast.

The argument continued, but Felix persisted in clinging to his berth, stupidly, from sheer fright of the storm—like an animal that won't leave a burning barn.

Teresa had no recourse but to do the deed herself. It was chancing certain death, since once out of the cabin she might be exposed to her worst fear—the open sea. But she went. Their cabin was the nearest to the deck companionway. The entrance had been shattered as though the hurricane had exploded from within. The heavy doors and most of the jamb had gone overboard, leaving a gaping hole for the storm to enter without check.

A portion of the passageway remained dry as if by a miracle. Teresa groped past the ruined doors of the first few cabins to that of Emilia and Miguel. Her pounding went unheard over the storm. Every ounce of her energy was consumed in forcing open the water-swollen panel.

The cabin was dry, blessedly dry. She screamed out her demands to the startled couple and went on to the next cabin without awaiting their reaction. Of the eight starboard cabins only five were occupied, with hers being the only one inundated by water. But the other passengers, upon peering down the passageway to the entering storm, caught her feeling of concern.

A burly Virginian, headed home to bring his family back to Texas, had been on the boat when Sam Houston had used it to move troops. "I know my way to the carpenter's bench," he volunteered. "I'll see what I can fetch."

The voices had brought Felix wading into the corridor. The wind was so fierce he had to plant his long legs wide to keep from being tumbled over.

"It's dry at this end," Miguel called, "but won't be for long if we don't get that hole closed off."

"Impossible," Felix shouted. "I can hardly stand against it."

Teresa started for him, her face a determined mask. Once before he had seen that selfsame set to her jaw. That time, too, she had been protecting him from certain death.

"Don't come any farther, Teresa," he said gruffly, knowing full well he had no recourse but to take over what she had begun. "Let the men do it. Hey, start bringing the mattresses off your bunks."

"Wait!" she commanded, still fully in charge. "The first three cabins are already soaked, use them first."

Felix, still a little awed by the authoritarian manner she had acquired in the past three years, turned back into his own cabin and began stripping the bunks of the soggy mattresses. He felt a little ashamed at not having listened to her in the first place.

He was the first back in the passageway. The water was now up to his calves and making the going difficult. With energy-sapping effort he got a mattress to the hole but was hardly able to hold it in place, the inward thrust was so great. Another mattress was thrust up to him, but his muscular arms were already aching with the effort. The plan was doomed, even if they had a thousand bunk mattresses.

"Lemme help," the big Virginian drawled, putting his broad shoulder against the sodden mess. "Here," he said, handing Felix a hammer and nails. "Already told 'em to start bringin' the slats from the bunks."

The slats were not long enough to reach across the exposed hole and Felix had to crisscross them as quickly as he could. Layer by layer, support by support, the barricade began to grow. With the wind thus reduced, they were able to work at a faster pace, exchanging jobs with every third mattress. The man proved to be a far better carpenter than Felix.

"Come by it natural like, Señor Escovarro," he said. "Done built me three cabin homes, and I ain't thirty yet."

"You know me?" Felix asked with genuine surprise.

"Reckon I see'd you and your brother enough times with the general. Saw y'all board, but the storm's kept me from sayin' a howdy-do. Bowditch, the name. Vince Bowditch. Course you wouldn't remember me."

"There were so many," Felix apologized. "Besides, I was only there the last couple of weeks. My brother might remember, though."

Bowditch laughed, deep and heartily. "Meaning no disrespect, sir, but he weren't too well known to the men, just the officers and Mexes."

A flash of anger almost made Felix correct the man, but they were once again fighting a common enemy, and he could not afford to lose the man's resourcefulness. Instead he remained quiet, stuffing the last two mattresses into the breach.

"That takes care of that," he said.

"Yep, till they get soaked through and start seepin' water. Them folks been working too hard to get it out to have it come right back in. Think I'll go back to the hold and search us up a length of canvas."

Felix had been paying no heed to what the others were doing, just accepting mattresses and plankings from them without question. When he stepped down, the water just barely covered his feet. The sand had been emptied from the fire buckets and used to bail the water out of the three

43

forward portholes. The six women on board had divorced themselves of petticoats and used them to sop up the water and squeeze it into additional pails.

Bowditch proved better than his word. He had found not only canvas but a bucket of pitch tar in the boiler room. Once the canvas was nailed securely into place, its base was painted with the tar to make it truly waterproof.

With unspoken but nodded thanks to each other, everyone seemed to melt back into their own cabins. No one talked, no one cared to talk; the storm raged on as before. They all sensed that they had only forestalled their destiny for a little while.

Felix changed into a dry suit of Miguel's, and Emilia opened one of her trunks to share with Teresa. It was all done in whispers, as though they were co-conspirators.

Bowditch was a curious man by nature, and now his curiosity was running rampant. After the battle at San Jacinto the involvement of Amarillo Rosa in helping to delay Santa Anna's attack became common knowledge among the soldiers. He had seen her that day and had marveled at her finery. His "old lady" had nothing to equal her silks and laces and hoops, but he vowed at that moment that she someday would. A strong family man, he did not condone "whoring" and was a little aghast to see the woman with the Escovarro brothers. Upon seeing the brothers on the boat, he had considered it a godsend, but now he questioned the wisdom of approaching them.

The war had not turned out to Vince Bowditch's liking. He had been offered a great wage and promise of land if he became a "mercenary" soldier to help kick the Mexicans back across the Rio Grande. The money had been skimpy and the land promise still unfulfilled. There was nothing for Vince to do now but go home to Virginia. His few hundred dollars would pay for a seed crop and food for months if he were careful, but Vince had no intention of remaining on his old farm that long. He would take the seed crop and his family and head again for Texas. He would make no more mistakes. The next time he would be ready to play the game on even terms—and when he won, he would show no mercy.

Finally he decided there was no time like the present to confront the brothers. From his knapsack he took an earthen jug he had been hoarding for months.

Miguel frowned upon opening the cabin door. In dry buckskins he recognized the man at once.

"Come in! Come in!" Felix called from the interior. "I was just telling my brother about you."

Upon seeing the two women, he hesitated. Somehow he expected them to have a cabin of their own.

"Don't want to intrude," he said.

"No intrusion," Felix said, coming to the door. "Besides I didn't get a chance to thank you for your help."

Bowditch hesitated a moment longer, then slowly entered. He needed their advice, and this might be his big chance to gain from them.

"This here," he said, extending the jug, "is from my farm in Virginia. My woman makes the best corn whiskey in those parts. Thought it might take some of the chill out of the storm."

"Our stomachs are hardly up to it," Miguel growled.

"Speak for yourself," Emilia laughed. "It sounds just right to me."

Bowditch was taken aback. He was not used to women drinking. Felix saw his discomfort but thought the reason for it was his brother's unfriendly manner.

"Forgive my rudeness," Felix said smoothly, "but I've failed to introduce you to our wives. May I present my wife, Doña Teresa Escovarro, and my brother's wife, Doña Emilia. Ladies, Vince Bowditch."

He nodded his head to each speechlessly, his mind totally shattered by this unexpected revelation.

"I, too, wish to thank you, Mr. Bowditch," Teresa said, rising from her stool. "Your resourcefulness in finding hammer, nails, and tarpaulins saved the day."

Bowditch was immediately captivated. Where Emilia's single utterance in English had been guttural and heavily laced with a Spanish accent, Teresa's use of the language was as soft and musical as when she spoke in her native tongue. He knew nothing about her. She had been somewhat of a mystery woman at San Jacinto, being whisked away almost as soon as the battle was over. He had just considered her to be another of Santa Anna's "whores" but now saw how mistaken he was. He had never seen such a beautiful woman.

"Please sit down again," he cautioned. "It's hard enough standing in this storm when you don't need to."

Miguel, who had retaken his seat next to Emilia on the lower bunk, saw in the man's own words an excuse to get rid of him.

"Sorry we can't offer you a seat, Bowditch. These cabins were not exactly designed for comfort."

Now that he was there, he was not going to be put off. "I'll just put my back here against the bulkhead, if it's all the same to you." As he slid down, he passed the jug to Felix.

"We don't have any utensils," Miguel said harshly.

Felix, not much of a drinking man, was growing irritated with the rudeness of his brother. He had never seen him like this before and couldn't understand it.

"We have your two broth mugs," he interjected quickly, before the man grew offended.

"Y'all can share them," Bowditch beamed. "Only one way for a farm boy like me to sip the corn."

He took the jug back from Felix, expertly popped out the cork with his teeth, and poured a dash of the crystal-clear liquid into the two offered mugs. Then he hoisted the jug to his shoulder, tilted his head to the side, and gave himself a half mouthful of the whiskey without spilling a drop.

"Bravo!" Emilia cheered. "Miguel, doesn't that take you right back to the Monte."

Miguel scowled and didn't answer. The last thing he wanted was for this man to learn she was ever connected with the cantina.

Felix sipped at the strong brew, but Teresa declined. This pleased Bowditch almost as much as Emilia's exclamation over its excellence. Now that he could really judge the women, he saw that Teresa was a real lady and Felix a courteous gentleman.

"What is it you grow on your farm?" Felix asked.

"Cotton," he said proudly. "Course I only got me 'bout twenty-five acres."

"Why would a man with a farm and family come to fight someone else's war?" Miguel asked.

Bowditch was still taking Miguel's measure. "Captain," he addressed him by rank and with respect, "y'all heard their big promises of money and land. I wanted me a piece of that land for the future. Twenty-five acres really ain't that much, not for cotton."

"I hardly see where cotton would be a suitable crop for Texas," Miguel retorted just as coolly as before. To his surprise this brought a toothy grin to the Virginian's face.

"What most people don't know about cotton would amaze them," he chuckled. "Did y'all know that cotton is a tree? A small tree, to be sure, but nevertheless a tree, not a grass or a grain. Well, to plant a tree from seed every year, cultivate and harvest it, and then let that tree die, is a right strange and uneconomical thing to my way of thinking."

"Then why let it die?" Felix asked, his curiosity aroused.

"Nature does it. Yes, sir, those trees can't take the winter, even in Georgia and Alabama."

"So," Miguel said, "why would Texas be different?"

A man, Bowditch thought, could starve to death trying to sell a new idea to that man.

Aloud he said: "As a young'un I went with the army down to fight the Seminoles in Florida. They don't get much winter, if any at all, and I saw the Indians' cotton trees that had been growing year after year. But it was a poor quality due to too much humidity. I ain't seen it, but I heard tell from some of the soldiers that the southwestern part of Texas don't get much winter and is drier than Florida."

"You're correct on that," Felix said. "That's the part of the country we are from."

"Do tell!" Bowditch exclaimed in mock amazement. It was just such an opening statement he had been angling for one of them to make. A man can't boast in the army without his words being spread about. He had heard some tall tales about the largeness and productivity of the Escovarro ranch and farms, and like every other man who had heard such fables, he had coveted a part of it for himself.

"Do tell," he repeated. "I'd sure like to see that area someday."

It was almost as though Miguel had read his mind. At the time he had seen nothing wrong in boasting about what the Escovarros had accomplished in the past three hundred years. It had been done out of pride and to show the Texans that the land would be better off out from under the control of Mexico City. He could see the greed in Bowditch's soul and it sickened him, for there were thousands more just like the man.

"Well," Miguel said smoothly, "if you're ever back in Texas, we'd be happy to show you *our* country."

"I'd like that, Captain Escovarro. My, you and your brother are right lucky, having a place to go right back to and not having to wait on the government to give you land because you fought."

Now the man had raised a point of interest in Miguel's mind. He had left Sam Houston right after the battle and was unaware of this development.

"With the amount of wagons we saw along the way, I assumed the land was being given out quite handily."

"No, sir, it ain't," he said seriously. "The most that's been given out has gone to people who already were living there before the war. You might say they were just getting back what was already rightfully theirs, such as you folk."

"You know this for a fact, Bowditch?"

"Heard one of Austin's men say as much in San Felipe."

"Perhaps there has been a policy change, Miguel," Felix volunteered.

"You didn't listen carefully," he growled. "Texans are getting their land back. That leaves only the Spanish grants to be fought over. Damn their sneaky hides."

This, Bowditch mused, was going much better than he had ever anticipated; but still he played naïve. "What y'all mean?"

When Felix started to answer, Miguel shot him a warning look, but Felix saw no harm in speaking the truth. "It's a small part of the new republic's constitution, Bowditch. All of the old land grants were supposed to become null and void."

"Damn!" the man roared. "That ain't right! You folk been on your land longer than the United States been a country. I'd fight such a dirty trick to my dyin' day, if'n it were my land."

Miguel eyed the man with new interest. His reaction had not been what he had expected from an Anglo. "Exactly," he said softly.

A sudden silence settled on the cabin. For the first time since his arrival they all became aware that the wind was not howling as fiercely and that the boat was on an even keel, although still being pitched about.

Bowditch offered the jug again, and this time Miguel shared the mug with Emilia.

"Captain," he said at last, "meanin' no offense, but we might be able to be of service to each other."

Miguel didn't see how but waited quietly for him to go on.

"Like I say, cotton is becoming king in the South. You help my family and my brother's family get a cotton plantation started in your part of the country, and that will give you twelve extra guns to help fight them off."

Miguel stared at Bowditch, his jaw mentally dropping. The man was either a fool or a sly fox. Didn't he realize that the Escovarros could muster a hundred guns or more from their own cattlemen and farmers? He had no need for the man, or his guns, but was intrigued.

"Interesting. Why do you place such importance on cotton, señor?"

Bowditch sat sprawled against the bulkhead, his big frame loose muscled and relaxed, but his face was incredulous.

"You don't know the product, do you?"

Miguel laughed. "Everyone knows it is for cloth and clothes."

"That's only the tip of it," Bowditch said quietly. "It's the only crop in the world that produces food, feed, and fiber. We eat cotton, drink it, write on it, shelter ourselves

49

with it, feed it to livestock, burn it in lamps, tie parcels with it, sit on it, sleep on it, use it in medicines, and shoot off guns with it."

"My God!" Emilia exclaimed. "I've never heard any of this before."

Neither had any of them.

"Interesting," Miguel said again, "but puzzling. How do you mean we eat cotton and use it as feed for livestock?"

"The cottonseed oil. You don't have it here, so you wouldn't know. It's made into lard, cooking oil, and salad oil, to name a few uses. The husks, back home, are then fed to the pigs and cows. Fats 'em up good and saves having to plant fields of hay for their winter fodder. That's the part where I thought we could be of the biggest use to each other. Think about your cattle feedin' on such fodder."

Think! Miguel laughed inside his mind, what thinking do I need, Vince Bowditch? *I* have been thinking. *I* have thought. Nobody else in my position would have listened to you. But I have. And why? Because you gave yourself away when you used the word "plantation." I like that. A man always knows where he stands with a blackguard. Ethical people are unpredictable. Besides, damn your hide, I see right through your scheme. Cotton requires more than just planting.

"As you say, Bowditch, I don't know the product well. But isn't it the main reason for slavery in the South?"

"Naturally," he said without hesitation. "Course my brother and I only own about eighteen slaves between us. But after a year or two they'd be able to train Mexican labor to pick the cotton."

"You own slaves, Mr. Bowditch?" Teresa asked with a gasp of surprise.

He laughed. "Why does that surprise you? Aren't the Mexican peons the same as slaves to you people? I was under the impression that the Escovarro ranch had many such."

Aha! Miguel thought. The scoundrel has revealed his hand and fallen into his own trap. Seeing that Felix was about to champion the family cause, he held his silence.

"I've never seen the black slaves," Felix said with a note

of heat in his voice, "but I do know our people, at least on our ranches and farms. First of all, they are not Mexicans. These are Spaniards who have been brought here, with their families, over the generations. They *are* a part of our family, and thus are not bought and sold like cattle."

With victory right at his fingertips, Bowditch saw it slowly evaporate. He cursed himself for ever having mentioned the slaves.

"I heard of it firsthand," Emilia said. "I have a servant, Mr. Bowditch, but he is a free black man. But he wasn't always free. You should see his back, sir. Those whip scars will never go away and have been on his back since he was seven. And why? Because at seven he just wasn't yet strong enough to pick one-hundred-twenty pounds of cotton a day. And so they whipped him and then sold him away from his family to a plantation in Mississippi. I somehow just can't picture someone whipping the Escovarro people to get them to pick cotton."

"Fair enough," he said. "Then the only other solution, Captain, is to bring enough slaves west to do all the work. They reproduce like rabbits and will grow as the acreage grows."

"Stop it!" Teresa cried. "I can't believe we are even on this subject. It would be just like the situation I found at the Casa del Sol. Oh, yes, Mr. Bowditch, slavery can be anywhere. But I, for one, never again want to see fear and hatred and misery in the eyes of human workhorses."

Bowditch shrugged. "It is all, of course, in how the master treats his slaves."

"Exactly," Miguel said, breaking his silence. "But the basic question, besides treatment, is one of ownership. Are your blacks able to return to their homes?"

Bowditch flushed crimson. He knew it would do no good to make them see that he had paid for his blacks. He decided to fight fire with fire.

"Are your people able to return to their homes?" he shot out hotly.

"At any time," Felix said calmly, "but, you see, they are home. This is now home, because they chose of their own free will to come here with my ancestors. Later others were recruited in Spain, by my grandfather and father. They could leave, but there is no need. As I said before, they are family."

But for how long, Miguel thought darkly. Already some of the younger hotheads, fearing a complete Texan takeover had slipped away in the night with their families. How many would still be there when they returned from New Orleans?

Bowditch looked out of the dirt-filmed porthole at the gale that was changing to rain, the waves beginning to recede.

"I reckon you're right," he said. "Only my slaves are treated as humans, too."

Miguel grunted. The sound held all the contempt in the world.

Bowditch left shortly thereafter, his mission in shambles. Never again did he want to go through the drudgery of clearing land and building a cabin before he could plant his crop. A union with the Escovarros would have saved him a good two to three years. He would not be content in just returning to his Virginia farm. He hated to even think of it. It was older, dirtier, and more dilapidated than any other in the county. It ran northward among the hills through country of depressing bleakness, wind-whipped even in the summer. Here and there shanties clung to the hillside, the homes of the people he treated as "humans." In the county he had a reputation for being "poor white trash," too damn dumb to sell his "darkies" and move away from the land that his "king" cotton had eroded right out from underneath him.

He sat on his bunk, sipping at the jug, until he was good and drunk. That's when Vince Bowditch did his best thinking. In a stupor he could put everything else out of his mind but the main thing he wanted to concentrate on. He had been vastly wrong about these people. They were not like the highly inbred Southerners who accepted life calmly and were gracious enough to let someone else do their dirty work for them.

Doña Teresa, to be sure, was a lady; but she had too many brains to suit his purpose. Felix came the nearest to measuring up in his mind as the "country gentleman" type: opposed to this and opposed to that but willing to turn his back and forget the opposition if it could keep him in a comfortable life-style. Emilia, in his mind, was not only a "whore," but something far worse—"a nigger lover."

But these three were put out of his drunken mind. He concentrated on Miguel Escovarro. Now here, he thought, is a polecat who hasn't yet learned how to attack. He was the type of man Bowditch loved to pit himself against—whether with bare fists or simple brain power. Neither of them were complex and yet extremely complex meeting one of their own. But how did one go about breaking down a Miguel Escovarro? How did one go about grabbing away some of his land and power?

The jug told Vince Bowditch one thing: neither question was going to be answered in faraway Virginia. He'd just have to use his last few hundred dollars for a return to Texas and a closer look at the Escovarro land. Something would work out for him; he knew it would.

The storm eased before morning; the next day the sky cleared, and the Gulf went down. By midmorning the mouth of the Mississippi River was spotted on the horizon.

CHAPTER FOUR

Fate was working against Vince Bowditch. The repairs to the *Yellow Stone* were extensive, dragging out from day to day. It was time and money that Bowditch could ill afford to lose. He loathed New Orleans right from the first. It was too urban and sophisticated for his country tastes; and, yet, it awed him as well. The bricked streets, shaded by wrought-iron balconied buildings, amazed him with their cleanliness. To him it seemed that every street was aromatically scented by the kitchens of the numerous restaurants. He would have loved to step into any one of them and taste their wares, but his pocketbook and clothing kept him out. He would have loved to sleep in one of the spacious and elegant rooms of the Maison Vieux Carré, as the Escovarros were doing, but again he had to guard his capital. Instead he took his meals in dingy waterfront cafés, and probably ate as succulent seafood dinners as those put on the tables in the French Quarter. Nor could he complain about the "Four Pennies a Night for Bed" he doled out for a small room over the Lafitte Concert Saloon.

Vince Bowditch's problem, when he came to realize it, was that he was jealous. He wanted to be one of the "grandees" in their fawn-colored suits and beaver hats walking the Vieux Carré streets with an Orleans belle on his arm. He wanted to ride about in the open landau carriage, escorting some of the most exquisite beauties he had ever beheld. It would have thrilled him to see inside of just one of the towering mansions on the Rue de la Cité, even though he had been momentarily shocked when the Lafitte barman had told him:

"The richest madams in L'osee-anna own dem 'omes.

Yah got de money and her gals'll turn yah every way but Sunday. Yah name's yah tune and she'll provide: white, black, 'nd eb'en sum yellow gals. Hears tell, dey eben gotta couple black studs lak me to service the rich white women."

"All seems to be for the rich," Bowditch scoffed.

"Oh, dere's plenty 'ouses dat ain't so high in price, but I'd stay 'way from dem, sur, if'n I were a fine geb'man lak you."

"Why is that?"

"Dey mostly got 'pirated' gals, ones stolen away from der 'omes up north and forced ta be 'ores."

The black barman had just given Bowditch a germ of an idea. He leaned over the bar and spoke softly:

"Do you know a couple of strong white boys who don't care how they make an honest dollar?"

The barman glared at him, suspicion written all over his black face.

"Wat dey gotta do for yah, man?" he demanded, looking Bowditch up and down, trying to determine if he was the type of man who liked to do "dis 'n' dat" with other men.

"I'll be honest with you," Bowditch began his lie. "I married me a Spanish gal while fighting the war next door in Texas. Her family didn't like it and brought her here to New Orleans. I needs me some help to get her back."

"Dat's different," the barman grinned. "I knows many such."

On the third day after he had gained the information from the barman, Bowditch was loitering outside a millinery shop in the Vieux Carré. He was not directly in front of it but lingered idly some two shops up the street, on the opposite side. This had been his habit pattern for days, tracing every movement of the Escovarro family. He had to make his plan succeed that morning, because the *Yellow Stone* was scheduled to sail that evening.

Damn it all! Bowditch was thinking. I didn't expect them to be this long! I wonder if I can head the boys off . . . He straightened up and was on the point of setting off when the door of the millinery shop opened and the Escovarro

56

women stepped into the street, followed by a muscular black boy carrying their parcels. Bowditch stiffened. The boy could ruin everything.

He saw at once that the boy was slovenly, lagging farther and farther behind Emilia and Teresa with a shuffling walk. Bowditch waited. Let them come! he thought. It's all the better, if they do come now. The boy would make a good witness to his bravery.

Then, suddenly, down the street, behind the Escovarros and the boy, dashed two villainous-looking thugs. Bowditch calmly started to cross the street, as though he, too, were going for a walk.

When he was within ten yards of them, he saw the thugs seize the two startled women and begin to force them into a carriage that had just driven up. The timing was perfect. Bowditch fell upon the two kidnappers like an avenging Jove. His great fists pumped out, delivering hammer blows. The men staggered back, releasing their victims. Bowditch squared off at one of the men, pivoting on his left foot, leaning forward with the blow, putting his weight behind it, hooking the thug's jaw so hard that it should have sent the man reeling. Instead he crumpled like a suddenly emptied sack. His confederate measured Bowditch briefly with his eye, then backed slowly toward the carriage, waving his hands as though in surrender. Bowditch advanced slowly, carefully, so that the next phase of his plan would go as smoothly as the first.

"Help the ladies from the carriage," he barked. "And you, boy, go back to your shop and tell the owner to send me some men to help guard these thugs."

"Yassuh, boss," he squeaked in a high-pitched voice and took off on the run.

Then, to Bowditch's astonishment, the man who was supposed to be helping the women exclaimed:

"Jesus! I know this one. I see'd her dance a hundred times in a cantina up Nacogdoches way."

Bowditch pretended not to hear him.

"Are you two all right?" he asked.

"We seem to be," Emilia answered. "What is this all about, Mr. Bowditch?"

He shrugged and looked nervously back at the shop front. He had to get the women out of the carriage before help came. Suspicion crystallized into certainty in Emilia's mind. Bowditch had made not the slightest attempt to secure the horse or demand that the driver step down. The man sat as though awaiting a signal. With a sudden motion she was able to bend over close to her original captor's ear.

"I'll double his offer for the truth."

The man grinned sheepishly. "He's gonna sell you for whores."

Emilia's black eyes widened, then her chin came up and she loosed her laughter.

Vince Bowditch jumped at the sound. "What the hell?"

The man whom Bowditch had downed jumped to his feet and made a dash for the carriage. Both confederates swung themselves up into it, and the driver brought his whip down on the horse's flanks. The carriage careened away through the empty street, and Bowditch stood in total bewilderment. The black boy came back, still clutching the Escovarro packages.

"Ain't no mens in dat shop, boss. Only womens."

Seeing the expression of confusion on the white man's face, he said: "Here am a rider, boss. Shall I tell 'im?"

Bowditch nodded as though he were in perfect agreement and then slowly started to walk away. His investment had incredibly vanished along with the prize. Damn the man for having recognized the whore, he thought bitterly. Instead of ending up being in the good graces of the Escovarro brothers, he would end up their enemy. He was only thankful that the *Yellow Stone*'s departure would let him vanish quickly. Once back in Texas he would just have to figure some other way of getting a hold of their land.

Three blocks away the carriage was slowed to a walk so as not to attract undo attention.

Teresa's face was gradually returning from a pasty gray to its own natural hue.

"Sir," she whispered, "how can we ever thank you."

Emilia cast her a sidelong glance filled with amused contempt.

58

"That has already been decided," she said. "We are going to double their present offer."

"Well, now, ma'am," he said slowly. "I don't think me and the boys should do that."

Charley Doone's eyes went round with astonishment. It was the first time he had ever seen Tim Fowles refuse easy money. He couldn't help but notice that the woman with the high yellow-brown complexion was studying Fowles with equal curiosity, her eyes narrow and shrewd.

Too shrewd, Charley realized suddenly. This one knows men, he thought. She was not about to show an ounce of fear.

"No money?" Charley said. "Hey, man, we're in deeper than we were supposed to be."

"Exactly," Tim said coolly. "But the lady, here, said she'd double his offer for truth. I can't charge her for the truth."

"Then speak the truth," Emilia said incisively.

"Me 'n' my pals here have been out of work for a long time. This guy paid us five each, and another fiver for the carriage, to play like we was kidnappers for one of the whorehouses, him becoming the hero by rescuing you. But I don't get it, seein' as how you are already in the business."

Charley's watery gray eyes moved quickly and took in Emilia's bosomy frame. My God! It had been five years since he had seen Amarillo Rosa dance in the Cantina del Monte, but in fact this was she.

"No longer, sir," Emilia whispered sweetly. "I am now a happily married woman."

Fowles turned brick red.

"Now," she went right on, "if you will just see us back to our hotel, I think your pals can induce you into considering some form of reward."

She had, she saw at once, struck the right note. Charley Doone snapped up every coin he could lay his hands upon. He was glaring Tim Fowles into an acceptance.

They were entering a residential street of handsome homes. No one paid any attention to the well-dressed grandee who rode passed on a strutting gray gelding.

"Going back to the hotel," Fowles said, after some thought, "could put us in harm's way, ma'am. Bound to have been an alarm raised by that nigger boy yah was with. I got me a lady friend who lives on this street. Would you mind stayin' with her and lettin' your menfolk come and fetch you here. She's got servant slaves who can run a message to them."

"I suppose you are right," Emilia sighed. "You still could be arrested for what you've done. Is it far?"

"It's right here."

Obediently Teresa and Emilia followed the two men up the steps to the front door of a mansion. Emilia was looking at the leaded glasswork of the door, but Teresa's mind was slightly troubled. It seemed a little out of keeping that the buckskin-clad man, who had admitted that he was out of work, could have a lady friend in such a lush neighborhood.

They went into a hallway with a tile floor, and Fowles hung his buckskin cap on an iron hat rack made in the shape of deer antlers. Doone stayed by the door, hat in hand, as though fearing he would get kicked out if he took another step. A mountainous black man appeared from out of nowhere and held a whispered conversation with Fowles, then, with a flourish, he threw open a door and ushered the ladies inside.

"Make yoreseff ta 'ome," he said in a surprisingly thin voice. "I'll bring refreshments soon as I've seed the geb-'mum to Miss Beatrice."

The room in which Teresa found herself was like no other she had ever seen in her life. A soft rosy glow spread itself over everything. After a moment Teresa saw the reason. All the windows were rose tinted.

Seeing the expression of wonder on her face, Emilia said: "It's supposed to make a person look younger, you know." That statement was supposed to explain everything. But seeing that Teresa still did not understand, she added quickly: "It's an old whore's trick."

"Do you mean this is a . . ."

"The whole room reeks of it," Emilia said expansively. "Just look about."

It was incredibly crowded. All the woodwork was carved in tortuous Cupid patterns. Scarves of every conceivable size and pattern and color lay over everything. Huge bows of rose satin ribbon were tied about the legs of the piano; in every corner sat tufted love seats. Three enormous couches formed a "U" in the center of the room. The coal scuttle, painted with fanciful scenes, stood before the fireplace which was covered with a fireboard bearing a remarkably bad reproduction of a heavy-hipped Flemish nude. Even the brass pokers and fire tongs had rose bows of ribbon around their handles, as did the whisk broom which hung above them. On the marble mantelpiece stood a statuary reproduction of "David," without the fig leaf.

On the walls were pictures dwarfed by their massive frames. What little space was left in the room was taken up by small tables and groupings of straight-backed chairs. On every table resided a decanter and tray of stemmed glasses.

Teresa experienced a vicarious thrill in seeing such a place, but, for the life of her, she could not repress the feeling that a person would have to go outside in order to breathe. Everything seemed to hold a stale tobacco odor.

Neither woman heard the faint click. Human eyes replaced painted ones in a picture that had a view of the entire room. They were each studied carefully for many long moments.

Emilia suddenly shivered.

"What's the matter?" Teresa asked with a note of alarm.

"It's nothing. I just had the oddest sensation that I was being watched."

Teresa turned, as though to see if they were alone, and gasped. The butler had silently stolen into the room.

"Miss Beatrice is dressing," he said. "She says y'all come to de upstairs parlor for refreshments."

Beatrice Beauvoir climbed down from her spying perch and reentered her bedroom-office combination. Normally she would have been cursing any one who roused her before late afternoon, and especially if his name was Tim

Fowles. But what she had just seen dampened the tirade.

"Well?" Tim asked expectantly.

She didn't answer. A tall woman, in her mid-forties, she strode with long steps to her bureau. Over her thin mousy-brown hair she fitted into place a jet-black wig, never once, in the mirror, taking her eyes off Tim or the silent Charley Doone.

"Don't have much use for Mexicans," she said smugly, painting harsh black lines on her forehead for eyebrows.

"But they are something special, Min!"

Without turning, she glared at him with open hatred. "Don't you dare use that name, Tim Fowles, ever again!"

He didn't answer, just hung his head.

Minerva Fowles was dead. She had died, as long as her family was concerned, when she had left their poverty-wracked bayou home thirty years before. She had vowed to have a better life than her sickly English mother and drunken Cajun father. Uneducated, but strikingly beautiful, she had been picked up on the streets of New Orleans by the original Beatrice Beauvoir who ran a small house of four girls on the riverfront. After two months of extensive training Beatrice leased Minnie out to one of the more fashionable houses. The girl's popularity soon allowed Beatrice to buy back the lease and open a better house. The madam, always thinking of the future, had Minnie educated and groomed.

Flush with money, she tried to buy back her family's affection. Tim, two years her senior, had been sent to bring her home. Old Beatrice was not about to lose her investment and bought him off. It was ten years before Minnie saw her brother again, and by then she was the new madam and had adopted the dead woman's name. Tim found his sister to be a harder businesswoman to deal with and usually left with little more than a "carry-you-over" handout.

"Now to business," Beatrice Beauvoir went on. "A woman in my position, unfortunately—and undeservedly—acquires enemies. Other houses don't keep their stables as well stocked or cared for as we do in this house. Envy, you know, makes people do strange things."

She lowered her voice to a tense conspiratorial whisper, all the time painting her lips and powdering her face.

"It will be all over town by nightfall that these two lovelies are gone. Only a damn fool would put them to work. Men, dear brother, are bigger gossips than women when it comes to a new wench in a house. Besides they would stick out like sore thumbs among my white and black girls. I just don't have that much call for Mexican girls."

Tim shrugged.

"Briefly," she went on, turning to face him, "my offer is this: they will have to be sold away from here. I have a good contact in Tampico."

Tim's blue eyes sparkled. He had anticipated that his sister would tell him to return them to their husbands.

"And our share?" he said.

"One hundred dollars!" Beatrice said grandly.

Tim was about to open his mouth to accept the price when Charley Doone spoke up for the first time.

"A nigger slave's worth more than that," he said calmly. "Them's fine women, and one of 'em already trained."

Beatrice's face purpled at his interference, but after a moment she recovered.

"All right," she quavered, "I'll double it."

Charley nodded and Tim beamed.

"When do we leave?"

Beatrice suddenly felt a little stir of uneasiness. She didn't trust her brother. He had already accepted Bowditch's money, had a promise of more from the women. She felt that he was quite capable of taking her money and returning the women to their hotel. Then, very softly, she began to laugh.

"All in good time," she said, going to open the big metal safe in a curtained alcove. "There are certain arrangements to be made."

"Can't take too long," Charley ventured. "They'll be screaming for their husbands within the hour. We still might stand a chance of getting them on the *Yellow Stone* this afternoon."

"Don't be an ass!" she growled. "Everything will be watched for the next several days." Extending the money, she grinned at them wickedly. "Terence is serving them refreshments by now. A couple of sips and they'll do no screaming for several hours. In the meantime get rid of that damn carriage and yourselves. I don't want to see you for at least a week."

"You won't," Tim grinned, " 'cause we'll be drunk 'bout that long."

They turned and fled her bedroom and house. From the window she watched the carriage race down the street, the laughter rumbling in her throat. Then she went to the roll-top desk and studied the appointment book for that evening. It was as she knew it would be, every girl was booked for the evening, and some of them twice. Terence would have little difficulty carrying the drugged women to the carriage house while the girls were at their busiest.

Only Terence, of her town staff, knew that she owned a sugarcane plantation out near Slidell. And the all-slave plantation staff only knew her as "Miss Minerva" and never dreamed of questioning her numerous female guests.

Now Beatrice pondered the problem of her latest "guests." That they would bring her at least a thousand dollars apiece, she did not doubt. But they were far different from the normal farm and country girls brought to her attention. She anticipated trouble from each of them, but for different reasons. The big one would be wily, already having been a whore. The prettier one, even more difficult, because she was a lady. But Beatrice had her own method of breaking down bodies and wills to do her bidding. She didn't know what the word failure meant.

A stir of excitement thrilled Felix Escovarro's heart as he entered the hotel lobby and was approached by the tall and imposing Creole gentleman. It was the man he had been waiting days to see.

"Señor Escovarro," he said, being courteous enough to speak in Spanish, "may I introduce myself. I am Yves de Beauveau."

"Monsieur," Felix replied in French, "the pleasure is mine. I am honored that you have taken the trouble to seek me out."

"Sir?" he said, slightly confused.

"I have been seeking an appointment with you for several days."

"Aha!" Beauveau exclaimed. "I have just this morning returned from Natchez and have yet to visit my office. Forgive," he shrugged. "But please, might I inquire as to the whereabouts of your brother?"

It was Felix's turn to be confused. Miguel had shown no interest, whatsoever, in the business side of this trip. "I would presume, monsieur, that he is in his room or sightseeing. I rarely see him but at the dinner hour."

"Then perhaps a word alone with you, señor? Shall we say over in that corner where the slave boy is guarding packages that I believe belong to your family."

"Sir, I don't understand."

His handsome face spread into a winning grin. "Sir, even the chairs in this city have ears to hear and tongues to gossip by; please trust me."

Yves de Beauveau had been born to riches but had worked hard to compound them into an uncountable fortune. His cotton plantations and sharecropping farms dotted the map from Natchez, Mississippi, down to the bayous. The rumor was that he owned nearly ten thousand slaves; a report he would scoff at, and then on a sly wink admit, "it is closer to fifteen thousand and growing daily."

But a sizable portion of his wealth came about through a sharing marriage: Luella Lambeau shared her bed with Yves, and he shared his wealth with his father-in-law to develop a lucrative trade route down the Natchez Trace from Memphis to the Mississippi and New Orleans. And all of this was accomplished while Yves was still under thirty years of age.

He was not the type of man who dallied long over any given problem and had made the black boy tell his story straight out.

Felix's thin sensuous mouth made a cavernous "O" in his golden face.

"What has become of them?"

"The boy's description of the carriage was most accurate. I was able to locate it in a nearby residential area."

"And?"

"That's the puzzlement," Yves said truthfully. "Neither had the look of a frightened, kidnapped woman. They seemed to be on quite friendly terms with their abductors."

Felix laughed. "Hardly a puzzlement to me, Monsieur Beauveau. Those two could talk their way right out of hell. They are probably paying their own ransom at this very moment."

Beauveau smiled at him quietly, coolly. "I stayed in the neighborhood for a spell, señor, as one of the men was known to me. A few years back I had trouble with the man when he was a Negro bounty hunter. He's mean and sadistic and will do anything to earn a dishonest wage."

A feeling of utter defeat overcame Felix. He visualized the precious equipment money vanishing for another cause.

"I'll pay their demand, of course. However, I am not a very wealthy man."

"If I am not mistaken, Señor Escovarro, no demands will be made of you." He was about to continue but stopped his next word in mid-flight.

Felix's big face was puzzled.

"Boy," Beauveau growled in English, "you speak French or Spanish?"

"No, massa," he gasped. His head had been swiveling back and forth as the two men had spouted different languages at each other.

Then Beauveau smiled at him softly. "You have done good work today. Later I will talk to your master about you. You may go."

Yves stood for a moment staring after him. "I saw no reason in giving him a chance to repeat what I was about to say, Señor Escovarro. The men in question left the mansion after a short time, and from their spirits I would say they had already been paid."

"Paid?" he asked.

"The mansion is owned by a very notorious madam. It is quite a common practice for such as she to buy the flesh of women so that she might resell it to the flesh of men."

Felix threw back his head and laughed merrily.

"She is in for a big shock," he said. "My sister-in-law will be able to see through her game at once."

"Sir!" Yves exploded. "It is hardly a laughing matter. Her women are as much slaves as are my blacks at Beauwood. I'm sure that Beatrice Beauvoir has her methods of making people do as she wishes, the same as have I."

Felix sobered. The man was a total stranger, but to gain his help, he had to be told the unvarnished truth.

"I'm sorry," he murmured. "My brother and I are already in your debt. But, you see, having been in the same business herself, before marriage, Doña Emilia should be wise to this woman's methods."

Beauveau was slim and blond, with hair not two shades lighter than Felix's own. He now studied Felix curiously. He was trying to picture in his mind which of the women in the carriage was the exceedingly handsome Spaniard's wife. And, at the same time, trying to determine which of the women had been a whore . . . a determination he was unable to make, for neither seemed to fit the role. It had been their regal beauty that had kept him tarrying in the street to ascertain their true danger. A worshiper of beauty, he could not stand to see it marred, whether it be human or material.

Yves, himself, was all grace and beauty, but it was the grace and beauty of a spirited male of a line whose breeding seemed to have been carefully planned for generations. Every ounce of his blood was French, just as he was now sure every ounce of Felix's blood was Spanish.

"Thank you for your honesty," he said. "However, it makes our task slightly more difficult. Beatrice is no fool. She will not keep the women in New Orleans, is my guess, but it will take time for her to sell them to someone in Mexico."

"Then we must call in the police!" Felix said, and his voice was genuinely angry.

"I think not," he said gravely. "They would find nothing; they never have before. The mansion is large, and I would assume your women drugged to silence. I've seen her use the trick on unsuspecting ribald customers not to her liking. They think their drink is a sociable one, and within seconds her big black butler is tossing the trouble-maker into a cab."

"Then," Felix said impatiently, "what do you suggest?"

He leaned forward confidentially. "I happen to have an appointment at the mansion this evening. It would not be uncommon for me to bring along two 'out-of-town business associates.' We should be able to learn more on the inside than sitting here."

Felix managed a dignified nod of his head, but once the arrangements for the evening were planned, he began to have doubts.

Miguel, after silently hearing the weird events of the afternoon, saw through his brother at once.

"You've never been in a whorehouse, have you, Felix?"

He flushed. "No," he growled, "and were it not for obvious reasons, I'd not be going tonight."

Miguel's laugh was ribald. "I'm looking forward to it. I've heard that these houses in New Orleans are legendary. If man has ever performed a stunt before, they can duplicate it here."

"That is enough," Felix snapped.

Miguel eyed him with contempt. "I'm surprised you even knew how to get it hard enough to screw Teresa!"

Felix grew crimson. He wasn't even going to acknowledge the insult with comment. With a disdainful hoot Miguel poured himself another drink.

"Haven't you had enough?" Felix barked. "Due to what we face tonight."

Miguel gulped the glass of tequila in a single swallow and then belligerently smashed the glass onto the floor.

"Damn you!" he bellowed. "For a little brother you're a pain in the ass. Santa Anna turned you into a priest in more ways than one. But I'm still alive, so stop trying to become the cardinal of this family!" Then he stormed from the room.

Yves Beauveau took an immediate liking to Miguel Escovarro. He admired the quiet beauty of Felix, but Miguel's smooth handsomeness reminded him of the Renaissance men: daring, bold swordsmen. They were men of the same breed who looked for the excitements in life, not content to sit back and accept them as they came along.

Yves had suggested that they wear black evening suits so that the Spanish cut of their clothing would be less noticeable. Although he was to ride in a neat little landau, he had hired black geldings for the brothers.

The street, which had been modestly quiet during the day, was now crowded with vehicular traffic. Every mansion on the block was aglow with life and the strains of music. Young black boys fought over the chance to tie the gentlemen's horses to the hitching posts, praying for a coin to be tossed in their direction.

To Yves's surprise Beatrice Beauvoir opened the door herself.

"Yves," she trilled, offering her hand, "it has been far too long, dear boy."

"Miss Beatrice," he said, his voice rich and deep, raising her waxen hand to his lips. "Forgive the intrusion, but these gentlemen only arrived this afternoon. As their host in New Orleans, I felt duty bound to bring them along. May I present Michael and Felix."

"You would pull this on me," she laughed, "and on one of my busiest nights."

"Why isn't Terence here to help you?"

"Lazy nigger!" Beatrice said, and her voice was genuinely angry. "Up and got sick on me this afternoon."

So, Yves said to himself, she has them under the care of the black butler. He found the idea oddly disturbing. It could also mean that the black had already left town with them.

"Sorry to hear that," he said indifferently. "And perhaps it would be best if I bring the gentlemen back tomorrow."

"Wait," she said impatiently, while studying the two strangers. She was a woman who judged men by their eyes, not their faces. The one indicated as Michael pleased her; his eyes burning with lustful desire. The other one had cold, indifferent eyes and something she couldn't quite read.

"I can't offer you gentlemen anything other than a refreshing drink at the moment, but there might be a cancelation. Of course, you are confirmed with Alisa, Yves. You'll find her in the salon. I'll bring these gentlemen, to get better acquainted with them."

Beatrice turned to Miguel and kissed him lightly on the cheek. But he glanced uneasily over his shoulder at Felix. Damn him to hell anyway, he thought. Even this painted old circus horse might have been fun if he hadn't been along.

When Yves entered the salon, he found Alisa seated at the piano, playing softly. He paused, pretending to listen, but actually taking in the whole room at a glance. A dozen men sat about, sipping drinks and holding whispered conversations with extremely overdressed and overpainted women of varying ages. He knew all of the women by sight and name and was disappointed not to see a particular face that he sought. When he approached the piano, Alisa stopped playing.

"Go on," he said sweetly. "I like to watch your fingers move so expertly over the keys."

She laughed. It was like the twitter of birds. "They are expert at other things as well, in case you've forgotten."

For the first time Yves smiled.

"How can one forget. Play some more of that piece. It's your kind of music—like you really are—not like you have to be around here."

But for a moment she did not play. "Are they with you?" she whispered.

"Business associates."

"Monstrous chaps, aren't they? I should hate to meet them in a dark alley."

"But you would like to meet them," Yves said mockingly.

"Just that *one* brute," Alisa said wickedly. "He looks like he's ready to go from dusk to dawn."

"Would you like the opportunity to learn how primordial a brute he might be?"

Alisa smiled, a slow, enigmatic smile. Hearts have been lost, Yves thought, because of such a smile.

"I said, would you?" he repeated, his voice hoarse and unnatural.

"Yes," Alisa said, looking straight at Miguel with open lust.

"If Beatrice can switch me over to Daphine, I'll arrange it."

Alisa frowned. "That may be difficult. She and the old bat had one hell of a screaming match this afternoon. Damn near woke up the whole house. Her *ladyship* isn't letting Daffy work tonight. Say, I didn't know you went for Daffy's specialty."

He winked slyly and strolled to the table where the brothers sat alone and silent.

"The absence of the butler makes me believe that the women have already been moved out of the house. I want to be sure, though, and am going to ask for a young woman who has a loose tongue. My excuse will be that Alisa finds you far more charming, *Michael*. As a matter of fact you make her feel delightfully wicked. Stroll over to the piano and engage her in conversation."

"Is that really necessary?" Felix asked piously.

"Quite," Yves said coolly, "and stop looking so shocked. This is a well-run house, and no couple gets to the second floor until Beatrice gives her stamp of approval. For reasons known only to her, she seems to be keeping everyone downstairs overly long tonight. Oh, there's Beatrice now."

As quickly as Yves made his exit to the foyer, Miguel scurried to the piano. Felix had never felt so uncomfortable in his life. The room was hot and stuffy even though the French doors to the garden stood ajar. The mere thought of why these men sat with the painted harlots nauseated him. He rose and strolled to the nearest French door. The moonlit night air was scented with blooming jasmine, a natural perfume he could enjoy and stood breathing deeply.

"Damned presumptuous of you," Beatrice muttered grimly. "Did you tell that handsome brute he might have Alisa?"

"Naturally not. I just told him to engage her in conversation while I discussed a certain business matter with you. What do you say?"

Despite herself, Beatrice could not keep from thinking of the profit margin. She could trust the talkative Daphine with Yves because the girl's mouth would be stuffed full of him during the session and besides, hadn't she bought some of her best black wenches from Yves Beauveau.

"Alisa's a fragile and expensive piece of property," she mused, "and that handsome lout must have a foot if he's got an inch. I'll have to charge extra."

"Put whatever it is on my account, Beatrice. But just get us upstairs as soon as possible."

"Oh, my God!" she flared. "Look at the time. I should have everyone upstairs by this time. See what happens when I have to do everything. Yves, you know your way to Daffy's room. Go on up. I'll see to your friend and Alisa after I get a few regulars on the road."

It was obvious to Yves that the girl had been crying bitter tears. Her moon eyes were nearly swollen shut, but they flared with fear upon seeing him.

"Massa Yves," she gasped. "She done sold me back ta yah, a'ready?"

"Hardly," he laughed. "I've purchased your services."

The room was awash in a silvery glow from the full moon. Knowing she was not working that night, Daffy had changed into a simple cotton nightgown. It clung to her brown supple body seductively, almost defiantly.

"Why you do dat?" she declared. "You get all de brown gals you want fur free back home."

"Why?" Yves grinned. "I just started remembering how good you could make a man feel."

"Ain't what you said at Beauwood," she sneered. "You sold me away 'cause I learned to love what you teached me ta do."

Yves Beauveau's blue eyes widened, then a slow flush of anger stole over his handsome face.

"That's because you were doing it with your own," he muttered grimly, "and depriving the plantation of those new births. I never could understand why you couldn't lie with your own men naturally."

"Ain't never and never shall," she declared. "Here, don't have to."

Yves sat down in the easy chair and stretched his long

legs out into a vee. He knew exactly how to calm her and make her talk.

"But are you happy here?" he asked calmly.

Daphine shrugged thin shoulders as she ambled across the room, never once taking her eyes from his crotch. She had been a nine-year-old house servant at Beauwood when Yves had first introduced her to his manhood. Yves was just twenty and recently engaged. His father still ran the plantation under the strict rule that "no white was to cut the meat of the black wenches" while he was alive. They both remembered that first day vividly.

The wooden tub had been carted up the back stairs and placed in the young master's bedroom. Buckets of steaming water had been dumped in to bring it half full. This was no time for the young master to bathe in the Mississippi; that afternoon he was to be married. Yves had been allowed to breakfast in bed while the bath preparations were taking place. As usual he paid the servants little mind, as though they were shadows he could walk right through. His mind, since awakening, had been on Luella Lambeau; a fragile little thing with no brains and no emotions—entirely passive. She, he knew, would enter the wedding bed 'as virginal as himself and would be a dutiful little wife, faithfully submitting to a repugnant ordeal of his masculine demands. Just once he wanted to be with an aggressive woman, like, he thought, the ones would be in those—those places in New Orleans his father would never let him attend. And as he thought of such women, his desire became unbearable, but he did not want to relieve himself and possibly ruin his wedding night.

Fully erected, he rose from bed and prepared to bathe. The water was near scalding, and his foot came out as quickly as it had entered. He pulled a straight chair to the tub side and wondered how long he was going to have to wait. Only his mother bathed in this fashion.

Suddenly he was aware of staring eyes. The skinny pig-tailed girl stood just inside the bedroom door with a stack of fresh towels. He didn't bother to scold or reprimand her unannounced entrance; he became too fascinated at the line of her stare.

Daffy had seen black men nude before, lots of them at the swimming hole. It had never crossed her young mind to think that white men might be different—quite different. Black men had a purplish rose of skin at the end of their "poles," which she had never thought much about. But she was awed by the pink helmetlike knob that rested atop this extension. She had never before seen an aroused black man and took this to be the white man's natural endowment.

Because of her awed expression Yves's arousal increased. Involuntarily his cock stiffened more and jumped.

Daffy jumped back and gasped: "How you do dat?"

Yves felt suddenly, deliciously wicked. "I didn't," he said pompously. "It has a mind of its own."

Her eyes flared until the pupils were brown pinpoints in a sea of white. "It do?"

"Of course. It is also getting ready for the wedding. Did you think this special bath was just for me?"

"Yassa."

Yves liked to play tricks on their simple, superstitious, uneducated minds. He toyed with what game he could play with this young thing.

"Well, the bath is mainly for *him*. But it is bad luck for anyone to see him before the wedding. They'll fall down and die before I say, 'I do.' Oh, you're doomed!"

The stack of towels fell to the floor, and she wrapped her arms about her head.

"Oh, Lawdy," she cried. "No one done told Daffy dat. Ain't no way I wants ta die, I'ze jest been born, almost."

Yves jutted his legs out into a vee, making his penis seem even larger and more animated as it swayed.

"There are ways you can make amends," he whispered.

Daffy's face was near ashen. "What dat mean, massa?"

"It means that if you come close and touch it and kiss it, you might be forgiven."

Wildly Daffy shook her head.

"My mammy'd kill me! Ain't supposed ta touch one of dem till I'm least twelve. I can't . . . I can't."

"Idiot," he snapped, "this isn't like a black one. White ones have power. Do it or die!"

She came like a shot and stood between his legs, her thin

hand trembling as it came in contact with his torrid, rigid flesh. Surprisingly she found it soft and enticing, even a little wicked.

"The kiss," he whispered.

As Daffy bent down to his stomach, he saw that her lips had parted even before they touched the head. He suddenly pushed upward, forcing immediate entry. He was aware, after a time, that she had not removed her mouth. He had never felt anything so exciting, but the fear of being discovered overcame passion. He attempted to draw her mouth away, but her lips fought for possession, clinging fiercely.

There was, Yves decided, only one thing to do about this. He allowed the storm brewing in his loins to build to its volcanic eruption.

Good-bye virginity! he exulted.

Daffy drew back, her lips swollen and trembling.

"That was good," he said dreamily. "It has saved you," he paused, lending bitter emphasis to his words, "—for the time being."

For the next ten years it became a wickedly dangerous game in Yves's mind. He would figure out the oddest places and strangest times for them to be together, as though flying in the face of his father's authority. But still he would not "cut" her, and when of age she refused to let the black men have her as well.

Yves's father was dead and the burden of Daffy squarely on his shoulders. The rumors were growing, and he wanted it stopped before the scandal reached his wife's ears and he was involved. He paid two black bucks to force her into oral sex and sold her to Beatrice Beauvoir on his next trip to New Orleans.

Daphine had never blamed Yves. In her eyes it was her own people who had forced him into selling her. The man would always be her idol.

She came and sank to the floor between his legs, letting her head rest lightly on his thigh, her hand dangerously close to his crotch.

"I'se happy here," she whispered, "when I get a chance to see yah in the parlor once in a while. I'm happiest now, 'cause you came to me."

"Why were you crying when I came in?"

She inched her hand closer, just like the game had been played in the old days. "Weren't too good a day, I 'spects. I mostly gets only one trick a night, 'cause of my color and what's I only does. I'm asleep hours 'fore dem and awake hours 'fore, too. Today, just da same, 'sept I seed sumptin' de old crow didn't lak."

"What was that?" Yves asked, controlling his excitement.

"Two ladies. Real ladies with fancy clothes like Miss Luella wears. But dey looked dead, with ole Terence carted 'em away on him shoulders. I watched him take 'em out back to the stables and he caught me."

"And he told Miss Beatrice?"

Her hand was now kneading him to arousal. "That ole nigger tell her eberything, 'cause he don't lak me. He don't 'cause I won't with him. Bet you didn't see him tonight."

"No, I didn't."

She laughed. " 'Cause dey got scared of what Daffy seed. When eberyone's having' their most fun tonight, he's goin' ta take 'em away in da farm wagon."

"Good girl!" he breathed, relaxing back in the chair. He now had time to give her her reward.

The room was suffocating Felix Escovarro, mentally and physically. He was blind with fury at his brother for having gone off with the fragile beauty, and equally incensed at the length of time it was taking Yves Beauveau to gain any information.

Suddenly he was aware that he was the only occupant of the garish room. He rose stiffly, still clutching his hat in knuckle-white hands and stole toward the foyer like an embarrassed little boy. He had to have fresh air before his stomach revolted on him. Almost too late, he spied the madam in a whispered conversation with a massive black man. He wheeled back into the parlor, but not before he was seen.

"Who's he?" Terence demanded.

"A guest of Yves Beauveau. I didn't have a girl for him, so just left him sitting in the parlor."

A sharp bang from the door knocker echoed through the foyer.

"Damn!" Beatrice cried. "The second stringers are arriving already. Get the wagon out of the carriage house and be gone before you're spotted. I'll ride out in a couple of days."

Their words had come to Felix only as a mumble. For one moment he remembered Yves's words about the butler. But the black in the foyer belied such a position, dressed as he was. His piercing eyes roved around the candlelit room, and his face was as hard and stern as chiseled bronze.

With a vengeful stride he was across the room to the French doors before Beatrice Beauvoir's next guests were ushered in. He found himself in a courtyard garden, surrounded by a high brick wall. The moon came from behind a scudding cloud and washed everything in silver. A wrought-iron gate sat in the far corner, leading to the back of the property, he assumed. Keeping to what shadows were available, he made it through the gate and onto the back driveway. He was determined now to round the house and await the other two men by the horses.

When he rounded the cookhouse extension, bringing into view the carriage house and the drive to the street, Felix saw a two-teamed wagon being led out. As the moon was clouding again and the light was fading, he could not distinguish the wagon's cargo, but there was no mistaking the black man silently urging the horses forward. Now his attire made sense to Felix. Who would question an old farmhand calmly returning to the countryside.

The black got onto the high seat and let the horses have their own head for an almost noiseless ramble down the drive. Felix had a fleeting glimpse into the bed of the wagon. Up near the driver were a couple of barrels and a wooden crate. The rest of the bed appeared to be a load of straw completely covered by a tarpaulin.

Felix's emotions were divided between growing alarm for the safety of Teresa and Emilia and a thrill and quickening of pulsebeat that tingled over him with the realization that he had surely found them. No action on his part could be taken immediately, he realized. An attack on the wagon would bring the black boys tending the horses and carriages to the driver's aid. He considered going and rousting Yves and Miguel from their pleasure. Then he discountenanced the thought. That would only arouse Beatrice Beauvoir's curiosity. He waited until the wagon was out of the drive, then set a fast pace for the street.

Felix lifted the roan's bridle and let it go. There was a crack and crunch of gravel, fire struck from stone, a low whinny, a snort, and then steady, short, clip-clop of iron hooves on hard brick. Felix could just discern the wagon and its driver outlined in shadowy gray before him. He held his horse back, measuring the distance he wanted to maintain until the city was no more.

A thick belt of thunderclouds obliterated the view, turning the Gulf air cool and moist. Felix now saw why Yves had insisted upon their attire; he was just a dark figure among the shadows. He almost laughed thinking of the other article Yves had pressed upon each of them. At the time it had struck him as almost comic-opera foolishness, now he thought he could put it to very good use.

The roan plunged into a gully, where sand and rough going made Felix stop planning his moves and attend more closely to riding. In the darkness the wagon was not so easy to keep in sight as on the even city streets, and now he had to be watchfully attentive to it. Then followed a long stretch through a mangrove swamp, denying Felix any move whatsoever without warning his quarry.

He lost track of time but judged they had been on the road for over two hours when they came out upon rolling pine-studded countryside. Felix veered his horse from the track and inland. The horse balked at having to break a new trail, and Felix had to keep it on a tight rein.

The farm track was old and seldom used, and it zigzagged and turned and twisted. The wagon team plodded along without urging. Terence, unaware of any danger, sat hunched over the reins, nearer asleep than awake.

Felix had circled the wagon and now came riding directly toward it down the track, his lower face now covered by the black handkerchief given him by Yves Beauveau. A

sudden instinct made him pat his breast pocket to make
sure he still possessed his derringer.

A dazzling blue blaze showed the countryside and the
storm-driven clouds. In the flare of light Felix saw the
driver clearly. His heart sank instantly. The man would
hardly be carrying the cargo Felix suspected and be asleep.

Then the thunderbolt racked the heavens, and as it
boomed away in lessening power, Terence came to with a
jolt. At first he couldn't tell if the horseman was riding
toward him or leading the way. In the next lightning flash
he saw the mask and hand-held derringer and knew the
worst.

"Wha' yah want from an ole farm nigger lak me?" he
cried.

"Your wagon," Felix replied simply.

"Ain't of no use, massa," Terence quavered.

"How strange! Then perhaps your cargo is of use."

A smile that was only a gleam flitted over his dark face.
His reply amazed Felix. The man's fear had suddenly vanished.

"Mask or no mask, I seed you 'fore," Terence spat.
"What's Miss Bea's cargo gotta do wid you?"

Before he could answer came the torrent of rain. It was a
cloudburst. It was like solid water tumbling down. Felix
had to shout to make himself heard.

"Everything! Now do you lift that tarp or do I after I've
shot you?"

The black sat frozen, his fear returning. Slowly he turned
to climb into the back of the wagon. But even as he did so,
a corner of the tarp began to move as though coming to life
and was thrust aside. A figure sat upright and then sput-
tered in the rain deluge.

Teresa's brain whirled. She had at first no control over
it, and a thousand thronging sensations came and went and
recurred with little logical relation. There was the attack;
the feeling of helplessness; the odd rescue; the garish
rooms in the mansion. Then after the refreshing drink she had felt
herself drifting. How black the room was—as black with
her eyes open as it was when they were shut! And the si-

lence—it was like a cloak. There was absolutely no sound. She knew she was dead.

When she awakened, she thought she was still dead. Under the tarp was as black as her drugged state. But a cool wind blowing under the covering caused her to put her hands up and fight for life. The rain brought her totally to her senses but confused her as to her whereabouts.

And the next instant she saw him, cool, smiling, devilish—saw him in the flash of lightning on the huge black roan; the next his bigness, his apparel, his physical being were vague as outlines in a dream. But, in spite of the mask, she knew her husband's eyes. Eyes that warned her to immediate silence.

"How is the other one?" Felix queried sharply.

"She be the same soon," Terence replied quickly.

"All right, down with you. You take my horse and I'll take the wagon. And don't let me catch you circling back around."

"Don' worry, massa," Terence cried, scrambling down. "Ah aims ta keep libin'."

With blacker gloom and deafening roar came the torrent of rain. One of the horses began screaming and kicking in terror.

Felix had no time for niceties. He hit the mare a blow on the side of the head that numbed his hand and staggered the horse, then backed the two around to make a turning. Both mares now balked, and he had to lash them with the whip to get them to move.

Another dazzling blue blaze showed the bayous being lashed into a fierce foam. In the flare of light Felix saw Teresa's face.

"Are you afraid?" he asked.

"Yes," she replied simply.

"Keep under the tarp," he called, vaulting up to the wagon seat.

The rain was so heavy he could see only the outlines of the horses. He snapped the reins and called out. The horses wouldn't move except to dance nervously in place. He took the whip and lashed them across their flanks. They reared and started off, fetlocks flying as they strained against the

mud and wind. Every mile he made now was worth two
when the rain had been on the ground long enough to soak
in. Then the road would be a foot deep in mud and impass-
able. The horses tried bravely to run. They actually did get
the wagon moving at a kind of half gallop. Felix didn't like
cutting them, but there was no choice. He leaned forward
and slashed at them again. The mare screamed as the whip
brought blood to her flanks. They'd never been lashed before, and terror brought strength to their legs. The wagon
lurched and slithered wildly.

In the back the straw matting kept the women's bodies
from being thrown against the sides, but the bone-
shattering jars brought Emilia around.

"What the hell?" she asked groggily.

Teresa moved close. "Hush, Em. It's all right now."

Emilia found Teresa's hand and clutched it. "What is
happening?"

"All I know for sure is that Felix has found us and is
driving this wagon."

Emilia was silent for a long moment. "God, what a fool I
was," she sighed. "I should have sensed the double cross
from the beginning."

Teresa shuddered. "You mean this was Bowditch's plan
all along?"

"Like hell!" she hissed. "We were sold to the madam of
that house by those two snakes."

Teresa was incredulous. "But what good would that do?
They'd never be able to force me to become a whore."

Emilia's laugh was harsh and cruel. "They would have
sold us to someone in Mexico, Teresa. There they have
many ways to force a mind, to control it. I know, I've seen
my mother 'train' her girls. A few times on peyote and they
don't even know what they are doing. Then they get
hooked. Then they will do anything the madam demands just
to get their daily little dose. After awhile they need a man
between their legs daily, and the peyote is only for a rosy
glow."

"Emilia," Teresa asked cautiously, "is that how your
mother started you?"

Emilia's rich mellow laugh returned. "I think she started

training me from the day I was born but was very careful to keep my mind and body untainted by drugs. By the time I was twelve, she had taught me to dance and sing and be very selective about the male customers. I knew no different so took that life for granted, except that if there is such a thing as a snob in a whorehouse, I was she." Then she sighed. "But it's all over now. For fifteen years, Teresa, I was very careful not to let a mistake happen. Now I don't have to fear. Oh. Teresa, what I'm trying to say is, thank God, we're safe. I would have killed before I'd have had my baby born in a whorehouse."

"Oh, Em," Teresa gasped. "Are you sure?"

"Very, very, sure," Emilia purred happily. "But I've said nothing to Miguel yet."

Teresa let out a little squeal, and the women hugged each other joyously.

The wagon suddenly acted as if it had taken wings. They came to the part of the road that ran beneath the mangrove trees. It had been raining less than twenty minutes. The road was soaked, but nowhere near as much rain had reached it as in the open. Beneath the top wetness it was hard as ever. The horses tore along, their flanks bleeding, their mouths flecked with foam. The rain drove down, but here it came in blasting gusts, and above their heads the trees bent almost double with the force of wind and water. Twice lightning crashed near them, but the horses were more frightened of the human terror behind them now than by anything else. They slewed wildly around a corner, the back right wheel went into the ditch, smashed over a rotten log, jounced off a stone outcropping, and ran smoothly once more.

Almost immediately after that Felix hauled the gasping horses to a stop. In front of them a huge windfall blocked the road. There was no way around. The swamp walled them in on either side—the great trees shrieking and bending to the weight of the storm, their moss-hung branches dancing like ghosts rising for their night on Bald Mountain.

"What is it?" Teresa called, peeking from beneath the tarp.

"Tree across the road," he shouted without turning. "We'll have to clear it out or walk."

He stood and lifted the seat of the wagon. He fumbled about in the darkness until his hand came to rest on a double-bladed ax. By the time he had waded into the tangle of wet wood and begun to slash at the broken branches, the two women had scrambled out of the wagon bed. In less than five minutes the massive trunk was clean for a width that was slightly broader than the width of the wagon. Teresa and Emilia had cleared his cuttings to the side of the road.

Felix unhitched the horses and dragged the mare up to the barrier. The horse shied and tried to get away. He climbed up on the log and dragged at the reins. She braced her feet. With nothing to hang onto, he was pulled off the tree and flat into the mud.

"Look out!" Teresa screamed as the horse started to rear and paw the air. In an instant she rushed to grab the loose reins and hold the horse's head down with all her strength.

When Felix got up, his mouth was bleeding.

"Bit my damn tongue," he growled. "Can you hold her steady?"

Teresa nodded, but she signaled with her head for Emilia to come and help her.

Felix looked to the right. Just off the road the underbrush was piled four feet deep. He pulled the second horse around so it was facing the brush, then went behind it and whacked it on the lacerated rump. The animal leaped forward crashing down the brush. Felix hit it again, and it floundered through. He plunged after it as it stood trembling and rolling its eyes under the big trees beyond. He led it around the broken trunk and back onto the road beyond the windfall. He shouted back for the women to lead the other horse through as he tied the mare to a tree, then climbed back over the log and dragged the wagon up until the tongues projected over the log and the front wheel almost touched.

Teresa and Emilia came back around the log, drenched and disheveled.

"We've got to get the wagon over the log," he said matter-of-factly.

"What about just riding the horses?" Emilia suggested.

Felix shook his head. "They've probably never had a human on their back and would be more dangerous. You two get behind the wagon and push when I tell you."

Teresa started to protest on Emilia's behalf, but a stern glance from the woman stilled her.

Felix got under the wagon and set his shoulders under the front seat, braced his legs, and began to straighten. The front wheels came up slowly ten times heavier than normal with their weight of mud. He set his teeth and lifted. The wheels passed the top of the log.

"Now!" he gasped, straining forward.

The women pushed and shoved and slipped in the mud. The back wheels moved a quarter of a turn—half a turn—three quarters. Then the front wheels rested on the log, the harness tongues pointing at the sky. Shaking with effort, he came from beneath the wagon and went behind the wagon.

"Rest," he said between heavy gasps.

But he would not rest. He set his back against the tailgate and shoved. The front wheels rolled off the log and came down with a splintering crash on the opposite side. The wagon was now straddling the log which came within a few inches of the black mud welded to its bottom. Together they shoved it forward until the back wheels touched the bark of the tree. Felix set his palms under the tailboard and lifted. His legs quivered with the effort. The veins popped into terrible relief on his arms and forehead. After a second blood gushed from his fingernails.

"You'll kill yourself, Felix," Teresa cried.

He ignored her, not wishing to waste energy with talk. The wheels came up but not high enough. His lungs were like molten fire, the pain in his arms excruciating. He closed his eyes, pulled lips flat against his teeth, and heaved. The wagon went up and forward. The wheel missed the log entirely and the tailboard crashed down on the far edge, ripping off a great chunk of bark.

Felix sank forward on one knee, gasping. There were silver flashes in front of his eyes, and his head was ringing. For a moment he forgot who he was or where he was.

Teresa sprang forward, scrambled over the log, and started to hitch the horses. Emilia came to stand by Felix. His heart was thundering and his breathing was harsh and unsteady.

"Now there is an amazing sight," she said. "I was unaware she had such capabilities."

Felix smiled weakly, blinking the water from his eyes. "Her months alone on Santa Anna's ranch forced her to learn many things, Emilia."

"A strange blessing in disguise. Still I hate to see her acting like a stable hand."

When the horses were harnessed, she came back to them. Felix's face was whiter than chalk, and the blood had begun to seep from the corner of his mouth. Cold fear gripped Teresa.

"Oh, my darling," she cried, "why did you lie to me? You didn't just bite your tongue. There's a deep gash from the corner of your mouth to the cheek."

She tore off a piece of her sodden petticoat and gently swabbed away the blood. She didn't like the amount of blood he was losing. Her eyes locked on Emilia's, and they communicated without speaking. Together they helped raise Felix to his feet and walk him toward the log. His head was so light he was unaware of movement. They forced him to slide under the tarpaulin.

"I'll drive," Teresa said with stern conviction. "You stay with him and keep his head raised."

Only one thought centered on her brain: how much blood could a person lose and still live? She had no way of knowing the answer. She climbed to the driver's seat and lashed out at the horses. Once more they went careening down the narrow road. Once a tree thundered to earth behind them, and twice more lightning smashed into the bayou swamp close by. The rain slashed at her and bits of branch and hanging moss pummeled horses and driver alike, but they passed out onto the delta without further delay. The horses were weakening rapidly now. Not even the whip could make them move faster. Teresa could see their chests heaving like bellows.

She was about to whip them again when a particularly brilliant flash of lightning lighted up the roadway. It was followed almost instantly by a clap of thunder that shook the wagon. Teresa blinked. It had only been a split second, but in that moment she could have sworn she saw movement on the road. Impossible, of course. No one would be abroad in this. A trick of the light probably.

The driver of the landau had experienced the same sensation, but being an experienced coachman, he began to pull his horse to an immediate stop and to the far right. He feared that both vehicles could not pass each other without crashing.

Whether by sight or sense, Teresa's horses knew the same. Their poor minds had taken all the fright they could stand and crashed off the roadway and toward the woods. Teresa screamed but could not control them. She was hurled from the wagon when it hit the gulley, her fall broken by the water-filled ravine.

Her scream had aroused Felix and Emilia, but as they rose from the wagon bed, a good-sized branch tore loose just in front of them and knocked both of them out the back of the wagon. Felix didn't feel either the shock of the blow or the pain of it. He twisted as he fell, keeping his body between Emilia's and the ground, and he never released his grip.

The wagon caught forcibly between two live oak trees and splintered, leaving the horses free to run out their fear until they would collapse and die of exhaustion.

In spite of his desperate mission Yves Beauveau could not leave the scene of such an accident without giving aid. He had seen the wagon driver's body being catapulted from its seat and ran toward the gulley. Teresa was just pulling herself to the edge of the muddy bank when he reached her and helped her onto solid ground. Instinctively, in spite of her muddied condition, he knew who he was pulling to safety.

"Madame Escovarro," he enthused, "thank God you are safe."

Teresa blinked at him foolishly.

"Oh, forgive me," he went right on, "I am Yves Beauveau, a friend of your husband."

"Felix," she said numbly, then on a rising wail. "Oh, dear Lord, he and Emilia are still on the wagon."

But even as she turned to flee toward the scene of the crash, they were confronted by a nightmare scene right out of hell. Felix approached half bent over and breathing like an animal. One dripping sleeve had been ripped off the shoulder of his coat and shirt and hung like a bloodstained rag from the buttoned wrist. The other sleeves were gone entirely, and the rest of the shirt was in tatters. His bare torso had been sluiced down by the rain, but now a dozen cuts, scratches, and abrasions were beginning to show blood. One boot was missing; the other was like a huge club foot packed into a great lump of black mud. His golden hair was matted with grime and leaves and there was a two-inch blood-soaked gash on his cheek. The water ran off, him making a muddy red pool at his feet as he stood desperately gripping the limp body of his sister-in-law.

Emilia's golden-brown limbs were bruised and lacerated where the tree limb had caught at her, and even her blouse and brassiere had been torn from her by its impact. He had her now under the knees and shoulders. Her hips sank deeply between his arms while her head lolled back over his forearm as if the neck were broken. The water ran in a steady stream from her tangled hair and her face had that faintly greenish hue of a corpse.

Together they tried to lift Emilia out of Felix's arms. It was like trying to get her out of a vise. Yves swore. Teresa wet her lips. "What is it?"

"Shock. Look at his eyes. He doesn't even know where he is. Señor Escovarro!" His words had no effect. He reached out and slapped Felix hard. The eyes didn't waver and the grip didn't relax. "Then let's lead him to my carriage. Quick!" He turned to his driver. "Get the medical kit and the brandy flask from the carriage."

The black man nodded, shaken by what he had seen. Yves tried to examine Emilia as they led Felix along.

"What's the matter with her?"

"I think it's only a faint."

"She looks dead."

"There's a pulse, señora. *Thomas, where's the kit!*"

Thomas ran back. "Here, massa." Yves snatched an earthenware bottle from the square leather satchel, pulled the cork loose with his teeth, and rammed the bottle under Felix's nose. Felix coughed and turned his head away.

"Watch him, Thomas. The ether will make him go all of a sudden!"

Felix did. Within seconds he quivered and went limp. Yves wrenched Emilia out of his arms, and Thomas and Teresa barely managed to keep Felix from plunging facedown into the mud. They started to drag him to the carriage, and Yves snapped, "Leave him! He'll be all right for a second." He carried Emilia to the carriage and laid her across the seat. His hands moved expertly over her body in a rapid search for serious injuries. "I don't find anything broken," he said hoarsely.

Yves took a bottle of smelling salts from the kit and bent over her. He moved the bottle beneath her nostrils several times, listening carefully, then he straightened up. "She's coming around." He waved the bottle again and glanced at Teresa. "Are you all right?"

Teresa nodded. She looked shakier now than when Yves had pulled her from the mud. "Come into the carriage and care for her. My man and I shall see to your husband."

Emilia moaned as he lifted her to a sitting position and then gently eased her back into Teresa's lap after she had taken a seat.

He went out, and Teresa put a hand on Emilia's forehead. The skin was still unnaturally cold and clammy. Unconsciously her mind took up a double prayer, for the lives of Felix and Emilia and for the life that Emilia carried in her womb.

The men placed Felix flat on the floorboard. Thomas put the carriage into a dead run. Yves took a scalpel from the kit and cut off the remnants of shirt and jacket. He worked swiftly and efficiently, cleaning him and treating the multiple scratches and cuts with antiseptic. Before he was finished, Felix was moaning.

Teresa said shakily, "Will he live?"

"He's lost an awful lot of blood, but he's a big man. Now let's see to your patient."

This time a single whiff of the smelling salts brought Emilia around. She opened her eyes and stared at an unfamiliar face. Her head ached with confusion. Every muscle in her body was stiff and sore. She tried to struggle upright and a hand restrained her gently. A far-off voice said, "Easy, Em, easy." She turned her head. She was lying in Teresa's lap.

"How do you feel?"

Emilia stared, frowned, and then remembrance flowed through her. She started up, thrusting Teresa's hands aside.

"It's all right, Emilia, *it's all right!*"

Emilia stopped struggling.

"Here, let her take a little sip of this brandy. Hold her head so she doesn't choke."

The burning warmth of the liquor took the tensions out of Emilia's muscles. She sank back slowly until her head touched Teresa's lap. She wet her lips. She said, "What of . . . what of Felix?"

Teresa nodded gently. "He'll be fine."

Emilia closed her eyes. A tremor ran over her face, and she flung an arm down to her stomach. After a second her lips moved. "My baby? What about my . . . ?" Again the tremor shook her.

Teresa felt a surge of helpless sympathy. She said quietly, "I'm sure it's going to be all right. Now, Em, this is a friend. Lie quiet and let him see to your wounds."

This time Yves's hands shook as he had to cut away part of the dress and brassiere. Not even in a whorehouse had he seen such an amply endowed woman. He was almost loath to cover her with a lap robe when he had completed the application of antiseptics.

"Now you need rest," he said, settling back on the opposite seat, preparing to put the articles back into the medical kit.

Emilia took her arm away from her forehead and opened her eyes. She said emptily, "Where is Miguel?"

There was a sharp snap from Yves's fingers. He looked down. He'd broken the scalpel in two. He flung the pieces into the kit irritably. He moved to the corner of the carriage and looked out. Keep your mouth shut, he told himself. No need to tell the woman that her husband had refused to leave the whorehouse to see to her rescue. There was anguish and desolation written in his face. Why would Miguel want to stay with Alisa when he had this remarkably beautiful woman for a wife? And why stay when she was in such danger? Still he had to offer some answer.

"He is probably looking for us right now."

Emilia had not been watching him, she had reclosed her eyes. But Teresa had noted everything, with growing puzzlement. Her mind whirled with a million questions. Questions she somehow knew she could not ask at the moment. Yves Beauveau met her eyes, and they each knew that he had lied.

"How did you come to be involved in our problem, señor?"

Yves felt on safe ground. He related the events as they had affected him without embellishment, stopping short when it came to their visit to the whorehouse.

"It's quite all right," Teresa said simply. "She's fast asleep."

Yves looked up. The rain had tightened her hair into tight ringlets, giving her a girlish, appealing look. Her soft brown eyes were filled with curiosity and the need to gain every scrap of information from him. God, he thought, how lucky were each of these brothers. They each possessed powerful women, but powerful in different ways. He would have given all his worldly wealth to lie with Emilia for a single night; he would have sold his soul to the devil to lie with Teresa forever. There was no bitterness in his voice when he spoke, only a kind of hollow finality. "Naturally," he said, "we had to go to where they were holding you. I've known Beatrice Beauvoir for some time and was able to get us easy entrance."

Teresa couldn't help it. She began to giggle. "Felix in that place? Oh, how shocking it must have been for him."

Yves's admiration for her soared. "And lucky for you that he was shocked. I assume that he saw the wagon leave the mansion while we were still seeking information from within."

Teresa took a breath. "And Miguel?"

"I'd rather not say."

"I'll make a guess, if you like."

"Make it."

"Fear."

"I'm not saying that's not possible, but it isn't likely."

"Oh, he hides it well with masculine brutishness, but surely, as a doctor, you sensed it."

Yves laughed. "I am hardly a doctor, señora. I am a landowner and merchant. Your husband wishes to buy farm equipment from me."

"But the kit and your expertise," she exclaimed in wonderment.

He laughed again, thankful the topic had gotten away from Miguel Escovarro. "Upriver, where I have my plantations, doctors are few and far between. To keep his people healthy, a man is smart to learn some doctoring. Slaves cost a great deal of money to replace."

She looked up startled and anxious. "You own slaves, Señor Beauveau?"

"Many," he replied simply. "It would be impossible to farm without them."

"Perhaps, but I can't help but feel sorry for them."

"You will see that their life is quite simple and nice."

"How is that?"

"It's part of the plan I worked out with your husband, Señora Escovarro. You're all coming directly to my plantation to await your husband's shipment of goods. I think you'll really like Beauwood."

Teresa sank back without answering. Love for Felix engulfed her. How like him to think of such a thing even before they were rescued. He had sensed that she would now have certain fears of New Orleans. Fears? She wondered now why she had been so forthright with this stranger, although she felt as comfortable with him as though they were old friends. Still the word had just come popping out. She had known at once that it was Felix rescuing her. He knew no fear. Miguel? She had to admit to herself that her brother-in-law was not afraid of anything where he could strike back. Sheer physical strain was a catharsis to him, by plunging into danger and lashing out at it. But when he was put into a situation where anger and muscle wouldn't help, he was useless. He would shrug his shoulders, go in the opposite direction, and leave the problem to Felix.

Rain fell steadily. The fury of the storm, however, had passed, and the roll of thunder diminished in volume. The air had wonderfully cleared and was growing cool. Teresa began to feel uncomfortably cold and wet. She pulled up the lap robe so that it would cover them both. Exhaustion overcame her and she slept.

Yves rose and opened the speaking hatch up to the driver. "Thomas," he whispered, "go directly to the *Natchez Belle* wharf. Then I have a special errand for you to run."

He sat back down, staring at the sleeping women. Suddenly his shoulders slumped, and his whole body seemed to go slack. He blamed himself for not being more forceful with Miguel Escovarro.

CHAPTER FIVE

Alisa had animalized him. Time after time, he had fought to resist another arousal, but she was an artful master at her trade. He lay spent atop her. He didn't move for three or four minutes, then as his strength began to flow back, he got to his knees and started to climb from the bed. The inward crash of the door startled him, but he didn't have time to turn.

One hundred and seven pounds of clawing fury landed full on his neck and shoulders. The impact knocked out his breath and half collapsed him to the floor.

"Dirty goddamn Mexican son of a bitch!" Beatrice bellowed.

Alisa began to shriek and cry.

Miguel fought to get his head up and was met by a rain of vicious stinging blows and raking scratches. He rolled and Beatrice left him only to leap at his throat. He held one arm across his face to fend off the attack and thrust out the other arm. His fingers closed on flesh. He got to his feet and held the thrashing woman at arm's length. Beatrice was crying with rage. "You've helped them get away," she screamed, "and cost me hundreds!"

Miguel dug his fingers deeper into the woman's bare shoulders and tried to shake her into submission. "You're crazy!" he gasped hoarsely. "I don't know what in the hell you're talking about."

Beatrice bent her head and sunk her teeth into Miguel's forearm.

"Dirty whore bitch," he swore, letting go of her. He cocked back his arm to smash her in the face. The woman

93

had fought many men in her life and darted past him to the door.

Miguel spun, his eyes flaring with fury. But he didn't take a single step forward. Standing in the open door, puddles of water forming around his feet, was a scowling Terence.

"One step, mistah," he bellowed, "and boff barrels of dis shotgun am fired!"

Miguel paled. "Now listen," he quavered, "there's been some mistake. Get M'sieu Beauveau."

Beatrice scoffed. "Fat chance! You know goddamn well he left hours ago!"

Miguel tried to steady his nerves. Without the shotgun he would not have hesitated to attack the black. Now he had to bluff his way. "What is the matter? Didn't my host pay for me? No problem, I can pay for myself."

"Oh, you're going to pay," Beatrice sneered, "and so is my old friend Yves Beauveau. Alisa, on your feet!"

"What is it?" she said, her voice trembling.

"Well," the madam said expansively, "it seems this big-cocked stud was screwing you while his accomplice was stealing away two of my recent purchases. I now have reason to believe that one of them was his wife."

"Nonsense," Miguel lied. "I am not even married."

Beatrice only glowered at him. No man had ever been able to successfully lie to her. "Go to him," she ordered the girl. "Take your long sharp fingernails and scratch his flaccid cock until it's bleeding raw. I want to make sure he can't use it for a long, long time. And don't make a move to stop her," she warned Miguel, "or Terence gets the order to fire. It makes me no mind, *mister*. I think you're just about the lowest, most disgusting creature I've ever met."

Miguel started to protest and then realized the hopelessness of it. He steeled himself for the ordeal, the pain of the nail bites more excruciating than he had anticipated. His eyes welled with tears, and he had to grit his teeth to keep from crying out. He would not give this madwoman the pleasure of seeing him cower. He could stand this pain, to lessen his fear of the shotgun. He did not want to die, and the look on the black man's face told him that Terence would consider it a pleasure to pull the twin triggers.

Triumphantly, as she barked orders to Alisa, Beatrice found his clothing and began to rip and shred them to tatters.

"No one makes a fool of Beatrice Beauvoir," she chortled. "Here, sucker, get dressed. We've really enjoyed your short stay. Oh, by the way, we've released your horse. Have a nice walk, you son of a bitch!"

Miguel Escovarro had never before known embarrassment. Try as he might, he was unable to keep the shredded clothing about him without revealing some portion of his anatomy. Unfortunately for him, Beatrice had let him leave just when the majority of the second stringers were leaving the various houses along the street. He became an instant target for abuse and defilement, without knowing that shredded clothing was a familiar sight along the street and instantly marked a man as not having had the means to pay for his night of entertainment.

With each step Miguel burned anew with fury and increasing pain. None of the passing carriages dared take pity upon him, although he lowered himself to plead and beg in a couple of instances. With each renunciation his rage soared. By the time Thomas found him and had him safely into the Beauveau carriage, Miguel was a seething torrent of fury. He wrapped the lap robe about him, unmindful of its wetness and contemplated dark thoughts of revenge.

Yves Beauveau had anticipated part of what Beatrice Beauvoir might attempt if Miguel were still within her mansion when Terence returned. He had not anticipated that she would be so cruel and brutal. As the owner of the *Natchez Belle* he had made arrangements for Miguel to be brought on board by Thomas without being seen. When the man was shown into Yves's private stateroom, he hardly recognized him. He was flushed, his eyes bloodshot and narrowed. Yves had seen the same look on the faces of runaway slaves on recapture, and it worried him.

"My friend," he said gently, "take off those rags. I've sent my man to gather up your things at the hotel."

Miguel grunted. "That woman is vicious."

"So I've been told." There was an edge of sarcasm in the voice. "You better clean up in here before I take you to your wife."

Miguel nodded. "I may have need of a doctor. Is there one on board?" In the amount of time it took him to speak, he had been able to strip naked.

The Creole came over, scowling. "That looks bad. I'd best get my medical kit."

"Are you a doctor?"

"No, m'sieu, but I seem to have become one to your family this evening."

"Oh?" Miguel said indifferently.

The tone angered Beauveau, but he restrained any comment due to the man's condition. As he retrieved the medical kit, he related its uses during the evening. Miguel remained calm and apparently uncaring throughout the narrative.

He nodded toward the washbasin and pitcher. "If you don't mind waiting, I can see to my own cleanup."

The Creole gave a Gallic shrug which seemed to indicate that how long he had to wait was of no particular importance.

"I'll look in on my other *patients*," he said flatly.

In spite of her fatigue Teresa had bathed Emilia and gotten her into a cabin bunk while Yves had overseen two crew members prepare the still unconscious Felix. Some time after that Teresa had managed to clean herself and crawl thankfully between the clean sheets. Yves found them all sleeping peacefully and returned to his cabin.

Miguel had just finished rinsing himself and reached for a towel. He said, "I'll kill that woman if I ever see her again."

Yves took a pipe from his desk and tamped it crisply with tobacco. "You should have realized the risk you were facing when I left."

Miguel tossed the towel away with a gesture that was elaborately casual. "She had no reason to do this to me."

Yves frowned and blew out a haze of smoke. "I know one thing. *She* thought she had a reason."

Miguel nodded thoughtfully. "Yes, I guess she did."

"But she can't pursue the matter without facing a kidnapping charge."

Miguel's eyes narrowed. "But we can pursue it."

"Don't you think it's better left dropped?"

The Spaniard's surprise was elaborate. "Why?"

"Only your brother is aware you stayed behind, and he is too much of a gentleman to raise the subject. Your wife and sister-in-law know nothing, and need to know nothing. Any comment on your part will only uncover the truth."

Miguel scowled. "Forget it, then. You got something to help take this damn pain away."

Yves nodded and picked up a jar of salve. He seized the lacerated penis between thumb and forefinger and applied the salve none too gently. He was accustomed to handling the black bucks who got the "sickness" and thought nothing of administering this aid to Miguel.

At his first touch Miguel felt a deadly excitement. No man had ever touched him before, and he had never before known such unusual pain. In his mind the two began to combine into a tantalizing experience, and he felt his blood begin to flow. As the pain and sting of the salve increased, so did his arousal and embarrassment.

Yves was quite accustomed to such a reaction and thought it best to laugh it off.

"Alisa must not have been up to par tonight," he laughed. "Most men can't raise it again for three days after having been with her. But then, again, you're not an ordinary man in an ordinary circumstance."

Miguel drew his eyebrows together and scowled. "What does that mean?"

"Your wife being with child, and all."

Miguel stared at him in astonishment. He reached for the towel and draped it about his waist as his mind whirled. For the moment it was the best of news and the worst of news. It would give him an opportunity to sexually stay away from Emilia until he was healed; but he was not quite sure that he wanted her to bear children that would carry his name.

97

* * *

Miguel Escovarro had a certain bloodless capacity to force his own errors, whatever they might be, onto the shoulders of others, quelling, by will alone, a forestalling of any discussion on the matter. By the time the paddle boat, in a calm and stately way, had meandered two hundred miles up the Mississippi, he had casually accepted the news from his wife of their impending parenthood, cowed his brother into a thin-lipped silence, and avoided his sister-in-law whenever possible. There was something in the chemistry of Miguel and Teresa that clashed, but each was wise enough to control an open battle. But the faint idea of revenge remained in Miguel's thoughts and mind, like dissolved mud in clear water.

However, upon docking at Natchez-Under-the-Hill, he became lightly affectionate toward Emilia and untroubled by Felix's and Teresa's coolness. It was the spirit which had first made him attractive to Yves Beauveau, and the host was relieved to see its return.

"This is the only time I'll deem an apology necessary," Yves said as he escorted them to an awaiting carriage. "Down here it's the riverman's town and the worst hellhole on earth. Ladies, even though it is just a little before noon, please close your ears to anything these dirty Hottentots might say; and gentlemen, we are hardly enough to fight the likes of them, so please restrain yourself."

An orchestra of drunken Indians, producing an ear-piercing cacophony on cane flutes and drums made from iron kettles, serenaded the paddle boat's arrival. The liveried coachman rolled the carriage slowly up the single-streeted town between gambling houses, saloons, pool-rooms, and brothels. Everywhere the doors were flung wide and raucous fiddle music bombarded the street. Before one gambling den the enterprising owner had constructed a wooden platform upon which ruffle-skirted dance-hall girls stomped to the music. Bear-pawed boatmen, who considered a man a sissy if he combed his beard, staggered drunkenly from clapboard building to clapboard building. The brothel girls hung out the windows, calling out their specialty and price.

It was more amusement than embarrassment that kept Teresa's head turning from side to side.

"Oh, Emilia," she exclaimed. "It's fascinating. They're selling the same thing as at Madame Beatrice's, but it's so different."

"And so is the clientele," Emilia laughed. Then with a wicked smirk she added: "As are the prices."

A steely glare from Miguel kept her from further comment. He wondered if the day would ever come that her past would not come back to haunt him. He was only thankful that Yves Beauveau was riding up with the driver and had not heard the exchange. As was his habit he had completely put out of his mind the knowledge that Yves was even aware of Emilia's past. Besides their chatter had broken into his train of thought. His eyes and ears had been just as searching as Teresa's but for far different reasons. If he were to be stuck in this place for several weeks, as Yves had suggested, he saw ahead ample opportunity to partake in the pleasure presented by the gambling dens and taverns and wished to spot their exact locations.

Felix had not even heard the exchange. As had been his custom for the past few days, his mind was totally absorbed with the business he had been discussing with Yves Beauveau. By coming upriver and having his equipment brought down by flatboat from Nashville, he would save several hundred dollars. Before the order went up the Natchez Trace, he had to decide whether to order additional equipment or hold fast to his aunt's money. It never occurred to him to consult Miguel on the matter.

After switchbacking up the two-hundred-foot bluff, they emerged into a different world. Bluff-top mansions held a commanding view of the wide river. The town, with its tree-lined streets, was serene and docile in comparison. Whitewashed picket fences stood like sentinels dividing the commercial areas from the middle-class homes. Land was the next dividing line. Vast fields spread like golden corduroy stretched to the horizon on either side of the deeply rutted dirt road. The wild grass in the gulleys and windbreaks was so vivid a green that its glare hurt the eye. Massive oaks dotted the land like mushrooms popping up in a cow pasture after a gentle spring rain.

But for all its pastoral beauty the humidity and dust were stifling. The women were now quite thankful that they had taken Yves's suggestion to dress simply and coolly for the ten-mile ride to the plantation.

Yves Beauveau was now on his own terrain. Like King Midas he boastfully had to point out and give the historical background on every piece of property he owned or controlled by sharecropping. But he did not need to verbalize on Beauwood; it spoke for itself.

For a quarter of a mile, after the turning from the farm road, they entered a shadowed and moss-hung tunnel of towering oaks. Here the roadway was raked smooth, and they seemed to glide along in the still and refreshing coolness. The end of the tunnel served as a dark green natural frame for the two-storied plantation house sitting atop an emerald-green knoll. Pillared in Doric columns, balconied in elaborate white wrought iron, it was far too magnificent to evoke comment.

Yves glowed at their reaction to his "simple" home. Silence was the greatest of compliments to the mansion; any word spoken would have been inadequate and an injustice to its graceful lines, sparkling windows, and many hued gardens.

"Someday, somewhere," Teresa gasped, "I wish a home exactly like this one."

"Then," Yves beamed, "I shall see that your husband receives a set of its plans. For people to wish to copy, it gives me the greatest of pleasure."

"It would hardly be practical in our part of the country," Miguel said realistically. "Timber wood is a scarce item in our part of Texas, Yves. Adobe brick is far more practical and economical."

"Still it would be nice," Teresa mused. "Don't you think so, Felix?"

"Hum? Oh yes, dear." But his eyes and mind had been for several minutes on an oddity that intrigued him. "That's most unusual," he exclaimed as they rounded the knoll and started the climb to the front portico.

"The slave quarters, M'sieu Felix," Yves answered the unasked question. "I bow to some of their ancient ways and allow them to build their cabins in communal circles; each circle sharing a common cook fire. Behind each cabin, as you can see, each woman is allowed to grow her own vegetable garden. The plantation supplies their meat from the smokehouse. Some of the circles eat from a common pot, while others tend to be more modern and eat as family units."

Felix had been counting. "Why are there twenty cabins to each circle?"

"Because they do not read or write or know figures, two is the most common number for them to calculate by. A husband and wife are two, two mules pull the plow, two cotton seeds are planted in each hole to make sure one survives, and each 'village group,' as they call the compounds, has two head men, each overseeing the needs of ten families each."

"My Lord!" Felix gasped. "At that rate you must have at least five hundred blacks on this plantation."

Yves laughed. "More or less, but it doesn't keep my wife from complaining that she never has enough household staff. Ah, and there she is to greet us."

Luella Beauveau stood between the central columns of the portico, flanked by a battery of starchly uniformed servants. It had amazed her when the messenger had ridden out from Natchez-Under-the-Hill to announce the impending arrival of her husband with guests. She had thrown her personal maids into a tizzy to prepare her in time, selecting a floor-length velvet gown adorned with a superb red and white candy-striped camellia blossom. Her soft accent and mild-mannered greeting of the guests belied the iron inside the velvet glove—the iron that kept the household slaves constantly fearful of her. Her orders were gently given, but made the butler, maids, and porters jump as though a drill sergeant had just barked. Like errant children the guests were taken in tow to be ushered quickly up the sweeping staircase to rooms which had been just as quickly assigned to them. And equally like errant children they had been informed that a "noonday repast would be set out within the half hour."

Emilia, still a little stiff and sore, clung to Teresa's arm as they ascended. A sly smirk played at the corners of her mouth.

"I feel like we've been through this all before," she whispered.

"I felt the same when she greeted us," Teresa whispered back. "It was just like when Señora Escovarro was forced to let us enter her home, cool and distant. And just like then, Miss Luella, as Yves calls her, is like nothing I expected him to be married to."

Emilia chuckled. "She must be two hundred pounds if she is an ounce."

"Should we change for lunch?"

"Mah dear," Emilia mocked, giving her voice a soft Southern drawl, "ah only dresses for dinner and not for a noon *reepast*."

In the foyer Luella Beauveau heard their laughter, and it angered her all the more. Much given to vapors and self-determined bouts of semi-invalidism, she was, in truth, quite a healthy lady of twenty-nine, with a greedy appetite. The kitchen slaves understood this; they discreetly left the pantry doors unlatched at night, leaving out a cold bird or pork roast, a crock of buttermilk, a slab of cheese, or the remains of a pie. No one asked who consumed them during the darker hours, by the light of a candle in the spacious brick kitchen. When Yves was at home, she would dine with him, eating sparingly. When he was away, she would take all her meals off a tray in her room, barely touching a bite, to make the servants believe that her stoutness was due to her illness and not her gorging at midnight.

Yves was well aware of the hypocrisy and pitied it. He knew that his wife was a foolish woman: selfish, avaricious, greedy, and self-indulgent, obsessed only with her own desires and vanities. She was incapable of giving love because she lacked the natural human quality of being able to accept it. To her mind, love was attention, and she made sure that her illness gave her plenty of that. As she was the wife of the richest man for a hundred miles around, she was given that attention and interest which would have been denied a more impecunious lady.

Yves followed docilely as she motioned him into the study. "Ah've been most ill, husband," she whimpered sharply. "Ah'm tryin' to build up my strength for the cotillion. But now, in your perverseness, you saddle me with extra guests. Have you all but forgotten that mah Aunt Emma Mae is comin' tomorrow from New Iberia? Never mind. You were always inconsiderate of mah family."

Yves sighed. "They are really business guests, Miss Luella. I shall see to their entertainment during the weeks they are here."

"Weeks?" Luella said peevishly, settling her plump frame onto the settee. She blinked angrily. "They'll be here for my cotillion and *bar-baa-que*? You have no consideration for me, at all. How insensible you are, Yves. A man of sensibility would have more sympathy for my position. Ah just know they'll ruin everything for me. Just look at their attire. Plain as mud fences."

"That was my suggestion," he said in his soft and chiseled voice. "Why ruin good clothing on that dusty ride out from town. Besides, I was thinking of you when I invited them. The Escovarros are from Texas and will give you someone new to show off."

"Really, husband, Mexicans," said Luella irritably.

"Spanish," he corrected. "Señora Teresa de Alarcon Escovarro's great-grandfather settled the city of San Antonio. She has been presented at the court of King Joseph of Spain. The Escovarro brothers' family have been upon their land for nearly three hundred years, as I understand it, and are titled. I will expect you to inform our other guests to address them as 'Don' and 'Doña.' "

Now that a touch of glamour surrounded the quartet, Luella was slightly soothed. She sighed, heavily, and touched her eyes with a laced cambric handkerchief.

"I do hope they've brought along proper clothing, husband. When I was at Aunt Emma Mae's last winter, for the elegant dinner party she gave for young Mr. Jefferson Davis, I was that heartsick for her."

Yves had not only heard the story a hundred times but

had been in attendance for the dinner. He had no recourse but to paint his face with an expression of interest.

Luella shook her head sadly. "New Orleans has become coarse, in spite of its charm, husband. Most of the frocks there had been worn at least two to three times. I told Aunt Emma Mae later, with much agitation, that not a one of those creatures would receive an invitation to my spring cotillion at Beauwood. Ah've been true to my word, ah surely have."

Yves was silent.

"Surely have," repeated Luella with malevolent emphasis. "And ah'll discuss clothing with these ladies at the first available opportunity."

There was a slight tightness about Yves's smile as he replied: "I'm sure they'll appreciate your interest, Miss Luella."

"They had better, husband," she said in a voice that was like a knife.

When the two women descended the stairs in their same traveling attire, Luella began to fear the worst. She picked at her food more sparingly than ever, her mind busily going over her own wardrobe to determine if anything she possessed could be altered in time to fit them.

After lunch, while Yves took Miguel and Felix on a ride around the plantation, Luella forwent her afternoon nap to strike at the heart of her problem. As a ruse, to gently lead up to her topic, she took Teresa and Emilia on a tour of the antebellum mansion. Throughout, as they glided through the high-ceilinged rooms agleam with mahogany and silver from Europe, lime-green rugs from Persia, swagged damask drapes from Italy, massive chandeliers from Switzerland, and hand-crafted and upholstered chairs and couches from France and Germany, Luella's chatter got no further along than what all must be done in the next twenty-four hours before her annual fete. She made it sound as though all of the laborious tasks would have to be performed by herself personally or never get accomplished. In spite of her instant dislike of the two women at their arrival, she was now finding it rather exciting and exhilarating to be able to use them as sounding boards for her elaborate plans rather than the undemonstrative household slaves.

"As some of mah guests must leave their homes before dawn," said Miss Luella in a pained voice, lifting her hand in an attitude of long-suffering patience, "we here at Beauwood have to rise the same and have a warm breakfast waitin' for them. By noon, when we serve the *bar-baa-que*, that road out yonder will be a steady stream of carriages bearing belles in crinoline and lace and handsome young bucks on snorting steeds. All of our bedrooms are given over to the ladies for the afternoon, while the menfolk sip whiskey and branch and talk over their menfolk talk. Near sundown, when the sky is a rosy glow and the lamps are getting their light, the orchestra begins to play and the dining room is laid out with a buffet. From then on it is dancing until the last guest leaves or dawn or whichever comes first."

"I'm sure that it will be very elegant," Emilia shrewdly observed, sensing the woman's need for flattery. "But really, Mrs. Beauveau, we feel like we will be intruding at this late date."

"Nonsense," said Luella with an unusual softness to her voice. Gratefully Emilia had opened the door for her to barge directly through. "Unless there is a problem. Is it clothing? I know how difficult it is to travel with an adequate wardrobe and *we do* dress for dinner at Beauwood."

"There is no problem," Emilia said expansively. "We just don't wish to put a burden on your guest list."

Luella sighed with relief, feeling she had gotten her clothing point across without embarrassment. "My dear woman," she said, almost joyously, "I invite two hundred and automatically prepare for three hundred. Four more will hardly be noticed."

Luella Beauveau's message had registered very plainly with Emilia.

"She thinks we're tatters and rags," she laughed when they were alone in Teresa's room. "This must be the crowning glory of her life each year, and she's scared to death that we are going to ruin it for her."

"Poor woman," Teresa sympathized. "Did you notice

them at lunch? There is not an ounce of love between them."

"It was a question of money marrying money, as Miguel tells me. Back in the 1780s Luella's father, with a man named Meriwether Lewis, surveyed the Trace from Nashville to Natchez. He had rafts and flatboats built to float down the Ohio and Mississippi rivers carrying wheat and flour, hides and furs, tobacco, hemp, barreled pork, and hardware. Here, they would be off-loaded and reloaded with the bales of cotton to go down to New Orleans and the ships for England. The rafts would be sold for lumber, the boatmen brought upstream by paddle wheel, and then the long trek back up the Trace would start all over again."

"You amaze me, Emilia," Teresa said with admiration. "You hear a thing a single time and you never forget it. By the way, what do they mean by 'trace'?"

"That," she chuckled, "I had to ask M'sieu Beauveau on my own. It's Old French for 'a line of footprints.' And it's not as romantic as it sounds. Up-country are cypress swamps where outlaws and renegade Indians prey upon the travelers. I heard Yves tell Miguel that if the mail rider didn't arrive after six weeks, then they automatically assumed that he was lost, a victim of bandits, drowning, a broken leg in a fall from his horse, or any of a dozen other perils."

"It almost makes you want to get back to the civilization of San Antonio, doesn't it."

"Civilization," Emilia bellowed with hearty laughter. "Were you blind to the elegance of this woman's home. Everything she casually took for granted today made my mouth water with envy."

"That part, yes," Teresa admitted. "But it is so isolated."

Emilia scoffed. "No more isolated than we will be on the Escovarro ranch."

"I beg to differ," Teresa insisted. "There we will be surrounded by our own people. Here we are a few specks of salt surrounded by a mass of pepper."

"Oh, really, Teresa," she chided. "You never felt uncomfortable around Big John."

"I know," she admitted, "and the thought might never

have crossed my mind if she hadn't taken us to that second-floor balcony today. Out across the fields they looked like a swarm of ants hoeing the furrows. Perhaps it was the chant that got to me. It was so sad and plaintive. And did you see the fear in that young black girl's eyes when she brought Miss Luella tonight's menu. I've never seen fright like that before, not even in the faces of the women of Saltillo when they thought Santa Anna's soldiers might rape them. It's a hopeless fright."

"And doesn't concern us," Emilia admonished. "So let's change the subject back to Miss Luella's dinner tonight. Where are those boxes of the last things we bought in New Orleans?"

Anticipating a fairly Spartan life on the ranch, the women had had the New Orleans seamstress prepare for them several dresses of a utilitarian nature. Although of fine-quality goods, they were devoid of ruffles and puffs, flat skirted and without the normal *passementerie* of appliquéd embroidery about the hemline.

Luella Beauveau took one look at the garments and took to her bed with the vapors. Teresa felt slightly guilty, but Emilia was exultant in putting the self-centered woman in her place.

During the feverish tumult of the next day Luella's pale and silent absence passed unnoticed by all save Teresa. It had been a lonely morning for her: Felix and Miguel had left before dawn with the Beauveau overseer to examine an experimental farm Yves had started several miles away, and Emilia had stayed abed, suffering from an acute case of "morning sickness." Teresa and Yves shared a simple lunch together.

"I do hope your wife will be well enough for her party tomorrow," she said with genuine concern.

He eyed her for a moment and then thrust back his head and laughed. "I'm sorry," he said, "but you may have noticed that you are the only one with such a concern. This is the eighth cotillion my wife has staged, and it shall be little different than the preceding ones. She always takes to her bed the day before, for some reason or another. It keeps her out from underneath Henry's feet. You really might say it is his party and not hers. He was the butler in this house when I was a boy and is the eyes, ears, and heart that keeps it running. Would you like to see the preparations?"

"Well . . . I . . ." She hesitated.

"I've finished the paper work on your husband's order and am quite free to escort you."

"Then I would love to," she said, her face radiating enthusiasm.

He could not help but wonder what Beauwood would be like with this vital and beautiful woman as its mistress.

In the kitchen they found a beehive of activity. Vast tubs of potatoes had been boiled and were being prepared for salad, pounds of butter were being churned, and corn ground into grits. Mountains of pole beans were being destringed, while the massive brick ovens were being worked overtime to produce bread, rolls, cakes, pies, and a dozen succulent-smelling hams.

In one corner bushels of yams awaited paring, collards their washing, and carrots their peeling. At twin chopping blocks butchers sliced thick slabs of bacon and dismembered a half-hundred chickens. In one corner a rotund black woman stuffed a row of a dozen turkeys, followed by another to sew up their flaps and another to butter them.

"They are really preparing the basics of three meals at once," Yves said with pride. "Tomorrow is a holiday for the slaves, as well."

"What about the serving of all of this?"

"Henry?" Yves said, encouraging the watchful butler to answer.

"Ain't no problem dere, Miss Teresa," he beamed. "We all look for'ard to dat. Am fun. Gib us de chance ta show all de ober plantation people how artful and skillful am de Beauwood folk."

Teresa's eyes were round with amazement. "It certainly seems like mountains and mountains of food."

Henry grinned broadly and turned away.

Yves also grinned and whispered: "That's Henry's little secret. Everything that is left over by tomorrow night goes to the slaves the next day."

Teresa giggled. "That's very sly."

Yves shrugged. "I really don't care. All of this is either raised or caught on my land because of them. It gives them all as much pride as it does the kitchen and serving staff. But there are some things I don't share with them. Come along."

Teresa had not noticed the intense heat in the kitchen until they stepped out into the wood-slated breezeway.

"Oh, that feels heavenly," she enthused, "and what is that delicious aroma."

"Mint," he replied, pointing to a half-dozen wooden buckets crammed full of the freshly cut stalks.

"Whatever for?"

"Mint juleps."

She frowned and he laughed.

"Tonight I shall have Henry prepare some so that y'all will be prepared for them tomorrow. That's all I'm going to say on the subject. Now here is the big surprise. It's the main reason I was down in New Orleans. Only Henry and I have a key for this storage room."

The oblong room, shelved from ceiling to floor, was cool and dim. In its center sat a vast slat-barreled tub holding a cake of ice.

Teresa gasped. "It's summertime! Where in the earth did this come from?"

Yves was captivated by her eagerness to know everything and was more than willing to answer.

"When the fresh-water pond freezes in the wintertime, we saw it into rectangular cakes and haul them to a building next to the smokehouse. They are covered in sawdust, layer after layer, and give us ice for most of the summer."

"That is something I'm going to remember."

"I'm sure that you will. You strike me as a very astute woman who never lets an educational opportunity slip through her fingers."

Flushing deeply and hastily brushing a stray hair off her face, she turned to give her full attention to the rows of jellies, jams, preserves, pickles, and relishes.

"Those are not the treasures I spoke of," he said, touching her arm to turn her about. Once touched, he did not want to release her. He wanted to pull her into his arms, to feel the touch of her soft lips. He had never craved anything as much in his life.

Teresa stepped away. She was intensely aware of his closeness. Her heart began to beat with great rapidity.

"These are the type of morsels that should only pass by lips like yours," said Yves, beaming at her affectionately. "I've had them shipped in from all over the world. Caviar from Turkey, tropical fruit from Veracruz and Tampico, and these jewels came all the way from the West Indies by clipper ship. Have you ever tasted a pineapple before?"

"Never," she murmured almost inaudibly.

"Ah, and here is something that had to be named for you."

She looked up to see what he was presenting to her, and her eyes gleamed like brown velvet. Her trembling fingers fumbled with the small round ball of fruit, and she tried to smile.

"What is it?"

"It's called passion fruit."

Teresa was silent. The beating of her heart did not subside. The strangest tears were making a bright dazzle before her eyes. She had the oddest impulse to run.

Then she stammered, her voice loud in her embarrassed ears: "What is this 'bar-be-que' your wife keeps speaking about?"

They looked at each other, as they stood in the coolness, apart from the hot and hurrying throngs on the plantation. He knew that she was a one-man woman, and he rued it. She was giving him an opportunity to save himself from embarrassment, and he rued that as well. If she had been Miguel's wife, he might not have faltered; but she wasn't.

After what appeared to be a long time, Yves said gently, not taking his eyes from hers: "That, we shall make the next step in your education on plantation life."

She began to laugh softly, quite without reason, and she felt her knees trembling. She was saved from having to say no to a man she had come to admire deeply. Her small, delicate face bloomed in tremulous beauty, and she rewarded his gallantry with a winning smile.

Yves Beaveau felt as though he had won a major battle,

if not the full prize he had sought. Just to be with her now was rapture. He prolonged his explanations of the preparations just to keep her with him.

Teresa didn't notice. She was now just as enthused over what she saw as she had been over the ice. She marveled over the length and depth of the pits the slaves had dug and the oak-chip fires built therein.

"When they turn to white embers," Yves exclaimed, "the gunnysack-wrapped sides of beef and pork will be put into the pits and covered with sand. They'll cook slowly there today, tonight, and tomorrow morning. Come, we'll go back this way."

They were halfway across the neatly raked circle of ground before Teresa realized he was taking her through one of the compounds. She stopped short, her heart skipping a beat.

He felt a strong tenderness for Teresa, a protectiveness and love. He took her arm to forestall her fright.

"In the daytime we call this the 'children's circle.' The lack of laughter and noise would suggest it must be nap time." He stuck his head into an open cabin door and called quietly: "Mama Abuela, you hear?"

In spite of herself Teresa had to giggle. "What an odd mixture of English and Spanish. Why?"

Yves grinned. "You'll see in a moment."

The woman had to duck to get out of the door. When she straightened, she towered over them both. The brightly colored bandanna tied about her head framed an angular face with high cheekbones, wide-set eyes, and a straight and narrow patrician nose. Although she was deep brown, her color was the only recognizable African feature about her.

To Teresa's amazement he spoke to the woman in Spanish.

"Mama Abuela, this is Señora Teresa Escovarro, who is our guest."

The stony face froze for a second, then the thin brown lips opened in a toothy grin.

"Mos' onta ten year since ah 'eard dat tongue, massa." Her English was deep and rich and mellow. Then she addressed Teresa in hesitant Spanish. "Welcome, señora. Abuela says welcome."

"Thank you. Forgive me if you heard me laugh. But I was curious as to why your name was 'grandmother.' Mama Grandmother, at that."

The laughter came from the pit of her stomach and was as deep and rich and mellow as her voice.

"*Niña*," she laughed, "when they sold me across the water from Cuba, I only knew Spanish. I had something like thirty years on me and already a grandmother. Fearing they wanted me for mating purposes, I kept telling them at the auction block that I was *abuela, abuela*—'a grandmother, a grandmother'—and they thought that was my name."

"That's delightful," Teresa laughed. "Mama Grandmother. I love it."

"And I love to hear Spanish again. No other Cuban black in these parts that I know of, is there Master Yves."

"If there were," he scowled good-naturedly, "I'd of had you married off these past ten years. You're a mean woman, and you know it."

"That's not meanness," she chortled, "that's being particular. Had me two husbands between ten and thirty, six boys and two grandboys. Besides, there's enough tar babies coming along on this plantation to last your lifetime."

"Never enough," he kidded, "never enough."

"How many do you care for?" Teresa asked.

"Fifty-nine," she exclaimed proudly. "Of course the older ones help a lot with the toddlers."

"Unlike most plantations," Yves interjected quickly, "I don't put the boys to work until they are ten and the girls twelve."

"That seems horribly young."

"Nonsense," Mama Abuela corrected. "Not for slaves. I'm considered an old woman already, but I don't feel it."

Yves tried to keep it light. "That's because you have the easiest job on the whole place."

"Get on with you, Master Yves," she laughed. "I'd like to see you chase these pickaninnies around for a day. They're all quiet now because I knocked them over the head to make them sleep. Would you like to see my children some-time, Señora Teresa."

"I would love to," Teresa said hesitantly.

For no apparent reason the woman switched back to English. "Yah 'range dat for Mama Abuela, massa?"

He nodded and led Teresa away.

When they were out of the compound, he said, "You don't have to go back."

"We'll see. It's just a little unusual for me. I'd only seen one black man in my life before coming to New Orleans. There are so many of them. How many whites are on the plantation?"

For a moment he seemed taken aback. "I've never really ever looked at it that way. There's the overseer and his family down at the dairy farm, three overseers and their families here, and a bachelor overseer at the sawmill. I'd say about a dozen of us."

"And there is never any trouble."

"Some of the young bucks try to run away now and again, but that's the way it is. I try to avoid trouble by keeping them happy."

"Yes," she mused, "Mama Abuela seemed happy enough. Why was she sold away from Cuba?"

Yves flushed but knew Teresa was the type of woman who would gain the information from the mulatto if he didn't speak.

"You could see for yourself that she is of mixed blood. She was raised as a house servant in a very wealthy home, which accounts for her flawless Spanish. When she said she had two husbands, that wasn't quite correct. She gave birth for the first time at age twelve. The father was her sixteen-year-old half brother. The family quickly married her to one of the housemen and thought that was that. It was for a time because she was busy giving him four sons right in a row. Her half brother, which of course was never acknowl-edged, was away in Spain for about ten years for his higher education. I gather that she was his secret mistress for the next several years, while her younger children were grow-ing up and making her a grandmother. Then she was with child again. It was born as golden hued as the father. The child was taken from her, and each member of her family sold and sent in different directions."

"No more," murmured Teresa. "I think it's a horribly cruel system."

"It does have its advantages."

"No more," she repeated, this time sternly.

Yves hated for such a pleasant afternoon to end on such a discordant note and was cheered when a gleeful shout greeted them as they entered the foyer.

"It's about time I was greeted by someone other than Henry," the white-haired rotund little woman chirped as she sailed out of the parlor with arms outstretched.

"Welcome, Aunt Emma Mae," he nearly shouted, hugging her and kissing her soundly on each cheek. "When did you arrive?"

"Oh, who cares," she kidded good-naturedly. "I'm here and that's all that matters. Oh my, either that niece of mine had gone and lost a hundred pounds or you've taken up with a new woman."

Teresa blushed as the introductions and explanations were made.

Emma Mae Lambeau was as warm of spirit as she was devilish behind her hazel-green Gallic eyes.

"My dear," she said, taking both of Teresa's hands, "I'm overly delighted that you have a husband. Now I've got something to look forward to. Any man who could capture a classic beauty like you must be the handsomest damn thing alive."

Teresa couldn't help but warm to the woman. "I certainly think so."

Emma Mae winked slyly. "Then look out for me, my dear. I'm a sixty-year-old spinster who's still looking for the right man."

"Then you're in deep trouble," Yves scowled darkly. "Both of the Escovarro brothers are here."

"The only man I want to see right at this moment is . . . Ah, Henry, you heard me. We'll take those juleps in the parlor, thank you."

"You see," Yves said, winking at Teresa, "five minutes after being in my house and the old nag takes over."

"Someone has to," the woman snapped without sting, "or poor Henry here would have it all on his shoulders. Isn't that right, Henry."

"If y'all say so, Missy Em," he chuckled.

"Aha!" she snorted, raising a warning hand in Teresa's direction. "Best you get the ground rules straight, my dear. I loathe my name and always shall. My niece and nephew insist upon calling me Aunt Emma Mae, but I forgive them because they both have soft brains." This brought a rousing laugh from Yves, who dearly loved the woman. "This old darky and I have known each other for far too long and is the only creature alive with the guts enough to call me Missy Em. I'm Emma to everyone else! Now where's that julep?"

The woman had so much of the spirit and joviality of Teresa's grandmother that she sat transfixed and enraptured. She sipped at the frosty julep glass, finding the contents cool and refreshing. The banter between the woman and her nephew deeply amused her.

"Yves, I've had Henry send the orchestra to sleep it off in one of the cabins. Really, a worse lot than last year, drunk all the way from Iberia."

"You mean your seductive charms didn't keep them sober?"

"Don't be a lout. I'm warning you now so you can keep them away from the punch bowl tomorrow. If there is one thing I can't stand, it's Luella's shrill voice, and she can be a real shrew when the orchestra in here sounds worse than the fiddler's music coming from the compound." Unexpectedly she agilely jumped to her feet. "Now don't no one say a word. I want to figure this out for myself."

Teresa and Yves eyed each other in confusion until they heard the front door close and saw Felix and Miguel enter the foyer and frame themselves in the parlor archway.

"Gentlemen," Yves said, heeding his aunt's warning, "may I present to you my aunt, Mademoiselle Emma Mae Lambeau."

They stood, a little disconcerted, as she advanced on them as though with a vengeful purpose in mind. Without hesitation she marched directly up to Felix and eyed him as though he were on a slave auction block.

"No mistaking it," she chortled, "you have to be the hunk of male flesh that belongs to this enchanting and beautiful girl." And immediately she whirled on Miguel. "But you're something, too. I can hardly wait to see the manner of beauty that captured you."

Felix flushed scarlet, and Miguel bent back his head and roared with amusement.

"Yves," he bellowed, "whatever your aunt is drinking, I'll have the same!"

Throughout the late afternoon and evening Emma Mae Lambeau sparkled up Beauwood. A favorite with the servants, she was showered with genuine love and attention. Felix, also, came to see certain similarities between the woman and Doña Clara, and it thawed the icy reserve he had maintained since their departure from New Orleans. Teresa just naturally loved her, and Miguel found her a much more amusing dinner conversationalist than his unusually quiet and restrained wife.

"What's the problem?" Teresa asked as they left the dining room to the men for cigars and brandy.

Emilia hesitated until Emma Mae's full-hooped figure had sailed regally into the parlor to supervise Henry in the pouring of the ladies' coffee.

"I don't know," Emilia answered abjectly. "That woman seems to look at me as though I don't have any clothes on."

Teresa laughed. "That has never bothered you before."

Emilia frowned. "I was never married before. I was never pregnant before."

"What has that to do with it?" Teresa scowled.

Emilia's eyes began to water. "Look at me. I'm the one who never cries. I'm strong Emilia Morillo, or should be. Oh, Teresa, for the very first time in my life I'm frightened."

"Frightened of what?"

"Myself, mainly. Or what I was. I so wanted these weeks

to be different. To be in a world where nobody would know of my past. To be accepted in a world such as this just for myself. I wanted that so much."

"I don't understand. Nothing has changed."

"It has," she said softly. "She's changed it. That woman reads me like I was an open book."

"Nonsense," Teresa scowled. "Now come on in and have coffee."

But Emilia was quite correct. When the thought first crossed Emma Mae's mind, she had dismissed it as foolishness, but when it persisted, because of Emilia's coolness toward her, she locked onto it like a bullet speeding toward the bull's-eye. Then she wasn't quite sure what she wanted to do with her newfound knowledge.

"I hope you don't mind," she said after she and Teresa had been chatting for some time, "if I impose myself with a personal question."

Emilia knew the question was directed at her and stiffened. "Not at all," she said coolly.

"No one has said, of course, but are you with child?"

Emilia nearly laughed aloud from her feeling of relief. "Yes, I am."

Emma Mae beamed. "Oh, that thrills me. You'll never know how I've prayed for the same event to bless this house. It won't, as long as my errant niece lets Yves waste himself and his money in the New Orleans houses."

Emilia's back went rigid. She was quite used to a subtle compliment being the forerunner of a snide dig.

"And thus you paint him as the black villain?" she said icily.

"On the contrary. There would be no need for those places if a woman were capable of keeping her man at home. Am I not right?"

Emilia took it personally, something she might never have done before. She rose slowly from the chair, her Aztec black eyes flashing lightning bolts. "How could you possibly know," she sneered, "you've never been capable of capturing even a single man."

A stunned silence filled the parlor as she stormed from the room and vaulted up the sweeping stairway.

"Oh my," Emma Mae gasped, "I really am an old fool when it comes to saying the wrong thing. Tomorrow I must figure out a way of making amends."

"Perhaps the least said the better," Teresa suggested.

"Leave that to me," she said gently and firmly. "I wish no enemy on earth, only friends."

Teresa suddenly shivered. She had a horrible feeling that the next day was going to be the worst kind of disaster.

CHAPTER SIX

Emilia awoke the next morning grateful that she was not troubled by nausea and morning sickness. She lay for a moment wondering where Miguel was and dreamily remembered him rising hours before. She arose and went to view the noise which had aroused her this time. The yard was alive with incoming carriages and chattering girls as they alighted. Her first impression was of nothing but bonnets: poke bonnets with a curved scoop like a coal shuttle, saucer ovals trimmed with lace, tallboys draped with veil, straws tied with wide ribbons under the chin, and all manner of feathers, lace, flowers, and ribbons to adorn them. She looked upon the country belles as young, frivolous, and unchallenging.

But the muscular bucks who escorted the carriages on their charging steeds in freshly pressed morning dress gave her a different opinion on the day. She was not about to let Emma Mae Lambeau get the better of her.

A half hour later, standing at the top of the stairs, she was able to view the foyer with a single sweep of her eyes. The guests were arriving in droves now, a bevy of ladies elaborately dressed and beribboned, fluttering their fans and conversing in the bright twitters suitable to the occasion, and elegant gentlemen as graceful out of the saddle as they were on. Greeting them, like a fat and jovial peahen, Luella beamed sunnily. Emma Mae assisted, virtually supplanting her niece as hostess. Next to them stood Teresa, in an unadorned dress of rose-hued linen with a high waistline emphasized by a sash a shade darker than the dress. She acknowledged every introduction with patrician dignity, her curtsy regal and graceful. Her breeding antagonized the ladies, charmed the gentlemen, but intimidated them. Her exquisite beauty put the ladies, for all their finery, quite in the shade, made their dull haughty faces appear plebeian and coarse, their studied manners affected. Her contained and perfect gestures seemed to make their own gauche and awkward, her cool tranquil voice, when she spoke, contrasting so acutely with the voices of the ladies that they sounded too shrill, too hard, and too loud.

Emma Mae gasped and hissed at her niece: "Luella, how dare you not tell me you invited that woman!"

Across the portico swept a mountain of a woman, her size emphasized by the immensity of her hooped skirt. Under the feathered and beribboned bonnet her pockmarked face was darkly flushed, her eyes glittered belligerently, and her big round head with its black curls was held in a defiant attitude. Lurking in her wake was a tall skinny girl whose gaudy beauty appeared overwhelmingly theatrical. She was obviously frightened, for her cheeks flushed and paled, and her large hands fumbled with the cherry bows on her purple velvet gown.

Luella blanched and felt the start of a vapor attack. "I purposely *didn't* invite her," she cried. "But I can't just slam the door in her face."

She had no choice but to step forward and paint a smile on her face.

"Why Arabella Eberhart," she cried, and it came out too shrill. "How nice of you to come."

The woman jutted out her cheek to be kissed and then said viciously: "Even without an invitation, Luella?"

Luella gulped and ignored the comment.

"And I see you've brought your dear Gracie Sue."

The girl took this opportunity to pluck fervidly at her mother's sleeve and point impolitely.

"Momma," she gasped, "look at her!"

Emilia was halfway down the stairway, and a deep silence fell over the foyer. She was suddenly transfixed by two dozen pairs of staring eyes and stunned faces.

"Who in the hell is she?" Arabella growled.

Luella waved her to silence and almost ran to the bottom

of the stairs, her arms outstretched. Never had her heart felt so joyously filled than at that moment.

"Doña Emilia," she trilled, "you look sublime, my dear. Come! There are hundreds of people dying to meet you."

Emilia knew exactly how she looked, but the genuine compliment was deeply appreciated. She descended slowly, tall and stately, the yards of turquoise moiré falling from her bustle making waves on the steps. The high-waisted gown was unhooped so that each step revealed the outline of her long and shapely legs. The neckline was high, of Mandarin cut, but tightly fitted to leave no doubt about her full-bosomed figure. The sleeves were plain and three quarter, coming to within an inch of the long matching gloves. Around her neck was a massive necklace of hammered silver embedded with unpolished chunks of turquoise gems. A matching ring adorned one of the gloved fingers of her right hand. Even though she was a tall woman, Emilia had increased the effect by pulling her raven black hair straight up, tying it tightly with a wide turquoise ribbon, and letting the curls fall pell-mell to form their own bonnet effect.

Luella guided her directly to the dining room without a backward glance at the front door.

Arabella Eberhart stood fuming, and it delighted Emma Mae.

"Arabella," she said, sugar sweetly, "may I present Doña Teresa de Alarcon Escovarro."

The harridan nodded but would not be put off.

"Emma Mae Lambeau," she hissed through tight lips, "who was that shocking creature?"

This brought the first involuntary smile to Teresa's face. She sensed exactly what Emilia was attempting, and she was proud of her. She put her hand on Emma Mae's arm to keep her from answering.

"Why, madam," she said regally, "that is my sister-in-law, *the* Doña Emilia Morillo Escovarro."

At this Arabella broke into a flutter. "Dear me, *royalty*! Come along, Gracie Sue. We must have a bite of breakfast."

Emma Mae took Teresa's hands and kissed each palm as she controlled her giggles.

"If I may paraphrase," Teresa laughed, "who was *that* shocking creature?"

"The countryside's biggest gate-crasher, gossip, and snob. Next to Yves she's about the wealthiest person around, but she nearly has a heart attack if she has to spend a penny. This is the third year in a row that I've seen Gracie Sue wear that natty purple velvet. Oh, but now here comes somebody I do especially want you to meet."

The voices in the dining room rose to an amiable confusion. Fans fluttered, hoops tilted and swept, tittering laughter mingled with the booming of men's mirth. The young ladies, as well as some of the older ones, had already lost their hearts to the Escovarro brothers; and men of all ages could not take their eyes off Emilia. Luella was radiant with happiness.

Although similarly admired by the men, they did not approach Teresa in the droves that they did Emilia. But still, later in the day, neither woman had to lift a finger during the bar-be-que.

"Oh, no!" Teresa laughed when Felix found her on the lawn in the shade of an oak. "One more bite and I'll pop."

"My, my," he exclaimed, sprawling down beside her, "you do seem well stocked. Where did it all come from?"

"From everywhere. Yves brought me a plate while you were still talking Henry into another mint julep. Then that redheaded lad, with the millions of freckles, insisted upon getting me more. Have you eaten?"

"A little."

"Then you help me with this plate."

He grinned. "I'd rather have another julep."

"Felix Escovarro! That is hardly like you at all!"

He rolled onto his back and shielded his eyes with his arm. "This whole day is unlike me. It is something like a fiesta but quieter and more relaxing. When we have our own home, we'll entertain like this."

Teresa laughed. "Not unless I get to take Henry with me. He's the mastermind behind all of this."

"I thought the only thing he knew how to do was mix juleps," he kidded.

"Oh, you!" She playfully kicked him. "I am glad you're having fun."

He rolled to his side and winked at her. "Part of the fun is watching the envy in men's eyes when they look at you."

"Me," she mocked. "Don't you mean Emilia?"

"That, my dear, is lust," he chortled, "not envy. And speaking of lust, why don't we take a long nap this afternoon."

"Felix!" she gasped. "I do believe those juleps have made you forward. However, it's a good idea if you don't mind an audience."

"What?"

"Why, honna-lamb," she mimicked, batting her eyelashes like Gracie Sue Eberhart, "we belles been assigned all the bedrooms so we can get out of our crinoline and rest up for the *coo-tee-llion*."

"Very funny," he sneered. "And what are we men supposed to do?"

"Talk and drink."

"I'll buy the last but not the first. If I have to tell about the Alamo and San Jacinto one more time, I think I'll vomit."

"How did all that come up?"

"My braggart brother and our host. We are being made out as heroes."

"Aha! Now I know why you're having so much fun."

Felix playfully stuck his tongue out at her. "Have I told you lately how much I love you?"

"No, as a matter of fact you haven't."

Felix jumped to his feet and started to run from her. "Then remind me to tell you if you figure out a way to keep our room vacant."

Teresa doubled over with laughter.

In the parlor Emma Mae was not laughing. She had been tracked down by the formidable Arabella Eberhart and forced to eat with her. The harridan planted herself near the window so that she could keep a watchful eye on the entire yard and make mental notes of anything she thought might be repeatable in the days to come. Emilia seemed to be her favorite target. To her way of thinking it was a disgrace that all of the eligible young men were hovering about a "married" woman and leaving her dear, sweet, available daughter quite on her own. Only when Emilia vanished from her line of sight did she dare raise her thoughts with Emma Mae.

"Of course," she intoned darkly, "you know that this evening is going to be a total disaster."

Emma Mae blinked, unsure of the woman's meaning.

"In my way of thinking," she went on meditatively, "a dance should only be for young people to get to know one another and pleasure themselves. The stag line will be long tonight because these men are going to continue to make fools of themselves over that hussy."

"Exactly of whom are you speaking?" Emma Mae asked icily.

"Don't give me that," she snapped. "You know damn well *of whom* I'm speaking. That Doña Emilia what's-her-name!"

Emilia had come into the house in search of Miguel to see if he had eaten. Just as she started into the parlor, she heard her name being snapped out and stepped back. At first she had thought it was Emma Mae Lambeau who had spoken, and her heart began to flutter. She had avoided the woman throughout the morning, letting her mind concentrate only on the enjoyment she was having. She feared that enjoyment would be short-lived if she was becoming the topic of Emma Mae's gossip.

"Oh, really!" Emma Mae flared in total disgust. "Aren't you the one who was calling her royalty earlier this morning?"

"That is beside the point," Arabella simpered. "There is only one kind of woman who can draw men to them the way that she has been doing."

"You're quite right," Emma Mae said softly.

Emilia's heart nearly stopped beating.

"You're quite right," she repeated. "A woman of exquisite beauty and form and breeding. Something you and I never possessed, Arabella, or we might have done better for ourselves. Our problem is that we envy her and so automatically must throw brickbats in her path. That you should even think such a thing of her thoroughly disgusts me. I would suggest that you and Gracie Sue make your excuses to my niece, or I might just be tempted to spit in your face!"

Emilia fled into the dining room, her heart a triphammer. Because of her own tumultuous emotions she could not at first distinguish or recognize any particular face.

"Doña Emilia," Henry whispered at her side. "Are you ill?"

"The sun," she stammered. "It blinded me when I came in from outside. Have you seen my husband?"

"Yes'm," he said even softer. "Saw him to his room awhile back. Henry thought he had more need of sleep 'an food."

"Thank you, Henry."

He beamed. "None needed, but ole Henry sure wants ta thank y'all."

"Oh?"

"Eight years ah've done dis shindig, and dis am the best 'cause of you."

Two champions in as many minutes elevated Emilia's spirits to the heights.

"Again, I thank you."

"You jes' watch, missy. When dese pasty-faced beauties come down ta dance, dey be aping you."

Exactly, Emilia thought. And I think I know how to give them an even greater surprise. But this time there would be no fear in her heart. She felt safe and secure.

Because of the snoring Miguel, Emilia was relieved of the burden of having to share her room with the visiting belles. She caught Teresa in the hall and whispered her plan, to which Teresa quickly agreed. Both forwent the turkey buffet supper to give them time to dress after their rooms were vacated by Miguel and the girls. And as Henry had reasoned out, the country belles upon donning their evening gowns for the ball made some subtle changes. In every bedroom of Beauwood mounds of crinoline petticoats and hoops had been left behind. For the majority the aping of Emilia's fashion trend became a burdensome problem. Their skirts were now too long, and they had to constantly kick the extra material out of the way or trip. Even those who were naturally graceful took on the guise of marionettes dangling from twisted strings.

Arabella Eberhart, who was incapable of being insulted, took one final look at Gracie Sue and marched the teary girl right back upstairs for redressing.

The spacious living room had been transformed into a magical grand ballroom. The five-piece orchestra was sober, tuxedoed, and partially hidden behind potted plants. The radiant lamplight gleamed down upon jewels, bare necks and arms, and dainty slippers gliding over the polished floor.

Luella was relieved that Emilia and Teresa had not yet arrived. She wanted them to be a part of the Grand March and had so informed Yves and their husbands.

Emma Mae, who had been trailing her since supper, finally was able to whisper into her small roseate ear.

"Luella, it's Arabella."

She halted abruptly and glared at her aunt. Her soft round face suddenly became suffused with hard lines. "Hush," she muttered. "I'll not hear a word about the matter." She paused and then said viciously: "No petty spat between you two is going to ruin my day. Ignore her, as I have been doing all day."

Emma Mae Lambeau's Cupid mouth flew open in surprise. For a moment Luella thought she had gone too far, then realized the woman's shock was brought about by something behind her. She turned slowly, almost hesitantly, and then her heart began to quiver with rapturous gratitude.

Emilia and Teresa stood framed in the double archway, their wide hooped skirts encompassing the entire opening. They were patrician Spanish in costume from head to foot, Teresa in white taffeta and a Swiss lace mantilla that cascaded down from the high ivory head comb like rapids on a rushing river. On her bare neck was a silver chain bearing a single diamond pendant.

Emilia was in her favorite pale yellow color, the gown of silk with a lace overlay, of the same design as her mantilla. Although cut daringly low, a necklace of yellow diamonds defused attention away from her cleavage.

With a flutter of her hand Luella signaled the orchestra to prepare for the Grand March and ushered the men to the archway.

"My plans have just been changed," she gushed. "Yves, please escort our dear and charming guests. Gentlemen, if you would do me an equal honor."

To ever increasing applause and cheers they circled the room to the strains of a rousing Strauss waltz. Born to dance, Emilia's hooped skirt was motionless, as though Yves were pulling her about on unseen wheels.

Not only was the stag line long, but by the first intermission the crinoline petticoats and hooped skirts from the bedrooms had mysteriously vanished and reappeared on the ballroom floor.

Emilia and Teresa were almost obligated to dance every dance, but seldon with Miguel or Felix. Gracie Sue Eberhart was not being asked to dance at all, and Emilia took pity upon her. Miguel seemed to be the favorite partner of the young belles, so she badgered him into dancing with the gaudy beauty in purple velvet.

Arabella saw it all and stormed down on Emilia at the end of the dance.

"Thank you for sharing your husband with my daughter," she said acidly, "but I prefer my daughter to dance with *eligible* young men."

Emilia was having too much fun to spoil it with a confrontation. "They all seem to be taken," she said indifferently.

"Obviously," Arabella pouted. "Because you seem to be quite an expert on the floor. Have you danced professionally?"

Emma Mae saw the two women together and came on

the run. Emilia was unsure exactly how to answer and avoid abuse by the harridan. The arrival, at her side, of Emma Mae gave her her answer.

"As a matter of fact I have," she said quietly.

Arabella exalted over the admission. "Well, Emma Mae Lambeau, didn't I tell you? She just admitted it."

Emma Mae, who had only heard Emilia's answer, paled and began to fan herself vigorously.

"What was there to admit?" Emilia said innocently, preparing her own trap.

Arabella sniffed. "Don't give me that stuff. I'm well aware of the type of woman who dances professionally."

"Oh?" she murmured. "Then you must have firsthand experience to be so well versed in such matters. You did seem to do quite well waltzing with Yves Beauveau."

Knowing that the woman was growing too incensed to answer, Emilia paused for several seconds before going on: "However, in my country, dancers, young dancers, are held in very high esteem. To the Spanish flamenco dancing is as high an art form as painting or music. But, then, we are an older, more cultured civilization than you here in the colonies."

Arabella would not give in. "Perhaps then," she sneered, "you wouldn't mind sharing some of that culture with us?"

Emilia still did not feel trapped. "It would be my pleasure. However, I doubt that those three violins, cello, and piano could reproduce the type of music that I would require."

Arabella puffed up importantly. "That is a minor matter. Please excuse me."

"Oh, dear," Emma Mae cried as Arabella sailed away toward Henry. "This is all my fault. I had a set-to with the woman this afternoon, and she's taking her spite out on you. I'm so sorry."

Emilia cupped the quivering woman's chin in her hand and smiled. "I heard it all, and I'm honored at the way you stood up for me. Besides you were both right. It's something I guess I'll never be able to run away from for my whole life."

"Oh, my dear," Emma Mae gushed with heartfelt compassion, "you're overlooking a very important part of you. You don't run, in spite of what you may have done in life. I was right when I told Arabella that we envy you. I've never had a man in my life, and she turned hers into a sniveling prig who finds his pleasure with the Nigresses. Besides I bet you're a beautiful dancer."

No one ever knew where Arabella Eberhart gained the vast knowledge she possessed of every person, black and white, in the Natchez area. After whispering to Henry, he had blinked at her stupidly, and he went with the information to Luella with a suspicious mind. Luella thought it was a superbly marvelous idea and sent Henry scurrying.

A half hour later Henry escorted Emilia to the study off the ballroom for an introduction to Mama Abuela. Instantly the two women recognized each other as mulattoes, although of different ethnic backgrounds, and an unspoken rapport was established.

"Doña Emilia," the black said, hesitantly, in Spanish, "this guitar is long unused, except for singing babies to sleep in the afternoon."

Emilia laughed. "And I am reduced to using four silver spoons as castanets. They have never heard our music, so they'll never know if we blunder."

"Our music," Mama Abuela said dreamily. "I never thought to really ever hear it again myself. I'll do my best."

Her best was some of the finest Emilia had heard in her life. Alone, ringed by faces respectful and anticipatory of the unusual, she had started slowly, depending only upon the beat of the makeshift castanets. But once Mama Abuela's strong fingers took command of the guitar strings, Emilia gave herself more and more to that beat. This was not the music of the cantina. This was classical. This was real Spain. This was flamenco at its finest. She forgot who she was, where she was, or why she was alone on the dance floor. She tapped and stomped and swayed and swirled; her hands and feet a constant pattern of rhythm and graceful motion. She was exquisite and spellbinding. Hardly a single breath was taken by the three-hundred-odd spectators during the entire performance. And it was to cheers of adulation and affection that she concluded.

Her spirited performance brought about urgent calls for "reels, and polkas" and more lively dancing for the remainder of the night.

But even before her highly successful dance was concluded, three people had angrily departed the ballroom. Arabella Eberhart snatched her daughter away as though she had been the one performing the dance to her displeasure; and Miguel Escovarro, in a dark and surly mood, snatched a bottle of brandy from Henry's startled hands and stormed to his room.

Oddly enough no one missed the trio.

CHAPTER SEVEN

It was nearly dawn before Emilia could break away and wearily return to her room. Miguel was still up, the brandy bottle lying empty beside his chair.

"I haven't danced this much in years."

"So I noticed," Miguel said, his voice heavy with sarcasm.

She knew that Miguel was suddenly and wildly ashamed of her, that some vast wretchedness and despair had taken possession of him, and that because of all this he was frantically enraged.

"When did you leave the party?" she asked quietly.

"When you made it impossible for me to stay," he answered through clenched teeth.

Emilia was stunned. The lamplight shone on Miguel's stiff features, which had a kind of contortion upon them as if he had been seized with physical anguish, with overpowering torture. Breath was suspended on his lifted and twisted lips.

She forgot her own stupefaction in her overwhelming compassion for him and touched his arm, murmuring to him. He started violently, thrusting her away so ferociously that her head crashed against the bed frame as she fell. He cried out, his hoarse voice broken by the most appalling dry sobs:

"Oh damn you, damn you, damn you! You'll never be anything but a whore!"

Yves Beauveau was just preparing to rap on the door when he heard Miguel cry out. He turned away, hesitated, spun back, and knocked soundly on the panel.

"Miguel, there is trouble in the compound. I need every man I can muster."

Not waiting for an answer, he strode to the next door and rapped gently. It was opened almost at once.

"Excuse me, Felix, for disturbing you," he said softly, "but some of the slaves have run off during the night. With fast action we can track them down shortly."

Felix did not answer him. Instinctively he wanted no part of hunting down human beings, but he was remiss in knowing how to decline. He nodded and closed the door.

"You heard?"

Teresa nodded. The brown brilliance of her eyes was suffused with tears.

"I loathe aiding this slave business in any way, but he is our host."

Teresa tried to smile and shrug. "I'd try to help them all get away if I had the choice."

He took her in his arms and kissed her tenderly. "Which is just another reason why I love you so deeply. Get some sleep. I'll be back soon."

He found his brother waiting for him in the hall. Miguel had torn off his coat and cravat and was in shirt-sleeves, which were rolled back, revealing his strong brown arms. His neck, so like a corded column of brown marble, was also fully displayed. He had run his distracted hands so often through his hair that every thick golden curl stood upright all over his big round skull in damp and vital springs. But it was his eyes which drew Felix's full attention. They were flaring wild with animal excitement. Felix misunderstood the look, thinking his brother still quite drunk. But Yves's summons had instantly sobered him, charging his blood with a physical challenge to dissipate his anguish and rage.

For two days, the prevailing features of plantation life for the whites were sleep and rest. Emilia slept through twenty-four hours, and then was so difficult to awaken that for a while Teresa was alarmed. When she did awaken, she was quiet and sullen. Her first fierce resolution was to blot Miguel from her life. With him away it was an easy resolution to master. The memory of his accusation and attack brought the angry blood mounting to her cheeks. She walked the floor in rage and dropped at last exhausted:

"I never should have married!"

The memory which stung deepest was the joy she had felt in his arms before marriage. She had thought of him then as a gentleman. In a flash of self-revelation she saw him simply as an animal. It unsettled her whole attitude toward him. For the first time she began to fear the darker side of his nature.

Yves had greatly miscalculated the easy nature of their task. The escape had been well planned and engineered. After two days they were still chasing shadows.

During the absence of the men Teresa was forced into almost daily contact with Luella. It was a different manner of woman who now stalked the rooms of Beauwood. She took it as a personal affront that some of the household slaves were among the missing. Henry was bitterly castigated for distributing the leftover food while she had been sleeping. By her law the majority were meant to suffer for the errors of the few. In her pique she cut off the daily supply of meat until every last slave was returned and properly punished. Teresa tried to avoid the woman, loathing herself for such deceit. After Emma Mae's departure, and Emilia's refusal to leave her room, she turned to the only other woman she felt she could communicate with.

"How many did run away, Mama Abuela?"

"One would have been too many" was the laconic response. "But this time is real bad. Eleven men, ten women, and thirty of my children. It will be bad for them and bad for us."

"Bad in what way?"

"Regardless of the women and children involved, the men were the ones who were becoming surly, unmanageable, and the quickest to stir up rebellion. Some still like them are here. When they are caught, they'll be forced to tell who helped them, and then they'll all be sold away, regardless of family ties."

"That's utterly inhuman," Teresa growled.

The large woman slowly squared her shoulders and faced the naïve visitor, erect, controlled, dignified:

"But the question is, Doña Teresa, who gave those hotheads the right to put us all into peril. There are no whippings here. Master Yves does not allow the white overseers to sleep with our wenches. The food is good and plentiful. No man is overworked."

"But you are still slaves," Teresa protested.

Mama Abuela's tall, rugged figure met the seated Teresa with the easy generous attitude of a mother ready to expose her daughter to the facts of life.

"We are also a family, my girl. A family that is an intricate network of law, order, and command. This is the first time since I've been here that so many have left at once. We are always going to be slaves, so must act like a family. They have done us all wrong."

"Then you would never run away if given the chance?"

"Rest assured, no," the quiet voice responded. "I never want to see a slave auction again."

It was not the creak of the wagons that aroused Teresa the next morning, but a sudden contraction of her heart, as though she had been given an omen as to what the day would bring. She shivered as she rose from the bed by inches, tiptoeing to the window and gently pulling aside the thick velour curtains. It was barely dawn, but she could plainly see the activity taking place in Mama Abuela's compound. A grim, hard giant of a black man was being chained to a post in the center of the circle. Silent women and children were being hauled from the wagon and marched into one of the cabins. There was, oddly, no sound from them.

In spite of her chagrin Teresa could not pull herself away from the scene. The hair suddenly tingled on the back of her neck, and she saw the black eyes, swimming in vast pools of clear, milky white, swing defiantly up to her window. As she started to turn away, she became aware that the glare had not been meant for her. Luella Beauveau, in a dressing robe, had come onto the second-floor balcony and stood starchy and erect, her face contorted by hatred.

Teresa gasped as the door came open behind her. With a slow shuffle Felix came into the room, his face ashen and gaunt, his eyes sunken and ringed by dark circles.

"Oh, my darling," she cried, running to him.

"Just help me to bed," he rasped. "I've never been so tired and sick at heart."

He slumped down on the bed, and she began to help him undress.

"Did you get them all?"

"No." His voice was hardly a whisper. "Miguel is still out with the other search party." He shuddered. "The bastard is enjoying every minute of this nightmare."

"I saw the ones you did bring back."

His laugh was hollow and horrible. "Hardly all. Yves has been selling them off piecemeal to different plantations on the way back. Oh, God, it was so disgusting. Children taken from their mothers, wives from their husbands. And eerie, because there were no protests; just the murderous hatred in their eyes and faces."

"Why were these brought back?"

"Because of the one they have chained. He's Henry's son and was one of the trusted black overseers."

"No more!" she snapped. "Lie back, and I'll get a basin to wash your face and hands."

He was sound asleep by the time she returned to the bed. Gently and lovingly she sponged off his face with a washcloth and kissed him on the forehead. She prayed that they could leave that place before Mama Abuela's worst fears started to come true.

For three days the search for the runaways had spread out into a mighty web of dogs and men as other plantation owners came to Yves's aid. It was one time that Yves wished that he employed more white overseers at Beauwood. His was an unusual plantation, founded on trust and not the bite of the whiplash.

Now, with the return of the captured rebel leader, he would impose new regulations and give them all a taste of the consequences of an attempted escape. He lay in his cool bed and calculated the details of every move he had to make to obtain the right effect. He would do nothing until Miguel Escovarro had returned with the other leader and the remaining women.

The silence came so suddenly that Miguel at first did not comprehend why the dogs had stopped baying and barking. He lifted his head and listened, the marvelous stillness pervading the cypress forest, and the stars seemed to blanket the distant clearing where the slaves had settled for the night with an assurance of everlasting security.

The search party came from behind the trees, spread out, perhaps purposely to make their numbers seem double. Only one man among them was an overseer from Beauwood.

"The dogs are muzzled to keep from setting up an alarm," said a voice.

Miguel smiled without looking around. He had come to know the voice and its owner very well in the past three days. It was a flat statement, but to his well-trained ears it had in it all the characteristics of stark greed. The little, shrill-toned man would profit handsomely from Yves's reward, whether this batch were returned dead or alive.

As though reading his thoughts, Wesley Thorpe chuckled. "They think that because they can't hear the hounds that we've gone off in a different direction. Bloody buggers are probably screwing up a storm."

"Why do you say that?"

"I know 'em and their ways and who is still unaccounted for. Big Frank has worked for me at the sawmill since he was fifteen. He loves to get the young wenches into the forest and show them some meat for the first time. That's what he got down there right now, four wenches and his old lady."

Miguel grunted. "I doubt that he would be doing anything with his mother along."

Thorpe chuckled wickedly. "Take it from me, she's the one who taught Big Frank everything he knows."

"You make the plantation sound a great deal different than your boss."

"Hell," Thorpe chortled, "he don't know half of what

goes on. We ain't supposed to touch them, but I'd much rather cut some of this black meat than take a chance with the sickness on them broads down at Natchez-Under-the-Hill. We got a saying 'round here that it changes your luck. You need your luck changed?"

Miguel started to answer, swallowed his words, his mouth remaining agape, as the whole forest exploded with the yapping of bloodhounds. It was not a sound emitted in aggressive assault; it was a vocal expression of the joy of having found the prey. The line of men became a ripple of movement, then a surging vortex that drove into the clearing, encircling it. The sound of the dogs enthused in Miguel the same expectant excitement. He ran forward, yelling excitedly, firing his pistol into the air.

The escapees were fully awake; screaming, scrambling for escape, and to the utter dismay of everyone firing back. Without being told, the search party began to use their firearms as protection instead of noisemakers to frighten and confuse.

Miguel had just entered the clearing when a young buck emerged from beneath a wagon totally naked; his bulbous mouth opened to spread the alarm, only to have it twist into a groan of agony as a rifle ball entered his face, separating even further his wide-nostriled nose.

And it was over as quickly as it began. As the captives were rounded up, silence came again, broken only by the moans of the dying. It was the silence that breeds the fear of death.

Miguel, exerting himself as if he alone had just done the entire battle, walked to the wagons. He found himself balancing on his toes with each step, as if he were afraid of waking the dead and near dead. He hung in the silence light as a feather, exhilarated, yet his muscles were so tense that he looked, too, like a man supporting tremendous weight.

"Big Frank!" Thorpe called out imperiously. "Where are you and your mama?"

"She am dead!" a booming voice wailed out of the gloom.

Miguel turned just in time to see two of the search-party

members push forward a huge strapping black youth of eighteen. By his side hovered a silent young girl.

The campfire was rekindled, and in that pale and uncertain firelight she was barely visible, for she blended with the darkness, was a part of it, and part of the bare and silent world surrounding the scene. Her quietness was its quietness; its stillness hers; its ebony hues were as those in her face and garment; its austerity and dignity and restraint were her own. She was not overly tall, for her fifteen years, but her slenderness had in it such serenity and pride that she seemed comparable to the young man at her side.

"Who is she?" Thorpe demanded, having never seen her with Big Frank at the sawmill.

"My sister Carrie," he answered sullenly.

Her dusky and serene face was oval and the color of well-polished saddle leather, delicately touched at the lips by a rosy shadow. This tenuous color was repeated in her bared breasts, somewhat sagged but beautifully shaped. She regarded the spellbound Miguel Escovarro with an expression which revealed her chilly hatred and loathing. The dead black buck was to have been her first mate.

She excited Miguel enormously. He had been watching her ever since the pair had come forward. She seemed to be surrounded by a sensuous glow, something he had not detected in any other black woman. The manner in which she clutched the skirt about her middle aroused him. A chance at having her display even more of her body excited him.

He was partially turned toward her, and the firelight illuminated his thick pulsing manhood plainly. He hauled her in close to him, unmindful of the search party, or her brother, and his trembling hands pressed over the dusky nipples of her rounded breasts. His desire was obvious, and her eyes told him that she would rather die than submit to his advances.

"Don't touch her," Big Frank growled darkly, taking a step forward.

"Chain him!" Thorpe barked, then winked at Miguel. "Have a go at it, mate."

Big Frank glowered as the white hand lifted away the

skirt; his youthful muscles fought against the handcuffs and chains as the invading hand stroked the never-before-seen ebony thigh of his sister. His anger boiled to near madness as Miguel brushed the tight curls concealing her virgin crotch; and Miguel unleashed himself, plunging sadistically into the girl, the young man split the air with horrible curses, pounding the chains so hard against his wrists that they turned the metal to wet scarlet.

The search party whooped and howled and urged Miguel to be even more animalistic. The sight was bringing out their basest nature, for there was not a man among them who had not taken a few black wenches in their life and were greatly disappointed that these two were the only survivors of the capture. They held the girl firmly, so that Miguel was given no resistance.

But Miguel heard nor saw any of it. His penis was aflame with fire from the still unhealed nail marks. He felt an instability of mind, a loss of focus; rational thought was almost beyond his reach. The girl became Alisa. The girl became every whore. The girl became Emilia. Animalistically he pounded out his fury at them all until the devilish pain subtly was transformed into exotic pleasure and he nearly fainted upon his completion. His place was taken immediately by another, and then another, until the girl was raw and bleeding.

Big Frank had paid no heed to them, knowing them his whole lifetime for what they really were—more animal than himself. His hatred centered mainly on the Spaniard, and he marked the man for death.

Miguel did not return with the party to Beauwood but headed directly for Natchez-Under-the-Hill. Yves, upon hearing what had transpired from Wesley Thorpe, was thankful for that. Because two of the most popular blacks on the plantation, Henry's son Amos and Big Frank had been the instigators of the escape, it was causing great consternation among the other slaves. Sides were being taken, and he was beginning to reevaluate the strict rules he had been considering. Still he sold Big Frank to the Carter Finnell plantation, closing his ears the very next day to the fact that the young buck had bolted from there the moment he had been released from chains and left alone. He nervously waited a day and then informed his wife that he could no longer postpone a business trip to New Orleans, in spite of the trouble on the plantation. To his utter amazement she did not try to hold him back.

Felix was more hesitant in broaching a similar plan to Teresa.

"There are still many things we need in New Orleans, Teresa. If we get them now, we can go direct by ship from Natchez to Corpus Christi without stopping there again."

"That sounds reasonable."

"Good. Then I'll tell Yves that we'll return with him."

"*You'll* return with him," Teresa said, her voice heavy with sarcasm. "I don't care if I ever see that place again."

Felix frowned thoughtfully.

"I suppose," he said quietly, "Yves wouldn't be leaving unless he thought the trouble was settled down. Yes, you stay here and see after Emilia."

"And who is to see after Miguel?" Teresa demanded suddenly.

Felix sighed. "I'll see what I can do before we board the boat at Natchez-Under-the-Hill."

Proctor Honeycutt came and bought the remaining runaway women and children before Yves's departure. In spite of Henry's pleading his daughter-in-law and grandchildren were included in the group, but Honeycutt wanted no part of Amos or the abused Carrie.

"After I'm gone," Yves told his wife, "have Thorpe lock Amos up in one of the cabins. Ten days without food and water might help break his spirit."

"You'll be back that soon?" she asked in surprise.

"My main purpose in going is to hire more overseers. I aim to get them back here as soon as possible."

Luella didn't trouble herself to inform Wesley Thorpe about Yves's wishes for Amos. She had wishes of her own about him and spent the afternoon contemplating them as she watched him from her bedroom window.

Amos moved about the restraining pole with the thrusting slowness of a lion; a broad, aggressive, king-of-the-jungle strut. When his Adonis face was soft, untroubled, he could touch one with a boyish quality. As the features hardened to mistrust and hate, his countenance doubled its actual twenty-two years. He had been born on the plantation, spent a more than happy childhood due to being raised mainly in the mansion because both of his parents were household servants. He never saw the fields until he was twenty, and Yves entrusted him with an overseer's position. Luella had wanted Amos trained to replace his father someday, but Yves was quietly adamant about the change. So adamant, in fact, that he purchased a bride for Amos in New Orleans.

Amos accepted the girl dutifully and his change in position gratefully. He was released from the mercurial temperament of Luella Beauveau. Then his bride began to subtly change him. A Virginia slave, Chulla became a runaway, with her family, at age fifteen. The Quakers in Pennsylvania saw them safely on the "underground railway" to Canada. For three years she had tasted the fruits of freedom and education before bounty hunters tracked down the family and spirited them back South. Her former master sent Chulla to New Orleans to be resold. At first she resented the imposed marriage to the big, lumbering Amos. Their first child softened her and made her start to plan. Her children were going to have the same benefits that she had had in Canada. Because it was illegal for blacks to know how to read and write and do figures, she had to secretly persuade Amos to let her teach him. And as she opened new vistas for him, she talked more and more about Canada and the good life there. Two years, and two children, later she finally controlled his mind. Not even to his father, who would have been furious with such a plan, did he discuss his innermost thoughts. But his attitude was becoming apparent to Big Frank, and they quietly joined forces.

Now, as Amos rested his back against the rough-hewn pole, the nearly dead cook fire bathed him in an almost effulgent whiteness. The shadows of the plantation were inky in contrast, and the lightless windows of the mansion stood out in bold relief. But the plantation was silent and, except for himself, seemed absolutely deserted.

For a time he stood looking at the curtained window of Luella's bedroom. From somewhere at his back, in the city-like circles of whitewashed cabins, drifted the heavy pungency of the pork that had been cooked with chickpeas for the slaves' dinner. To win silence that night, Luella had relented on the "no meat" rule.

His ears were alert for the sounds that might, in their drifting inconsequences, mean everything. Then he heard something like a subdued ejaculation and opened his eyes upon a startling spectacle.

Leaning against one of the cabin walls stood Luella, whose face in the firelight showed a strange mingling of savagery and hatred.

"I presume," she said icily, "you're aware of the state of turmoil you have caused on this plantation?" The shadowy figure paused, then marched defiantly to the pole, her voice charged with a bravado that somehow seemed to lack genuineness.

"I'm at a loss to understand why you have done this to my husband, to your father, and mainly to me. You were treated very well in my home—even treated like family after your mother died. When you wanted freedom from household duties, you were given a position of responsibility and respect. Why throw all that away and end up in chains?"

"Chains didn't hold Big Frank for long," Amos said evenly.

Luella looked at him steadily, almost insultingly, with deep blue eyes, then laughed.

"It could all be the same as it once was, Amos."

"Never," he said coldly. "My wife and babies are already gone."

She looked at him bitterly and said, "I was speaking of before she came on the scene. Do you think me stupid? Niggers love to gossip, and I know all about her educated glibness and how she turned you against me. That's the whole thing, isn't it? Just like when Yves took you away from me when he began to suspect something. She was afraid you'd come back to me sometime, wasn't she?"

He was disgusted with her. The same disgust he had felt

each time she had cowed him into climbing atop her since he was a boy. It was a horrible dark secret that he had kept hidden from everyone, and now he wanted to say something that would hurt her womanly vanity: "She never knew of the ugly things you used to make me do."

She blushed angrily, blood coursing across her face.

"You bastard," she snarled. "You never thought them ugly after you were sixteen and came to me of your own accord."

"Any young man needs release, and you said you'd sell me away if I was caught with any of the wenches. I had no other choice."

"I treated you well," she temporized. "Just listen to yourself. You're hardly a black man. I kept you away from the compounds and taught you to speak as we speak."

"Dat don' change de color of mah skin," he mocked arrogantly in argot.

"Shut up, you fool! I'm giving you a chance no other runaway ever gets."

"You can force me to remain here, even to bed with you, but you will never break my will to go and seek out my wife and babies."

A scowl crossed her face, a harsh, belligerent scowl, and she could not kid herself into thinking that she was dealing with the naïve young mind she had once been able to frighten into doing her bidding. He had become a man! The only black man she had ever wanted to possess as her very own.

They stared at each other for some time, and he saw in her eyes hatred, bitterness, confusion, and love. But as he continued to look at her, those attributes vanished, and he saw only that she was the slave and he the master. He wondered what his wise wife would advise him at this moment.

"My husband will be gone for ten days. Thorpe is to lock you into a cabin tomorrow morning. I'm sure that by the time he returns, we can convince him that you have had a change of heart due to the dedicated loyalty your father has shown this plantation for his entire life."

She stepped out of the bonfire's umbra and was quickly gone.

He realized that she was quite capable of doing as she said. She was the real master of Beauwood. Sold away, it could take him years to escape again. Here he could live the easy life by training under his father and quickly regain trust. He was going to escape again and, suddenly he knew that Yves Beauveau's Achilles' heel would help him. Years ago he had overheard the doctor tell Yves that Luella was childless because of his sterility and not Luella's. At the time he had not understood. As Yves had hurt him, by taking away his wife and children, he would hurt Yves, by taking his wife at a time when she could not reject his seed.

His second visitor came when the fire was cold ash. He listened to the whispered plan and agreed. Anything to keep him out of Luella's bed. Even that!

CHAPTER EIGHT

It was at first a terribly horrifying experience for the young girl, because she did not at first recognize the savagely beaten man she stumbled over in the gulley a few miles from Beauwood. She gasped and clasped the small bundle of clothing to her breast, thinking the man dead.

That was exactly how Big Frank thought he had left Miguel—dead. Coming cross-country from his escape from the Finnell plantation, he had seen the horse and rider coming up the road at a slow walk and scurried into the trees at the roadside. The moon was full, and he did not want to be spotted, no matter who the rider might be. His only desire at the moment was to get to Beauwood, find his sister, and be off again. But when the rider drew near, his eyes flared in disbelief and his heart thundered savagely. His hatred had burned Miguel's image into his brain so that he knew he was not mistaken. Still he was cautious, knowing the man to be armed with a pistol. But as the horse passed him by, he knew vengeance was his—Miguel was drunkenly asleep in the saddle, almost in the same position as when Felix and Yves had placed him there and Yves had instructed the horse to make for home.

The first crash of the tree limb wielded by Big Frank caught Miguel in the small of the back, bringing him awake with bewilderment even as he tumbled from the saddle into the gulley. For only a second he saw his assailant and knew he was looking death in the face. His reflexes were too benumbed by drink to act fast enough, and the weapon crashed onto his head before his arms were half raised. Blackness closed over him almost immediately. Again and again Big Frank maliciously battered at the fallen body until the dry wood of the limb was splintered into kindling and no longer effective. His eyes wildly gleeful, the big man quickly snatched off Miguel's money pouch, thrust the pistol into the waistband of his pants, and started running up the gulley, keeping well into the shadows cast by the oak trees. He was too smart to capture the startled horse, which had cantered up the road and was now slowly returning to see what had become of its rider. He would not in any way be connected with what would be taken as a robbery-murder. No runaway slave ever returned to the plantation they have just been sold away from, but to be caught with a stolen horse meant an immediate lynching.

The girl started to skirt the body when Miguel moaned and rolled onto his back.

"Lawdy, me, oh my," Daphine wailed. "I knows you from Miss Bea's!"

Because Beatrice Beauvoir had immediately suspected that Yves had gained information from his former slave girl, she had had the girl whipped to tell her the truth, but Daffy had kept her heart and lips steadfastly loyal to Yves Beauveau. Then, when the house was at its busiest the next night, she wrapped a few possessions in a headkerchief and began to walk. Sleeping by day, wherever she felt it was safe, she would walk by night—keeping the smell of the river to her left and the North Star constantly in front of her. It took her twelve days to reach this familiar spot and what she thought was safety.

In spite of her fear of horses, but because of her ability in handling loose-limbed drunks, she was able to get Miguel up into the saddle and lead the horse to Beauwood.

It took five minutes of steady pounding on the front door of the mansion before lamplight came into the foyer and the large door barely cracked.

"Daffy?" Henry blinked in disbelief.

"It's de Spanish man, Missah Henry," she exclaimed. "He don' been robbed."

"Go to da cabins, Daffy, and wake a couple of men and Mama Abuela."

Henry took the lamp out to the tethered horse and set it

146

on the hitching post. Miguel started to slump out of the saddle, and it took the old man's full strength to ease the comatose body to the ground without being crushed.

The strident knocks had aroused everyone who hadn't been sleeping and brought them on the run. Luella had only returned to the house minutes before from her talk with Amos and came waddling, expecting trouble. Emilia had been pacing the floor when she heard Luella's heavy tread in the hallway, at what the obese woman could muster as a run. Instinct made her spin toward the window just in time to see Henry stretch the heavy bulk out on the ground. She came flying down the stairs, passed Luella in the foyer, her lovely face ashen.

"Miguel," she whispered, "oh, Miguel . . ."

"He's been attacked and robbed," Henry explained. "I've sent for some men—"

Emilia swayed dizzily, and for a moment Henry thought she was going to faint. But she crouched down beside her husband and started to feel of his arms and chest and legs; and when she spoke, her voice was very quiet.

"Nothing seems broken," she said.

Four blacks came running up, and Luella took charge. With their bulky cargo, they met a startled Teresa on the stairway.

"Come help me undress him," Emilia said.

Together they pulled off his bloodstained clothes and dropped them in a sodden heap on the floor. Henry filled the washbasin and brought it and towels to the nightstand. Luella hovered about like a field foreman. They bathed at the wounds, which were mainly abrasions and bruises.

Miguel's eyes opened.

"Take me home, Em," he muttered. "I'm sick of this black man's world."

Luella pushed forward to the bed. "Are you saying a nigger did this?" she asked grimly.

He nodded. "The one we just captured."

Her eyes glinted like flints striking on stone, and she spun toward the hall where the four blacks were waiting to be dismissed. "That would be Big Frank," she snapped, "who escaped from the Finnell plantation." Then she dropped her voice to a low, warning pitch. "By morning I want the word spread that if he is on my property and anyone is caught feeding or aiding him. they will be whipped and given free for life to the poorest sharecroppers I can find in the county. Now go!"

Mama Abuela came scurrying down the hall carrying Yves's medical bag. At first Luella thought little about the young woman following in her wake. Mama Abuela took one look at the wounds and shooed everyone into the hall. Only when Daffy didn't stay to aid her did Luella recognize her.

"Daphine," she gasped. "What in the world are you doing here?"

Henry intervened. "She's da one found him and brought 'im 'ome, Miss Luella."

"That hardly answers my question," she said icily.

"Ah run away," Daffy said weakly, hanging her head.

"Oh, my Lord," Luella exclaimed. "It isn't bad enough that we have slaves running away, but now I'm faced with one running back. Well, it will do you no good, young lady. You'll just have to go right back to where you were sold to, and at once!"

The girl's face clouded, and she began to cry. "She'll kill me if you do dat," she whimpered. "Miss Beatrice will kill Daffy fur sure 'cause wat Massa Yves did fur des ladies."

Luella had been told nothing of Teresa and Emilia's adventure and was totally mystified. "Whatever are you talking about?"

"Of course," Emilia exclaimed, "you're the girl who passed us in the hall that day. But how in the world did you ever recognize Miguel tonight."

With no reason to lie Daffy was bluntly honest. " 'Cause he were wid Miss Alisa while Massa Yves were in mah room gettin' information 'bout where Miss Bea were hidin' y'all. Den when her main man come back without y'all, dey done shed his clothes and sent 'im out near bare-assed. Daffy saw it all."

Luella looked from one to the other in total confusion. It was exactly as Teresa had suspected the night Yves had saved them after the accident. But just as she had done then, she again held her thoughts silent.

"It seems that you surely did," Emilia said testily, "but it's hardly a story I wish to dwell on any longer tonight. Madam Beauveau, my husband will need undisturbed sleep. Is there another room I might use for the night?"

Still confused, but anxious now to get Daphine alone for the full telling, she nodded toward the door directly across the hall. Without a further word Emilia approached it and entered with great dignity. A moment before she had been ready to forgive Miguel anything. That he had stayed behind in the whorehouse and had not come to aid in her rescue was a stunning blow to her vanity. She grasped one of the bedposts, shaking all over with weeping.

After hearing the full story from Daphine, Luella knew she had little choice but to keep the girl at the plantation until she could dump the entire matter in her husband's lap. Her heart ached for Emilia, but she had little experience in dealing with other women and so held her silence and her distance. She knew exactly how the Spanish woman was feeling, for hadn't she, too, spent many nights in a cold and lonely bed, as well as loveless bed, while having the full knowledge that Yves was in the bed of some New Orleans whore.

But when the new breath of scandal reached her ears, she was insatiable with fury toward Miguel.

"All right, Amy," she said quietly, "it was wise of you to come to me. Now tell me slowly how you came to learn this thing."

The pig-tailed black girl felt proud to be the central figure of Luella's attention. She saw this as a golden opportunity to get out of the fields and assigned to household chores, so she was very careful not to lie to or embellish the tale, as she was normally prone to do.

"Las' night," she drawled, "ah was takin' care Carrie, juz Mama Abuela tell me. Big Frank he come in, thinkin' Amy sleep. He want 'is sista ta leab wid 'im. O Carrie, she say, too sick 'n' hurt ta much. Den he tell 'er dat he kilt de Spanish man who'd kilt der mama 'n' raped Carrie. He says fur Carrie ta rest up, dat he be 'round 'n' dat he gonna let ebery nigger 'ere know wat 'appen 'n' der women ain't safe from de white cocks no more."

To safeguard the girl and insure her from spreading the gossip, she was assigned to the house staff at once.

Armed with her knowledge, Luella pounced on Wesley Thorpe the moment he came for his orders. Faced with the facts, he could not deny them but tried to keep his own skirts clean.

"You mean to tell me," she said in utter disbelief, "that you did not partake in the festivities?"

"No, ma'am," he insisted hotly. "And I couldn't stop them, either. That Spaniard is some mean and ugly man when he's drunk and fired up."

"All right, it's past tense. I want Amos padlocked into a cabin and the entire plantation searched for Big Frank."

"Think these niggers will turn him over if they find him?"

"If they know what's good for them!"

But those who had helped Big Frank gather his supplies for his first escape had already heard his story and made sure that he was safely hidden before they began to pass along the news of what had happened to his sister. By nightfall there wasn't a single soul at Beauwood who had not heard the story, in one form or another. It was unfortunate that some had to learn the facts at all.

Mama Abuela, coming back to check on the patient in the late afternoon, purposely spoke to Teresa in Spanish so that no other ears would understand.

"I wish he were well enough to move, Doña Teresa."

"Why?"

"He's going to bring us all big trouble. Don't know if Big Frank is right in blaming him for his mammy's death, but the other . . ." She shrugged. She was hesitant to discuss such a vulgar matter with such a gentle lady.

"It's quite all right," Teresa said gently, taking the big woman's hand. "Every time I've gone to the kitchen today for Don Miguel's broth, they all stop whispering the moment I enter the room. I think I'd best know the worst so I know how to handle it."

Mama Abuela was still reluctant, choosing her words slowly and carefully, until the whole sordid tale had been told.

"Dear God," Teresa cried weakly, "we must keep this from Doña Emilia's ears."

"That won't be necessary," a fierce, cold voice said from the doorway.

Teresa turned to her quietly. "Em," she whispered, "I'm sorry you heard."

Emilia stood staring at the bed and the waxen body that appeared more dead than alive. There was no emotion on her face or in her voice. "Leave me alone with him for a moment." She sat down beside the bed, thinking: I said I would never love again with my heart after Sam Houston, but you changed all that, my great *macho* darling. I'd do anything for you—anything at all, except return to what I was before. I'd do that too, but only for you. If you have done these things to spite me and throw my past in my face, you've succeeded. No man has ever made me cry before. In time I may be able to forgive you but don't ask that of me right now. That I cannot do.

She rose very slowly and went back into the hall. To her relief, Teresa was still waiting for her.

"You would do me the greatest service, Teresa, if you would see to his care for a few days. I'm afraid my sharp tongue will say the wrong things at the wrong time."

Teresa wasn't so sure she might not do the selfsame thing.

Luella had not received any "repentant" message from Amos throughout the day and that evening put into effect a new stratagem. Henry was triumphant. With a tin of hot food right from Miss Luella's own table, his heart sang with the news he was carrying to his son. So absorbed was he in speculation that he paid scant attention to a group of slaves strolling aimlessly about in the first compound. His mind was quickly returned to reality by a gigantic roar. A wooden shed full of baled cotton, crates, and he knew not what else, burst into a blaze so suddenly that he thought the earth had opened to let an avenging fire consume the structure. No one seemed to be in a hurry to extinguish the flames.

It had been hopeless from the very first. The flames had leaped high, driven everybody back, lighted up everything—and collapsed. By the time the white overseers arrived, the shed was already a heap of embers glowing fiercely. Ian Danton shrugged and said he was going back to his dinner. As they passed, Henry wished him a good evening.

"Ain' nothin' good 'bout it," he drawled and walked off.

Skirting the glow to get to his son's compound, he found himself behind men who were talking. He heard the name of Big Frank pronounced, then the words, "tak 'vantage of de massa not being back." Henry didn't like such disloyalty and let it show in his face.

It was noticed by the other overseer, Todd Barrow. Young, aggressive, with a forked little beard and a hook to his nose, he had always been standoffish with the blacks, not friendly like Thorpe and Danton; and the blacks on their side said the man had a devil in him just waiting to spring out. As for Barrow, he had never before seen the butler in the compound area, and he was curious.

He motioned over one of his field bosses, Jamie.

"Mighty fine-lookin' supper ole Henry's carrin' there." Jamie shuffled his feet in the dust. "Am fur 'is boy, reckon."

With each mention of Amos, Jamie would twist his answers. It was evident Jamie was a perfectly shameless prevaricator and a strong supporter of Amos and Big Frank. At last Todd got angry, and to conceal a movement of furious annoyance, he yawned and then suddenly turned away without wishing Jamie good night.

In the next compound he looked around the row of cabins and was startled to see that they all appeared deserted. Cutting across the compound, he headed for the back of the main house to report to Luella on the fire. He was amazed. Then he had to look at the front mighty quick, because upward of twenty blacks were forming a circle about the entranceway.

He strode forward. Sticks and little stones began flying

about—thick: they were whizzing before his nose, dropping below him, striking behind him against the trees. All this time the slave quarters, the main house, the woods, the gardens, were very quiet—perfectly quiet. He was being warned away and knew it would do no good to yell at the blacks.

He darted into the mulberry bushes to determine how best to get to the house. He resented Yves's strict order that the overseers were not allowed to carry weapons. He was defenseless. He saw a face amongst the leaves on a level with his own, looking at him very fierce and steady; and then suddenly, as though a veil had been removed from his eyes, he made out, deep in the tangled gloom, naked chests, arms, legs, glaring eyes—the garden was swarming with human limbs in movement, glistening, of a midnight color. He was being surrounded and cut off from the house, and it made his blood run cold. They would all be dead if the slaves gained access to the main house and Beauwood's supply of firearms.

The silence was broken by the sharp rattle of rifle fire. Into the long Beauwood drive five horsemen swept forward at a gallop, their rifle reports meant only to frighten. But halfway up the drive shots rang out from the bordering oaks, and two men and horses crumpled to the gravel. The remaining horsemen veered into the trees, and the air began to grow heavy with the noise of volleys, and yet the main house was silent.

Todd Barrow saw his chance and started running toward the main house. Halfway there a horseman swept past. Todd recognized Alvin Finnell and shouted, but the young man shook his head wildly, and went on firing indiscriminately at any black moving figure.

Todd crashed through the front door and slammed it shut, almost colliding with Luella.

"Good God!" she breathed. "What does it mean?"

"Riot!" he shouted. "Get the keys for the firearm locker while I bar the doors."

"Who are the riders?"

"Finnells! Probably tracked Big Frank here and stumbled into this mess."

A grim-faced Henry came stumbling in from the kitchen, his clothing tattered and torn. "Mah boy weren't dar, Miss Luella. De lock were smashed and de cabin empty." Then his face contorted in disbelief. "An' mah own people weren't goin' ta let me come warn yah," he sobbed.

"Shut up, old man," Barrow barked. "You may be fighting them for your own life before this night is over. Go help Miss Luella get the guns."

Big Frank and Amos, with twenty loyal blacks, had not counted on the Finnells' arrival. They possessed eight rifles and Miguel's pistol between them. Firepower enough, they reasoned, to shoot down the remaining horsemen and storm the house. Then the house turned black, and the horsemen vanished. Amos, fearing their small ammunition supply was also vanishing, sent out word to cease firing.

The brilliant moon came from its cloud cover and flooded the field of blood and death with an eerie glory. From every nook and corner, from every shadow and across every open space, through the hot breath of the night, came the overpowering moans of the wounded.

The Finnell brothers waited in the shadow of the trees to ascertain the rebels' firepower. Through the uncanny "slave grapevine" the news of the attack on Miguel Escovarro had reached their plantation in the late afternoon. Two of the brothers had been with Miguel in the capture of Big Frank and reasoned things out quickly. When they rode onto Beauwood land, they were puzzled to see the women scurrying the children into the fields, even though dusk was falling. They held off riding into the grounds until they could see what the black men were about, counting on launching a surprise blow, paralyzing the presumed weaponless slaves. Instead, they had two of their overseers killed.

The wide square remained quiet, Alvin Finnell directing his brothers to dismount and spread out. An occasional balcony window would open cautiously as Todd Barrow positioned those within the house and instructed them on the use of the firearms. Even Miguel, weak and bewildered, sat by a window, his eyes roaming blurredly up and down the length of the driveway. The kitchen help and maids were frightened of the guns and balked against using them on their kin and friends. Todd thought it was just as well to keep them weaponless, although it gave him only six people to defend the house.

It became a waiting game, with only an occasional sniper firing at a moving shadow. Then it became a jungle game as the hours wore on. Two of the Finnell brothers were caught in the dark and silently stabbed to death. Alvin Finnell had made it unseen to the back of the house. Toeing and fingering his way, he made it to the roof via the kitchen chimney. No one thought to look up so his sniping position went undetected. When a third white man was felled by a knife, the news elated Big Frank. In the darkness the blacks had not noticed that the cautiously approaching man was their own overseer, Ian Danton.

"Dey only one man and three woman left," Big Frank chortled. "Fire all yah wan' at de windows and door."

The continuing volley was so massive that those within the house were forced to squat down and not return the fire. Only Alvin was able to be on the attack, picking his targets carefully by the flash from their guns.

And as suddenly as it started, it was over again. Death and lack of ammunition had stilled the black guns. Every window in the front of the house had been rifle bored and smashed, and the great main door stood ajar, hanging precariously by a single hinge.

"Listen me!" Big Frank yelled. "Gib me de Spanish man 'n' papers ob freedom fur us all. Do dat 'n' you lib."

Before anyone could answer, Alvin yelled down from his perch. "Go ta hell, nigger! It's Alvin Finnell, and the only place you're going is to your grave."

"Thought he was dead," Amos gasped.

Big Frank fumed. "How'n de hell he git into da house?"

"Doesn't matter," Amos sighed deeply, knowing it was all but over. "We're out of bullets. We'd better make a run for it before they find out we're gone. It'll take Barrow a long time to round up a search party."

Big Frank smiled broadly, patting his waistband. "Still got me dis unfired pistol 'n' a surprise ah don't tell yah 'bout. Jamie, am time."

The hero-worshiping young black slithered off into the shadows. Again it became a time of waiting, although Big Frank was directing the collection of the ammunitionless rifles and giving directions as to how they would be used.

Within fifteen minutes a mass of shadowy figures began to emerge from the nearest compound and shuffle toward the main house. Among them was Mama Abuela. She was haggard and distraught. Not until the group was directly in front of the house was it apparent that she was the only woman in a crowd of frightened, wide-eyed, bewildered children.

"Hold yah fire!" Big Frank yelled. He rose and walked forward with Amos and eight blacks bearing the rifles. When they reached the group, they circled it and aimed the rifles at the children, and Big Frank placed the nose of Miguel's pistol against Mama Abuela's temple.

Alvin lay frozen on the peak of the roof. He could easily pick off the black man but did not want to be responsible for the bloodbath it would bring about.

"Hear me," the black shouted, "des 'ere am de chillen ob you household women in dar. You best talk Miss Luella inta doin' wat ah wants or dey 'n' Mama Abuela am dead."

A horrible wail erupted from the kitchen where the ten women sat huddled together on the floor.

Luella flung herself from her room and stood teetering on Miguel's threshold.

"What am I to do?" she wailed.

Miguel eyed her with total contempt. "I am not about to place myself back in that madman's hands, if that's what you mean."

She spun away, confused and bewildered. Teresa caught her when she almost fell.

"Amos would never let that happen to children," she muttered.

Teresa's mind was also almost numb with the shock of what might happen. But there had to be some sanity in this nightmare, she reasoned.

"Would they settle for just their freedom?" she asked.

Luella blinked at her as though it were a lunatic suggestion.

"Good God!" Teresa snapped. "You've got to at least try it! Come on, I'll go with you!"

As they stepped past the battered door, Teresa realized she still held a pistol in her hands and had to quickly hide her hand in the folds of her skirt.

Funereal silence surrounded them as they came to the edge of the porch.

Her throat clenched with emotion, Luella croaked out: "You are free to go!"

"We're free," a voice sang out of the crowd. An audible murmur spread throughout the slaves, regardless of whether they had supported the rebels or not.

Big Frank threw up both hands with a gesture of rage. He knew what the wily woman was up to.

"Don' listen ta her!" he growled. "Ah don' see no paper sayin' dat—'n' she ain' de Spanish man."

Teresa had not been paying that much attention to him. She had been around soldiers enough in Mexico and Texas to note that there was something peculiar about the eight blacks and the way they held the rifles. They were not tense, like men ready to shoot, and not a one of them held their finger in the trigger ring. But when she saw that not a single rifle was cocked for firing, she decided to take a desperate gamble. She held Luella back from answering.

Teresa faced him a moment, and the two looked at each other tense, erect, unyielding.

"How would she have had time to write such a document," she said in a quiet voice, "when it cannot be a single paper for all of you."

"She's right," Amos said. "Each of us—man, woman, and child—must have a paper of our own."

"Aw right!" Big Frank scowled. "But what about yah husband, lady?"

Teresa blinked. The man was taking her to be Miguel's wife. "My husband is no longer here."

"Ah don' understand," he snapped, his ears not accustomed to the Spanish accent of her voice.

"It's simple," Mama Abuela said, stepping away and eyeing him contemptuously. "It mean dat he dead."

He accepted the lie from the woman who had seen him

born and doctored him. But in the time he had been watching Mama Abuela, it gave Teresa the courage to raise the pistol and aim it directly at the big man's chest.

"Tell your men to lay down their arms," she commanded, "or I will fire."

"Na, such," he bellowed, putting the gun back against Mama Abuela's head. "Dey gonna pop off soon as you do."

Teresa eyed him coldly. "I don't think so. Their rifles are not cocked, and you'd be dead before they could cock and fire them."

"Den ah shoot dis ole hag," he screamed at her, knowing that his options were being quickly narrowed.

Unafraid, the woman turned until she was looking down the dark hole of the barrel. "Do dat, if'm it'll sab my chillen."

With a horrible scream he whipped the pistol toward Teresa as Amos leaped forward to restrain him.

Two shots rang out. Big Frank looked stunned that none of them had come from his pistol. His wide eyes flared. He dropped the pistol to claw at his inflamed chest before falling lifeless at Teresa's feet. Amazingly Amos was still standing, a bloodless hole in his forehead, his eyes raised to where Alvin stood poised, ready to fire again. Then he crumpled like a deflated balloon. Teresa began to shake, then let her smoking pistol clatter to the driveway.

One by one the others let the useless rifles slip from their hands, melting into the coming dawn shadows.

With a borrowed wagon Alvin Finnell rode away with his comrades, stupefied by how he was going to explain their deaths to his father.

CHAPTER NINE

During the next few days the rubble was removed, new windowpanes inserted, the door rehung, bullet holes filled with doling and painted over, until outwardly Beauwood looked peaceful and tranquil.

The blacks buried their dead, thirty-eight in all, and waited. Teresa silently saw to the needs of the rapidly healing Miguel, and waited. Emilia stayed mainly to herself, and waited.

Luella sat alone, lonely. Her meals cooled without being touched. She felt she had nothing left to wait for or think about. She had grieved over Amos's pine coffin even more than Henry. Almost gladly she named Todd Barrow to replace Ian Danton as the head overseer and gave him free rein.

With almost sadistic pleasure he shipped the eight rifle-bearing blacks to the Finnell plantation as indemnity for the lives they had lost. The blacks stoically accepted their fate, knowing that one way or another the Finnells would not let them live out the month. And then Barrow began to systematically weed out the other troublemakers and sell them off.

It was the black women who suffered the most. Still linked to their African traditions, they were looked upon by their men as little more than bearers of children and beasts of burden. They had not been consulted when the riot was planned but paid the heaviest price when their families were split asunder. And what confounded Todd Barrow the most, as he skillfully pieced together the true essence of the plot, was that the husbands of the household servants were among the main instigators with Amos and

Big Frank. How, he wondered, could they have been so savage as to let the black leader use their children in his final revolt. He didn't understand them as a people and never would. They were, to his way of thinking, little more than animals and had to be treated as such. Without Yves there to stop him, he began to drastically alter the Beauwood mode of living.

Teresa lay tensely in her bed night after night, unable to sleep but in snatches for the feverish throbbing of her thoughts. She felt so remorsefully guilty for having taken a life, regardless of the circumstances. But the voice that haunted her the most was that of Luella's after the woman had come out of the shock of seeing Amos fall. She had actually turned on Teresa like a tigress protecting her cubs, pounding with her fists and cursing and accusing Teresa of being the cause of his death. The woman had become momentarily deranged, and it had frightened Teresa more than facing up to the black man.

Nor did Luella's attitude alter greatly with the passage of time. Whenever Teresa would enter a room, Luella would flounce out, growling vile curses. Teresa would try to avoid her but was unable to avoid the things the nearly demented woman began to subject her to. One afternoon, after returning from changing Miguel's dressings, she found the dress she had worn for the cotillion shredded in the middle of her bedroom floor. She refrained from discussing the matter with Emilia and Miguel until the next day, when she found a strangled cat on her pillows. When she told Miguel, he laughed.

"What can you expect? You caused her lover to be taken from her."

"Oh, really. Wherever did you get such a notion?"

"From Amy."

"Amy?"

"The girl who brings my meals. She's a wealth of information. This Amos, it seems, had been Luella's secret lover since he was a boy."

"How disgusting, and I don't believe it. Nor do I believe

that I caused his death. I have trouble enough living with
the one that I did cause."

"That was foolish of you, of course, but I wouldn't let it
worry you."

Foolish, she thought. She had saved his life, and he now
thought it was foolish of her. She did not trouble him with
any more of the odd little things that happened after that,
and they happened almost daily. Little things, annoying
things, that did no harm to her personally but grated on
her nerves until they were ragged and raw and she was
near exhaustion. Finally her body could stand it no longer,
and a healing portion of her mind took command, shutting
off her thinking processes and memory; the muscles were
told to automatically relax, the limbs to unwind, and she
slept. She slept throughout the night and the next day and
again into night.

"She's totally exhausted from caring for the rest of us,"
Emilia told Miguel, forced to speak to him for the first
time in a week. "It's time that we cared for her for a
while."

"Yes, it certainly is," he said, looking at Teresa's peaceful, beautiful face. "I napped this afternoon, so I'll look in
on her later."

"Miguel . . ." Emilia said and then paused.

"I know," he said as though she were the one who had
the confessing to do. "We are going to have to talk, sooner
or later. But not now, Em. Not in this horrible place that
seems to bring out the worst in all of us. Please."

She nodded and went back to her room, thinking that he
was at least facing up to what was the worst in him. It was a
beginning; she wouldn't push him farther.

In the wee hours before dawn Teresa began to dream.
She could hear the squeak of wagon wheels on the hard
gravel and Felix's voice as he spoke to Yves. But still she
could not make her senses awaken enough to rise and prepare to greet him. Then she felt his presence in the room,
could almost see him undressing and preparing for bed.
She felt the weight of his body tilt the mattress as he sat on
the edge and then spring back as he crawled beneath the

sheets and molded against her full length. Instinctively she
sensed by his touch that he had come to bed stark naked,
and this amazed her because of his sensitive shyness to sex.
But another portion of her brain laughed and told her that
this was only a dream and Felix was only doing as her
secret self wished him to do.

That's why she was more amused than alarmed when the
dream fantasy continued, and he began to cup and mold
her breasts with his hands, smoothe his hand down over
her torso and belly, and begin to pull her nightgown up to
expose her thighs.

She moaned and rolled to greet him. His hands became
rough and demanding, pulling her forcefully into a locking.
Once entered, he began to drive his hips with hammerlike
thrusts.

Teresa came instantly awake in wide-eyed alarm. Frantically she began to push away the male form which had
been so familiar in her dream world but was utterly foreign
to her in the world of reality. For a second she was unsure
if it were reality or a dreamlike drop into nightmare. But
when her blurry eyes were able to focus on the leering face
opposite her, it became both reality and nightmare.

"Relax, baby," Miguel chuckled, "you seem to need it
as much as I do."

They lay silent for a moment, still entwined. Her mind
swirled with the word pictures she had heard of his last
two encounters, and her stomach churned with nausea.

Before he could react, she quickly rolled away and
jumped off the bed. There was nowhere to run, no one to
run to, so she cowered behind the nearest chair, quaking.

It amused rather than angered Miguel. Languidly he
rose and came to pose before her. He was almost of equal
height to his brother, narrower of shoulder and far greater
in waist. But in Miguel Escovarro's mind there was only
one measurement that was of importance.

"Yes," he sneered, "I am much more of a man than he,
right? Oh, don't blush, my dear, I know. As youths, on a
lonely *ranchero*, Felix and I had no one else but each other
to experiment on. But he became most pious to such youthful daredevilry upon his return from Spain, no doubt due

to the strict education he'd received there, and poor Miguel was left to his own adventures. Do I shock you? Perhaps that is my intent. Well at least you have now seen me and felt me. There will come a time—and who knows where or when—when you will want me again. I'm quite willing to wait."

With maddening slowness he draped his dressing robe about himself and arrogantly strutted from the room.

Teresa stood, her throat and chest burning with the screams she had been forcing back from eruption, and her mind wildly insisting: never, never, never, never . . . never . . .

Felix's and Yves's scheduled ten-day return was delayed by a week and then another. It was time enough for Todd Barrow to transform Beauwood into a wall-less prison, based on a system of whippings, informers, and favoritism. All but those children up to age six were taken from Mama Abuela and trained as hoers in the fields. Her pleas on their behalf fell upon deaf ears.

But the oddest transformation on the plantation came about the day before Yves's return. It was probably the cruelest aftermath of the riot.

The furious bellow brought Teresa and Emilia flying from their rooms.

"Jesus Christ!" Miguel stormed, standing fully dressed in his doorway. "Where in the hell is that slut of a girl with my breakfast. I was supposed to ride over to the Donnelly plantation with Barrow this morning, and I think I just heard the wagon depart."

Just then a teary-eyed Amy came shuffling down the hall.

"About time," Miguel barked, snatching the tray from her hand and wheeling into his room.

The girl's face pouted, and a river of tears rolled down her brown cheeks.

"Now, now," Teresa soothed, taking Amy's hands. "Whatever is the matter?"

"Eberthing," she wailed.

Teresa looked at Emilia and sighed. "It's going to be

another one of those days. I wonder what tirade the old harridan is up to now."

"Probably a carry-over from last night's dinner. I thought she was going to kill poor Henry when he filled her wineglass too full."

At the mention of the butler's name the girl wailed louder.

"Das it," she moaned. "Nobody know wat ta do. Eberthing a mess. De oberseer don' put Missah Henry on de wagon fur de Donnelly place."

Teresa and Emilia stared at each other speechless, then Teresa turned and stormed down to the dining room.

Luella was so absorbed in her thoughts that she started when Teresa repeated impatiently: "Luella, I have been talking to you, and you have been staring at me as if I were not here."

"That's as I wish," she said coldly.

Teresa came directly to the table, rigid and straight, her face a mask of glacial calm.

"I wish to know one simple thing. Is it too late for my husband and I to buy Henry instead of the Donnellys?"

She was surprised and incredulous. She regarded Teresa intently, but her moments of lucidity were fewer and fewer of late.

She shrugged. "Teresa, I always thought you would come to your senses and see the wisdom of slavery. Why is it that you wish to purchase Henry?"

"To give him manumission." Immediately she knew the mistake of her words.

Luella's smile was very unpleasant, its amusement malicious.

"Then I could never agree to it," she said, deliberately lowering her voice to a murmur so that it was almost inaudible. "The man must pay for his sins."

Teresa flushed. "Please!"

"Please? You begin to beg exactly like Henry," she pointed out in a hard thin voice. "Please, Miss Luella, save my boy Amos. Please, Miss Luella, don't let the overseer be so cruel to the people. Please, Miss Luella, don't sell Henry away, I'll find you another young buck to replace

Amos. Please! Please! Please! I'm sick to death of nigger begging."

Luella paused. Their eyes clashed. Luella retained her smile, a little disdainful, and very removed and untouched. Teresa started to speak but thought better of it.

"Nothing further to plead," Luella urged nastily. "That's just as well for I have little more time for you. I must begin an immediate search for a new butler. Actually the prospect is a little thrilling. As the examination must be most complete, I'll kindly ask you to confine yourself to the second floor. I would hate to have your prudish, sensitive mind offended. And until I have obtained the services of a new butler, we shall all take our meals in our rooms. You are now excused."

Teresa moved mechanically across the floor to the doorway. There, she paused, looked back at the fat woman with pity. Then she closed the door firmly behind her.

Luella rose, laughed softly to herself, gave herself a brief inspection in the mirror over the mantel, and, humming under her breath, turned with a smile to the closed door.

"Come in, come in," she said gently. "No reason to be afraid. Don't slouch! Walk tall and with dignity; you are quite manly for just sixteen. Now let me hear you speak."

The room was vacant except for Luella and the image she had conjured up. She was once again in the past. Yves was off on a trip, and she would soon have Amos all to herself.

It was to be their last meal at Beauwood and Yves wanted it to be perfect for his guests. Out of respect for the man the women dressed elegantly but simply.

Back less than twenty-four hours he had infused some of the old serene and graceful charm to the plantation. His delay in returning had been due to the careful selection of the six new overseers. Burly Irishmen, the sod smell of Cork still clinging to their clothing, they were each a man with a large and growing family who could be stern and honest and yet humanely sympathetic. Beauwood could never go back to what it was before the riot, but it would be just.

And the riot, of course, was all Yves seemed to want to discuss as they took their cocktails from Amy's tray in the salon before dinner, even though he had already received varying versions from Alvin Finnell, Todd Barrow, and Mama Abuela.

Yves was sensitive enough to avoid bringing up Miguel's involvement in the cause or aftermath. Without making them relive the nightmare in their minds, he dug only for basic facts that would help him avoid such a bloodbath ever again.

Miguel had little to offer and moodily sat drinking julep after julep. Emilia ignored him and answered very few questions. It was mainly left to Teresa to fill in the pieces. She was slightly embarrassed and greatly downplayed the role she had taken. Felix sat stonily silent, his heart an admixture of dread and loving pride.

"Well," Yves said, "that is that. We shall close off the topic for good."

"Except . . ." Teresa started, then stopped.

"Yes?"

"It's hard for me to believe, sometimes, that I am alive; why his gun never fired." She shuddered.

"Poor Big Frank," Yves laughed, and they all stared at him. "He must never have checked the pistol after he stole it. Felix took the bullets out of it before we sent Miguel home from Natchez-Under-the-Hill."

Teresa put out a slim hand and caught her husband's. Her eyes swam with thankfulness and love.

"One last word," Yves said with deep warmth and respect. "Doña Teresa, my undying gratitude for saving my home and livelihood. It is all yours for the asking."

Teresa laughed. "Then it would have been no good for me to save it for you, if you offer it up so quickly."

"But surely there is something I can do for you."

"It is quite unnecessary," she said. "However—" She stopped abruptly, her cheeks a bright scarlet.

"However what?" Yves demanded. "Name it and it's yours."

"Henry and Mama Abuela," she whispered. "You could give them manumission."

Yves's face was suddenly black as a thundercloud.

"I think it is time we adjourned to the dining room. We shall discuss the matter later."

"That was quite a request," Felix whispered as they crossed the foyer.

"I don't think so," she said quietly. "I don't think I would have had the courage to face the man without Mama Abuela being there."

It was obvious at once that the table had been laid for only the five of them. The thundercloud was now gone, and a sad smile crossed Yves's face.

"My wife sends down her regrets," he said flatly. "She is not well this evening."

They all took their seats without comment. They were all aware that Luella Beauveau had not even recognized her husband upon his return. She had closed herself up in her bedroom, content to live forever with her fantasy.

"Henry!" Yves roared.

The old man came scurrying fearfully out of the kitchen.

"Oh Henry!" Teresa cried, her eyes welling with joy at seeing him again.

"Do you ever want to leave Beauwood again?" Yves demanded.

"Na, sah, Massa Yves," Henry quavered.

"And never shall you," he said. "You're the only one who keeps this place running properly. Now off with you and bring our dinner."

Henry's brimming face, as he fled back into the kitchen, was a study in joy.

Yves rocked back in his chair, his big face flushed with contentment.

"I'm sorry to disappoint you, Doña Teresa, but I had him back here a half hour after my return. Although Marion Donnelly is livid with rage and threatening to sue."

Teresa looked at Yves, thinking: he wins them over—all his people, no matter how lowly. Even when they don't like being a slave, like Mama Abuela, they remain loyal to him personally.

The dinner conversation centered around the arrival of their equipment that afternoon and their departure the next morning. Even Miguel became animated and excited over the prospect of going home.

Before dessert and coffee were served, Yves excused himself to go look in on his wife. When he returned, he placed a folded piece of paper in front of Teresa.

"Were I to grant manumission to one," he said gently, "many others would start expecting it and demanding it. It could be the fuse to set off another riot, so I will not chance it. That, however, is a bill of sale. Mama Abuela is now the sole property of Doña Teresa de Alarcon Escovarro."

She bowed her head over the empty coffee cup, her eyes blinded with sudden tears. Her heart filled with emotion.

"One more thing," she whispered.

Yves roared with laughter. "Isn't that just like a woman. Name it!"

"Will you teach me to write a manumission paper?"

"Without hesitation! Come, we'll do it now. Felix, we'll need your signature as a witness."

Emilia and Miguel sat for a moment alone. They were each uncomfortable with their own thoughts, and each other.

"I'll be glad to get home," Emilia whispered, breaking the ice.

"The ranch can be a very lonely, dull place," he growled.

"I won't have time to think about it. I'll be too busy having this baby. And then I want another one right after that."

"Maybe we'd better work on it," he grinned, "starting right now!"

Emilia shook her head.

"Not in this place," she said gently.

Miguel stiffened.

"Don't be angry. At home it will be different. Soon you'll have a son to love. And Miguel, I don't want you to ever look at him and think—" She stopped, glancing warily at her husband.

"Go on," Miguel said ominously.

Emilia's head came up. There was a flare about her fine nostrils, the face was proud and haughty as ever it was.

"That his mother was a whore!" she said firmly.

Miguel got up slowly. From where Emilia sat, he seemed to tower into the candlelight umbra. She could not see the fury in his face.

Emilia looked up at him, her face taut and still.

"Where are you going?" she whispered.

"Out!" Miguel said curtly and marched from the room.

Hearing the crash of the outer door as Miguel slammed it, Emilia thought: damn, you're a fool! You had to go and remind him. You had to harp on the subject—and deny him when he started to get into a good humor. You surely spoiled the moment. Now he'll ride down to those saloons and come back drunk and ugly. Or he may even . . .

She stopped, jealous of the thought. For, even as she shaped it, she knew it was precisely what Miguel would do. He would go to the first whore he could find.

And then, on a long sigh, she thought: I'm getting paid back by all the women who damned me for sleeping with their husbands. They must be smiling tonight.

When Teresa reached Mama Abuela's cabin, the door was ajar. Inside, by the light of a cone candle, she could see the tall woman, her back to Teresa, busily putting away her supper dishes.

She stepped inside the door and watched her. She turned, holding up the candle to see who had come to visit her. Her grin widened until her cheeks were dominated by it.

"Child," she beamed, "come in." It was automatic for her to speak only Spanish with Teresa now. "I thought not to see you till morning, then it would have been too quick a good-bye. You pleasure me."

Teresa laughed. "I hope to pleasure you even more. Because I know that you read Spanish, and not English, I wrote this so you could read it."

She took the offered paper and held it to the candle. She read it through twice before speaking.

"Dear child," she whispered. "I love you for thinking of this old woman, but it changes little."

"It sets you free!"

"Freedom doesn't make any difference. I still couldn't go home to Cuba."

"Why in thunderation couldn't you. The law says—"

"The law," Mama Abuela said slowly, patiently, as though she were talking to one of the children, "hasn't anything to do with it. My folk are no longer on the island. I'd be a free black in a sea of slavery. It'd get mighty lonesome, I think. I can stay right here and do the same but will at least know the people around me."

"But you can go wherever you want. Up North you'd be with free blacks."

"A few years ago that would have been fine, when I was young and could have got myself another man."

"I'm sorry," Teresa muttered. "Perhaps I've done the wrong thing."

"Wrong thing!" she exploded. "You did it because you've got a good and loving heart. You just don't know how that makes me feel . . . I guess you don't know how it is to be sick inside, miserable from being a piece of human flesh that can be sold and resold, from wanting to be free. I'll cherish this piece of paper for all of my days."

"That's all you may be able to do with it," she said sadly. "You'll never be able to let anyone know, or it could cause trouble. Others will demand it if they know you have it. They could even resent you for having it and staying."

She studied the thought in her mind for a long time, then grinned.

"Child," she chuckled, "you got yourself a problem, not Mama Abuela. That paper says I have the right to refuse manumission if I want; but only a damn fool would do that. Still I think you just found someone who's going to be a mammy to your children when you start having them."

The thought had never occurred to Teresa, but it was a glorious one. She grabbed Mama Abuela in her arms, hugging her, and crying: "Oh, yes! Oh, yes!"

CHAPTER TEN

Felix had been highly hesitant about taking the woman to Texas—free or not. But halfway down the Mississippi—and again in Corpus Christi—he was grateful for her doctoring ability. Although a smooth passage, Emilia did not take it well. She suffered violently from massive leg and stomach cramps of such fierce and prolonged pain that she nearly ground the crowns right off her back teeth. Only Mama Abuela was able to knead them away and soothe her.

"Ain't the child causing them," she warned Emilia, tapping her on the heart and head, "but what is troubling you here and here. If the trouble don't stop, you'll never see this child alive."

"He doesn't help my problem none," Emilia hissed, her muscles going taut.

Mama Abuela knew that sympathy was sometimes the wrong type of medicine, although she sympathized with Emilia. She had seen the anguish on her proud face as Felix and a barman had had to drag the drunken Miguel on board ship at Natchez-Under-The-Hill so that they could depart. And from some mysterious source of supply, which none of them could detect, he was able to remain drunk for most of the voyage.

"You take it from this old woman," she scolded, "once the seed becomes a child, a woman has one and only one obligation. You make sure that child is going to be healthy, whole-limbed, and alive. And from the looks of you, not quite three months along, he's going to be as big as his father and uncle at birth."

It brought a smile and light laugh to Emilia's mouth.

171

"You're right," she chuckled. "Nothing seems to fit me any more but my nightgowns."

"Then it's time for old Mama Abuela to get out her sewing kit and let out a few waistlines."

Emilia studied the woman intently and curiously. There was nothing in her face to suggest age. Nor was it the youthful beauty that it once must have been. It was more a serene, mature handsomeness.

"Why do you always make yourself out to be so old?"

"Because, child, when I arrived at Beauwood, without my family, I felt to be a thousand. I knew that was the place where I was only going to get older and die. If you think old, you get old. If you think young, only the wrinkles and gray hair give you away."

This time Emilia laughed genuinely and happily. "I somehow get the impression that you are starting to think young again."

She winked slyly. "I'm starting to give it a try."

Emilia frowned. "Then we have a problem."

"What's that?" she asked seriously.

"This 'Mama Grandmother' title. You are now going to be back among only Spanish-speaking people, and it will become 'Mamacita Abuela.' It's confusing. What was your name in Cuba?"

The woman had been sitting pulling threading out of a pleated waistband and now studied her silent fingers as though they would revive her memory. "It was a name I once loved," she said quietly, her fingers starting to work again. "I was born into the de Lama household, though I was never allowed to use that name. But the master gave me the Christian name of Maritza. I have not uttered it in nearly a decade."

"Oh," Emilia exclaimed, "I think it is beautiful. Maritza de Lama. You were Mama Abuela in Mississippi, but in Texas you are to be Maritza de Lama. Understand?"

"Another manumission," she chuckled. And Maritza it was for the rest of her life, until finally she herself forgot that her name for many years was Mama Abuela.

* * *

The bay and seaport of Corpus Christi for the majority of its life had been a sleepy Spanish settlement of adobe huts with tin roofs and an out-of-the-way harbor at times for pirates willing to sell their booty. The battle of San Jacinto altered that. For the affluent emigrants it was the fastest way to reach Texas from New Orleans, Mobile, and Gulfport.

Felix, who had come into the port on his return from Spain, eager to return once more to the freer atmosphere of America, after his further education and "broadening" travels, stood at the rail in openmouthed disbelief. The harbor was dotted by anchored clipper ships and paddle-wheelers awaiting a berth at the wharf. From the shoreline came the constant tattoo of hammers erecting new buildings and sledge hammers pounding down pilings to support new wharfs.

"A madhouse, eh?" the first mate said at Felix's elbow.

"Not as I remember it as a youth. The only excitement they saw then was when a pirate ship hoved to."

The man laughed, "The pirates are still here, señor, but now they fly a different flag. It's called the Lone Star. Don't worry about our docking or unloading. We are a scheduled line and have priority at the wharf. The new buccaneers, as we call those ships that bring the Georgia and Alabama farmers here at a hell of a price, have to stand to and await their turn."

Still it seemed to take forever to dock, unload—and then to face an unexpected delay. In spite of its youth the Republic of Texas had already spawned a formidable bureaucracy.

The scrawny man, perched atop a high stoool, behind a slant-top desk, eyed their approach with malicious contempt.

"No Mexicans allowed," he barked before Felix could open his mouth.

Felix wisely answered in English and quite evenly. "We are residents, sir. Have been since the 1500s."

The man scoffed. "You hardly look that old."

Felix hardly saw the humor. "I was speaking of my ancestry. Here are our papers and the manumission papers on this woman."

Without even looking at them, the man flatly stated, "No good, no more. Many fled and are now trying to get back on these old Mex papers."

"Listen here," Miguel stormed forward, drunkenly, "papers be damned. We fought that goddamn stinking war for independence and where were you?"

The man nearly jumped from his perch and fled.

"Hush," Felix snarled. "The man is only a new kind of soldier following orders. Sir, can you tell me if Señor Manuel Cruz is still the mayor of this city?"

"He is," the man said, keeping a watchful eye on Miguel.

"Then that settles it. He can vouch for us, for he has been a friend of the family for years."

The man shrugged, as though it would carry little weight with him. "He'll be sent for, and in the meantime let me see your bills of lading."

Felix produced the documents and the beady-eyed man scanned them as though he had been remiss in not requesting them first, keeping a scrawled account sheet busy as he went down the columns.

"Very handsome," he wheezed. "As we have yet to print our own currency, you will be given an opportunity to pay this import tax in either Mexican or American—providing you are who you say you are.

"Import tax," Felix bellowed. "That equipment is nothing more than replacement for what Santa Anna destroyed marching through our ranch and farms. How much is it?"

The man thrust his work sheet forward. Felix eyed the page and blanched at the total. He went livid with rage.

"Impossible!" he snorted. "That is more than I paid for the goods new!"

"Yep!" the man said simply. "But you'll be makin' two to three hundred times that amount on them when you set up your business."

Felix was angry. With a muffled "damn!" he threw down the ledger, his face heavy with frowning.

"I am opening no business," he said fiercely. "I have ten

thousand acres of ranchland and two thousand acres of farmland that this equipment and supplies are to be used upon. Can you understand that?"

"Nope," the man said without blinking an eyelash. "Ain't ever been able to farm more'n ten acres myself. Any man who makes a claim like you just did is nothing more than a damn liar."

With a low-throated growl Miguel went directly for the man's throat. Only Emilia's swoon, in the humid tin thatched shed and Felix's restraining arm kept the man from instant death.

Felix's luck that day was miserable. Ten minutes after the arrival of Señor Cruz, they were allowed to leave the customs shed, but their cargo was impounded until Felix could take up the tax matter with a higher authority. In the overcrowded town they were only able to find accommodations in the poorest section of town. The rooms were filthy and within an hour after having been put to bed, Emilia's legs were a mass of red welts from bedbug bites. When Felix returned to Señor Cruz's carriage. Miguel had vanished. He kept his anger from the thin, little old man.

"It was kind of you to wait, señor."

The man shrugged his bony shoulders. "It has given me something to do, Don Felix. The Anglos have taken over everything, and I am mayor in name only."

Don Manuel Cruz was tired. He had been tired before, but never like this. His world was dying before his eyes, and he was unwilling to rise and fight against it. History was largely a long series of *faits accomplis*.

His name and presence did, however, get Felix an immediate hearing with the port officer. It took the man, with great concentration, less than an hour to rough out new tax figures. They still seemed excessive to Felix, but he told the man he would pay them the next day after he had purchased wagons for their cartage.

"Look at these people, Don Manuel," he said when they were back at the carriage. "How are they able to pay such stiff taxes?"

The frail old man chuckled. "Who says they are being taxed? They are welcome because they are coming to populate Sam Houston's new kingdom. We are no longer wanted. If they cannot drive us out, then they will find ways to squeeze our pocketbooks until we give up."

"I am already beginning to feel the squeeze. That tax and the cost of two wagons and horses will fairly well wipe out my ready cash."

Miguel came down the street toward them, pushing roughly through the crowds and paying no attention to the angry scowls he was receiving in return. His face was flushed, but not from drink. His experiences in the past hour had turned him cold sober.

"Where have you been?" Felix said stiffly.

"Trying to save us some time," he said darkly, flinging himself up into the carriage. "I was not about to spend a single night in that flea trap."

"Hardly any different than the whorehouse I hauled you out of a few nights back," Felix said scornfully in English so that Don Manuel would not understand.

The old man hid a smile behind a parchment-thin hand. He had been forced to learn some of the language since the coming of the Anglos.

"That's beside the point now," Miguel said with a show of calm, but Felix could see his chest expanding with contempt. "I've been to three liveries and the wagon-master's shed. There are no wagons to be had, of any size or description, and they're asking five times the proper price for broken-down nags."

"What of Señor Torres?"

"I went there first, remembering the wagons he built for Father when we came here to pick you up from Spain. He's no longer there. It's now run by a nasty-mouthed Kaintuck who only laughed. He's got people who have been waiting four weeks for wagons, and I won't even scare you with the price the bastards are getting for them."

Felix slumped back in despair. "It's a hundred and forty miles to San Antonio. That seems the only answer."

"It's the same distance to the ranch," Miguel pointed out. "There we know we have horses and wagons."

"I was thinking of the women," Felix said wearily. "We can get them there on a stage. One of us, of course, would have to stay here and guard the equipment. Besides, with what they are demanding for taxes, I may have to hit Aunt Patricia up for another loan."

"They didn't come down in their figure?"

"Damn little," Felix said. "Well, just sitting here isn't helping. Don Manuel, is there a stage today for San Antonio?"

"A moment!" he gasped, his thin face lighting up on a thought. "Just the day before yesterday Don Carlos Castro was in town to put his wife and family on board a ship for Tampico. He is selling off his land and equipment and moving south. I have a riding horse at my house you may borrow. It is the least I can do for not being able to offer you hospitality in my small home. I will give you a letter of introduction to Don Carlos."

By unspoken agreement Miguel took the horse and followed the old man's directions to get to the Castro ranch. It was not as large and grand as the Escovarro lands, but the buildings were neat and the yard clean. Next to the barn sat two buckboards and a carriage. The corral housed a couple dozen horses. Miguel's spirits began to rise.

As he rode into the ranch from one direction, a shaggy, dusty horse bearing a lean, ragged rider rode into the barnyard and halted. Two men came out of the barn and greeted the rider. One pointed toward the house, and the rider slid from the saddle and headed toward the porch. Then they saw Miguel's approach and headed for the house themselves. That they were Anglos, there was no mistaking. Pretty rummy outfit Don Carlos has working for him, Miguel thought.

By the time he had reached the porch, the trio had been joined by another Anglo and a Mexican.

"*Buenos días*, señor," ceremoniously said the Mexican.

Miguel looked down, and the men looked up. There was something uncomfortable about the way they stood, as though expecting trouble.

Miguel answered the greeting in Spanish, and, waving his hand at the Anglos, added in English, "And good day to you. I am looking for Don Carlos Castro."

The Mexican's graceful bow indicated that he was such, otherwise Miguel would never have recognized the former elegant vaquero in his rough peon dress.

"Señor, I have a letter of introduction from the mayor of Corpus Christi."

A big-boned man with a bullethead and a blistered red face of evil coarseness stepped off the porch and extended his hand.

"Ah'll take it for him."

Miguel handed it over and said: "Don Manuel informed me that you are selling out. My brother and I have great need to purchase two wagons and four horses."

Don Carlos started to open his mouth, but the bullet-headed man silenced him with a single look.

"Ain't nothin' ta sell," he drawled. "Me and *my* brothers jest bought the whole she-bang—lock, stock, and barrel."

Don Carlos shrugged as though the matter was now out of his hands.

"Then, perhaps, you'd consider a sale."

The man laughed sarcastically. "Y'all ain't too smart, mistah. Ah got this land to get rid of a Mex. Why'd ah let two more come in wid wagons ah sold 'em?"

Miguel gritted his teeth to keep from losing his temper. "We already have land," he said evenly. "Don Carlos can inform you of that from the letter."

The Mexican nodded that it was so.

"Don' make a damn bit of difference," the man insisted. "Ah ain't sellin'."

"I'm sorry, Don Miguel," the Mexican said ruefully. "Had you come but an hour earlier, things might have been different. Give my regards to Don Manuel."

Miguel was so bitterly disappointed that he flung the horse's head about and spurred the mare into a full gallop. Two miles down the road he veered the horse off the track and toward the mud huts of the village of San Leon.

By midnight Miguel Escovarro was drunk—meanly, savagely drunk. He was very quiet about it, so that even the cantina owner who repeatedly filled his glass was unaware of his condition. Tequila, which normally put him in a jovial mood, tonight curdled in him sourly. He felt thwarted, frustrated, mocked. The desire inside him now was elemental and brutal, mingled with anger. He cursed Don Carlos for selling to the Anglos. He cursed the Anglos for robbing them on the tax charges.

"Gringo *putas!*" he growled.

"You echo all our thinking, señor," the barkeep said, pouring him another drink.

"Any wagons for sale in this village?"

The fat Mexican laughed as though it were a good joke. "We are a poor village, señor. The most you might find is a donkey cart or two. Horses, yes, for the men of the village are riders for Don Carlos Castro."

"Fuck him!" Miguel said savagely. "He sold out to the gringos."

"*Caramba!*" the man gasped, his brown face going ashen. "That is the end of this village. Our people will not work for the gringos."

"Will they," Miguel said with drunken craftiness, "work against them—for a price?"

"A man will do what he must do," he answered with a sly smile, "to survive."

He squared himself suddenly, tossed a five-dollar gold piece on the bar, and held the man in a steely glare.

"That should be more than enough to hold four strong men in drink until I return. I want men who can wake up the next morning and not remember what they did the night before."

The Castro ranch was dark and appeared almost deserted. Miguel slid from the horse and tied it in the deep shadows of a grove of trees. There was only a slight sway in his walk as he skirted the house to come up on the side of the barn where the wagons stood. He stumbled, then straightened up, swearing. But drunk as he was, he traveled straight as an arrow to the barn door and the horse harnesses he'd need.

Miguel opened the right-hand barn door a few feet and froze. The haggard-looking Anglo was standing there waiting for him. He gave Miguel one long, malignant stare; then threw back his head, swept a six-shooter from its holster, and his evil smile showed gleaming teeth.

"We all thought you'd be tryin'—" he began.

With a magnificent bound Miguel was upon him. The Anglo's cry was throttled in his throat. A fierce wrestling ensued, then heavy, sodden blows, and the Anglo was beaten to the ground. Miguel squeezed the gun from the man's hand and smashed it into the side of his head. The man gasped and went limp.

A shadow crossing the path of his vision made Miguel crouch and palm the butt of the gun. It took his vision a moment to fully determine what it was he was being cautious of. Don Carlos was swaying from the end of a rope in the center of the barn, his eyes bulged and his tongue lallygagging from the corner of his mouth. His drunken mind cleared to the horrible truth of the matter, and he swore at himself for being a fool and not recognizing the truth that afternoon.

Running feet echoed across the yard. He spun for the open door, crouched with both hands holding the gun steady, then yelled at the murderers. He had been quicker than a panther, and now his voice was so terrible that it curdled their blood, and the menace of deadly violence in his crouching position made them stop in their tracks.

"There are lawmen all around you," he screamed, "so drop whatever guns you have."

Two of the three started to unbuckle their holster belts, but the bullet-headed man was not that easily intimidated. His piercing yell that they show themselves was stilled by the roar of rage from Miguel and the sharp report of his pistol. The velocity of the bullet smacking into his chest lifted him from the ground and threw him backward.

With belts half off the other two wavered and then threw their arms into the air. Miguel eyed them, the blood in his veins cold. The silence of the man crouching like a tiger about to leap was more menacing than his former roar of rage.

"Get over here," whispered Miguel breathlessly. He became conscious that he was weak and shaken. In the war he had shot soldiers, but they had been Mexican. He had just shot one Anglo, and possibly killed another, and there was no guilt as he had felt on the battlefields. Nor did he feel that he was avenging the death of Don Carlos. The man could have given Miguel far clearer clues as to the danger he faced. He felt no remorse for the foolish man, even though he had come to steal from him.

"Don't make a wrong move," he said, firmness coming back into his voice. "I want those two wagons hitched together and four horses harnessed and put on the lead wagon."

"Shit, Elmo," one of them barked, "ain't nobody 'ere but 'imself."

"Exactly," Miguel snarled, "and it started out as four to one. Do you want to change the odds?"

They did as they were told silently, although reluctantly. The one named Elmo became curious about his fate. He kept looking back at the house as though it held the answer for him.

"Hey, Mex," he called as the last horse was backed into place. "Of the money laying on the old man's table five thou of it is our'n and not his'n. Jest let us ride away with that and no questions asked."

Until that moment Miguel had been unsure of the final outcome himself. There was, his father had often said, a black devil inside Miguel Escovarro. It reared up now, brazen and angry. The gun roared twice, and the odds were now totally in his favor.

With uncommon calm he walked to the ranch house and belted less than the amount of money the robbers had claimed as their own. And just as calmly drove the wagons to where he had tethered the horse and then back to San Leon.

The cantina owner, upon seeing the pile of gold coins Miguel casually poured out upon his bar, immediately included himself as one of the men Miguel needed.

It was nearly three in the morning when the two wagons rolled onto the bay wharf. The single guard, left to watch the unclaimed cargo, came forward hesitantly. Miguel, who had left the wagons fifty feet back and circled around was just preparing to knock him in the head when he sang out:

"Felipe, why are you upon a wagon at this hour?"

The barkeep stared down into the gloom. "Who is there?" he stammered, a quaver in his voice at having been recognized.

"Pablo Diaz, from your village."

Felipe Romero sighed deeply, coming off of the driver's perch with quaking legs. "Then you will be happy to know that I have with me your brother and uncle."

"And that news," Miguel said gleefully, stepping from the shadows, "makes me exceedingly happy."

The young man started and stared, confused and mystified. Left in the wise counsel of his uncle, the young guard was not asked but told what he must do to further the betterment of his family *and himself* in this venture.

Miguel was so elated over this happy turn of events that he hit the young man on the head only hard enough to make a welt that would be convincing.

Miguel looked so haggard and weary and sober that Felix took pity on him.

"I've been the whole night over the countryside," Miguel said, without really lying, "and no wagons are available. Don Carlos has sold out to Anglos, and they would not sell. We had best have Don Manuel help us find storage space for the equipment or those bastards will figure out a way of charging us a storage cost."

"You're right," Felix said wearily. "My folly in wanting this new equipment is going to cost us more than it will ever return."

To his disgust the port officer had no choice but to allow the mayor and the Escovarro brothers into his office when they arrived. He sat morosely behind his desk, a disheveled Pablo Diaz cowering in the corner. That morning he had been exulting in his good fortune in being able to levy such a heavy tax against such rich Spaniards—his good fortune that was now his misfortune, the worst that he could imagine.

"Where is my equipment?" Felix roared, storming to his desk. "It is not on the wharf."

"Gentlemen! Gentlemen, please be seated!" He started to wheeze and regretted the day he had deserted his wife and children in Boston and headed west. Nothing approaching this calamity had ever befallen him in the years he had worked the wharfs at Boston.

"We have had," he said when they were settled, "a slight misfortune during the night. A theft, you might say."

"Damn!" Felix stormed, instantly realizing the worst.

"Really?" Miguel exclaimed so mildly that Felix blanched at his calmness.

Oscar Feldman was not paying attention to either of them but nervously motioning the Mexican boy forward to become the focal point of attention.

"He will tell you all we know to date," he said nervously.

Pablo Diaz's account was as letter perfect as if he had been rehearsed.

"They were four. Anglos." Then he gave an exact description of the robbers on the Castro ranch. "They said they had papers for the Escovarro cargo, but when I reached for them, they fell upon me. That is all that I know."

Felix sat stunned, benumbed.

"And what of the authorities?" Miguel asked on a rising note.

"They are looking into it, of course," Feldman fluttered.

"Rubbish," Miguel snorted. "They will find nothing, as usual. We, in the meantime, are out a considerable amount of equipment, as you are well aware from the paper work," and he paused and smiled cynically, "and from the taxes due on it. We shall not stand such a loss."

Feldman cringed. "The republic will make good, of course. However, it will take time. We are young, and you must understand; I even have problems getting them to make the payroll on time."

"Come," Miguel said, rising grandly, "we must get our wives out of this hellhole and deal with this incompetent government later."

Felix followed like a man drugged. Miguel was fully in charge. To obtain the use of the mayor's carriage, he quietly told the old man what the authorities would find at the Castro ranch. Without exactly saying so, the impression was strong in the man's mind that the robbers had killed each other fighting over the loot and Miguel had "borrowed" the wagons. Then he raised a blue-veined hand for silence. Officially he would believe the tale told by Pablo Diaz; unofficially it gave him heart that Miguel had stolen back his own property to thwart the Anglos' tax.

Felix stared at the loaded wagons in openmouthed wonderment.

"How—?" he stammered.

"It doesn't matter now," Miguel said gruffly.

"You might have told me."

Miguel's sigh was gusty with disgust. "And have you ruin everything. You never were a very convincing liar, little brother."

"We'll never get away with it, you know."

Miguel set his teeth and glared. "I've had just about all of the bullshit I'm going to take from you. Once before I told you to stop acting like you were the boss. We are back now and will conform to the Escovarro customs. There can be only one male voice giving commands on those one hundred and fifteen thousand acres. As our father told his brother: you can stay and work with me or get your ass off the land!"

"I see," Felix said despondently. He did not mention the matter again.

A bed of mattresses had been prepared for Emilia and at the head of it a box seat for Maritza. Miguel's intention was to drive the teams day and night until they were on Escovarro land.

But riding along the track at night was an additional strain on their already tense emotions. In the hamlet of Diego they learned that a band of Mexican guerrillas were robbing and looting the countryside at will. The box of new percussion rifles were broken open and made ready. Food baskets were purchased for each wagon so that they would not have to stop and eat along the track. In the Diego cantina Miguel purchased a clay jug of tequila. Felix started to comment and then stopped himself.

The moon, coming out from behind a night-blue tracery of clouds, burnished the face of the Nueces River with silvery mist. Through it fireflies were fairy lights on the surface of the water, and the rolling hills stood up black and forbidding, crowned with a ragged fringe of trees.

The slow clopping of the horses drawing the buckboards made a rhythm like a double heartbeat, and looking at Felix, Teresa could see his tense profile. He lighted a cheroot, and it glowed redly in the dark, its fragrant smoke climbing upward about his head, visible in the darkness.

He sat hunched over, brooding over Miguel, and once more Teresa knew the feeling that he was something traditional and ancient and grand, something beyond the commonality of ordinary men.

Timidly she put out her hand and touched his thigh. "It will be all right once we get home," she whispered.

"How?" he growled.

How, she thought bitterly, must you ask "how"?

Then, without conscious volition, her arms flew up around his neck, and she dragged his face to the side, locking his mouth to hers in a savage kiss. She laid her head on his shoulder, her lips bruised and swollen, the unashamed tears falling from the oval of her upturned face. She studied him gravely, her eyes searching his face as though she would memorize his image.

Then she said very quietly: "Because we have each other, Felix. He can't take that away from us."

CHAPTER ELEVEN

"As far as the eye can see," Felix had told Teresa the first time he had brought her upon Escovarro land. But that time she had not seen the land, so occupied was her mind with running away from Santa Anna and herself. Now the land meant something completely different to her as the wagons slipped down to the edge of the plain, following the track in among the boxtrees that masked the maze of channels skirting the Río Frío. In and out, down and across, the track took the easiest way and the hardest surface. Crossing at a natural ford, they rounded a spur of timber to reach the main track which consisted of deep twin ruts made by many wagons—lines the buckboards must follow as a train must follow the iron rails.

The sky was a bowl, blue varnished, sweeping down to the northern timber stands, elongating them by the mirage to the likeness of Eastern date palms, its rim resting on the humps of distant purplish hills to the west.

The tranquil verdant plain was dotted with activity. Cattle milling, cattle munching, cattle gathering like black and brown islands in the sea of green; cattle complaining to high heaven in one continuous low. Now and then a vaquero, riding the herd, would spot the wagons and wave joyously. Even the cattle seemed to sense that the Escovarro brothers were home. A massive bull snorted, pawing the ground with his hoof and bowing his head low; a playful, devilish calf ran the track beside them; now a matron, who looked as though she would give them a piece of her mind for being gone so long; then a pert yearly wench full of conceit. Each seemed to have a distinct personality, for all had in their veins the blue blood of the aristocratic toros of ancient Spain.

The cattle on that range, numbering twenty thousand, were recently rounded up from the western grazing lands and foothills. For weeks they had been driven by men and horses, herded and branded, and now before them were long months of peace and fattening on the summer heavy grasses. In other years, when the first cool breezes blew out of the north, many would be driven to San Antonio and Mexico City. This year the cattle were unaware that the latter might prove to be a problem.

It was a matter the vaqueros and farmers did not take on their shoulders either. Those who had remained were playing a waiting game. Once, when Raymundo Escovarro had been alive, they numbered over twelve hundred people. They had a hamlet of their own—Escovarro, a happy contented village that loved to fiesta. Because of the name that it bore, Santa Anna had ordered it pillaged and burned. Those who did not die fled to the Ranchero de Oro. They remained only one step in front of the marauding army. The pink adobe villa was surrounded and put to the torch with Don and Doña Escovarro and their household staff locked inside and disallowed to escape the holocaust. Because Santa Anna's army was marching on San Antonio and the Alamo, many fled south to immerse themselves in the Mexican population and be forgotten.

One who could not do that was Guido Herrera. He, like the returning brothers, was fourth generation on the land. A decade their senior, he had no authority when the old don was killed. He, like many others, turned to the cow foreman, Manuel Rodriguez, to guide them. Rodriguez sent word of the events to the brothers in San Antonio and sat down to await orders. The reply he received from Felix did not please him:

"For the moment, I leave everything to your best judgment."

Rodriguez's best judgment was to pack up his family and depart the next day.

Guido had family buried on the land, children and a

grandchild to think of. Although there were older men still on the ranch, none seemed willing to step forward and exert authority.

His face and hands were tanned by wind and sun, and the manner in which he walked with his toes slightly turned inward proclaimed the many years he had lived on the back of a horse.

"Morning," he had said, drawing near his comrades.

"Morning, Guido. Morning."

Absently the cowman scratched his head. He frowned with seeming perplexity. A stranger would have thought that the bane of his life was finding work for many more hands than he needed.

"Rodriguez has left," he had said flatly and without further comment on the matter. "Pedro, the windmill needs grease. It isn't pumping."

Nodding assent, old Pedro departed for the tall wooden structure and its reservoir tanks set high on the next hill. From them water was piped to all the watering troughs, as well as to the garden, and at one time to the villa itself.

"Fernando, I want you to round up as many brick forms as are available. Those that are rotted out destroy and make new ones. The adobe bricks Don Raymundo had planned for a new smokehouse will give us a good start. Noel, you and your crew better prepare to head into the hills and start rounding up the calves and strays. Rubin, the air tells me that it is already a couple of weeks past the time for planting the hay and oats. My woman's vegetable garden is already greening out of the ground."

There was always plenty of work to be done on a ranch and farm of that size and magnitude. With less than a third of the original work force, Guido feared he would fail. But the three hundred eighty-one men, women, and children who had remained considered themselves as family. They accomplished their normal tasks handily and with a quiet reverence gave extra of themselves to Guido's pet project.

The gutted pink villa was demolished and the land raked clean of any sign of fire. A new structure began to rise, not as grand as the original but designed so that additions could be put on as the new occupants desired.

Then the news reached the ranch of the victory at San Jacinto, that Santa Anna was a captive, and of the impending marriage and honeymoon of *both* Escovarro brothers. The ranch hands became jubilant with happiness. It was the first time in months that they had something to look forward to: planning and celebrating fiesta.

Two weeks before he anticipated their arrival, Guido's heart sank. A dust cloud was spotted coming down the track. He looked at his surprise and sighed. The walls were all up, the roof secure and waterproof; but the interior walls were still being plastered and whitewashed. The humid July heat was not letting them dry properly.

"Unbelievable," Doña Patricia exclaimed as she sailed from empty room to empty room. "Guido, you are a marvel."

His weathered face beamed into near smoothness.

"What do you think, Big John," Doña Patricia demanded of Emilia's black butler and coachman.

"Mighty empty," he grinned.

"But not for long," she enthused. "Oh, Big John, Emilia may kill me for what I did, but I couldn't help it at the time."

"Seem's ta me yah did da right thing. Mighty empty."

Guido looked around and for the first time began to realize that all of the furnishings of the villa had also vanished in the fire, and he had not given a single thought to their replacement.

But the whirlwind Irishwoman was not giving his brain a chance to even worry on the subject.

"These rooms seem quite ready to decorate, although the plaster is drying in cracks on that one bedroom on the south side and the dining room floor could stand a second coat of beeswax. Other than that I think the wagons can be unloaded and Big John and I can start decorating."

Guido was momentarily stunned. "When are they arriving?"

"I can't say for sure. I've had two posts from them. Teresa, who is Felix's bride, wrote to say they were going to someplace called Natchez for four weeks and then returning here. A week or so later I had a post from Emilia, who is Miguel's bride, asking me to sell her house and furnishings in San Antonio. She may kill me, but I couldn't bring myself to sell her lovely things, and now I know why. I can just see every stick of her furniture in this house. Well, let's get started."

Emilia was flabbergasted and deeply moved to walk into a near replica of her former grand San Antonio home. It amused Teresa and Felix, but Miguel was darkly angry. He looked upon the furniture as just another glaring reminder of Emilia's former life.

"Oh, Felix, look," Teresa called gleefully as she came to the rooms that would be theirs. "It's my grandmother's four-poster."

She ran to touch the bedpost lovingly, then to reacquaint herself with the bureau, clothes press, and her father's picturesque old desk. But the furniture in the airy sitting room was new to her eyes.

"Just some things I had lying about the attic," Doña Patricia said, trying to pass it off lightly.

"You are just too good to us," Teresa cried, running to the small woman.

"And why not," she said, hugging Teresa tenderly. "It's about time I had someone to spoil."

"You will soon have a grandniece or nephew to spoil as well."

Doña Patricia held her at arm's length, beaming. "Oh, my dear child."

"No," Teresa laughed, "not me. Not as yet, anyway. It's Emilia."

"Well," she gasped, "if that doesn't beat all. Still it's marvelous news. So why is the proud father so glum?"

Felix scowled. "Miguel's been a bit off his feed, Tía."

"Typical," his aunt laughed. "Being the middle child, he always felt left out of things and pouted his way into being noticed. Once a pouter, always a pouter. Well, come along and have some dinner. Out of all the women on this ranch I have finally found one who can prepare something other than tortillas and beans. And I am just bursting with news."

In the kitchen Maritza began to feel the first faint pangs of loneliness. She had been so busy caring for Emilia that she had not had time to consider what her new life would be like. She was not a guest, she was not an employee, she was just an extra body standing around.

Big John had taken one look at her, and a deep suspicion began to grow in his brain—a suspicion he found hard to put into words.

"Did yah come along jest ta nurse Miss Emilia?" he asked, the long unused Virginia argot sounding strange even to his ears.

"It wasn't planned that way," she answered coolly in Spanish.

"Where yah learn ta talk like dat?" he asked on a note of surprise, automatically switching to Spanish.

Maritza reared back her head and laughed. "In Cuba where I was born. But where did you learn *your* Spanish? You sound like your mouth is still full of pone."

Big John cocked his head haughtily. "Ah learned on my own, woman, when ah run away and come ta this place." Then he eyed her rudely. "You a runaway or did they buy you and bring you here?"

The man was aggravating Maritza. "Neither," she snapped. "I was given to Miss Teresa by my former master and she gave me manumission."

"Lordy, Lordy," Big John sighed, "am that a load off my mind. Ah was afraid they was starting to bring slaves here, and slaves would mean bounty hunters and trouble for Big John."

"There is no slavery here?"

"Not yet, but the talk in San Antonio is that if this Texas becomes a state, then there might jest be."

Maritza had been eyeing the rotund woman working at the stove.

"Are you the butler here?"

Big John preened proudly. "Nobody's said, but ah 'spects so."

"Then might I suggest that that woman is going to have that meat as tough as shoe leather frying it in the pan that way."

In the two weeks that he had been there Big John had seen a half-dozen women come and go in the kitchen. He couldn't afford to have another one storm out with dinner only half prepared. But when the woman didn't turn in anger, he realized Maritza had made the statement in English so that it wouldn't offend.

"Ah suppose you know a better way."

"I saw orange trees as we drove in. Have any of them gotten old and soured?"

"How'd ah know a thing like dat?"

Maritza very graciously asked the same question of the woman and learned that it was so. The woman's child, who had been pounding flour into strips of steak, was sent to find some. Careful not to rile the woman, Maritza explained how she could be of help. Big John sighed with relief when the woman began to bubble with gratitude. She was scared to death of the assignment but her husband, who feared losing face with the Escovarros, had forced her to come. She began to chat animatedly with Maritza, and Maritza subtly began to taste and reseason and artfully change the menu. When there was little left to do, the woman was released to go home and prepare her own supper. Big John was also a diplomat.

"To save you time at home," he said, "why don't you take along the steaks you cooked. We have more than enough."

"*Gracias,* señor," she beamed. "Is just the way my husband loves it."

After the dining room table was set, Big John began to lay two places at the breakfast table in the kitchen alcove. He did it so hesitantly that Maritza had to smile to herself. So used to eating her solitary meal in her cabin, she thought it might be fun to have a man across the table again.

"I . . . ah . . . well," Big John stammered.

They stared at each other a moment, then burst into laughter.

It was a fine, gay meal. The musicians among the vaqueros stood on the patio and serenaded them with music that had been remembered by their fathers and grandfathers from old Spain, and the food kept coming from the kitchen: thin slices of beef that had been lightly fried in the juice of the sour oranges, fluffy white rice laced with raisins and a touch of brandy, spring peas and mushrooms, a platter of paella made with trout from the Rio Frío and eggs *a la flamenca*. And throughout it all Doña Patricia was a wealth of news.

"That's interesting," Felix said, "I was unaware Houston was in New Orleans at the same time as we."

"Almost didn't live to get there," she went on. "President Burnet refused his passage on a Texas naval vessel, and he had to cross the Gulf in a dirty little trading schooner. What's more, Burnet dismissed Surgeon Ewing from the service for wanting to go with him."

"Sounds just like the petty man he is," Miguel supplied. "He gave Houston nothing but trouble throughout the campaign."

Doña Patricia chuckled. "He's starting to get some of it back now. Confusion prevails in this republic. His Cabinet changes so fast that no one can keep track of it. The man is impotent."

Miguel laughed. It was doing him good to hear of these troubles. "In more ways than one is he impotent. He'll never last."

"Miguel!" Doña Patricia snapped. "Don't get me ahead of my story. I have over two months worth of news to catch you up on. Now . . . ah yes, the scandal. Burnet negotiated two treaties with General Santa Anna—one public, the other secret. A secret that lasted exactly an hour. The first would end all hostilities and return the Mexican to his people. The second is a promise from Santa Anna to prepare the way for Mexican recognition of the independence of Texas."

"Damn," Felix growled. "They let him get away."

"Yes and no," Doña Patricia laughed, enjoying being the center of attention. "They put him aboard the *Invincile* to sail him to Veracruz, but it was stormed by some adventurers who brought him back ashore in manacles. The mob shouted their approval of his death and jeered Burnet. In spite of his humiliation he was able to get Santa Anna returned to jail under heavy guard. The army is so against the man that he has called for a general election to choose a new president and to ratify the constitution."

"Which will be our undoing," Miguel said darkly.

Doña Patricia smiled wickedly. "If they can find it."

"What do you mean?" both men asked in unison.

"There isn't a copy of the document in the files. It seems that Mr. Kimble, the secretary of the convention, had the only copy of the manuscript, and he left Texas when it appeared that Santa Anna would win and can't be found."

Felix laughed. "Well, Teresa, you're beginning to get your wish. It will take them months if they have to call a whole new convention. Who is running, Tía?"

"Stephen Austin and ex-Governor Henry Smith."

"Not Houston?"

"No, he's back home in San Augustine recuperating."

"What do you make of that, Miguel?" Felix asked.

Miguel pursed his lips. "Interesting. Either Austin or Smith would be more lenient on the land-grant issue. Both are in the same boat as we are with large holdings from Spain and Mexico. Interesting."

"Well," Doña Patricia insisted, "let's put a period on any further politicial talk for this evening so that we can get these two lovelies to open their pretty mouths. Let's talk fiesta."

"Grand," Teresa enthused.

"Miguel," his aunt said sternly, "I hope you won't mind that I have already gone ahead with some of the preparations."

"Why should I mind?" he said blandly.

"Don't give me that pussy-won't-drink-cream expression, young man. You are now the Escovarro don, and I didn't want you to think that you were going to be controlled by skirts as was your father."

He had feared only two people in his whole life—his mother and his aunt. "Fiestas," he laughed weakly, "have always been the province of the ladies. I leave every aspect of it in your three pairs of capable hands."

Big John came in with more coffee.

"Thank you," Doña Patricia said, "and thank Carlota for a surprisingly excellent meal."

Big John grinned. "Best you be thanking Maritza. Most was her doing," he said as he left the dining room.

"Oh dear," Teresa gasped, "I had all but forgotten about her in the excitement. Whatever are we going to do with her?"

"That's obvious," Doña Patricia chirped. "Miguel, you had best hire her to run your kitchen for you."

He scowled. "She belongs to Teresa."

"No, she doesn't," Teresa insisted. "She is a free black."

"As is Big John," Emilia injected. "Unless Doña Patricia is going to try to steal him for good, you'd best talk employment with him as well."

Miguel had been cold sober for the past twenty-four hours, and the dinner wine had been like so much water to his craving need. His nerves were frayed and the constant chatter had become a growing irritant. He had to escape them and find a drink or go crazy. He rose from the table so quickly that he knocked over his chair. It was a little thing, but it irritated him the most.

"This damn house," he barked, "like the fiesta, I leave to the women to run!"

It was unfortunate that just before he barked, the musicians had finished one number and were preparing to begin another. A sudden silence fell on the room with suffocating embarrassment.

Felix cleared his throat and said softly: "I'll see what we can work out about their salaries."

Miguel glowered at him with utter contempt and stalked from the room.

Emilia rose calmly and gracefully, but her Aztec black eyes were spitting fire.

"I think it's about time—"

Felix stayed her with his hand. "Teresa, why don't you and Tía Patricia go and see if those arrangements would be suitable to Maritza and Big John. I can discuss salary with them later." He rose and offered his arm to Emilia. On the patio he graciously thanked the musicians and excused them for the evening.

"Thank you for not going after him," he said gently.

She scoffed. "I doubt it would have done any good."

"Care to discuss it?"

"Not really." She was silent for a long moment. "What is that scent in the air?"

Felix laughed. "It surprised me too. Orange blossoms. I guess because of the cold winter, they are late in blooming."

"But I saw fruit on the trees."

"If it was orange, that was last year's crop and most likely sour. The new fruit won't be ready until next November or December."

She turned and appraised him carefully. "You know a lot about this land, don't you?"

"I tried to learn everything about it as a child, until I nearly drove my father wild. Like those oranges. My great-grandfather brought twelve tender young seedling from Valencia and nurtured and grafted them until he had a whole grove. It's the same with the grape arbors and the apple orchard. Everything had to come from the land to make it like the old country, or you did without."

"And you love it?"

"Dearly."

She asked suddenly: "Did Miguel, ever?"

"I—I really can't say. I know he was resentful when Father let me go to Spain to study when it should have been his turn, although I didn't learn it until my return. He insisted, at the time, that he loved the ranch."

"That seems to be his nature. Love something and then grow resentful when he's obtained it. That's our problem right now, and I'm sorry that it is giving you difficulty."

For once in his life Felix knew when to keep his mouth shut.

"Ever since we have been married," she went on candidly, "I have tried to be a wife to him and not a whore. He even accused me of advertising the fact when I danced at Beauwood."

"Damn idiot!" he declared. "It was magnificent. It took me right back to the Zarzuela Theater in Madrid. But there you had thirty or more señoritas in flouncing skirts clattering their castanets as Antonio Sobrino led the ballet to flamenco rhythms. My Lord, the stage actually quivered with the staccato of their pounding feet. I got the same thrill out of watching you. If to dance like that makes a woman a whore, then all Spanish women would be whores."

Emilia laughed lightly. "You know, Felix Escovarro, perhaps I don't hate you as much as I thought I did."

Felix grinned.

"We seem to have been traveling the same street," he said. "I've been taking your quietness to be sullenness. I can see now that it was hurt pride."

"I—I find myself in the strange position of being the other woman."

"Look, Emilia, he has never been an easy person to deal with. But you've got to save yourself. In the long run that's Miguel's best chance too. If the one who's got the brains and the ability goes down, what chance have the poor devils who are depending on her to come to their rescue later? You wouldn't have achieved what you have in life if you acted as you have been lately."

"There's sense in that," Emilia said thoughtfully. "Still—"

"Listen," he said firmly. "Our people need this fiesta badly to take the taste of death out of their mouths. We can do that for them. I want you and Maritza to recreate for them the show you gave at Beauwood."

"No," she glowered. "I'm trying hard enough to close that wound as it is."

"To hell with what Miguel will think," he sneered. "You will be among only Spanish people—your people. People who will be thrilled by your artistry and take you to their hearts. Win them over, and Miguel will become the fool if he dares speak against you."

"I—I—"

"You do what I tell you!" Felix ordered.

Emilia stared at him. "All right, Felix," she whispered.

"Good! Now let's go see what other plans have already been made."

On the day they had arrived back at the Ranchero de Oro, Vince Bowditch came into General Thomas Jefferson

Green's tent on the outskirts of the new capital city of Columbia, his thin face gray with misery. Green took one look at him and jumped from his seat.

"Don't tell me you were wrong!" he roared.

"No, sir," Vince whispered. "The land is just as the Escovarros described it—even more so. It isn't that."

"Then what the devil is it?"

"It's their people, sir—more than I expected. They could raise an army of a hundred guns right from their ranch hands. The rumors were false that everyone had deserted the place after Santa Anna had sacked it. Must be four hundred people there, and they've rebuilt the main house."

"Jehosaphat!" Green exploded. "That means the report out of Corpus Christi is true. The Escovarro brothers brought back thousands of dollars worth of equipment from New Orleans. Thinking they were going to resell it, a large import tax was levied against it. It was stolen right off the wharf, and they put in a claim against the government."

"They'd never sell their equipment," Vince said soberly.

"I am not a fool, Bowditch," Green stormed. "A month ago I wasn't even in the army, and now I am a general. I got where I am because I'm not timid. Was I timid with you when you came to me about this little scheme? I staked you to horse and capital to get out there and put our claim in on that land. Is this how in hellfire you deliver?"

Vince's face paled, then the red came back, deeper than ever.

"How was I to know the land was still occupied?"

Green nodded grimly. "Perhaps there is a different way," he said quietly. "I have a hunch the Escovarro brothers are very much aware of exactly where all that stolen equipment is at this very moment. Now, should it be located upon their land, they would be in danger of trying to defraud the government with their claim. I do have the power to provide you with orders for just such a search. Of course, even if you find nothing, you will report back to me that you did."

"That," Vince said, "is downright dishonest!"

Green grinned. "You could say that the whole proposal you brought to me in the first place was dishonest," he said. "Should Austin or Smith become president, and should we enter the Union, the land-grant issue will be fought in the courts for years. Possession, dear fellow, is still nine tenths of the law."

"Whichever way you look at it, we're never going to get our hands on that land," Bowditch reminded him.

"Not so," Green said. "The arrest of a man can work wonders on those around him. How long will the peons remain if the masters are arrested and taken away in disgrace? If the government should confiscate the land for the unpaid taxes on the equipment *you will find?*"

"They know me," he said sourly. "They won't buy it."

Green smiled smugly. "I don't intend to send you alone this time. I'll handpick the soldiers I want to go with you."

"But will it stick? Whoever is elected could overrule us on the land after they are in office."

"I've been thinking on that," Green said quietly, "and I think I have the proper answer. One man could have put Burnet out of office and taken charge of Texas under any title that would have suited his whim. I think it's time for the men of this army to start letting their voices be heard on whom they wish to be president. Of course, you know, their wholehearted choice will be the recluse of San Augustine."

"That stubborn jackass would never run."

"Perhaps," he said, "it is time for us to make the situation such that Sam Houston cannot refuse to run."

Carlos Escovarro de Madria first saw the land as a member of the Alonso de Pineda expedition in 1519. The next year he returned from Spain with three workers, a dozen horses, and a dream. After a decade of near impossible toil and strife with the Indians, he sought and received a land grant from Charles I. On his return from Spain he brought along his new bride, a small herd of cattle, and a dozen working men and their families.

On the first day of August, 1620, to honor his memory and celebrate their centennial on the land, the family held a fiesta. Because of the distances the conquistadors had to travel from their own great landed estates, it was automatically assumed that they would remain as guests for a week to ten days. It established a precedent that survived for the next two hundred and sixteen years.

Overnight the vast lawns of Ranchero de Oro mushroomed with brightly colored tents and marquees jutting from the sides of covered wagons. Many had traveled as far as the ancient conquistadors for the mere pleasure of being with people of their own caste.

There were old friends of wealth and power, such as the Esparza family who had helped Teresa and Felix flee Saltillo and Santa Anna. There were old friends of no wealth and power, such as Anna-Maria and Pedro who had come to make Teresa the godmother of their first child.

It afforded Felix exceeding pleasure to have from one and all of his guests varied encomiums of his beautiful wife, and a real and warm interest in what promised to be a delightful and memorable fiesta.

The Esparza party was smaller than Felix had expected it to be. The old don had been careful to leave his eldest son at home.

"Nightly they raid and steal my horses," he quietly told Felix and Miguel. "I've lost three vaqueros from gunshots in their back and a dozen more out of fear. Because of Santa Anna I fled New Spain for *Tejas*. Now, again because of him, I am making preparations to go to the northwest into New Mexico." Then he brightened. "But we are not here to discuss politics. My wife and daughters have been longing for this since we received word of your marriage."

Malita Esparza was a patrician brunette, a serious, soft-voiced woman of twenty-two, sweet and kindly, despite a rather bitter experience that had left her worldly wise and unwed. Dorotea, a plain, lively girl of twenty, made up in spirit and charm for what she lacked in beauty. Doña Marta Esparza still reminded Teresa greatly of her grandmother, but the events of the past year and a half had left a strained look to her eyes and mouth. The fifth and last of the Esparza contingent was nineteen-year-old Carlos—a strapping youth of near feminine prettiness. He had a cream and brown complexion, a small golden moustache, and his heavy eyelids, always drooping, made him look sensuous. His attire, cut to what appeared to be exaggerated "caballero" style, attracted attention to his handsomely muscular frame, although he stood no more than about five feet six inches tall. He was immaculate and fastidious, with the careless smile of the youth for whom life had been easy and pleasant.

By the evening of the second day over two hundred guests had arrived. As near as they could, they duplicated the Beauwood bar-be-que. It was a happy afternoon, especially for the Spanish women Maritza had trained to serve it, and who could not fail to note its success. The mingling of low voices and laughter, the old, gay, superficial talk, the graciousness of a class which lived for the pleasure of things and to make time pass pleasurably for others—all took Teresa far back into the past. She did not want to let go of it, but she saw in the faces of her people and friends that they were well aware that their world had suddenly tilted, and a time such as this might never be seen again. There was a new breed upon the land, loud and boisterous and strident in their demands. They wanted *mañana* today. They wanted to still the vibrant heart of this rich culture.

When the fiesta adjourned to the paddock where the clay earth had been raked and watered to harden into a dance floor, the red sun was sinking over the near hills and the vaqueros began to light tallow torches while their women loaded the tables with refreshments. Just as the last curve of red rim vanished beyond the dim mountains and the normal golden flashes of heat lightning began to flare brighter, Maritza joined the musicians with her guitar.

"It needed only this touch. Ah, how that music pleases my ears. And what is this surprise? Who is the dancer?"

Miguel knew before he looked the identity of the woman swirling her way to the center of the paddock. A bitter sensation knotted his stomach and his ears began to burn with humiliation. But this time there was no escaping the scene. Of all the young women in attendance, only one had stirred Miguel's interest—Malita Esparza. He had just joined their family group when the music had begun and chose to suffer humiliation rather than lose favor in the patrician beauty's eyes by a rude departure. Emilia glided along the rim of the spectators and out to the center again, where, castanets held high above her head, she poised momentarily in bold relief.

"What an exceptional gown. Who is she?" inquired the curious Malita.

"That is Emilia, my wife," replied Miguel emotionlessly. To have answered otherwise would have been fatal, because he was aware Malita's parents had already met Emilia.

"Is she from Spain?" asked Malita.

"Hardly!" replied Miguel with a little laugh.

He found it necessary to explain that she had been born in San Antonio and had visited France but not Spain.

"That is hard to believe," Señor Esparza enthused. "She is classical."

"More than that," Doña Marta corrected her husband. "She is superb. I have seen none like her since I was a girl in Spain. Oh, how I longed to be that graceful and fluid of motion."

"*Mamacita*," Carlos roared with mirth, "you have danced like that?"

Doña Marta blinked at her son unabashedly. "In my day, young man," she said sternly, "a young lady was not a young lady until she mastered the arts of the flamenco rhythms and movements. It is a shame that Doña Emilia does not live closer so that some of her culture could rub off on your sisters."

"Oh, Momma," Malita laughed, "I can't picture you dancing at all."

"And why didn't you teach us?" demanded Dorotea. "I would have loved to have danced like that. She *is* superb!"

"Marta," Señor Esparza said with a sly wink. "The music is familiar, no? The solo is near ended and comes near to the strains of invitation. If not to amaze the children, please me again."

Señora Esparza started to protest and suddenly decided differently. The strain marks evaporated from her face, and she stepped forward and poised with her arms arching over her mantilla. Without castanets she used her fingers to snap sharply three times, followed immediately by three staccato beats of her heels and toes. Emilia spun around, momentarily stunned, and automatically aped the woman's movements.

It was the ancient *gallina picotear*—hen peck—whereby one woman, and then others, would challenge the lead dancer to win supremacy before the *gallo*—rooster—would stomp his way onto the floor and with frantically building movements dance among the women until he had selected one to compete with him in the "flamenco fin."

Long forgotten skills and desires stirred through the throng like wildfire at midnight. Soon the torchlight circle was ablaze with the color of swirling skirts, snapping fingers, and rapidly moving feet. However, the men hung back and seemed reluctantly afraid, or ashamed, to assume their role in the old ritual. Finally Señor Esparza felt the obligation rested upon his shoulders. He entered the crowded floor of dancing women and played the *gallo* to their *gallina*. By comparison of ability, Emilia should have been his choice for a finale partner, but he won popular approval when he weeded out all but his wife. To wildly exciting cheers they concluded the dance as the only participants in the paddock. When it was over, Malita turned hesitantly to Miguel.

"Señor, would you see me to a refreshment table?" she asked of Miguel. She was restless, nervous, and did not seem to be able to stand still a moment.

"My pleasure. But I can easily bring you back what you desire."

"No," she insisted, "I want to get away from this throng for a moment."

He was more than happy to present his arm to her and get away himself. Carlos Esparza started to follow them and then hesitated. He had been enjoying the company of Miguel Escovarro and resented his sister for taking the man away. He had so little contact with sophisticated men that he had found the encounter with Miguel exhilarating. Almost at once he began to ape Miguel's stance and manner of walking and use of his hands. He was a novice at the game of hero-worship, although he respected his father with an arm's-length approach. Other than the Mexican laborers on his father's land, he had only one other male to measure the masculine world by—his oldest brother, Guillerno. He never realized how much he hated and despised Guillerno until he met the suave Miguel Escovarro.

Malita was experiencing a like emotion. "I'm sorry," she murmured, "but I suddenly grew very embarrassed seeing my parents dance in that fashion. It became so intimate at the end that I began to blush."

"I was blushing from the first," Miguel said honestly, "that my wife started the whole thing."

"But she was marvelous," protested Malita. "I'm just glad my brother Guillerno wasn't here."

"Why is that?"

"He would have been the first to try to play—" She stopped and flushed.

"The rooster?"

"Sometimes he thinks he is the only rooster in the whole world," she replied softly.

There was in the plaintive reply, accompanied by a dark and eloquent glance of eyes, what told Miguel all he needed to know about her quietness, of her misery, and perhaps a betrayal of her unquiet soul. It heartened Miguel. The other young fillies at the fiesta might have the longing to break down the bars of their cage, but had not the spirit. Someone, and he suspected who, had broken her spirit, and she was now longing.

"I am also a rooster," he said, leaving no doubt as to what he meant.

"A married one," she replied promptly and ruefully.

Miguel started to flare and then softened. "The rooster has the choice of more than one hen. If you agree, don't close your tent flap tonight."

He stalked away, arrogantly sure that she was his for the night. Because Emilia had become an instantaneous success with his contemporaries and family friends, he devoted the remainder of the evening to being by her side, basking in the reflected rays of her glory. Because of the return of his warmth and attention she prepared her mind to grant him that night any wish he might desire of her, but close to eleven, when the party was at it fullest, violent cramps doubled Emilia over. It took Maritza an hour to ease them, while Miguel stalked the floor with hand-wringing false concern, downing glass after glass of tequila. When the pain eased, and Emilia lapsed into sleep, Maritza bid Miguel a cool good night.

"Who's he trying to fool," she muttered to herself, as she wandered back to her quarters. "He hasn't shown this concern before. Devious, devious, and dangerous man."

Miguel stood for another two hours by the bedroom window until the noise of the last merrymakers had subsided and the numerous campfires had turned to white embers. Keeping well within the shadows, he sliced his way from tent to tent until he came to those of the Esparza family. The larger structure, he reasoned, was for the parents, while the three lesser A-frame tenting were for their children. Two, of the latter, were flapped down and secured for the night, but the third was open and seductively inviting. His heart began to sing with joyous conquest as he ducked down and entered the small enclosure, bringing the flap down over the opening.

Enough moonlight still invaded the tent to give him an image of her stretched-out form. She lay with her back to him, the cut of her nightgown molding about her buttocks in such a fashion to instantly arouse him. Without comment he stripped away his clothing and nestled down beside her. She nestled back, bringing the cleavage of her buttocks in horizontal contact with his arousing manhood. He reached across her shoulder to make contact with her breasts, but his hand was restrained before it made contact and was forced back. But her hand did not retreat. It coursed down between their back and belly until it came in contact with his turgid length and closed around it. With a sigh of gratitude he rolled onto his back and waited for what he had been demanding from Emilia and not been receiving. He did not have to wait long. The warm, moist sensation of lips and mouth encompassing him sent exotic vibrations shimmering through his body. It was more than he had anticipated, it was sublime. Built to erotic peaks, he reached out for what he next sought of the woman.

His mind boggled. He had come in contact with the same structure that he was supplying to the overeager mouth. Frantically he pushed the body away and stared into the darkness in drunken confusion.

"You!" he gasped.

Carlos Esparza grinned back at him with deep-lidded sensuality. "Malita secured her tent so carefully that I took a chance by leaving mine quite open."

"You're perverted," Miguel growled, trying to find his pants and shirt.

"You wouldn't be saying that," Carlos chortled, "if you had reached your peak, because you were loving every minute of it."

"Because I thought——"

"It was my sister," he sneered, cutting him short. "Don't delude yourself. After two unsuccessful attempts by my older brother to seduce her, he turned to me as the next alternative. I proved to be far more satisfactory." And as though to prove his point, he rolled onto his stomach and raised up his buns.

Miguel was enraged with fury. Because of drink and other circumstances he had not reached a full and satisfactory climax in nearly six weeks.

Maddened by that insatiable animal that was becoming a part of his very being, he pulled the belt from his pants and began to beat the boy on the buttocks, cursing him with lascivious phrases. Then he stopped, stunned. Carlos was laughing and urging him on.

Miguel, his face immobile, his body rigid, blinked once and began to hurriedly don his clothing. He felt as though he were going to vomit.

Carlos turned, his pretty face a mocking leer. "Finished?" he giggled.

"Fuck you!" Miguel growled, pulling on his boots.

Carlos put back his head and roared with laughter. "You use the acronym incorrectly, señor. It is a British law term—'For Unlawful Carnal Knowledge.' F.U.C.K. Give me back your length, and I will show you its true meaning."

Miguel reached down and slapped Carlos with a quick, stinging cuff blow. Carlos blinked, not fully aware of what had happened. Then it hit him with almost as much impact as the blow itself.

"The more brutal you are, the more I like it."

"Shut up! You make me sick! Now listen! I don't give a good goddamn how you get your thrills, but I do know I'll kill you if you ever try to touch me again."

A silly grin crossed the boy's mouth. His heavy-lidded eyes remained fixed on Miguel. Then, with deliberate desire to anger Miguel further, he began to fondle himself.

Miguel spun from the tent, his mind a seething rage. Had it been any other family than the Esparzas, he might have ordered them off the ranch that very night. But he didn't want that, either. He wanted Malita now more than ever. Then he stopped and grinned on a sadistic thought. His knowledge of the incest among the Esparza children gave him a valuable tool for revenge.

And Carlos Esparza's mind was traveling a similar course. I'll make him want it again, he thought gleefully, or he'll never get near Malita.

CHAPTER TWELVE

"Jesus!" Vince Bowditch exploded, looking down on the ranch from the Marcos hills. "What in hell is happening here?"

The soldiers came in a single line over the crest of the hill, stopped, and the lead rider rode up next to Bowditch. He sat silently a moment, mentally counting the campfires.

"Got himself a little army up, hey, Mistah Bowditch."

Vince scowled without looking around. Captain Harlan Guth had irritated him since their departure from Columbia. The little shrill-toned man was a kinsman of General Green and had made sure that Bowditch was well aware of the fact.

"You see any of the equipment?"

Bowditch grunted, unable to see very much at all through the field glasses. The ranch seemed peaceful, tranquil, almost deserted. He was unaware that this had been the next to last night of the fiesta and the celebrants were nearly sated from a week's worth of food and drink. They needed a good night's sleep to carry them through the next day.

Guth said crisply, "The thing is, Bowditch, we are only fifty, and he must have a couple hundred more men down there than you led us to believe."

Now he emitted a sulky grunt. "Fifty can do a lot of damage if we take them by surprise in their sleep."

"No, sir, we need the Escovarro brothers arrested to make this look like a military operation and not just another bloody guerrilla raid."

Bowditch looked away, and Guth continued, "Do you fully understand?"

"More than you seem to," he said icily. "You don't know these greasers. They might have bought it if all the brothers had around them were their peons. Now, if they've got some real guns on their side, you'd need five hundred men to ride in and take them away. Your brother-in-law ain't going to like us coming back empty-handed. He wants all these greasers off the land."

Bowditch saw that Guth had understood the part about his brother-in-law. He wondered how much of the land Green had offered Guth. He hated to think of having the man as a neighbor for the rest of his life.

"We'd best get to it."

Bowditch grinned and spurred his horse forward.

It took them an hour to descend to the plain and come close to the ranch compound. The sliver of a moon kept them in darkness and undetected. They avoided the vaqueros' adobe huts, knowing they would scatter in fear at the first report of gunfire. To bring the Escovarros to bay, they concentrated their assault upon the tent city.

The horsemen broke fast on the area, the first using the butt end of their rifles to knock away retaining lines and tent poles. The next began firing point-blank into the collapsed fabric with rifles and pistols. A third group charged the main house, concentrating their fire on the second-floor bedroom windows.

The ranch was fully awake; screaming, scrambling to disentangle themselves and find their own firearms. It was such a shock that no one knew for sure exactly what was happening.

The Escovarro brothers crawled on the floor to the hallway and stared at each other in total disbelief. Then they rose and raced downstairs for their own guns.

Señor Esparza had learned to sleep with a pistol beneath his pillow years before and had it in hand with the first rifle reports. When his tent began to collapse inward, he rolled deftly from his pallet and clawed up the hem of the canvas. His head and arm were barely outside when he saw the horseman bearing down on his tent, his rifle aimed at the moving hump that was his wife. He fired without aim-

ing and burst the rifle right out of the man's hands. He saw
Carlos emerge from his tent and shouted the boy down.
Instead, Carlos squatted, using his knee as a balance base
for his five-chamber Colt percussion pistol, and began to
fire. Three of his five shots brought men tumbling out of
their saddles, and then he had to tumble himself under the
canvas for more ammunition.

In spite of their surprise advantage Guth's men were far-
ing poorly. They assumed they were killing and wounding
many of the tented people while actually only slightly
wounding a few. With each passing minute more and more
guns were being brought into play against them, and over a
dozen of his men were down. And from the vaqueros'
quarters he could see the Spaniards start to swarm from
their huts.

He spun his horse about, raised his arm, and shouted
for retreat. His men would have to plow their way through
the vaqueros or be annihilated. Just then Miguel got a bead
on him from the parlor window and fired. The horse kept
charging forward, Guth's pistol held at the ready, his beady
eyes transfixed. But his brain was no longer functioning,
half of it had been blown away. Amazingly he stayed in the
saddle, the vaqueros jumping out of the way of his galloping horse and men.

At first it was automatically assumed that it had been a
guerrilla raid, as many of the guests had been experiencing
on their own property—discontented soldiers banding together to maraud and plunder. To warn them off, the
campfires were built higher and sentries were posted for
the remainder of the night.

Everyone feared that the assault had been a near-massa-
cre. Dawn brought with it joyous truth. The wounds to the
guests were superficial, and no one was dead. Of the
twenty-seven "bandits" dead and wounded, only one survived until dawn.

"Felix, come here!" Miguel called out imperiously.
"Look at him! Wasn't he with us at San Jacinto?"

"Good God, yes," Felix gasped. "That's young Jimmy
Yerby, the drummer boy."

As though the mention of his name was a summons, the scrawny blond youth came around and stared at them with pale green eyes.

"Capt'n," he said weakly, focusing on Miguel, "did we beat Santa Anna."

The boy was in shock, but Miguel was anxious for immediate truth. "We did," he said harshly, "months ago. What is your present mission, soldier?"

The eyes darkened to emerald. He blinked and sighed, awareness of the moment returning. "We ain't volunteers, sir; we was picked by General Green himself."

"And the reason?"

The boy looked ashamed. "I didn't know till tonight. We are here to arrest you and your brother for stealing and not paying taxes."

Miguel caught Felix's eye, as though to say that it all didn't add up.

"But why, then," he said gently, "didn't you just ride in for the arrest?"

"I don't know," he said remorsefully. "We didn't get the order to fire until we were right on the ranch. I couldn't do it, and I don't think Capt'n Guth wanted to either. It was all the doing of that civilian."

"Who is that?"

"Man named Bowditch. Vince Bowditch, I think."

Again the brothers locked eyes, and Felix warned Miguel to silence.

"You'd best rest now," Miguel said calmly and spun from the room.

Felix found him in the yard shaking with fury. "Goddamn that bastard," he stormed. "How dare he come here with such gall after what he did in New Orleans?"

Felix eyed him with utter contempt but was smart enough not to open the ticklish subject of Miguel's lack of concern over the man at the time of the incident.

"He has, so forget it," he said coolly. "Come, we have to figure out if he is going to return."

As though it were his right, Felix became the spokesman before their guests. He was openly candid with them about the wounded soldier and why the attack came about, and why they would be able to depart that day without fear of attack from these "bandits" on their return home. He was not about to put their lives in jeopardy should another attack occur.

They split evenly on whether he was right or wrong, the former already packing their wagons for a hasty departure and the latter wanting to stay and help him fight.

"Their ranks have been reduced," he advised, even as the first wagons were leaving without as much as a good-bye.

"And they can see," Señor Esparza countered sternly, "that your ranks are diminishing, as well. It will buoy them for another attack tonight. I, for one, am not going to leave you to such a fate."

"Nor I!" Carlos echoed his father.

Miguel, who had been leaning languidly on his rifle, laughed derisively. He had been unable to get near Malita throughout the entire fiesta because of her brother's constant attendance with the young woman, and he felt justified in calling the boy's bluff.

"Really," he scoffed, "and how do you expect to 'man-handle' them?"

The true meaning of the words were apparent only to Miguel and Carlos. The boy fumed, charged forward, tore the rifle from Miguel's grasp, and fired at the barn. The weather vane toppled neatly from its perch.

Felix was furious. He snatched the rifle from Carlos's hands and growled: "What are you up to? Do you want to give them a signal that we are preparing for them?"

"Hardly!" he snapped. "Just make some people realize that they are not the only *men* in the world."

Miguel chuckled inwardly. It proved nothing more to him than that firearms were little more than sexual symbols and that was why Carlos was so expert with them.

"I think," Señor Esparza said calmly to break the tension, "that Don Felix has a sound point in wishing us all to depart. That is, our wagons, carriages, and womenfolk. Quietly I advise the best shooters to stay behind."

* * *

Throughout the day, in the cover of the hilltop trees, Vince Bowditch had fumed and paced. He had been heartened by the disbanding of the tents and the rapid departure of the wagons and carriages. And the reports of the soldiers that they had ridden through the vaqueros without a single shot being fired had been somewhat reassuring, but still he hesitated on the next step. Captain Harlan Guth was dead, a fact that would not set well with General Thomas Jefferson Green. The men were grumbling that Vince's plan had led them into a near trap. The officers were all dead, only a sergeant remained in command of the rest of the troops. The man was a French-Canadian, with a questionable past.

"Lambeau," Bowditch barked, "what do you see down there?"

"A mass exodus," the burly man chuckled.

"Besides that?" he demanded.

"*Oui*," he chortled, "a rich purse for the right man."

"Or *men*," Bowditch quickly amended. "How do you judge the scene?" He thrust his field glasses at the man before he could reply. A vast row of bodies had been covered with blankets and sheets, and peons had begun to dig a mass grave in a far field.

Felipe Lambeau whistled. "We took a great toll, it seems."

"Great enough that they will not fight if you march in and demand surrender?"

"*Oui*," he said confidently. "But what of yourself?"

It was something Bowditch had not discussed with Captain Guth. Lambeau, he felt, was too wily to be fooled. "I am known to them. The first look at my face would queer the whole deal. Then there is no land for anyone, if you get my drift."

Lambeau's ugly face contorted into a leering mask.

"I see," he smirked, "no arrest, no captives, no witnesses."

"As near as possible, Sergeant. As near as possible."

They rode onto the ranch as an organized military unit, rank and file smartly spaced and in seeming calm. They were not molested by the vaqueros, who let them ride through their hut area and then silently shuffled after them, apparently without arms, to Lambeau's relief.

In the main courtyard, standing on the house steps, the Escovarro brothers awaited them, also unarmed. It increased Lambeau's courage. In the gathering dusk he counted over a hundred bodies that had not as yet been buried. He considered a three-to-one loss on the previous night's raid a great advantage. Even though his men held their guns at the ready, he now anticipated a quick capitulation.

Miguel did not recognize any of the riders. He was unaware of the vast change in the Texas army. The veterans he had fought with had been mostly family men and were even then harvesting their first crop of San Jacinto corn. They had been replaced by mercenary adventurers thirsting for battle with the Mexicans.

"I don't see Bowditch," Miguel whispered as the riders broke rank and formed a semicircle in front of the porch.

"Which proves my point."

Lambeau gave them a crude salute, keeping his face as fierce looking as a gorilla and as repulsive.

"My captain is dead," he said grimly, "which will add another charge to your arrest."

"To whom are you speaking?" Felix asked calmly.

"Both of you," he replied curtly.

"On what charge?"

"Stealing and tax evasion."

"Interesting charges," replied Miguel angrily. "Hardly the type of crimes to warrant the sneak attack that took place here last night. If that is the brand of law and order your kind is bringing to this republic, then we'll have to start arming our vaqueros to safeguard our land. Go ahead and try to arrest me!"

Miguel took one mighty stride off the porch. His last words had been cold. His rage appeared to have been transferred to Lambeau. The sergeant had begun to stutter and shake a lanky red hand at him when one of his men shouted: "Look out! The dead's moving!"

Without waiting for orders, the soldier spun his horse

and began to fire at the covered bodies. His comrades began to follow suit, as Miguel leaped up and caught Lambeau's arm just as he was ready to fire. With a jerk he twisted the pistol hand back against the man's potbelly just as the percussion cap exploded. Miguel staggered back, his hand black with powder burns. Felix caught him and hauled him to the ground as the frightened horse began to rear and paw the air madly. Lambeau cursed violently, dropping the reins and using both hands to hold his stomach together. He started to faint and lost his balance. His weight sent him crashing toward the ground, but his foot twisted and got locked into the stirrup. This sent the snorting horse into greater panic. It charged away at a full gallop, further scattering the huddled knots of vaqueros and bouncing the screaming man along the ground like a rag doll.

Everything had happened so quickly that it took several moments to realize that his receding cries were the only sounds to be heard. Everyone gazed upon the scene in stupefied benumbedness. It had not been planned this way. Here and there among the actual dead and some blanket-covered logs, the conquistadors had lain silently with their rifles ready. Each had been able to peek and select a soldier to concentrate upon. Their only desire was to disarm the soldiers and keep the Escovarro brothers from being taken away. And should they be discovered, the vaqueros were secretly armed and would block the way. But so quickly had the twenty-three soldiers fallen, that not a single vaquero had been able to get his pistol out of his cumbersome waistband.

And again, because of their speed, not a single conquistador was touched.

"How did it happen?" queried Felix with sudden swift start of passion.

Miguel did not hear his brother; he was gazing at his badly burned hand in a kind of imploring amazement.

Señor Esparza was the first to reach them.

"Well, this will certainly bring more soldiers and more war." There was now no trace of the courteous, kindly old don. He looked harder than stone. "I'll let the sneaking coyotes have my damn land. Gentlemen, we may not meet again. I shall move my family to Santa Fe at once. I would strongly urge you to do the same."

"No," replied Felix steadily. "It will take more than this to put me off the land. Thanks, señor, for the way you and the others stuck by us. Come, Miguel, we'd best let Maritza have a look at that hand."

As he ceased speaking, he seemed suddenly to become spiritless. He knew that this was just the beginning of the end, no matter what he could do. Now it wouldn't be just fifty soldiers they would send, but ten times as many. Was it worth it? Was it worth risking all of their lives for a piece of land? But where would they go?

Teresa saw him bring Miguel into the house and sensed his misery. A vague riot in her breast leaped into conscious fury—a woman's passionate repudiation of her husband's broken spirit. It was not that she would have him to be a lawbreaker; it was that she could not bear to see him so broken. After all, it was Miguel's land and not theirs. Let him shoulder the burden and strain.

In the time it took her to make the few steps to their side, she not only felt her anger and sense of justice and pride summoning forces to her command, but there was something else calling—a deep, passionate desire to set the record straight with Miguel.

"Come, darling," she said softly, taking Felix by his free arm. "You're dead tired and need rest."

"I have to get Maritza for Miguel."

"He has a wife who can see to his needs, in case he's forgotten."

Felix dropped Miguel's arm. His face took on a chalky whiteness. The last thing he needed at that moment was another family feud. Miguel, in a slow, stupid embarrassment beyond his control, nodded his head at Teresa in a respect that seemed wrenched from him.

"I think you'll find Maritza with Emilia in your room. I don't want Felix disturbed, for any reason, for the rest of the day. It's not his responsibility anyway."

Miguel's stare underwent a blinking change. He coughed, stammered, and tried to speak. Manifestly he had been thrown completely off his balance. Astonishment slowly merged into discomfiture. The last few hours had proven that he was incapable of running the ranch without Felix. He watched them go up the stairs without him. He was not long disconcerted, but his discomfiture wore to a sullen fury, and his sharp features fixed in an expression of craft.

"Have it your way, Doña Teresa," he said to himself. "Have it your way for now, but I'm putting a price tag on it. I'll get back into your bed yet!"

Thomas Jefferson Green stepped slowly from behind his desk, his breath making a loud rustle in the room.

"All of them dead," he said quietly, "and you now say they were only neighbors there for a fiesta?"

"That's right," Bowditch said sorrowfully. "I holed up for a couple of days, because the Escovarro brothers didn't know I was with the troop. I ran across a nigger and an old Irishwoman on their way back to San Antonio. The nigger was glad to have me ride along with them, and I learned the old woman is the Escovarros' aunt."

The general pondered the point for a long moment.

"It hardly seems necessary for her to lie." Then he grinned. "But very necessary for you to do so."

"I didn't lie," Bowditch roared.

"Shut up, you sniveling idiot! You never listen to what people really say. *Now listen*! For the time being you are to forget that you were at the Escovarros' ranch. Your report will state that the troop was ambushed and killed by Mexican soldiers. Leave the rest to me."

Bowditch sat silent, his face white and still.

Green growled. "Damn it man, I never did see a longer face on a man who'd just given us a golden opportunity to get all the Mexicans out of our hair."

Bowditch's face cleared, but only momentarily.

"But the land," he said, half to himself, "they are still on the land."

"Forget that damn postage-stamp-sized ranch," he stormed. "That's only one family out of hundreds who own vast estates. By the time I finish letting the army know about their fifty dead comrades, they'll be ready to march immediately against the town of Matamoros. They will be led to believe that there are six thousand Mexican troops there preparing for an invasion. My soldiers will carry the town and burn and destroy the main people if they resist and retreat, before they can have time to recover from their panic. After that the Spanish and Mexicans will have little heart to remain in Texas."

Because the ragtag army was nurtured on rumors, it was soon common knowledge that the Mexican invasion force numbered six thousand troops at Veracruz, four thousand at Matamoros. But as Green had slyly anticipated, nothing was done about it. The Texans were without supplies. But his rumor had the exact effect he had been seeking. Confusion prevailed with the thought of further warfare. People grew suspicious of the Spaniards and Mexicans among them, and acts of violence and terror began to flare up throughout the republic. As more and more of the landed people fled, the desertions in the unpaid and underfed army grew. They wanted to take over the deserted farms and ranches before the constitution could be rewritten.

But the constitution came back to Texas in a strange, if not original, way. The errant Mr. Kimble ended his retreat in Nashville, Tennessee. Upon hearing of the San Jacinto victory, he gave the constitution to an editor who published it but lost the original. A Cincinnati paper copied it from the Nashville sheet. An Ohio man, seeking some of that pioneering land, brought a copy with him. A journalist and printer by trade, he was chagrined to learn that the serviceable *Texas Telegraph* was a thriving enterprise. He exchanged the newspaper for the promise of a job, and the next day the *Telegraph* reprinted the constitution. President Burnet put a copy of the paper in his desk, and the republic was ready to move on to the election.

But with men like Green and Felix Huston stirring up the army, little thought was being given to the election. Also, with east Texas denuded of most of its soldiers, the Indians took advantage of the situation and began to attack the increasing number of wagon trains moving into the area. Then eleven days before the election, the republic became electrified with the news that there would be a third candidate.

Sam Houston's reason for running was the soul of brevity: "The crisis requires it."

On the fifth of September he received 5,119 votes to 743 for Smith and 587 for Austin. The constitution was adopted, and a proposal of annexation to the United States was carried almost unanimously.

But his victory looked dangerously into the jaws of defeat. The army wanted war, but his navy was detained in the Baltimore shipyards for nonpayment of repair bills. Santa Anna was still confined on a plantation near Columbia, and the Mexican government was putting pressure on the Jackson administration to secure his release. Houston wanted him released, but the First Congress of the Texas Republic, mostly Smith and Austin men who felt cheated by his election, declined, passing an inflammatory resolution. Houston vetoed the resolution, gave Santa Anna a fine horse, and sent him on his way under a military escort.

This only increased the rancor of the people against anyone who spoke Spanish. With Santa Anna free to raise new armies against them, they wished no spies and traitors amongst them. They, who had been on the land for mere months, were growing strong enough to force people from the land who had been there for centuries.

CHAPTER THIRTEEN

Emilia lay snugly in her four-poster with its ball-fringe curtains half closed to keep her warm against the bitter January winds. She could watch the swirling dust through the crack left open in the curtains of the window opposite her bed. She could not sleep for sheer discontent.

Her thoughts went back to San Antonio, to the fun and excitement of the life she had once led. She had looked forward to her marriage to Miguel Escovarro, feeling it would not just be sensual ecstasy but a sublime marriage of the spirit. She found nothing in it but unhappiness. And the past five months had been the unhappiest of all. He had become meaner and more sadistic than ever, demanding sexual license with her in every way but the one she was no longer able to give. She had tried, but the acts which had once been so natural for her to perform were now repulsive. She tried to hide her emotions, but her noninterest in satisfying his needs orally or anally were apparent, and he would storm from the room. And then she grew too large and physically uncomfortable to even approach. The four-poster became her prison. During her ninth month she was ill for so many days at a time that she refused to see anyone but Maritza, and even with her she was tense and snappish.

It was a prevailing mood about the ranch. Everyone moved and acted like they were prisoners locked within the stocks and unsure of exactly when the guillotine blade would start to fall toward their neck.

Teresa nestled against Felix's warm nude body, rubbing her hand over the golden down of his chest until it tickled her palm. It was not done as a matter of arousal, for they

221

had just finished lovemaking and rolled away from each other.

Felix chuckled. "You're growing less subtle, my dear."

"Oh?"

"Don't be coy," he said, drawing her close. "Of late your amorous nature has always been followed by some profound statement."

Teresa giggled. "That obvious, huh? Well, I do think you are taking over more and more and Miguel doing less and less."

He kissed the top of her head. "That, my little conniver, I thought was your object. He is inept, isn't he?"

"Except in one area," she said forlornly. "I would give anything to change places with Emilia right now."

"Give it time," he soothed. "The doctor will be right, you'll see, and it isn't as though we weren't really trying. As a matter of fact . . ."

She sat up suddenly. "What was that?"

He was instantly alert, expecting to hear the distant report of hoofbeats. Then he heard what feminine instinct must have alerted her to. Teresa was instantly out of bed and donning a robe. "I'll go to her; you find your brother."

The baby was already filling the room with its wail by the time she entered.

"It's a man-child," the Spanish midwife exalted.

"There's another one in there," Maritza cautioned.

"My God, not twins!" Emilia whimpered. "I can't do it again. I'm exhausted."

"We all are, child," she soothed. "Just keep pushing."

"Is there something I could do to help," Teresa asked.

"Sponge her face and arms, please. That first rascal gave us all a devil of a time."

"How long have you been here?" she asked, wringing out a cloth from the basin.

"Seems like forever," Emilia said weakly. "Oh, thank you, Teresa. That feels so good."

"You should have called me."

"No use disturbing the whole place," Maritza said. "Babies come when they are ready to come and not a moment before. And I think this tyke isn't going to be as stubborn as the first. Push now! That's the way. He's coming out straight, so it won't take long."

"Him?"

"Yes, another son. Push, Emilia, push!"

"Oh, God! Oh God, God, God! He's cracking me wide open!" she screamed.

"Stop tensing up! Try to relax and push. Knead her belly, Teresa. Help push him down past the breech, his feet are tangled in the umbilical cord."

"*Hurry!*"

"Don't stop, child. *Force* it!"

Deftly the mulatto pulled forth the wrinkled mass of reddish skin, tied and cut the cord, and gave the child a resounding slap on its pear-shaped behind. It did not respond. Again and again she spanked, praying for the slightest wail.

"Oil!" she demanded of the cowering midwife. "Hot oil!"

"What is it?" Emilia demanded with sudden fright.

"It'll be all right," Teresa soothed, again sponging her perspiration-covered face.

The tiny lips were already turning blue when Maritza pressed her own mouth onto it, pulling with all of her might to clear the small throat passage.

Once, twice, three times she pulled away, spitting out a milky fluid. With her hands she motioned for the midwife to rub the hot oil over the child as she pushed her own air in and out of the small lungs.

"His feet were wrapped around the cord almost too long," she panted. "Quickly, Teresa, that basin of cold water." She raised the infant boy by his heels, preparatory to another swat. "Throw it! Throw it all over him!" There was a weak gasp as the water hit his small nude body, then Maritza struck, leaving a red welt on his behind. But she didn't care; he was filling the room with his undoubtedly male cry.

"That's my boy," she chortled. "Almost did yourself in by wanting to get out of that dark hole, but you be fine now. You be just fine. Here, señora, clean him up. Teresa, tell the father to give me fifteen minutes to change the bed and tidy up Emilia and then he can come in."

Miguel was boyishly jubilant. For hours he had paced the parlor floor, drinking uncountable cups of black coffee laced with brandy, telling himself that he didn't want the child. But one look at Teresa's radiantly beaming face ignited the godlike reflex inbred to every male: he had created a living thing that would bear his image. He didn't even wait to hear what manner of child he was responsible for, but raced up the stairs, burst open the door, and hurled himself into the room. Maritza was laying a tiny, wrinkled little object next to Emilia to feed. Miguel inched forward and looked at it.

"A boy," Maritza said. "Congratulations, señor."

It was small and mottled and as ugly as all new babies are. But it was not bald. Its tiny head was crowned with a mass of golden curls, as light as Miguel's.

A scolding wail erupted behind him and spun him about. Stupefied he watched the midwife lift another small body off the towel-covered bureau and march triumphantly to place it at Emilia's other breast.

"Oh my," he gasped so breathlessly that it made Maritza and Señora Diaz laugh.

"Sí, Don Miguel," the midwife chuckled. "Two niños. And each his own person."

This child was not bald either. His large round head, which had given Emilia so much trouble, was carpeted with straight raven black hair. Together, eagerly demanding nourishment, they were like night and day.

Miguel bent down to Emilia's white, pain-ravaged face.

"You said you wanted another child right away," he whispered, "but you didn't say you were going to do it all at once."

Emilia smiled—a soft delicate smile, with only the slightest hint of mockery in it.

"A son," she whispered. "I knew it would be a boy because of all the kicking. Didn't know it was four little feet pounding at me. I have a name for one, but none for the other."

"Which one?"

"The first one born, I guess. This golden-haired rascal who's trying to drain me dry in one feeding."

"What are you going to call him?" Miguel said.

"Raoul," Emilia whispered.

"Raoul?" Miguel echoed. "Hmmmm . . . Raoul Escovarro. There has never been a Raoul in the family. I like it. For the other lad can we honor my great-grandfather? Ramon—Ramon Escovarro."

"Bless you, Miguel," she sighed. "They go very well together—Raoul and Ramon. *Ouch!* Maritza, I think our friend Raoul has had quite enough."

"And I think," Maritza said sternly, "that we're going to have to check among the women to find a wet nurse."

Miguel chuckled. "You have to be kidding. She must have gallons to spare in those two mountains."

Taking the child from Emilia, she straightened up, towering at an equal height to Miguel. She did not like crude talk in her presence and refused to chuckle as the midwife was doing. Although she had remained stoically silent, she had been very much aware of the misery and strain he had caused his wife. It wasn't exactly hatred she felt for Miguel, but it came very close. She knew exactly how to get the man out from underneath her feet. She started to place the child in Miguel's arms.

He backed away in near panic. "Hell," he said with gruff tenderness, "I'd probably break him." He turned and fled.

To Emilia's unending delight Miguel took a deep interest in his sons and tapered off on his drinking. When her body felt mended, she allowed him to come back to her bed. He was at first slightly hesitant, as though she had become as fragile a thing as one of the infants. She accepted his gentleness as a welcome sign and gave of herself freely and lovingly. His new attitude eased many tensions on the ranch.

In March, 1837, Big John returned to the ranch, supervising three Mexican-driven Conestoga wagons.

"Never saw anyone make up their mind so fast," he told the family, still slightly amazed himself. "Doña Patricia got the letter from New Mexico one day and started packing the next. She said that all of her furnishings were to go to

Felix and Teresa so that they might start a home of their own some day."

Miguel snickered. "I must have been about thirteen when Mother's cousin stopped off on his way back from Spain with a new bride. Do you remember him, Felix?"

He looked puzzled. "You don't mean that bumbling little fat man who always slobbered at the dinner table?"

"The very same," he laughed. "It's hard to picture Don Ricardo de Sanchez as the governor-general of New Mexico. He was such an incompetent."

"I think he must be very brilliant," Emilia said abruptly.

"Oh, really," Miguel said fretfully. "The man would do nothing without getting the simpering approval of his wife— a woman ten years his senior, I might add."

"My point exactly," she said. "What with his wife now a hopeless invalid, I think it is a brilliant move to ask Doña Patricia to come and act as his official hostess. She'll be running the governor's palace and his fiefdom in nothing flat, I'll bet you."

"I wouldn't take that bet," Teresa laughed, "if I were you, Miguel."

Felix was still puzzling over the matter.

"There must be something more to it," he said thoughtfully. "She was never one to act on impulse alone. Big John?"

"Well, Mistah Felix, from Christmas on everything started to depress her. Wasn't a day go by that some of her old friends didn't come by to say farewell. Then she took Mistah Austin's death badly."

"Stephen Austin dead!" he said in surprise.

"Yas, suh, some say it was because President Jackson told Congress not to recognize Texas as an independent republic or as a state."

"Damn," Miguel exploded gleefully, "that puts everything in limbo. The treaties Burnet signed with Santa Anna are worth no more than the paper they're written on."

"That's what Miss Patricia say too, suh," Big John beamed, taking full advantage of the fact that he had been the woman's main sounding board for the past several months. "She say it'll mean war soon as ole Santa Anna gets back to Mexico."

"Back?" Miguel's face was filled with astonishment.

"He making a tour of the United States. Folk back East calling him a hero for opposin' de rebels and tryin' ta keep slavery from dis area."

Miguel opened his mouth to ask a further question, but the parlor door opened suddenly and Maritza ushered in a panting and eagerly excited Guido Herrera.

"Excuse, please, señor and señoras," he gasped, dropping a brass-cornered wooden box on the floor. "I find in one of the carcasses in the smokehouse."

The corners of Miguel's mouth worked, but try as he would he could not speak. Felix stood for a long time, looking at the box, his handsome face filled with tenderness. Then he stooped and undid the bolt of the lid. Miguel surged from his chair all at once and began to examine the contents, whispering over and over: "Oh, thank God! Thank God!"

"What is it?" Teresa asked.

"Father's strongbox," Felix replied with amazement. "We automatically assumed it was destroyed in the fire. Thank you, Guido."

Maritza caught Big John's eye, motioning him from the room as though to imply that they were intruding on a family matter. Guido bowed his way out after them, his heart swelled with joy.

"Look at all this money," Miguel exclaimed, "and here are the land-grant documents."

"Neither of which may do us any good," Felix murmured.

"Good?" Miguel said. "We can always take the money to Mexico City and exchange it for gold. And the documents give us evidence to fight them in court. Oh God, I feel good! We've got to celebrate. At last I have something to leave to my sons."

Felix's face darkened.

Miguel had turned happily to Emilia and didn't see the look. "When we were children," he enthused, "we were not allowed to see or touch these documents. Aren't they beau-

tiful? Just look at that parchment and ornate lettering."
Slowly he began to read aloud the stilted language and the
grandiose phrases to extoll the reasons why a grateful king
was showing so much largess to so faithful a soldier and
servant. Then came laborious legal phrases giving the lon-
gitude and latitude lines of the land granted. Then he
stopped suddenly.

"Felix," he said, "I never was any good with all this gib-
berish. Why so many directional clauses?"

Felix hadn't been fully listening. He had been experiencing what Doña Patricia's husband must have once felt like.
There was a form of slavery in their Spanish world: he
would always be a slave to Miguel's prior birth.

"What?" he started. "Oh, I don't know. Let me see."

He studied the figures with a deepening frown. "I'm no
engineer or navigator," he said slowly, "and I wish father's
globe hadn't been destroyed. Still there's no doubt that there
are three different sets of figures here. Do you ever recall
father giving the location of this property?"

"If he ever did, I didn't pay any attention. Now how in
the hell do we figure it out?"

"Would—" Teresa hesitated. "—knowing the location of
New Orleans help any?"

"A great deal," Felix said. "We know that we are west
and south of it."

"Then I hope I've remembered correctly," she laughed.
"While we were keeping the water out, during the hurricane, I remember that man Bowditch saying something
about our being all right if the captain just kept the boat
heading thirty degrees north and ninety west."

"Good girl," Miguel enthused, pouring back over the
document. "This must be it, Felix. The one that starts
twenty-nine degrees north and ninety-nine degrees west."

"Then I don't understand these next two," Felix scowled.
"They are similar, as if adjoining, but are six degrees farther west and about the same north."

"That doesn't sound like much," Teresa said.

"A degree, darling," Felix explained patiently, "is about
sixty miles. In other words, somewhere about five to six
hundred miles northwest of here."

"Felix," Miguel cried, "do you realize what you just said? What it really means? We've got land grants in New Mexico."

The salvation of the moment was that Miguel had said "we've got." the burden seemed to lift from Felix's heart and shoulders. There was, after all, some place to run to if their present situation became too intolerable.

"Oh God!" he breathed. "And unless I'm mistaken, they each appear to be much larger than this present ranch. If only we knew what the land was like."

Miguel was on his feet now. Then with a gesture that was absurd and touching at the same time, he dropped to his knees in front of Emilia.

"Em," he said slowly, "I know the boys are young—that it would take me away for several months—but I've just got to see what this land would be worth to their future and the future of Felix's children."

Emilia laughed unexpectedly. "I think it might be a very good time for you to go away," she smiled. "If I'm not mistaken, I'm going to have another child."

In April 1837, Jimmy Yerby finally made it to the banks of the bayou where the new capital, Houston City, was springing up. He might have stayed with the Escovarros forever, after his wounds had healed, but he had a burning ambition to repay them for their many months of kindness.

It was raining, and he had to wade through water above his ankles to get to the president's mansion. It was little more than a small log house consisting of two rooms and a passage through, after the Southern fashion. He entered the anteroom timidly and saw there was no need to clean his boots as the floor was muddy and filthy. A large fire was burning, and a small table, covered with paper and writing material, was in the center. Camp beds, trunks, and different materials were strewn around the room.

"Pardon," he said softly to a young man seated on a stool. "My name's Jimmy Yerby. I was the general's drummer boy and would be grateful for a moment of his time."

"Are you aware of the hour?" he sniffed indignantly.

Jimmy blushed. "Not rightly. I got myself lost in the swamp trying to find this place."

"Well, that's an honest answer, at least. You may be in luck. The president just returned from a ball at the capitol building and may not have retired yet."

Jimmy blinked. "Y'all got a capitol building already."

The young orderly roared with laughter. "It's only a barn and leaks like a sieve, much to the discomfort of the congressmen and the ladies trying to dance around the mud holes on the floor. Wait here."

A moment later Jimmy was ushered in to be presented to His Excellency. Houston wore a velvet suit and cravat, somewhat in the style of his flamboyant youth. Jimmy hardly recognized the man.

"Jimmy, my boy," Houston roared, "you're a welcome sight."

"Don't mean to disturb, Gen'rl," he stammered.

"It's my standing order," he boasted, "to see every man who asks of my time. Besides, it ain't often I get to talk to a ghost." Then he scowled. "Or are you a wee bit of a deserter?"

"Neither," he quickly protested. "That's why I'm here."

Houston eyed him suspiciously. "Pull a stool to the fire, son, the night is chill. Last I heard tell of you was that you had perished with the rest of your patrol. Now what can I do for you?"

Now that he was in the presence of the great man, his throat and mouth became cottony. "You could oblige me first, sir, with a drink of water."

"If only all requests of me were so simple," Houston sighed, going to the back door of his room and calling out to the adjoining lean-to that served as a kitchen and servants' hall for his two Negro retainers, Esau and Tom Blue.

"Esau! You, Esau!"

"Yes, Marse Gen'l."

"Fetch some water for my young guest."

"Where ah gonna find wattah dis time ob night?" Esau inquired.

"If we have none," Houston said impatiently, "then go down the street to Aunt Lucy's. If that aged Negress had water to wash my clothes, she sould have some for me to drink."

While he was gone, which was a considerable amount of time, Jimmy was able to inform Houston of every event that had taken place.

"Neat trick," Houston said with admiration, "but I would expect little different from the Escovarro brothers. You like them, don't you?"

"I guess that's why I came to you. They treated me square, and I think what our soldiers were trying to do to them was dishonest."

"To say the least," he scowled. "It saddens me, on what was supposed to be a happy night. We were celebrating, my boy, the fact that President Jackson changed his mind on his last day in office. We will be recognized." Then he amended sadly, "In time. Another former president, John Quincy Adams, is trying to talk us to death in Congress. Oh, Esau, there you are. Where's the water?"

The old Negro went into a lengthy excuse on why he returned without it.

"Esau," Houston said dejectedly, "can you believe that this is I, Sam Houston, protégé of Andrew Jackson, ex-governor of Tennessee, the beloved of Coleto and his savage hosts, the hero of San Jacinto and the president of the Republic of Texas, standing at the dead hour of midnight in the heart of his own capital, with the myriad of rain-drops falling down outside my window, begging for water at the door of an old nigger wench's shanty—*and-can't-get-a-drop*?"

Esau reflected upon the words of his master. "Dat's jest right, Marse Gen'l. We sho' ain't got no wattah."

"Get the hell outta here!"

"It's all right, sir," Jimmy grinned. "Gettin' that misery off my mind seemed to have quenched my thirst."

"Thank you for coming, son. I will personally put a right to this wrong immediately."

And even before Jimmy was fully out of the room, Houston was carrying a candle to his littered table and running terse phrases over in his mind. But after he had addressed the letter to Thomas Jefferson Green, he paused. To accuse the man Bowditch in written words could cause scandal and make it appear that he was against land-reform measures. The young republic was near bankrupt, and he could not chance scandal or the influx of new people and their money. He chose his words carefully so that General Green would see that this was an individual case that had been very badly handled.

"In the case of the east Texas land of the Escovarro family, it will be henceforth unmolested."

Near the bottom of the page he signed his name. Sam Houston enjoyed doing that, for his swelling autograph was a work of art. And because the republic still did not have a great seal of its own, he continued to use his personal cufflink to impress in wax its engraved heraldry of the Scottish barons of Houston.

"Marse Gen'l," Esau came flying in. "Ah held a mug in de rain ta get yah wattah."

But in his excitement to please, he had filled it to the very brim, and it slouched over onto the letter.

"Damn," Houston fumed, blotting at the paper with the sleeve of his velvet suit. "You'd best find some bourbon to go into it now. I may have to sit up longer redoing this spoiled letter."

But on closer inspection he saw that his ornate signature was intact and only the last word of the letter slightly blurred. The letter would stand, but he would still accept the bourbon. He folded the letter and called in the orderly to deliver it that night, even if it meant waking General Green.

Green was still awake, and Bowditch in his company. An obstreperous army had upset the Texas government of Burnet and were hardly impressed with Houston to date and were discussing how to make him look more ridiculous. Green read the letter and scoffed.

Bowditch paled upon reading it. "He knows everything!"

"Bullshit! He probably got a plea from the Escovarro brothers and no more. They are too smart to tell him the whole truth or else he would be demanding an investigation. I'm tired now, Bowditch. Send Thackery in as you leave."

But General Green did not retire. He and his aide studied the document for over an hour before the general nodded his agreement and dismissed the man for the night.

A jubilant Vince Bowditch arrived back at General Green's tent early the next morning, only moments after Thackery had placed the document before a beaming General Green.

"What is it, Bowditch?" Green growled.

"This," Bowditch boasted, pushing a frightened Jimmy Yerby into the office before him. "I found him wandering around this morning looking for his outfit. He's a survivor of the patrol."

Green didn't alter his facial expression, but at that moment he loathed Bowditch's stupidity with a consuming rage. With a curt order he commanded Jimmy to be seated and Thackery to escort Bowditch outside the tent.

He instantly mellowed into a fatherly pose, grateful to see Jimmy alive and overly concerned as to what had happened to his brother-in-law's patrol. His manner put the youth entirely at ease, and the exact story he had told Sam Houston was repeated. Green was a natural-born con artist; he grew morose over the telling and indignant that he had been betrayed by Bowditch. In a storm of fury, that was not all show, he left Jimmy sitting alone in his tent while he went to confront Bowditch.

"Bastard," he whispered through clenched teeth. "This kid has told everything to Houston. Don't let him see you, but get your damn butt back here in five minutes. Thackery! Take the kid away as though you were leading him to his new outfit. Jail him with the hard-core deserters. I don't want him alive by sundown!"

Jimmy Yerby had been impressed by General Green and the rapid efficiency of Sam Houston. Even as they had spoken, he had seen the large signature of the president on the letter before the general and decided he could be quite honest and truthful with the man. He felt proud that he had in a small way been able to help the Escovarros for saving his life and decided to take a quick peek at the written words. Then his heart froze as he laboriously read:

"In the case of the east Texas land of the Escovarro family, it will be henceforth undertaken by General Thomas Jefferson Green and his agent Vincent Bowditch."

Unaware of the clever forgery performed by Thackery, Jimmy's head spun in utter confusion. In less than eight hours he had been betrayed by two men he had put his confidence in, and the words of the letter were burned into his brain. When Captain Thackery came for him, he departed calmly, still slightly stunned. He had heard the talk about the Escovarro ranch but had not fully understood it. Now he was fully aware but unsure if he had been wise to come to this place at all.

"There," Green growled, thrusting the letter at Bowditch.

The man's grin broadened as he read. "Son of a bitch," he howled. "How in the hell you'd bring this off?"

"It hardly matters," Green said with icy calm. "It's a sealed document, but can't be revealed. How many men will you need to present it *properly*?"

"None," Bowditch barked. "This time we do it my way."

"And how," Green said airily, "is that?"

"I'm goin' home. The next time I see that land, I'll be backed up by wagonloads of my family, my equipment, and my slaves. With this document and that, then they'll know I've come to stay."

"You don't read too good," Green sneered. "It says you are only my agent."

"Readin' don't change facts, large-mouth! I know how to make that land make money for us out of cotton. You don't. Think that over while I'm gone."

A quarter of a mile away Jimmy quickly put his fists together and violently swung his arms back into the stomach of Captain Thackery. The man fell instantly to the ground, his sight and breath momentarily suspended. He sat stunned, a vague image of the youth darting into the swamp before his eyes. Then he relaxed, without raising an alarm. More rescuers, he reasoned, had vanished in that swamp than deserters they had been sent in to find. He considered it a far more appropriate fate than that which the handsome young youth would have experienced in the jail among cutthroats who had been without a woman for months. After all, he was an expert forger and could counterfeit a death report on the youth for General Green before sundown.

CHAPTER FOURTEEN

Felix kept Jimmy Yerby's news to himself and prayed for Miguel's quick return. He hired the lad to ride the eastern range to give them early warning of the approach of soldiers or wagon trains.

The violet haze of bluebonnet spring slipped away to humid summer. A normally busy time of the year was made busier by Felix. Quietly determined to move on his brother's return, he had wagons repaired, old equipment altered or discarded, and began a careful selection of the better bulls and cows. He understood the science of breeding on that land and prayed he'd selected the type of beasts that would thrive best farther north.

At the end of the fall roundup he was forced to make a major decision without the absent Miguel. Culling the cows and bulls he did not want, he had the vaqueros divide them into two herds. Fearing to leave the ranch himself, he put his trust in Jimmy Yerby to head the drive of beef cattle to San Antonio. The bulls and yearlings would be headed south by Guido Herrera and a band of vaqueros. South of Laredo he was sure the Mexican ranchers would quickly buy the two thousand head of prime reproducers.

These were months that slipped quickly away for some. With this child Emilia suffered not at all and was not the least bit worried or discontented over Miguel's long absence. In November she gave birth to another son, so quickly and painlessly that it amazed Maritza. The woman had "three darlings" to care for and a strange beating in her heart that she had thought she'd never feel again: she was falling in love with Big John.

In mid-December a Santa Fe family passing through to

237

Monterrey for Christmas brought the first news of Miguel.

"The land," he wrote, "is vaster than imagined. The two parcels are cut through by a common river . . . and though quite cold at present was warm and fertile this past summer. It lies about ten miles from the Esparzas, who all send their regards. It is about a quarter-day ride from Santa Fe, which is a charming city laid in a bowl of mountains. Tía Patricia sends her love. My delay is due to problems with Cousin Ricardo's fear that we are taking too great a bite of land, and it will hurt him politically. He is as he always was, a buffoon. With warmer weather I shall have the whole grant surveyed."

Everyone chose to overlook the fact that he had not asked after his wife and children or sent them his love. In actual fact it had never crossed his mind. He had been far too busy with a survey of his own—a complete and thorough survey of the anatomy of Malita Esparza.

These were months that seemed to stretch into an eternity for others. Teresa remained barren and began to fear that the doctor had been wrong about her being able to have children after her unfortunate miscarriage. Outwardly she was loving and caring for her husband, but that seed of fear was a hard stone in her heart.

On the banks of the Buffalo Bayou Sam Houston was serving out the last days of his first term. Friend and foe alike advised him against the humiliation he would suffer in being soundly defeated for a second term. He took their advice by remaining nearly continuously drunk. Lone Star money fell to fifty cents.

General Mirabeau Buonaparte Lamar was elected with ex-President Burnet as his vice-president. Things didn't move fast enough for the cavalry officer at San Jacinto. He ceased negotiations for annexation to the United States and pressed to make Texas a separate country. A Georgia boy, he saw nothing wrong with slavery. He declared war on the Indians to purge them from the land, recruited an army to make menacing gestures across the Rio Grande and make life miserable for the "native" Mexicans. He loathed Houston City and began to build a new capital on the upper Colorado, which he named Austin.

Thomas Jefferson Green had fallen into disfavor when Lamar was secretary of the army. Prudence being the better part of valor, he retired for the duration of Lamar's term to a plantation he had secretly acquired near Houston City.

Vince Bowditch was learning that time had stopped for him in Virginia, and he was having a hard time making it start up again. His death at San Jacinto had been falsely reported to his wife. For months she refused to believe it, but at the end of a year she gave up all hope and married Vince's brother Edward, who was a widower. Three months before his return Edward deserted the near spent farms and took his family away. Vince was ill prepared to let his brother keep his wife and started a frantic search that would consume a year of his life and end in failure.

Samuel Thackery, upon sorting out General Green's papers, came across the forged Houston letter. He deftly stuck it into his own portfolio for future consideration.

Estavar Escovarro was six months old when his father returned. Miguel hardly recognized the twins and was suddenly aware of something that had not been apparent at birth. Raoul, for all his golden locks and coloring, bore Emilia's Aztec black eyes, high forehead, and cheekbones, a thin nose, square jaw and full, sensuous mouth. And like his mother was a proud and haughty extrovert. Ramon was quiet and sensitive. His raven black hair made his milk-chocolate eyes seem even lighter. Although he would wear to the grave the patrician Escovarro nose, the rest of his features were Germanic.

Estavar was unmistakably a carbon copy of his father in every aspect. Miguel could only stare at him in wonderment. Even though the ranch was now in a frenzy of departure arrangements, he would sneak away and come to gaze down into the cradle.

Emilia came into the room and paused just inside the door. She had a letter in her hand.

"An army messenger just brought this," she said.

Miguel turned away from the cradle and took the letter. Swiftly he tore it open and read it.

"Now," he said, when he had finished, his voice heavy with disgust, "we know the Houston letter to be the truth."

Emilia looked up in surprise.

"Letter?" she asked. "For what?"

"This land. The letter introduces a Samuel Thackery as an agent for a General Green. Houston has ordered the land undertaken."

"Do you want me to find Felix for you?"

"Hardly!" he snapped. "I can handle the matter quite alone. Besides I want to let the man sit and stew for a while."

"I thought things would be different," she said morosely, "but you have done nothing but bully Felix since you've been back."

"He had no right to sell off so much cattle," he protested.

"No, Miguel," Emilia said quietly, "that isn't all there is to it. Even before you knew about that, you said what a hard trip it was going to be. Harder, now that we know not all of the families want to go with us. You want to be the center of everything but can't do it without Felix. I didn't understand the family power structure until I was grown, but I do understand now. I don't want that kind of life for my sons. I don't want Raoul and Ramon growing to hate each other because one is five minutes older than the other."

"But, Emilia," Miguel protested, "that's the way it's always been."

"Then it's time for a change," she said evenly. "Felix's request was reasonable, I thought. Why not let him have one of the two land grants?"

"Now you're talking foolishness!"

"Am I? I'm sorry. Only, Miguel, I don't want the same strained emotions in our new home as we have here. And the situation would only get worse when Teresa starts having children. In time our children and their children would be fighting just as much as you and Felix."

"You don't understand," he growled. "It's a simple matter. Life is not going to be easy up there at first. The biggest and toughest ranch we can build will win out. You can't change that."

"I think I can. Do you know why?"

"No—why?"

"Because I'll leave you if you don't do something to give Felix something to strive for. Oh, I know that doesn't bother you. You'd have another woman in your bed before my carriage was out of sight . . . only, Miguel, I'll take the children with me, and you'll never see them again as long as you live."

Emilia could see the livid spots of rage appearing on Miguel's cheeks. But she could see something else, too, the tiny glow of fear in his eyes; and she sensed the smell of victory.

Miguel crossed over to the crib and stood looking down at the baby. Then he put out one thick finger, and Estavar caught it in his chubby fist, cooing with delight.

"You—you wouldn't," he said gruffly.

"Perhaps for Estavar, more than any, I would do it. Twenty years from now, do you want him hating his brothers because one of them has to be the focal point of attention?"

"No!" Miguel roared.

It's strange what a hold the baby has on him, Emilia thought. Thank God for that. Now I really have a weapon I can use against him.

Miguel stood looking at Estavar. He's so like me, he thought, so very much like me. Montezuma's gold on his head and eyes like chips of fresh-hewn oak. I think, little fellow, that I am in awe of your brothers because they are two. But you are really the firstborn in my heart. His own thought stunned Miguel for a moment. Estavar would be the Felix of his family, the third male child. No, he wanted much more than that for this child.

"You win," Miguel croaked. "I'll talk it over with Felix."

"See that you do," Emilia said serenely.

Samuel Thackery was astounded by the size and apparent wealth of the ranch. He had come alone, determined to play the whole matter low key. As there was as yet no physical evidence of a move, he felt doomed from the start. Taking stock of the situation, he saw they had enough manpower to hold off a small army. Even if they accepted the Houston letter as fact, it didn't mean they would meekly pack up and depart.

"Well, Thackery," Miguel cackled, "I should know that signature well enough. It's as brazen as the letter itself. Exactly how are you supposed to be acting as General Green's agent?"

Thackery leaned forward, his eyes bright and eager. This was capitulation. He had to think quickly.

"Captain Escovarro," he said smoothly, "I am only a middle man and wish no rancor."

"That is a slight improvement over the last agent sent here."

Thackery flushed. He had misjudged Miguel.

"That, sir," he said quietly, "was unfortunate. The man acted quite on his own and has been sent back to his home in Virginia."

"When I was with General Houston, a man would have been shot for such an act."

"I don't believe," Thackery murmured, "he was informed of all of the facts."

Unless Jimmy Yerby had lied, Miguel knew quite differently. And because he knew, word for word, exactly what the letter was going to say, he had to believe Jimmy had seen Houston.

"Why then," Miguel grinned, "did he write this letter? It's almost open thievery." He tapped on the letter with his fingers in a show of contempt. "Of course, now that he is out of office I could prosecute. I believe it was General Green who persuaded the army, almost to a man, to vote him into office. This is a very handsome political payoff, is it not?"

"Oh—no!" Thackery gasped. "Nothing like that!"

He was slowly being trapped. There was no way he wanted the matter to go to court, no matter how shoddy the court system was, because the forgery would be exposed at once.

"What then?" Miguel said evenly.

"There are many land problems," Thackery spluttered, fishing for words. "People fighting and killing each other over the breakup of the deserted plantations and ranches. I think the intent was to keep this beautiful spread as a single unit."

Miguel frowned. Then his face cleared up. He remembered how taken Sam Houston had been with the ranch when he had visited it during the days of his father. It was becoming very clear to him now. General Green was nothing more than a stalking horse for Sam Houston. As long as the man had been president, he could not openly take the land he coveted, but would do it through another.

"That still tells me nothing," he growled. "It shall remain a single unit as long as I have both feet upon the land."

Samuel Thackery fingered the brim of his hat and glanced uneasily at the man. A desperation move had entered his head, and he saw no reason not to give it a try.

"My client does not want to be looked upon as a thief," he got out hoarsely. "I am authorized to offer you ten thousand for the land."

Miguel eyed the man icily. "Your generosity overwhelms me." Then he roared. "That's less than ten cents an acre, to say nothing about the buildings and the crops already in the ground for this year. Thief! Goddamn robbers!"

Thackery sat back, satisfied it had not been a flat refusal. He was no longer thinking of Green or Bowditch. He knew where he could get his hands on twice the amount he mentioned. Then it would be a legal sale. Then he could destroy the forgery and let it become a misplaced page in history.

"I am willing," he said firmly, "to take back to my client your proposal for a rate you would consider decent."

Miguel decided to be conciliatory, while biding his time. Later, after Houston met his demand, he would strike. Sam Houston would have to be brought to heel once and for all: he now realized, after serving so long with the man, that he was not only greedy but dangerous.

"Tell the man triple," he announced.

"Sorry," Thackery said ruefully. "I'd like to take that

report to them, but I can't. Double is about as high as they might go."

"Between us," Miguel said, leaning forward confidentially, "that was the figure I had in mind. Any amount over that you are able to squeeze out of them, I'll pay you the commission at any rate you specify."

A gleam stole into Thackery's eye. He would be making money back on his own money.

"Seven percent?" he suggested.

"All right," Miguel agreed at once. "How soon can you be back here?"

"I'll have to go into the states for the money. A matter of four to six weeks."

"All right," Miguel said slyly, "I'll be here waiting."

Samuel Thackery rode away with dreams of glory spinning in his head. Everywhere he looked he began to feel the pride of ownership swelling his breast. He had no fear that he would be able to raise the additional capital.

Miguel watched him depart, a gleam in his eye. He was well aware, because of the constant flow of news that came down the Santa Fe Trail, that Sam Houston was on a tour of the United States. Thackery's assessment of four to six weeks seemed to confirm for Miguel the fact that that there was where the money was coming from, for he suspected that General Green was still in Texas. He knew that he could have held out and bargained for more money, but money was no longer an object in his mind.

There was, perhaps, reason enough for Felix's jubilant mood. Miguel had not only agreed to give him one of the New Mexico land grants but had informed him of the possible sale of the present ranch, although the price seemed incredibly low. There was, however, something that puzzled him. Miguel wanted the ranch ready to move in no less than three weeks. Felix was to lead the emigrants, while Miguel remained behind with the vaqueros who had decided to move back to Old Spain. Miguel's reasoning was that the fields and ranch had to be kept in order until the purchaser arrived, and although it sounded reasonable, Felix was still troubled by it. But a new thought pushed it far back into his mind.

He sat down at Teresa's father's old desk, in their sitting-room alcove, and undid a thick roll of papers so long tightly rolled that the pages refused to lie flat. He took the inkwell and some ledgers from a cubbyhole to secure the edges.

Gingerly he began to turn back each of the flimsy sheets and examine them. He was not very proficient at it. But he began to understand more as he went along. He had never built anything in his life but knew that Guido Herrera would be unable to read the plans.

He became so absorbed in his task that he didn't hear Teresa enter the room.

"Felix," she whispered. "Oh, Felix, Emilia just told me!"

"She could have left that to me," he said testily, folding the sheets back to the first and trying to cover them with his arms.

"But, Felix," Teresa said with gentle insistence, "it wouldn't have come about without her. What are you up to?"

He didn't answer but reluctantly removed his arms from the desk. The finely inked lines were brisk and easily recognizable.

The color slowly left her cheeks, so that the dimple pits stood out vividly against her pale skin. At the corners of her mouth a little tremor started. She stood still, looking at the drawing, then all at once she was against him, clutching at his shoulders.

"Felix," she whispered. "Oh, my darling Felix . . ."

He bent her down and sought her mouth, deep pink, soft fleshed, wide and generous. He was surprised, when he opened his eyes, to see that she was crying.

"Isn't that what you asked for? The blueprints for Beauwood."

"Yes," she said suddenly, fiercely, "but I wanted to fill it with our children."

"Teresa! Oh, Teresa, honey, we'll have them."

But she pulled away from him wildly. "I wonder? Emilia already has three and with little effort on Miguel's part."

Felix laughed. "Remember that one of them was an extra bonus."

Teresa came back, dejected. "I'm sorry. I just haven't been myself lately. I should be feeling happy for you that Miguel gave in."

"Or happy for yourself that you'll at last get the home you dreamed of."

"It is beautiful, isn't it?" she said, sitting down on the arm of the chair.

Together they began to leaf through the plans. He was acutely conscious of her slim hands tracing about the floor plans. Each time he glanced at Teresa, an aching void formed in his middle and expanded and contracted with his breathing.

I want her child, he told himself. Oh, my God, how I want her to have children! He had begun to comprehend, dimly, how vast a change had overcome Emilia. She had become motherly, witty, warm, and enduring. He wanted all those things for Teresa and more—much more. He not only would build her home for her, he would build her the finest ranch in New Mexico.

"Honey," he said suddenly, "you look so funny! What's the matter?"

"Just a little hot flash, that's all."

"You don't mean?"

"No, Felix."

"No, Felix!" he said bitterly. "Isn't the answer ever going to be 'Yes'?"

"Yes, darling. My heart prays for that answer all of the time. But I think this is just a little stomach disorder."

In the three weeks before their departure the "stomach disorder" became so frequent an occurrence that Maritza began to grin knowingly. By the morning of their departure it was a forgone conclusion that Teresa was with child, and the vaqueros looked on it as a great omen for the journey.

"You'll have no trouble following my charts," Miguel boasted. "Just follow the Pecos River north. Here I have marked where it joins the Santa Fe River. That is where our land starts, north and south of the Santa Fe. About here, where the cottonwoods are thickest in this glen, I thought would be a good place for the ranch."

"We'll see," Felix said huskily, "when you get there. How long will you be?"

"Two to three weeks. I should meet up with you on the trail. You're not going to make more than ten miles a day with this crew."

Felix looked at the thirty-six heavily laden wagons and the saddled vaqueros and sighed: "I wish they all would have come with us."

"Shit!" Miguel said hoarsely, "we only lost a little over a hundred. Cousin Ricardo is going to piss his velvet pants when he hears you are arriving with two hundred fifty-eight men, women, and children; two hundred hogs, chickens and goats; seven thousand head of prime cattle and wagons full of the type of farm and ranch equipment they have never seen before. You've done well, little brother, putting it all together so successfully."

"Thank you," Felix said without a trace of warmth. "How many men are you keeping here to help run the ranch until the purchaser arrives?"

"No more than twenty," he answered indifferently. "But none that are coming north with us. I hired only single vaqueros who want to return to Spain."

He did not tell Felix that part of their wage was to include their passage money home or that they had been sworn to secrecy.

Felix looked at him wonderingly. "As many as that? For what?"

"Do you want me to meet them alone?" he snapped. "They would murder me, take the money, and still have the land."

Felix put out his hand.

"Then I hope you've kept enough. I don't want the responsibility of raising your brood."

Slowly Miguel put out his hand, and Felix crushed it in his big paw.

"Look out for them," Miguel said gruffly. "Especially, young Estavar."

Controlling the wagon train, Felix found, was surprisingly simple for the first eight days as they rambled across the fertile plains to the point where the Rio Grande and Pecos rivers converged. Then came fifteen hard and tortuous days of climbing up between the Stockton and Edwards plateaus and onto the bleak west Texas plain.

Anyone watching the ranch during that time would have witnessed a strange scene: old plows, drag lines, broken axles, lengths of timber of every sort were lashed to the backs of the vaqueros' horses. It had taken three months for the greening fields to be plowed and seeded and cultivated, but it took only five hours for twenty men to lay them clean and demolished. Day after day other areas of the ranch were destroyed, and the vaqueros received gifts of hard liquor that left them totally incapable of remembering what they had done from one day to the next.

The cattle salt licks, too weighty and cumbersome to be carted to New Mexico, were pounded to powder and sown upon the farmlands, the orchards and vineyards chopped and hewn so that they would never sprout again. Storehouses, barns, and the vaqueros' old houses became pyres of white hot flame. What adobe walls still stood after the holocaust were pulled down and smashed back to clumps of clay. Then, on the last night of the drunken spree, the vaqueros sat around a bonfire made by the burning of every last piece of old equipment that had been left behind. Their pockets were filled with Miguel's money, their bellies and minds overpowered by the liquor. They laughed and joked and sang and danced and wrestled with each other. They were going home, and that was all that mattered. They were Basques, mainly, brought with their small herds of sheep to the New World no more than a decade before by Raymundo Escovarro. The raising of sheep was one of his few failures, and the herds were at last eaten, perished on loco weed, or became the targets of the coyotes. But the Basque shepherds had been forced to stay and become farmers or vaqueros; but Don Miguel was now setting them free, and nothing he requested was illegal in their minds.

In the after-midnight darkness, Miguel stumbled through the debris that had once been the Ranchero de Oro. In his pack he carried several bulky objects, but he walked calmly through the rubble as though he were strolling along a residential street. When he came to the last structure still standing on the ranch, he leaned against the porch columns that supported the second-floor balcony. It was strong, built to last a century or more.

Miguel hunched his shoulders and entered the house he had hated from the first moment he had seen it. Now that it was devoid of Emilia's furniture, it no longer seemed such a threat to him. The rooms were now cold, impersonal, lifeless. Ruefully, he thought, just like his life with Emilia unless she wanted a child.

Sadistically he went first to the room he had shared with Emilia. Then, suddenly remembering that this was the room in which he had produced Estavar, he darted across the hall to Felix and Teresa's room. He pulled out several of the long, bulky objects from his pack that were like great sticks tied together and fastened them under the supporting arches of their room and alcove, making sure the fuse was long and trailed after him. He left that fuse in the foyer. He walked through the darkness until he came to the support wall between dining room and kitchen and placed more sticks. He retraced his steps until he came back to the archway between living room and parlor. Again he fastened some sticks on the support columns for the center of the house, wiring them securely.

He came back to the foyer, knelt, and a brimstone match flared in his hand as he cupped it, shaking it until it blazed, and lighted the first fuse. Then with a sadistic chuckle he walked to the next fuse, and the next, lighting each fuse calmly. He left the house, still walking slowly, joyously. He knew how long each of the fuses had been cut.

Sitting down on a pile of adobe which had been the barn base some five hundred yards from the house, he waited. He did not have long to wait. It happened very cleanly, just as he had planned. All four corners of the house lifted at the same time, and the hollow booming shook the hills. Then a second later the roof flashed fire, and the house buckled inward slowly.

Miguel sat very still until the air was no longer filled with bits of adobe and flying timbers.

Then he stood up, grinning.

"Well, Sam Houston," he said. "How much are you willing to pay for it now? My only regret, you son of a bitch, is that I won't get a chance to see your face."

The Basques began departing before dawn. They began to fear that a madness had overcome Don Miguel and that they might be killed to assure their silence.

Miguel was too drunk to leave that day. He sat beside his pitched tent and surveyed all the black, arid ugliness he had created. It delighted and saddened him, all at the same time. With each drink his hatred grew for all men who thought they had the right to take another man's property because they were stronger or had been victorious in a war. On a drunken oath he vowed that never again would he let any man take a single thing from him.

A week later another oath was uttered on the land. The speaker was gaunt and travel worn, his face a study in near apoplexy.

"I'll build it back!" Vince Bowditch screeched. "I won't let them do this to me!"

"It's hardly how you described it to me," Thomas Jefferson Green chuckled.

"I'll have the law on them!" Bowditch shrieked. "I'll put them in jail for so long that—"

"What law, Bowditch? I know of no law which says a man can't destroy his own property."

"It wasn't theirs," he screeched. "It was mine! Mine!"

Green shook his head sympathetically. Bowditch had returned to Texas without finding his wife or children. It had altered the man, making him harder and crueler than ever. Green had come with the man only because he thought he would be in a better position to bargain over the land, after he couldn't find the Houston letter in his portfolio. He had fully expected to find his former aide, Samuel Thackery, using the letter for his own needs. He found, instead, no one to bargain with and nothing to bargain over. He found it a rather wry joke. Without even saying good-bye, he turned his horse and began the long ride back to east Texas.

A week later Vince Bowditch knew it was useless. It

would take the land a decade to recover from the salting, he discovered, and he was a man alone with no capital to replenish the herds or orchards. He felt so lonely and dejected. The thought of the ranch was the only thing that had kept him going after failing to find his wife and children. Now he had nothing to live for but the burning hatred in his heart. The Escovarros had cheated him of *his* land. If it was the last thing he did, he would repay them for his misery.

He saw the rider from a long way off, a slow-moving, shimmering mirage in the heavy summer air. He had nothing better to do but watch the advance and note the apparent change of emotions as the horse was spurred to a trot and then a full gallop. The horse and rider churned about the former compound as though they had accidentally stumbled into the wrong place and couldn't find an exit.

"What—what happened?" Samuel Thackery gasped, slipping quickly from his horse to stand beside Bowditch. "Was it an Indian raid?"

"Fucking bastards did it themselves!"

Thackery turned an amazed face toward the man.

"Impossible," he gasped again. "Don Miguel agreed to a sale price."

"With whom?" Bowditch growled.

Thackery, like all con artists, was able to sort out his mind quickly. Bowditch was alone, in a horrible unkempt condition, and seemed to be disoriented of mind.

"When you did not return for so long," he answered smoothly, "General Green had my name added as his agent. I have the letter to prove it. The Escovarros would have fought an outright take-over, so I negotiated a sale price to take back for approval."

"With Green?"

"Who else?"

Bowditch was confused. His mind was dull from misery and unsure if Thackery or Green were the liar.

"Where is he now?" he asked to pinpoint the matter.

Thackery shrugged. "I had to go to Louisiana to raise the necessary funds, and he was not at his plantation when

I returned. I came directly here so that the Escovarros wouldn't back out on the deal."

"The bastard!" Bowditch got out. "He was going to cut me out without a word."

"He didn't hear from you," he said, feeling more comfortable in the lie. "What happened?"

"None of your damn business," he barked. He now had a score to settle with Green as well as the Escovarros. "There's beans and bacon in the kettle, if you've a mind. I'm turnin' in, 'cause I want to ride out early."

Thackery had been looking forward to the luxury of a good meal and a soft bed—after he had offered Miguel Escovarro the twenty-five thousand dollars in gold. He reluctantly settled for the overly salty beans and pondered what manner of madness would make a people cause such destruction and havoc when a sale was pending. He could only surmise that Bowditch had returned and somehow screwed up the deal. Sunset turned the adobe piles to near flame color, and it only saddened him more. Waste, he thought sadly, what a horrible waste. It was the last thought he had.

Bowditch had plunged the knife deeply, twisted it so that it would tear at the heart, and jumped back, prepared for a counterattack. The man slumped forward and didn't move. Bowditch kicked the body twice to make sure and sat down to finish off the beans and bacon. He had accomplished the only thing he had in mind; to make sure the man didn't get back to Green before he had a chance to.

He spat out the salty beans in disgust. He rose and went to see if the man had anything different to eat in his saddlebags. He was delighted to find a couple of strings of beef jerky and began gnawing on one while his other hand rummaged deeper into the leather pouch. He withdrew the man's calfskin money bag without giving it much thought. He took it near the fire to dump it out and count his find.

Bowditch's eyes turned as round as moons in his thin face.

"Of course, you ass," he cursed himself. "He said he was coming here to buy the place."

Frantically, he took the saddlebags from the tethered

horse and dumped their contents on the ground. Trembling, he retrieved three similar money bags and dumped them with the first. Never one who had been good at arithmetic, he laboriously stacked the gold coins in piles of ten. A gleam stole into his eye.

"Hundred-dollar coins," he gasped. "Two hundred and fifty of them!"

He hardly seemed interested in the pile of five and ten and twenty-dollar gold coins, although they amounted to another five hundred dollars.

"I just beat you, Gen'l Green," he chortled. "I got your money, and you ain't got nothing. Time I forgot about you and put your money to helpin' me get even for what they did to my land."

But with more money than he had ever had in his life, Vince Bowditch was unsure of what exactly he would do. He was unsure if the Escovarros had gone north or south. He was unsure what he would do when he did find them.

Then he became sure of one thing. He was a rich man. Rich enough to afford the time to hunt down his wife and kick his brother's butt for having married her. He was also rich enough to buy slaves to do his work for him. Suddenly the Escovarros had become third place in his priorities.

On that same evening Miguel Escovarro looked down from a red bluff ridge at the encircled campfires of the wagon train. The cattle, divided into herds of a thousand each, looked like huge black blotches. He, too, was sorting his desires and wishes into one, two, three order. The wagon train had been on the trail for over twenty days—halfway there, he determined. He could join them and help with the more difficult days of creeping into the foothills that would climb to become the Rocky Mountains. Or he could spur his horse northward, making the distance in less than a third of the time it would take them. This would give him an opportunity to make sure that his name was recorded for the larger, more fertile land grant on the southern banks of the river; leaving Felix with the rising, rocky hill section to the north. He knew he could persuade them that he had missed them in transit; after all, it was a very large and vast area they were traversing. Besides, he reasoned, it would give him ample opportunity to borrow help from the Esparzas and have a structure nearly ready for his family by their arrival. That would scotch any doubts or questions of impropriety.

Impropriety? Suddenly his last thought for wishing to press onward became first place in his desires. His body hungered so for Malita Esparza that he knew he would never join the wagon train. For nearly a year he had carefully turned her into the seductive-type bedmate that Emilia had once been. He had been able to do it without further complications from either of the Esparza brothers, and she had been a constant ache in his heart during his days at the ranch. These days, before Emilia arrived, might be the very last he would be able to spend with Malita. He turned north, without giving another thought to the wagon train or what problems it might be undergoing.

He was unaware that this was the second night for the train to remain at the same campsite—a position they would hold for a further five days.

Teresa had miscarried. Far more severe than the first time and they feared that if she were moved, she would die; they feared that even if she wasn't moved.

On the fourth morning, near dawn, the cattle began lowing and moving about restlessly. The vaqueros rode slowly among them, soothing the herd with gentle words and searching out the reason for their discontent. There were no rattlesnakes about nor sign of coyotes. Water was plentiful from the river, and the summer range was full of wild grass. It mystified the men.

"Madre Mía!" Guido Herrera gasped, squinting at the eastern horizon. For four days he had looked to that rise of land in anticipation of spotting Miguel Escovarro. But this morning, as the sky streaked gray, the barren horizontal line separating earth and sky had vanished. Overnight a forest had sprouted and was silhouetted against the dawn mantle.

The vaqueros now knew the reason for the cattle's unrest but were still unsure of what it was that they were looking at. Not even Felix could reassure them. He had never seen anything like it, but he had an uneasy suspicion in the pit of his stomach. They stood staring, until their eyes hurt from the ball of summer fire that seemed to spring up behind the phenomenon. The coolness of night vanished, replaced more by the warmth of human fear than the sun's rays. Silently Felix gave the signal to keep all firearms at the ready.

Cascading down the slope, a tightly packed throng of Indians stood staring back at them, their cook fires laid but unlit, their two to three hundred wigwams emerging as the cone-shaped forest that Guido had first spotted.

Each side seemed to be weighing and measuring the strength of the other. It was easier for Felix to calculate, because the Indians were all standing in the open; his own people were mainly still within the close-packed tongue to tailgate enclosure made by the wagons and carriages. He knew he was outnumbered by at least ten to one.

As the sun cleared the wigwam spires, six of the Indians jumped to their horses and began moving cautiously forward. One brave held aloft a staff, attached to which was a white cloth that hung limply in the breezeless morning air.

"I don't want them too close," Felix said. "Guido. Pick four men to walk out with us."

"Sir," Jimmy Yerby said, pushing forward, "might I be one of them. I lived for three years with the Cherokees and might understand their dialect."

Felix nodded his wholehearted approval of the offer. But when the walkers and riders were within fifty yards of each other, it appeared his offer would not be needed for the moment.

"Greetings, brothers of the brown skin," a powerfully built brave shouted in musical Spanish, urging his horse forward from the others. "We wish you no harm."

Felix motioned the men to stop and walked forward alone. The brave slid gracefully from the pinto pony and came to within five yards of Felix.

"Señor," he said, "I am Ta-Tak-To, son of the chief of the Santo Domingos. We reside in our pueblos near the great waters that you call the Rio Grande."

"I am Felix Escovarro. My people go to reside near the

Great River on waters called the Sante Fe. You and your people are a long way from home."

The Indian nodded grimly.

"These are not my people, señor," he said. "This is all that remains of the Quapaw nation. Their chief is dead. Behind me are his five sons, of which one will become chief on this last day of mourning for their father."

"How do you come to be with them?"

"It is a story," Ta-Tak-To said slyly, "better repeated if we sit in council. My Quapaw brothers are still wary that men such as you are different from the pale-faced ones."

The twelve men solemnly sat down in a cross-legged circle. Ta-Tak-To took from his pouch a handful of ground cornmeal and threw it into the center of the ring.

"Maize is the Mother of all earthly life," he intoned in his Shoshonean tongue and then repeated the phrase in Spanish. The Quapaw braves could understand his words for it was not unlike their Siouan dialect. Also it was so similar to the Iroquoian language of the Cherokee people that Jimmy Yerby understood almost everything said.

"My Pueblo people are agricultural," the Indian went on, continually repeating himself twice. "My brothers of the brown skin are also men who plant and herd their cattle. Now that the Mother of earthly life is with us, no fork-tongued words may be spoken, or she will make the crops fail."

As though the men had been through the ritual before, they all nodded that it was a fair statement.

In the Indian tradition of having to relate a full tale, even if only one of the group had not heard it before, Ta-Tak-To went slowly over the facts as though the teacher of primary students.

His people were also traders. A month before, when the first corn of the season was harvested, Ta-Tak-To's father saw that it would be a bountiful year, and the blessing had to be shared or it would bring misfortune. He sent his son and twenty-five braves, their horses laden with woven strands of corn ears, to the Red River valley and the wigwams of the Quapaw. The corn was a gift, and he expected nothing in return. But a gift could not be accepted unless a

gift was given in return. Po-Nee-Chee coveted the wild
horses the Quapaw tribe rounded up on the plains of east
Texas and used as barter with other tribes.

The day after his arrival at the Quapaw village they
learned of the war the new chief of the Texas pale faces
was waging against the Cherokee. It had amazed the chief
of the Quapaw, for he had gone and sat in Buffalo robes
with the chief called The Raven. Sam Houston had promised them, as he had the Cherokee and other tribal chief-
tains, that there would be no war. The Indians could not
understand how there could be a new chief when the old
chief wasn't dead.

Without warning the Texan army stormed the Quapaw
village. It was a savage, brutal battle. The Quapaws were
horsemen and had little use for the white men's "fire
sticks." Their bows and arrows were near useless against
the heavy firepower of the army, and over half of the tribe
was annihilated, including the twenty-five Santo Domingo
braves. They fled, with the army constantly attacking them
until they were out of Texas territory.

Day and night they had moved westward and were near
exhaustion when they spotted the fires of the wagon train.
Fearing it was the army, they pitched every available wigwam to make their numbers seem larger by the light of
dawn.

"It certainly had that effect," Felix agreed at once.
"However, you could have lighted your fires and made us
tremble at their number."

Ta-Tak-To grinned broadly. His teeth were straight and
even and so white that they contrasted vividly with his burnished copper coloring. Now that he was relaxed, Felix
could see that he was younger than he'd first appeared—a
man in his early twenties. His shimmering black hair was
carefully parted in the middle and held back by a colorful
band tied around his forehead. When he grinned, his black
eyes took on diamond sparks and his wide nostrils flared.
He was one solid piece of muscle from his bull neck to the
wide ankles that disappeared into doeskin moccasins.

"The fires," he laughed, "were not lighted out of fear of

you, señor. They will only be rekindled when the tribe has a new chief and new life. Besides, after our scouting party determined that you were Spanish, I was able to calm the fears of my Quapaw brothers. I had to tell them that the fathers of our fathers' father smoked the pipe of peace when we allowed your men of the brown robes to come and build their missions. I had to tell them that the men of the brown skin had helped our Pueblo people many times against the murderous attacks of the treacherous Apache and Navajo peoples to the west. I had to tell them that your people do not bring their cattle with them when they wish to make war."

Felix sat back, looking at the brave with real admiration in his eyes.

"I thank you for reassuring them," he said softly. "What will become of them now?"

"When they have a new chief, they will go north from this place to the land that lies below the mountains that are forever white and know no summer. There the wild horses still roam and the buffalo can still blot out the sun with a dust cloud from their stampeding hooves. For a while yet, it is still too wild a place for the men of the pale face. And now, as is custom, my friends will expect the story of how you come to this place."

Felix's telling was simple, blunt, and to the point. Ta-Tak-To's translation was more lyrical.

"For as many moons," he told the Quapaw braves, "as there are eyes in the night sky, this man's people have lived upon the land known as Texas. As it happened to you, the long rifles came and said they wanted the land. The one of the golden hair, like corn silk at autumn, had his men fight them and win. But being a wise chief, he knew they would come back against him with as many numbers as they came against the Quapaw people. And like you, he gathered up his people to take them to a place where men would rather grow things out of the ground than spill blood into it."

"I didn't say that much," Felix whispered to Jimmy Yerby.

"Hush!" Jimmy croaked, his throat tight with emotion. "His translation was the truth."

The five sons of the dead chief thought so as well. They put their palms on the bare thighs of their crossed legs and began to beat vigorously.

It was a welcome sound to the Quapaw people. The council was peaceful, and they began to rhythmically slap their hands together in approval and give their negotiators encouragement.

The sound also pleased Ta-Tak-To, although his face remained immobile. Although his own tribe might never hear of this day, it would remain in his heart. His people were famous for their ability to be the mediators in squabbles between various tribes. He considered the day a marvelous learning process. He was twenty-four and also the fifth of five brothers. Since the day of his rites into manhood he had been fully aware that he would never become chief of the Santo Domingo, so had directed his talents toward tribal rites, healing, and intratribal diplomacy. This day, which would be shared only with the ears of his father, might help atone for the loss of twenty-five braves on his first mission.

But like all people of his race, there was a point still unmentioned that held him in curiosity.

"Señor," he said, "the Quapaw scouts traced back your trail during the night. Is there reason why you have not moved in four moons?"

Felix's face darkened suddenly. The council had been going on for over an hour. Teresa had been in a grave condition during the night and here he sat with Indians instead of her. He saw no reason to lie.

"My wife," he said ominously. "She has lost a child and a great amount of blood. We are afraid to move her."

Ta-Tak-To's head came up. There was a flare about his wide nostrils.

"Have you no medicine man with you?" he demanded.

"We have a woman with some knowledge."

"Bah!" he growled. "Squaws are good to give birth but know nothing if there is trouble. You take me to her, at once!"

Felix got up slowly, slightly confused. Although a tall man himself, Ta-Tak-To seemed to tower over him when he rose. The five Quapaw braves rose but did not move away.

Ta-Tak-To, in his concern for the woman's health, had almost forgotten the immediate need of the council in the first place.

"Señor," he said, "we will walk away from the Mother of earthly life in peace. As a token for your desire for such peace, it would be generous of you to show your goodwill by helping these people who are near to starving."

Felix blinked. "Of course. I have some barrels of shelled corn that I was going to use for planting, and I'll have the men cut out a few head of cattle for slaughter."

Ta-Tak-To translated quickly and began laughing before the answer was fully given by one of the brothers.

"Excuse my laughter," he said, "it is not meant as disrespect to your generous offer. The corn, my own people will repay you so that you do not go without a harvest. The white man's cattle, my Quapaw brothers say, tastes very wild to their peoples' tongues, but they accept it gratefully. Now, to the sick one."

It was almost as great a shock for Maritza to hear the Indian speak Spanish as it was for Ta-Tak-To to view his first black person.

Although leery of what manner of medicine he might practice, Maritza was respectful and gave him a complete description of what had happened and of Teresa's condition.

Upon entering the tent, he again dug into his pouch and began sprinkling cornmeal all around Teresa's cot. The act not only raised Maritza's suspicions but her eyebrows. The man was so silent in his performance that Teresa was unaware of his presence. But never once, as he rounded the cot, did Ta-Tak-To take his eyes away from her.

In his life he had seen many Spanish women. They would come to his adobe pueblo village with their brown-skinned husbands: the men to purchase the better grade Santo Domingo corn and squash for their own planting; the women to barter for the intricately woven baskets and handsome pottery of the Pueblo women. But a woman such as this, even though her face was ashen and pain wracked, he had never seen before. He could not allow such beauty to be taken on the never-ending journey. He motioned Maritza outside.

Emilia had heard from Felix about the Indian and had come to see if she could be of any assistance. She looked up at the man, her face taut and still.

Ta-Tak-To sensed rather than saw that there was Indian blood in the woman. He felt instantly at ease with her, as though he had just gained an ally.

"Señora," he said to Maritza, "cattle are to be slaughtered to feed the Quapaw people. I shall require at least four cups of the first-drawn neck blood, as warm and fresh as you are able."

Maritza looked at Emilia as though she had just been ordered to worship the devil.

"Do it," she said softly. "Señor, I am the woman's sister-in-law. Is there anything I can do to help?"

He thought her voice as lovely as her face. Thinking back on the men in the circle, he could not imagine her being the wife of any of them.

"You may," he said. "I go to the riverbank. When I return, I will instruct you and the black one. I am yet without squaw and cannot look upon the body of another man's squaw."

The man interested Emilia but not in a sexual sense. He was so powerful looking, but his voice had been as soothing and reassuring as a gentle hand laid upon her arm. Deep in his eyes she had seen the soul of the man's fear for Teresa's life and the stubborn determination that it would not be taken. She instantly gave her full confidence to him.

Ta-Tak-To prayed to the God-husband of the Mother of earthly life that the mud of this bank would be the same as that of the Great River. He cut the wider blades of the saw grass and laid them crisscross until he had a platter. Then he lay belly down on the levee and intently studied the crystal-clear water. His shadow disturbed the trout, but it was as he hoped, because his intent was not to fish. He watched them disappear into the mud bank, as though by magic the brown curtain had swallowed them up. Quickly he thrust his arm into the icy water and closed his fingers around the oozing mud. Time and time again he would extract his hand, let the excess water drain away as he expertly studied his catch, and would plop it gently onto the saw grass. When he felt that the mound was sufficient, he rinsed off his hands and took his cargo back to the tent.

Maritza was awaiting him, bearing a pottery bowl nearly filled with an almost black liquid, and her stomach near ready to retch at its pungent aroma.

"You may set it down," he instructed, "for I have yet to prepare it. Señora," he said to Emilia and suddenly felt a little embarrassed, "I—I wish for you to pack this around her . . . ah . . . where—"

"I think I know," she said quickly, saving him further embarrassment.

He saw Maritza stiffen, her whole body rigid suddenly, and her face blank with incredulity.

"Mud?" she gasped.

He ignored her. "It must be applied gently and then fanned. Watch it carefully, señora. The moment the top crust starts to dry, it must be taken away and I will bring fresh."

Slowly Emilia shook her head.

"It's—it's not the mud," he said to win Maritza's support, "but what is in it. It is only a covering to keep the fish eggs from drying too quickly. It is their substance which will help make her thin blood become thick enough to stop flowing."

Maritza still snorted her disapproval and a few moments later really felt her stomach retch as he poured cornmeal from the pouch into the bowl and stirred it with his hand. The already thick blood became a liquid paste.

"Now," he advised, "you must make her drink at least four cups of this. If it makes her ill, let her rid herself of it, and then make her drink again. Soon her body will accept it, and it will help make the fish eggs do their work."

Maritza was tempted to dump the mess out the back of the tent but knew Emilia wouldn't allow her. Teresa was so weak and feeble that she was hardly aware of what they were doing to her. The first cup was barely a quarter consumed when she did become violently ill. Once it was out of her system, she lay back convulsing.

"No more of this madness," Maritza scowled.

"Come here and fan," Emilia commanded sternly, taking the cup from her. She lifted Teresa up and supported her to control the shaking. With soothing words she got Teresa to start drinking again. This time she had nearly finished the cup when Emilia sensed what was happening in her system and quickly grabbed a basin.

"No more," Teresa pleaded as Emilia wiped her face with a cloth.

"Take a sip of water to wash out your mouth," Emilia said, without relenting, "and spit it into the basin."

"This mess is drying," Maritza warned.

"Let him know and then clean it off." She dipped the mug into the bowl and held it again to Teresa's lips. Teresa stubbornly locked her jaws and refused any more. Emilia grabbed her about the neck, just below the jawbone, and squeezed until the lips and teeth parted. She poured the liquid quickly, massaging Teresa's neck until she was forced to swallow. In spite of the fact that the sticky substance was gagging her, her stomach did not revolt against it. By the time she had consumed a third cup, a new mud pack had been placed between her legs. She collapsed against Emilia. Tenderly she was laid back and her hair stroked with a loving hand. Within moments she was having her first normal sleep in days.

Until midafternoon she was unaware that the mud dressing was changed five more times.

"She's no longer bleeding," Maritza said with mild surprise. "It has worked."

"We should never have doubted," Emilia said tiredly. "Something similar was probably known to my Aztec ancestors and yours along the banks of the Niger."

Maritza did not answer her. She stood there, staring down at Teresa's peaceful face. In old Cuba what she had just done would have been called voodoo. She had vowed when Teresa took her away from Beauwood that she would never again look backward. Emilia's words were trying to force her to go against that vow, and she would not have it. To keep from thinking, she turned her mind to another matter that had her more concerned than Teresa. To keep from going backward, she was aware there was only one way to go forward. She would tell Big John that she would become his wife.

That night the Quapaw fires burned brightly. They had corn and meat and a new chief. It was a night of rejoicing and ceremony. When the sun had set in its western nest, they said good-bye to it and the past. Dawn would bring them a new sun and a new beginning. They said special prayers for the Spaniards for helping change their fortune. They would set their eyes northward, saying good-bye to their Santo Domingo friend and adding ten ponies to the twenty-five he arrived with. Ta-Tak-To would join the wagon train and lead it to its own future.

"The gift," Ta-Tak-To informed Felix, "was given very grave thought and consideration. The horse was selected for the new chief because it was the finest of the entire herd. Chief Oo-La-Te bids me to present it to the don of this tribe. To show his respect, he will select a lesser mount."

The horse was a magnificent creature, its coat and mane like polished black onyx. There was no other marking on the proud beast, just solid black from head to tail. It stood as though fully aware of its ancestry and would willingly accept a conquistador upon its back again. Its eyes measured Felix as he took the guide rope as if to question whether one of the man's kin had ridden his own to this land before the Indians knew that such beasts existed.

"He is a most handsome gift," Felix said graciously. "So that this day and this friendship shall never be forgotten, I shall call him Quapaw."

When Oo-La-Te told his people what name the horse had been given, they knew that his first official act had been a wise one and that he would be a strong, loving, and unselfish leader.

Felix Escovarro was just as strong and loving and unselfish. The moment he saw the animal, he knew that there was only one person in the world who could sit its back and match its nobleness. Quapaw would be for Teresa alone.

Because Ta-Tak-To was well acquainted with the area, they left the twisting, turning Pecos River and moved in an almost straight hundred-and-fifty-mile line from water hole to water hole.

From berries and herbs collected by the Indian, Maritza reluctantly made nasty-smelling teas for Teresa. But her strength and health came back so rapidly that the woman kept her thoughts to herself.

Teresa felt an awesome gratitude toward Ta-Tak-To, although he would not let her utter a single word of thanks. Now that she was again vital and healthy, his heart was crushed that she belonged to another. He knew he would never be able to find such a woman for himself among his own tribe.

But another male did steal away Teresa's love. At their first meeting Quapaw came directly to Teresa and nuzzled her cheek with his velvety nose.

"Oh, Felix," she squealed, "he's gorgeous."

He laughed. "We're going to have to build a ladder to get you that high."

Ta-Tak-To grunted and did an impulsive thing. He put his powerful hands about Teresa's waist and deftly lifted her to sit sidesaddle on the bare back. Upon realizing that he had actually touched her, his heart nearly stopped and a cold sweat broke out on his broad forehead.

Quapaw looked back as though to approve of her being there, and then his nodding head and mane made Teresa and Felix laugh. The woman and beast were inseparable for the rest of the trip.

CHAPTER FIFTEEN

By the early spring of 1839, the Ranchero de los Dos Hermanos—the Ranch of the Two Brothers—was a reality. For a time, among the other ranchers, it was considered a single unit. It was not so for Felix and Miguel. The division caused more bickering and fighting than had they remained as one.

The first contention was over the division of the land, which Miguel won. Then came a struggle over the livestock, which was an even draw. Hostilities intensified over the equipment until it was recalled that Doña Patricia was still owed for the majority of it. This brought about a real clash over the purchase price of the old ranch. Miguel flatly refused to discuss the matter or to share the profit.

The biggest donnybrook, however, involved other people.

"You can't just divide them like the cattle!" Felix roared. "We don't own them, you know!"

"Don't we?" Miguel whispered maliciously. "Then let's see who can outbid the other for their services."

There was no bidding for Maritza and Big John, who had spoken words of mutual love and respect to each other and considered themselves married. Maritza would not leave the children, and Big John wouldn't consider leaving Emilia.

Because of the composition of the two ranches, the majority of the farmers and a couple dozen of the vaquero families stayed with Felix on the hilly northern side of the river. To the majority of the vaqueros the southern foothills and gently sloping plain seemed more suited to their type of cattle raising. Because of the prices Miguel offered, several farmers remained with him to produce the hay and grain and fodder plants that would be required.

One other used common sense to make his choice.

"I'm sorry, Don Felix," Guido Herrera said with great embarrassment. "It's not the money that he offers that will keep me on that side of the river. You may hate me forever for saying this, but you are quite capable of running your own ranch and affairs, Don Miguel is not. Besides he is hardly ever there."

And also because of the composition of the two ranches, they took on a completely different look. Because he had the room, Miguel laid out his ranch exactly as his father's had been: the adobe homes of the vaqueros and farmers erected in straight, streetlike rows; the barns and pens and coops and smokehouse of the same size and dimensions; and, in time, even the pink adobe villa he had known as a child began to rise on a grassy knoll. He told himself that he was doing it for Estavar's future, but in truth it was a vainglorious attempt to prove that he was *the* don of the Escovarro clan.

On the northern bank it was impossible to find a spot that would have been suitable for the erection of a second Beauwood. Although the home Felix designed and built was spacious and airy and comfortable, its two-story sprawl seemed humbled by the towering pink walls that glared down at it mockingly from across the river. The house had two saving graces over its pink counterpart: it sat quite alone on its terraced hillside, the farm and ranch buildings nestled down in the dell behind. Nor was there a jumble of family quarters. Because the farms had to be carved out an acre at a time from the slopes and numerous small valleys, each farmer built his adobe home nearest the fields he would work in the growing patchwork-quilt landscape. A mile inland, where the country became a gently rolling mesa that stretched to the base of the towering Rocky Mountains, the vaqueros built their corrals, holding pens, barns, and family units.

The majority of this was accomplished before Ta-Tak-To came across the Rio Grande from the Santo Domingo Pueblo with an equivalent amount of seed corn that Felix had given the Quapaws. He was duly impressed by what he saw but was more uncomfortable around Teresa than ever before. She truly loved her home, even if it wasn't her cherished dream house. She truly loved this new land, and it seemed to return that love by making her strong and constantly healthy. Used to much lower elevations, nearly everyone else on the two ranches had suffered through the winter months with constant bouts of colds and grippe. It was so hard on Emilia that she went through her worst pregnancy of all and gave birth to a scrawny, sickly little girl.

But the mile-high clime, the brisk refreshing air, the crystal-clear snow water she would bathe her face in, returned to Teresa that look that could at one moment be as fair and dainty as an innocent twelve-year-old and at other times as aristocratically beautiful as a Goya painting of a Madrid matron.

Ta-Tak-To had tried to put her out of his mind, even winning disfavor with his father because he refused to take a squaw. Now her face was etched on his brain as though with acid, and he could not stand the longing in his heart. He made his excuses and stayed with them only part of the day, vowing he would bend to his father's demands no matter who the squaw might be. He would leave behind his unspoken heart.

Miguel Escovarro had watched the progress through unseeing eyes. He had become a vacant shell, his mind tormented by the memory of the night before their arrival and the nights he had spent away from the ranch since then. He loathed himself each time he departed the Esparza ranch, vowing never to return again. But his flesh would weaken, and he would return. He did not loathe himself for the lies to cover his absent nights. He was becoming an expert at self-deception.

Then Emilia, without knowing it, added insult to injury.

"Damn!" he breathed. "Why do you want to call that ugly brat that?"

"All newborn babies are ugly," Emilia said slowly, although she had never seen one as pinch-faced and fierce looking as this child. "And I've always considered Malita to be an uncommonly beautiful name."

"I think it's as ugly as she is, and I'll never call her that," he screeched and stormed from the room.

Emilia lifted her fine head proudly. And, even as her heart sank, she knew what she must do.

An hour after Guido Herrera found Jimmy Yerby droving cattle for Felix, the young cowboy shyly entered Emilia's room.

"I understand," she said after greeting him warmly, "that you are visiting the Esparza ranch a couple of times a week."

Jimmy blushed crimson. "Yes, ma'am," he stuttered. "I ain't exactly welcome except to one party over there."

That was exactly the information Emilia sought, but she was not quite ready to spring her trap.

"Still," she said slowly, "because you do visit them, I would be thankful if you would carry an invitation for me. I'm planning a fiesta to celebrate my daughter's birth. As you go there regularly, it will save me sending someone."

"Well . . . I . . . sure."

His hesitation, the crimson skin turning scarlet, and the fact that he could not look her in the eye, told her that he was well aware that someone closer to her had much more opportunity to deliver such a message than he.

She hid the gathered information behind a mirthful laugh. "You young swains are all alike. Embarrassed to admit that you've grown sweet on a girl. I have only met them once, you know. Which one is it?"

"Dorothy," he stammered, ". . . Dorotea."

"I seem to recall," she mused, "that she was the younger one. What was the other girl called?"

"Malita," he offered, without knowing how damaging his evidence had been.

"Yes, that's right," she smiled. "And I believe two boys, correct?"

Jimmy's face darkened. "Yes," he said sullenly, "Guillerno and Carlos."

He feared the one and loathed the other, and it was totally evident in his face and voice.

Emilia sat back and nodded, greatly pleased. "Then I shall make the invitation for six. When do you next anticipate visiting them?"

"Not until the weekend, ma'am."

"Plenty of time," she cooed, "plenty of time."

After he was gone, she thought it was a simple matter on the surface. There had been a time when Miguel's big fingers had but to touch her hand and the wild sweet madness started. He could kiss her casually, unthinkingly, his thoughts far away, and she went down fathoms deep in tenderness and rose to leaping flame. It was no longer like that. Mother of God, it was no longer like that! She was now a mother first and a wife second. Once she had threatened to leave him and take away his children. That, she now saw, would not be the answer. She wanted a home, *this home,* and stability for her children. She was not above fighting dirty to keep it that way.

The next morning came graying in. Miguel Escovarro ran a hand over his jaw, feeling the bristles that had sprouted during the night. He was aware, too, that his mind and body were a flaming torch, but the sensation was not new to him. He had been experiencing something similar each time he left the Esparza ranch. But this time he had no remembrance of the ride home. He could not even remember climbing from his horse and staggering toward the villa veranda.

Surely no man had ever been called upon to bear anything like the guilt that was sanding him down like a sharp rasp. Even as he stumbled and fell against the front door, the reality of the nightmare he had been living began to close over him.

"What is it?" Emilia asked anxiously after Big John had him in bed and Maritza was examining him.

"Mumps," Maritza said sourly, "from the feel of his glands."

"But he's too old," she protested.

"Worst time. If we don't keep him warm, they'll move down."

"To where?"

Without speaking Maritza nodded toward his groin. Emilia had to quickly turn away, a sly smile of poetic justice on her lips. Perhaps, she thought, that is the exact place where he should suffer.

But when they were unable to control the disease and he did begin to grow like two enflamed balloons, it was his mind that suffered more than his ball sac.

Again and again and again the visions of the last few month's experiences would come into focus, defuse, and then get entangled with the next scene.

In the secrecy of Malita's wide four-poster bed he would be well aware of her artful sating of his every desire. Then the intruder would come slithering into the bed and attempt to join. Even in his feverish condition, Miguel could hear himself screaming at Carlos to leave them alone. But it was not the effeminate Carlos seeking Miguel; it was the masculinely built Guillerno who wished no male contact with Miguel. His desires were even more depraved, the sharing of Malita at the same time.

Something salacious in Miguel's makeup made him give silent consent, and only at the conclusion did he begin to feel sullen and guilty. He tried to forestall a second happening, while secretly desiring it. He tried to tell himself that he needed such a contact because Emilia had arrived on the new land pregnant again.

The game was now being played solely by Guillerno Esparza's rules or not at all. Sexually sadistic in nature he would flaunt his sister's body in front of the sex-starved man and then only offer him a slim portion of it. Miguel wanted Malita completely alone and sensed that she desired the same. When it was denied, he stormed from the room and crashed over Carlos who had been spying on the other side of the panel. To bring Malita to her senses, Miguel's mind became a vengeful thing. He grabbed the boy by the hair and forced his engorgement upon him until he was fully sated. The only reward he received was Guillerno's mocking laughter.

Miguel vowed to never return again. After a month he began to see that it was not so much the sexual satisfaction he had received that enticed him but the danger it represented. At any moment, in the hall or Malita's room, the

272

elder Esparzas could have come upon them. It was the excitement of that danger that made him return, made him share an all-giving bed with the three of them, made him go away more disgusted with himself than ever. Like a child who cannot stay away from a forbidden candy dish, he came back again and again until he was doing things out of craven desire that he never dreamed he would do in his life.

And never once, in or out of his feverish condition, did he consider he was capable of never having let it happen. He blamed, instead, Emilia's pregnancies for denying him his manly due. He blamed Malita for having two brothers who desired her body and his body in any manner, way, shape, or form they could obtain it. In his troubled mind he was the put-upon victim of it all.

And when a mind is that troubled, it seems to slip cogs and combine hatreds. When his fever reached the point where it was either going to kill him or break, a single face was all he was capable of holding in his troubled brain. Felix was his tormentor and the bane of his existence.

When the mumps began to recede, the fever did not. He was unaware that summer slipped into autumn and then winter. He was unaware that his hair began to fall out by the handfuls and that the fever had eaten away fifty pounds, his weight returning to the trim hundred and seventy that it had been when he was a youth. On his large-boned frame that weight was virtual emaciation, and those who saw him now were shocked at the change in him.

He became aware of it all by Christmas, and his heart became as bitterly cold as the snow on the Sangre de Cristo range. He fretted and swore at his total baldness and was a very bad patient, continually trying Maritza's patience. Even when it became possible for him to get out of bed, he refused. Day after day he would sit in his shuttered room, a nightcap continually on his bald head, his mind centered on a single new worry. The first day of February, when he could stand the worry no longer, he sent Maritza for Emilia.

Emilia came—out of curiosity, for she had abided by his

wishes and had not seen him since he had regained consciousness.

She stood back, her jaw sagging, seeing Miguel thin, bent, his cheeks hollow, great dark rings around his eyes. She stood still, her dark eyes somber and questioning, knowing his present condition had little to do with his illness.

"Emilia, I—" Miguel began.

"Yes?" she said quietly. "Yes, Miguel?"

"I've been a fool! Forgive me. Say you'll forgive me, darling, and never again as long as I live will I—"

"There is no need to go into the details. You made a mistake. Granted. But I'm not God. He seems to know how to handle his own form of punishment."

"Punishment," he whispered. "What do you mean?"

She knew no other way to tell him but straight out. Her motive was not revenge, but the epidemic of mumps which had swept from ranch to ranch and into Santa Fe had eliminated her need to expose Miguel's affair with Malita.

"It would seem," she said slowly, "the Esparza family were already exposed to the mumps when you paid your last visit." There was an icy finality to her last three words.

"All four of the Esparza children came down with them," she went on hurriedly. "But so did ours. The boys, being toddlers passed them off quickly and handily, but the baby had a little rougher time of it." Ever since she had learned the full truth from Jimmy Yerby, she had not been able to bring herself to call her daughter by her given name.

"No one could have had a rougher time than me."

"Many did," she said emphatically. "It was hardest on the adults and many died. Guillerno Esparza was one of them. His sister, Malita, learned of it while still in a fevered state. They say that her mind went and she tried to take her own life. Señora Esparza has taken her back to Spain to be institutionalized."

Miguel did not move. His face was as still and white as though it had been carved from stone; his eyes were wide, staring into space, their expression unchanged except that now they filled up slowly with tears.

Emilia stood still in the silent room, listening to the

sound of her own breathing. She might not have learned any of the sordid details if Jimmy Yerby had not taken sick while visiting Dorotea Esparza and been quarantined with the family. The whole household had been able to hear Malita's screaming laments over Guillerno's death. It was a horrible way for the family to learn such ghastly truths. Jimmy's heart went out to the innocent Dorotea, and he wanted to kill Carlos. He never got a chance because Señor Esparza banished his son to Mexico City as soon as he was able to travel. Jimmy Yerby now felt two obligations. Because he was not allowed to see Dorotea without her parents being present, he was looked upon as an honest man. When he asked for her hand in marriage, the grief-stricken parents granted the request immediately, seeing it as a way to protect her from some of the gossip.

Gossip is what brought about Jimmy's second obligation. The household servants had heard everything that he had heard, and he did not want it spreading and catching Emilia unawares. It was the hardest thing he had ever had to do in his life, and he was wringing wet with perspiration by the time he was finished. It was only Emilia's calm, gracious way of accepting the truth that kept him from feeling like a cheap tattletale. He sensed that she would handle her husband in the same manner, and he went away with the hope in his heart that some day his future wife could mature into the same type of lady.

Miguel sighed. "You know, don't you?"

"Yes," she whispered. "I've a feeling you've all paid a heavy price for what you've done."

Her words brought his greatest fear flooding back. His feeling was that he had paid the dearest price of all. He put out his arms to her and she came to him, but not like a wife or lover. She took his hands as a mother would take the hands of a child to soothe away the fears of a nightmare.

"I want it put behind us, Miguel. I don't ever want the children to learn of it."

"They won't from us," he said gruffly, "but I do have enemies, you know."

"You are your own worst enemy, if I'm not mistaken."

Emilia smiled softly at him and kissed him on each cheek.

"Now," she said, rising, " I have something for you. Tía Patricia has made the trip out to see you twice but understood why you weren't receiving visitors. I really should say that she has something for you. They have been entertaining the Count Alphonse de Saligny, the French chargé d'affaires. She purchased this from him."

She handed him a box and a hand mirror.

"You must think I'm crazy," he exploded. "I'll not wear that damn thing."

"Powdered wigs," she laughed, "are all the rage again, the count tells Doña Patricia."

"Get out!" he screamed, throwing the box and hand mirror at her.

Emilia sank back against the door when she had it closed and said a short and simple prayer. "Don't let me hate, God," she murmured. "For the sake of the children, don't let me hate . . ."

Miguel threw the sheet from his legs in disgust and looked at the flat flannel nightgown. At any other time the touch of her hand, her kiss, her very presence would have caused his arousal to tent the fabric. There was nothing. There had been nothing. For over a week he had been trying to arouse himself, but there had been nothing. It was dead, as dead as Guillerno Esparza's penis lying six feet under the New Mexico soil.

The tear drops brimmed in Miguel's eyes, spilling over his lashes and making slow streams down his hollow cheeks. He felt tired and old and useless. He was thirty-two years old, and his life was over. He didn't even have to think about how miserable an existence it was going to be without sex. Suddenly he saw why Emilia had been so quick to forgive. She never had to worry about him cheating again. The hardness in his heart now turned to cold stone. He would not be miserable alone.

On a cool, crisp March dawn Felix Escovarro came storming across the river and caught his brother and a vaquero just ready to ride out.

"Jesus Christ!" he growled. "I didn't believe it when Jimmy just told me. Miguel, you're both madmen."

"That's your opinion," he said icily. "The man sent his note challenging me to a duel and I have my honor to consider."

"Honor?" Felix exploded. "Were you thinking of your honor while you were screwing away in that wild manner?"

"You're going to make me late," he answered indifferently.

"Late?" Felix echoed blankly. "My intention is to make you see the stupidity of going at all. Señor Esparza, in spite of his age, is very handy with pistols. And Jimmy tells me that he has purchased a new brace of Colts. You're not used to those new weapons, Miguel."

"Good," he laughed sardonically, "then maybe you won't have me around to fight with by breakfast time."

Felix looked at him quietly, almost pityingly. "If you're going to be a fool," he said, "I might as well go along as your second."

"This vaquero will do quite nicely," he sneered. "But I guess I can't keep you from riding along."

Jimmy Yerby had gone back to try to dissuade Señor Esparza in the same manner Felix was trying with Miguel. He was also failing. What he could not understand was the timing. This was to be his wedding day. The old man could not give his future son-in-law a logical answer for why he wanted Miguel Escovarro eliminated before the wedding. He advised the boy to leave the dueling field, but Jimmy stubbornly stayed.

An hour later Señor Esparza was unable to advise Jimmy further. Miguel, in spite of his still weakened condition, had been swifter on the turn and fire. But it was a moment that created even more enemies for Miguel Escovarro. The fault might have been laid at the feet of Samuel Colt for having invented a dueling pistol that carried more than a single shot. The fault of Miguel involved the purity of the "code"; he had fired and rehammered three times to Esparza's single shot. According to Señor Esparza's second, Miguel's first shot caught the man in the shoulder and should have settled the bad blood between them without death. But the second and third shot fatally entered the old man's heart and stomach. The second vowed to remember the facts well.

On a single day Jimmy Yerby would be attending a funeral, his own wedding, cancel a fiesta, and ponder the fact that he was now the owner of a great and prosperous ranch. But, in spite of his good fortune, he did not thank Miguel for bringing it about.

Felix rode back to the ranch with his brother and the vaquero, his dark eyes blank and unseeing. He felt a forlorn helplessness for Señor Esparza and wondered if deep in his heart he didn't wish that the outcome had been reversed.

"You!" Miguel barked halfway back. "Your name!"

"Estaban, señor," the vaquero answered, slightly surprised. His family had been with the Escovarros for two generations and he had considered that was why he had been selected to be Don Miguel's second. In actual fact Miguel had appointed him because he seemed the strongest of the four vaqueros working in the stable that morning.

"All right," Miguel barked, without using the young man's name. "From now on, in the eastern sector, where we normally let the Esparza cattle use our water holes, they will be disallowed."

Felix came instantly out of his gloom.

"Miguel," he said, "you haven't been out and about to see that this has been an unusual winter. There is hardly any snow on the mountains, and we have had little down here. Young Jimmy is going to be saddled with a big enough problem as it is. Without the use of those water holes he'll have to drive the Esparza cattle ten miles around your property line."

"As you say," Miguel said candidly, "it is Jimmy Yerby's problem and not mine. If the weather has been as bad as you say, then I'll need every drop of water for my own cattle."

Miguel spurred his horse away at a gallop before Felix could argue back. Felix's sudden arrival, and where he had obtained his information from, had stirred an interest in his mind. It was not until he was on the dueling field and learned that Jimmy Yerby was to become Esparza's son-in-law that his rage had exploded. For a month he had been contemplating how he could end his own useless life with the least amount of pain, when the duel challenge had given him his answer. He had fully anticipated that Señor Esparza would kill him.

But Jimmy Yerby altered that thought. It was very obvious to him now where Emilia had received her information—had probably been receiving it all the time he was having his affair with Malita. He had made sure that he had anticipated the call and began to turn even before the order started to emerge from the referee's lips. The pistol was new to him, but he had studied it carefully during the solemn moments of instructions. He had made sure to hit Esparza's right shoulder first, so that the man's own shot would be jerked out of his range. Then, coldly and deliberately, he murdered the man. He had no hatred in his heart for the man, but suddenly, in Miguel's mind, he was a barrier to his real target. He wanted Jimmy Yerby to suddenly find himself the "don" of a great estate. Blown up with vanity, he would be a much easier target.

Contemplating how he would financially ruin the boy gave Miguel a sated feeling that came near to the trembling sensation of a sexual climax. Sadistically he savored the moment and knew he wanted to repeat it again and again. It was like when he was a youth and had first experimented with himself. It had felt good, but he had known that there had to been far more enticing feelings ahead. He looked forward to a mental sensual growth based upon casting his miseries onto the shoulders of others.

In the next year his name was not mentioned, it was spat. He would not allow the other ranchers to join his vaqueros on their cattle drives up the Santa Fe Trail to Independence, including his own brother. During the drought of the summer of 1840, he had channels dug on the upper regions of his property to bring irrigation water onto his farmlands. Below that point the Santa Fe became a mere trickle, adding little to the spring runoff to the Rio Grande. Felix's land, too high for irrigation, suffered greatly from the rainless summer, but his wells, which depended greatly on the water seepage from the Santa Fe, began to be stagnant and dry.

Downstream, where the Santa Fe converged with the Rio Grande, Miguel's greed was far more evident. The Great River, unfed by its own mouth or that of the Santa Fe, was becoming a parched and arid cracked expanse. The women of the Santo Domingo Pueblo labored tirelessly carrying jugs of its murky brown liquid to try and save the annual corn crop. Finally, in despair, their chief told them to stop and harvest what crop was already on the stalks, no matter how puny. He thanked the Mother of all living things for one saving grace, the bull and twenty head of cattle that had been presented to his son for saving the life of a brown-skinned squaw had been reproductive and would supply meat should it prove to be a hard winter.

It was a devastating and yet hopeful winter. The heavy, wet snows began early in September in the higher elevations. By October the mountains were covered in a mantle of pure white. Then winter descended to the mesas, blanketing everything for four solid months in a wonderland facade of whiteness.

For Emilia it was a period of quiet contentment. Miguel barely stirred from the house; his hair was beginning to grow back in, his pallor diminished, and his interest in his sons was renewed. He never asked for sexual license with her, and she accepted the fact with a relieved sigh. She was unsure if she were able to bear him another child and that would be the only reason for which her bed would be opened to him again. Her only problem was the manner in which he continually avoided the baby of the family. Because she could not bring herself to call the child Malita ever again, she fell into the habit of calling her Marta—Mary—without ever once realizing that that had been Señora Esparza's name.

Miguel could not believe Emilia would play such a sadistic joke on him, and he silently fumed.

His own name was also a sadistic joke to his cousin Ricardo de Sanchez, but the governor-general of New Mexico did not silently fume.

"Madness," he shrieked, strutting back and forth in his ornate office. "The Texan army is no more than a two-day march away from here with an overture from this President Lamar, and the only advice I can wring from you men is put Miguel Escovarro onto the matter. You're worthless!"

"Your Excellency!" the Mexican officer in charge of the city's defenses pleaded. "We are a small force, since the last war, and are really quite unsure of the intentions of this advancing army. We have not the time to raise and train an army. Señor Escovarro and his brother have such manpower immediately at their disposal."

The governor-general turned to the one person whose advice he knew he could trust.

Doña Patricia had been trying to maintain a disinterested position throughout.

"That they could mount a hundred or so men is true," she said slowly. "But it is summertime and the men widely scattered."

What she was not saying was that she did not have that much faith in the leadership ability of Miguel.

"But, señora," Major Cuesta pleaded, "you overlook the main advantage of my request. Don Miguel soldiered with the Texans and will be better equipped to learn their true intentions."

"A point," Don Ricardo chirped. "A very valid point. Will you speak with him, Doña Patricia?"

She nodded without enthusiasm.

"But," Don Ricardo scolded, "this does not let you off the hook, Major. You must still start raising volunteers should Miguel be unable to persuade them to countermarch."

It was a challenge that stirred Miguel's vanity. In such a venture he could prove his manliness. Never once did he consider taking on the task for the protection of his family and property.

Grinning, he ran to a wagon in the ranch yard and mounted it.

"Vaqueros of Escovarro!" he cried. "To horse! The day of vengeance is at hand for having been forced off our land!"

It made Felix a little sick to listen to Miguel's exultant estimate of the advantages that would accrue to their ranches as a result of his being asked to raise an immediate army. He had no qualms about protecting his own land once again. Try as he would, the idea of depleting both ranches of all their protective force seemed foolhardy.

"But what if you fail?" he demanded. "You're not even sure of what size force you will be facing."

"Must you always be so damn negative."

Felix was tired of fighting. Almost every day Miguel seemed to find a new bone of contention to raise between them and the two ranches.

"I think I'm being reasonable," he said dully. "Take my vaqueros, but I will keep the farmers here with me in case you are overwhelmed and we must fight."

"Coward!" Miguel screamed, his face purpling with rage. "I'm going to make you rue this day!"

President Mirabeau Buonaparte Lamar had received a similar warning from Sam Houston when the scheme for the expedition was presented to the Texas Congress. Lamar was a desperate and anxious man. All of his schemes had failed. Texas money was worth twenty cents on the dollar, millions had been added to the public debt, and her credit was gone. In a few months he faced reelection and needed something spectacular to reassure it.

In the drafty frame tabernacle in Austin called the Hall of Congress, he appeared to fight his own battle.

"It is our destiny," he cried, "to capture the rich revenues of the Santa Fe Trail. It is our right to plant the Lone Star of Texas on the gray towers of *el Palacio Real*. *Gentlemen*, look at the map! Look at the map that was drawn up at the close of our victorious 1836 campaign! Santa Fe and most of New Mexico lie within the boundaries of our republic, but the previous administration did not attempt to assert its dominion there."

Senator Sam Houston pounded his desk for recognition. When it was ignored by Vice-president Burnet, Houston shouted over the speaker's words:

"To attempt so would have been foolhardy!"

With the energy of despair Lamar brought forward others to speak on behalf of the scheme. Houston sat whittling sticks and crushing the orators with ridicule.

Just before the vote the Bible-thumping Burnet had no recourse but to recognize Houston.

"I've little to say," Houston drawled slowly, "damn little. To me this whole scheme is highly suspect as a glittering trick to assure someone's reelection. Now, gentlemen," he chided when several began to boo and pound their desks, "no need for all this racket. You didn't hear me mention any names, did you? *But now I will!* Lamar, if you and your hog-thief vice-president push this bill through Congress, I might just decide to run against you and make you rue this day!"

When Congress declined to sanction the expedition, the president was in no position to sustain the defeat. He knew deep in his heart that Houston was going to run again, although he denied it in public. He decided to proceed on his own responsibility and ordered a half-million dollars from a New Orleans printer. This dropped the Lone Star to three cents on the dollar.

Horses were purchased for a thousand dollars apiece—Texas currency—and the troops newly uniformed to make a brave showing. In June of 1841, the cavalcade marched.

Miguel Escovarro was duly impressed. The Texas soldiers were quite handsome in their forest-green trousers, white tunics with scarlet piping, and plumed caps of a Prussian military cut. But the fine show and the respectable caliber of their ranks made them appear to be little more than an escort for the rest of the gallant facade Lamar had put together. The cavalcade was composed mainly of merchants with rich stores, financiers, diplomats, and an editor of the New Orleans *Picayune*—come to report on what he considered was a mission of goodwill.

He continued to believe such was the case when white flags were unfurled upon the sighting of Miguel's force. Lamar wanted a quick and bloodless conquest. Force was to be used only to repel attack.

Major General Jack Henderson had been a cavalryman

under Lamar at San Jacinto. He greeted Miguel Escovarro like a long-lost brother.

Henderson wore an all-white uniform—with gold braid over forest-green piping—with a jeweled sword case lying gracefully along his slender leg. The uniform was impractical, Miguel decided, noting the travel stains on closer inspection. But the young man wore it with an exotic quality, almost imperial. After his first warm greeting the haughtiness of his bearing seemed to emphasize this: his dark eyes, meeting Miguel's over the proud arch of his Roman nose, were utterly cold and suggested a master-servant relationship.

"Well, Miguel," he said, "I'm mighty glad to see you. It's been a long time."

"Five years," Miguel said.

"It seems much longer," Henderson mused.

"Married?"

"No. Frankly I haven't seen the girl who interests me enough. Besides I'm much too busy. Thirty years old and a major general."

Now Miguel recalled the man completely. As a young officer he had made no bones about stepping on anyone who got in his way for attention and advancement. He considered him little changed, and it gave Miguel an advantage.

"But even as a general," he went on, "I am exposed to incompetence. We seem to be without maps for this area. Can you inform me how near we are to Santa Fe?"

"A day's ride. You are on the eastern portion of my ranch."

"Your land?" Henderson looked at Miguel shrewdly. "I was under the impression that your land was in west Texas."

"It is," he answered soberly, "but my brother and I have holdings here as well."

Henderson's thin lips curled slightly.

"Ah, yes, Felix, isn't it? The man and I never did see eye to eye. He was constantly going against General Lamar's brilliant plans for the cavalry."

Miguel laughed sourly. "Then you will find him little

changed. I have become the Lamar he constantly goes against."

"Well," Henderson said, turning suddenly businesslike. "I was under the impression you were a troop of Mexican soldiers. But these are your ranch hands, is that so?"

"It is so." Miguel wasn't ready to play out his full hand as yet. "However, I have been sent by the governor-general to greet you and learn your purpose. But here is not the place to get into such a discussion. A quarter mile ahead is one of my water holes. It is tree shaded and will make an excellent place for you to camp for the night."

"We'll follow your lead, Captain Escovarro," he said and put out his hand.

Miguel took it, a germ of a plan starting to jell in his brain.

Once General Henderson's tent had been erected at what he called "an oasis in this vast landscape," the two men were left alone over brandy. Miguel, his face emotionless, listened to Henderson outline Lamar's grandiose scheme for the bloodless conquest of New Mexico.

"They have given you a nearly impossible task, General," Miguel said seriously. "Granted, there are some, such as myself, who have been able to work and live in harmony with you Texans. We are of Spanish heritage and see little reason to give our allegiance to Santa Anna and the Mexicans."

"Has he a strong grip on the area?" Henderson asked as though the answer hardly mattered.

"On the surface, no," Miguel said. Then: "But I am aware of the fact that for months he has been sending troops north, in peons' dress, to prepare for an invasion. While you Texans keep your eyes peeled across the Rio Grande, he will slip out of the northwest and have dirks in your back before you can turn."

Henderson was hardly an idiot. His suspicions were immediately honed sharp.

"Why do you tell me this?" he asked icily.

"Damn it!" Miguel shouted, slamming his brandy mug to the ground. "I'm a rancher, not a soldier. I'm sick and tired of seeing my land overrun by unnecessary warfare.

Houston was incapable of stamping out Santa Anna. He let him vanish back to Mexico. Will Lamar do any better?"

Henderson was momentarily confused. "My mission is not to use force unless attacked," he stammered.

"But your main purpose," Miguel sneered, "is to persuade the people of New Mexico to rebel against Santa Anna and join Texas. If you do not strike against the main leader Santa Anna has in this area, then your mission is doomed before it ever starts. That you are here is not a very well kept secret."

Henderson sat back and eyed Miguel shrewdly. "You seem to have your finger on the pulse of the entire matter."

"That's why I am as successful in my line as you are in yours. We don't let people or their petty desires get in our way."

Henderson spread his thin hands expansively. "You haven't quite gotten to the bottom line, Don Escovarro. You must have a *fee* in mind."

Miguel's face remained motionless, but his heart was a trip-hammer of victorious beats. Henderson had started to give up the battle by elevating him back to an equal rank. He had the man near the point of doing his bidding without ever realizing the degenerate reason behind it.

"I have *several* in mind," he growled. "I want an assurance that should you Texans try a land-reform scheme in this area, as you did in Texas, my lands will go untouched. Next, as the representative of Lamar, you will name me the governor-general of New Mexico."

Henderson started to balk, but Miguel was ready for him.

"Good God," he stormed, "don't be an asshole. This area and the Californias added to Texas will make it larger and stronger than the United States. It can become a United States of its own. And who will have been responsible? You! We are not exactly in the Dark Ages up here, Henderson. We get news quite regularly and know of Lamar's difficulties. A man who comes home with a golden plum could easily replace him and overshadow Houston."

Henderson had felt from the day he set foot on Texas soil that it held his destiny. He had always dreamed of becoming a great man, and Miguel Escovarro had just opened a providential door. He was unaware that it was grossly similar to Satan offering Jesus of Nazareth the command of the world.

His throat was bone dry and his palms sticky with sweat. "What is your plan?" he rasped.

Miguel was cunningly prepared for that moment. The plan was so simple, and yet devious, that it left Henderson stunned and unable to agree except with short, bewildered nods of his head.

"You were right," Miguel apologized a little ashamedly to Felix. "It's not that large a force, but handsomely attired and equipped. On the surface they appear to be no more than an escort for a trade mission, but Jack Henderson ran true to form and gave away his true intent."

"Henderson," Felix echoed. "If he's in command, you shouldn't have any trouble. He rattles easily."

"My point exactly. You know him and what he might do to break out of a trap. I've left my vaqueros camped to the northeast of him and have sent word to Major Cuesta to bring down from Santa Fe any forces he can get here by dawn. If you bring your farmers in from this direction, you'll be on the high ground and can signal us as to what you expect him to do. He wanted a bloodless conquest; I think we can assure him of a bloodless retreat."

It seemed reasonable to Felix, and he was relieved that they had been able to have one meeting without bickering. He agreed to bring the rest of his men into the wooded hills at dawn. Miguel rode back to where his vaqueros were camped, a joyous singing in his heart. Instead of being northeast of Henderson's camp, as he had told Miguel, the rich red glow of the twin campfires almost touched in their closeness.

After sending word to Henderson that all was arranged for dawn, he spent the rest of the night instructing his men, quietly in small groups, on their specific assignments in the morning.

He had not lied about sending word to Santa Fe, but Major Cuesta puzzled over the strange orders before beginning to gather the men and supplies Miguel Escovarro had demanded. He departed the city at midnight, giving him ample time to reach the water hole by dawn.

When Estaban Duran could no longer abide working for Miguel Escovarro as a vaquero, he had sought a return to a farmer's position with Felix and a return to his parents' home. Now he found himself in the saddle again, riding next to a man he trusted and admired.

It was still dark when they reached the wooded hilltop that looked down on the water hole. The campfires were barely discernible starry embers. The vaqueros' campfires, at Miguel's instructions, had been smothered by dirt an hour before.

Felix motioned the men to dismount and rest, seeing Miguel's mistake on demanding such an early arrival for him and his men.

It was none too early for Henderson and his men lying in ambush to Felix's rear. He squatted in the shadowy cover of the undergrowth and intently studied the mounted figure silhouetted against the early morning sky. He heard his own whispered voice, awed and incredulous, saying: "Why, it's his own brother! It's Felix!"

His men had been ordered to total silence until he gave the command to fire. His mumbled words were taken as such. At once the guns from the bushes and tree limbs opened up. Henderson saw the shadowy figure stumble from the saddle, but remain on his feet, until finally one of the soldiers began to fire his brace of Colt pistols, and the ugly weapons set up their furious constant stutter. Felix stopped short as though he had run up against an invisible wall. Henderson saw his body jerk again and again as the torrent of slugs tore into him. Then he crumpled slowly, like an actor taking a bow, and went down upon the earth, and still the pistols poured bullets into him, shaking his pitiful body with the repeated impact of its fire. Then all the guns were still.

Unbelievingly Felix's men had been too surprised and stunned to fire back. Then Estaban Duran began to run toward the broken figure on the ground. Others were just behind him. Then the men were gathering Felix up, and one by one they took off their sombreros. Henderson watched them drape the body over the horse and bear it away. He had neither the heart nor the inclination to tell his men to move. He had seen men borne from the field of battle by their comrades before but never with such loving dignity and respect. He instinctively felt that he had just committed murder. He could think of nothing else as he led his men back down to the camp.

"Oh, hell," he groaned, upon seeing what had transpired during his absence.

His troops stood stark naked, shackled one to the other, and closely guarded. His own small force faced a battery of poised rifles and began to drop their own weapons with feverish haste. Major General Andrew Jackson Henderson could not allow himself to face such a disgrace. He quickly whipped his pistol from its holster and fired it almost as soon as it entered his mouth.

"Let him lie!" Miguel roared sadistically. "The buzzards haven't had their breakfast yet."

His heart was near rhapsodic. He had pitted enemy against enemy and witnessed each man's destruction. In triumph he made the cavalcade march to Santa Fe. Through the streets he paraded the naked men and their mercantile-laden wagons. Soon the Texans were bruised, dirty, and torn, for they were the vanquished left to the mercy of the howling, frenzied mobs intent on no other object than their destruction. They were spat at, cursed, kicked, whipped, and taunted. Daring women of the street would race forward to grab at their manhood and then slap it away with an insulting remark. Then the people took a greater interest in material rewards.

Don Ricardo stood on the covered entryway to the palace, his stomach turning over, as women he recognized ran past, their arms loaded with bolts of silk and lace. There were other men and women carrying barrels and crates, dress goods, hats, and foodstuffs of all sorts. Still others had corked bottles and jugs of wines and liquors.

Are these my people, de Sanchez thought bitterly. whom I have looked out for so lovingly? These depraved, thieving monsters! Who has brought them to this?

His answer instantly rode up before him.

"There they are, Cousin Ricardo," Miguel chortled. "Your invasion army, as requested."

The sensitive little man turned away; he was aghast. But as he turned, he saw two beefy Spanish women engaged in a tug-of-war over a bolt of dotted Swiss lace. They had ripped away each other's clothing to the waist, and their huge, pendulous breasts were covered with bloody scratches.

"Get them out of here," he screamed, turning back to Miguel. "Take them south to Santa Anna before they cause the ruination of my lovely town."

"Is that a command?" Miguel spat.

The governor-general was quieter now. Though he trembled all over, he was regaining control of himself.

"It is a request, Don Miguel," he whispered. "Please, take them away."

Miguel sat his horse looking at his aging cousin for a long time. Then he slowly motioned Guido Herrera and Major Cuesta forward.

"Guido," he growled, "take our men home. Tell my wife I am on my way to Mexico. Major, I will use your men for the march. It will start at once."

Guido Herrera obeyed with heartsick gratitude. He had never lived through such a terrible day and felt mortally sick and ashamed. Major Cuesta was internally furious. He felt that as the commander of the Mexican forces in New Mexico he should be afforded the honor of taking the prisoners to Santa Anna. He had already begun to feel the gold braid of a generalship on his shoulders for this day's venture.

The glory, Miguel egotistically measured, belonged to him alone. He had not only dispatched one of Santa Anna's enemies—his brother Felix—but would bring to his doorstep the *crème de la crème* of the Texan army. He saw himself returning from Mexico City with the same laurels he had demanded from General Henderson: the governor-generalship of New Mexico. But this time he would be demanding it from a man who had the genuine power to grant it.

* * *

When men write the history of tragic or sordid events, they attempt to protect future readers from the true horrors that man is capable of perpetrating upon his fellow man. In this instance two weird elements combined that men of that era were never fully able to comprehend—only men of a century later would fathom that such things could transpire.

Miguel Escovarro was nearly mad with his crazed notion of victory over the forces he felt had been taunting him— and he was in command of a guarding force for his prisoners that he was unaware of. When Major Cuesta had been unable to secure sufficient volunteers to meet Governor de Sanchez's demands, he had opened the doors of the jails and offered the prisoners freedom if they accomplished the mission.

Without knowing it, or really caring, Miguel was leading a pack of murderers, horse thieves, robbers, and brigands. They only cared that freedom lay at the end of the road.

The "naked march" to Mexico City became the cruelest, most sadistic degradation to that date. The prisoners were forced to fornicate with their guards and themselves; because of inadequate food supplies they began to gorge on their own stool. Soldiers forgot how to march; merchants gave up their forlorn crying over the goods they had lost; financiers soon lost count of the number of steps that they were taking southward; diplomats no longer had the words to convince the leader of the sadistic mob that reason should prevail, and the editor of the New Orleans *Picayune*'s mind became so swamped with the editorials he was going to write about the atrocities he had experienced that his mind snapped and he trudged forward, repeating over and over again the last sensible sentence that had come to his mind:

"What have we ever done to warrant such treacherous treatment from these savages . . ."

CHAPTER SIXTEEN

The sophisticated people of Mexico City, at least, were of no mind to be a part of such depravity. They rushed into the street and covered the men's nakedness with shawls, ponchos, sheets, and blankets.

Their disgust was shared by Santa Anna, but for different reasons.

"Get out," he said. His voice was very quiet, but so deep that Miguel could feel it. It reverberated through the presidential office like an organ chord held long and piercingly.

It was a moment before Miguel recovered.

" 'Get out,' he says! I bring you a great victory, and all you can do is tell me to—"

"*Victory?*" Santa Anna stormed, cutting him short. "In Texas they are likening this to the Alamo. You have brought us to the point of war."

Miguel blinked stupidly. "Isn't that what you wanted?"

"On my terms," he ranted. "I had them on the brink of bankruptcy, and soldiers don't fight well unless they are paid. You have given them a moral issue that will make them fight with or without pay." Then his voice dropped to a scathing snarl. "But the most insidious thing you have done is pave the way for the gringos to vote overwhelmingly to restore the presidency to Sam Houston. A war against Lamar would have been a simple matter."

He shrugged, without speaking his thoughts on waging another war against Sam Houston.

"Then strike now," Miguel demanded, "while Lamar is still their leader. If you're afraid, give me an army to lead across the Rio Grande."

It was a strange moment for Santa Anna. He held the

Escovarro brothers, and especially Miguel, responsible for his San Jacinto defeat. He would have loved to incarcerate the man, but his advisers thought differently. Miguel was being lauded as a hero in Santa Fe. Santa Anna could not afford to lose their support in a new war with Texas. Still, he wanted nothing to do with this two-faced man.

Santa Anna grinned at him. "If you had your choice," he said softly, "would you rather walk out that door—or be thrown in prison?"

Miguel Escovarro's face was a battleground for his emotions. Fear and rage struggled with each other. Because his temperament was now so near that of the fiery Santa Anna, he knew the man to be quite capable of throwing him in prison and forgetting about him forever. Fear won out.

He clamped his dirty hat on his new grown hair and stalked to the door. But then he turned, quivering with fury.

"I did one other thing for you, Santa Anna!" he got out. "I made sure that Felix didn't come out of the battle alive! Teresa is free!"

"How thoughtful of you," Santa Anna simpered sweetly, ";but I can't help but wonder if you did it *just* for me."

"You'll never have her now," Miguel screamed. "I'll make sure that you never have her again."

Santa Anna knew only too well that that was solely up to Teresa, but he couldn't let the threat go unchallenged and started to reach for the bell cord. Miguel Escovarro, fearing he had talked himself right back into prison, turned and scurried through the door like a ragpicker right off the street.

Santa Anna sat down slowly behind his desk, drumming his fingers on its polished surface. In spite of the bad blood that had developed between them, he felt genuine loss over the news. Felix had been one of the few men he had ever respected in life, before he became an enemy. Sam Houston, too, had been an enemy, then had become a respected adversary. Now he was going to become an enemy again. For once in his life Santa Anna felt sad.

* * *

Teresa sat before the fire in her living room and looked at Felix's rocking chair. It was a habit she had acquired ever since the morning Estaban Duran had brought him home. It would remain motionless, she thought bitterly, just as he would remain motionless.

The string of cowbells rattled at the front door.

Teresa stood up—though to describe the motion thus is wrong. Rather she stiffened erect, her body expressing the emotion that she was tired of having people intrude upon her troubled mind.

She turned the knob and opened the door.

Anna-Maria Perez stood looking at her, her lips trembling foolishly.

"Anna-Maria!" she whispered, gathering the old friend into her arms. "Wherever in the world did you come from?"

"Saltillo," Anna-Maria murmured. "I—I'm sorry to hear about Felix. I came up by stage. Only I stopped by to say hello to Doña Patricia in Santa Fe. That's how I learned."

"I see," Teresa said steadily.

"I—I'll come back again—some other time. I didn't know . . ."

"Nonsense," she said, pulling her through the door. "How did you get out to the ranch?"

Anna-Maria glanced uneasily over her shoulder. "Doña Patricia arranged a carriage for me."

"That was thoughtful," she said, guiding her into the parlor and indicating a seat. "Oh, Anna-Maria, I'm awfully glad to see you. You look fine. Pedro must be so proud. Where is he?"

"In Saltillo, with the children. We have three. *Thankfully* all boys." She paused for a moment, as though searching for the right words.

"It's all right," Teresa said quickly to save her guest embarrassment. "Doña Patricia could only give you the bare facts, because she has been out only once since it happened. She's had enough troubles of her own since Santa Anna sent a new governor-general to Santa Fe. The man must be a monster. He showed her no sympathy when Don

Ricardo killed his poor wife and committed suicide; he ordered her to vacate the palace at once."

"She told me, but the house she bought is quite lovely."

"I wanted her to come here, but . . ." She had to stop a moment to control the tremor in her voice. "Four months," she went on dryly. "Four long horrible months and he somehow still clings to a narrow thread of life. I have to have someone with him day and night. The doctor holds out little or no hope." She clenched her fists until the knuckles were white. "Perhaps it would be best for him. He's paralyzed and can't speak. When he is lucid, which isn't often, his poor eyes are constantly moving as though he's desperately trying to tell me something. It was tearing me up so, the doctors will only let me spend a few minutes at a time with him."

"I'm so sorry," Anna-Maria breathed.

"Well, enough of that," she said crisply. "What brings you all the way up here alone?"

Anna-Maria glanced at her uneasily. Then she launched into her reasons, blurting it out awkwardly, forgetting the careful approach she had planned.

"I'm sorry to hear that your mother is dead," Teresa said without feeling any emotion. "But what does this child she was caring for have to do with me?"

"It was my child," she said quietly. "My child by Fernando Martin Flores."

Teresa frowned. "But he's been dead for almost ten years," she declared.

Now it was Anna-Maria who frowned. "Yes," she said. "I gave birth to the child a month before you were captured and brought to the cantina. It was being wet-nursed by a woman on that street while Fernando was deciding what to do with the child."

"He was going to take the child?" she demanded.

She laughed uneasily. "By trying to be nice, he was brutal. He said that he was not about to have a child with his patrician blood running through its veins raised in a brothel. He and Mama fought like lunatics over the matter."

"She wanted him to marry you?"

"Hardly," she said candidly. "They fought over how much he would have to pay her to take the child away. Of course, she saw him shot by the firing squad before she had a chance to get a peso out of him. I couldn't let Pedro know. so Mama just kept the child after I married."

"Child! Child!" Teresa flared irritably. "Hasn't it a name?"

Anna-Maria hung her head. "She has never been christened. Mama just called her Niña."

"How cruel." Teresa scolded. "To live for ten years and be called nothing more than 'little girl.' I am surprised at Pedro though. Are you sure that he won't let you keep her?"

She shook her head furiously. "He's that mad at me for not telling him before. Besides they hated each other while Mama was still alive. I guess they just sensed that they were rivals for my affection. Neither of them wants to be together."

Teresa sat back and sighed. "Why did you think I would take her, Anna-Maria?"

"First," she said shrewdly, "because you have no children of your own. Second, because you are the only one who comes near to being a relative of the child's father."

Teresa laughed throatily.

"You will never know, Anna-Maria, how close I was to calling off that engagement the nearer our carriage came to Saltillo. I knew then that I didn't love the man, could never love him. I hardly consider myself anywhere near to being a relative. I'm sorry, Anna-Maria, but as you can see, my full-time obligation right now is to Felix."

"Perhaps," Anna-Maria muttered, "you could think on it. I—I'm not leaving on the stage until tomorrow morning."

"My God!" she gasped. "You didn't drag the poor child all the way up here on the vain hope that I couldn't refuse you."

"I—I—no!" But that was not exactly the truth; it had not been a vain hope.

"Well, thank God for that," she sighed. "It must be hard enough on the tyke being pulled from pillar to post as it is." Then she softened, as Anna-Maria knew she would, but not quite as much as she had expected. "All right, give me some time to think it out and handle my present problems. I'll send word to you in Saltillo as soon as I've made a deicision."

At once Anna-Maria was abject.

"I hope it is soon," she said miserably. "Pedro is going back into the army because of the big bonuses Santa Anna is offering. We shall be on the move, I fear."

Teresa began to feel trapped. Another outright refusal would keep the woman there pleading and begging. Teresa, at that moment, wanted nothing more than to be left alone.

"Perhaps," she muttered. "I don't know. I—I've got to come into town tomorrow for some supplies . . ."

"Make it before my stage leaves at eleven," Anna-Maria begged. But the next morning was November 18, 1841, and New Mexico was in the grip of a blizzard that was not to be equaled for another fifty years.

For two days the ranch was cut off from the rest of the world, and almost from the various segments of itself. The blizzard gave Teresa a righteous excuse for not going into Santa Fe. She knew that she would not have been able to go and say yes, even if it had been a sunny day. She wanted the solace of a child, but her own child.

By the third morning the storm had subsided enough so that Estaban was able to plow a path to the main house from the barns and hen coops. Except for the two women who took shifts seeing after Felix, Teresa had been caught in the house without servants. The larder was growing bare, and she went with Estaban to replenish it.

Halfway to the barn she caught him by the coat sleeve suddenly and leaned against him, shuddering.

Estaban looked past her and saw the frozen sticks that had once been legs sticking out of the snow drift, while nearby other cattle stood hunched together to ward off the whiplashes of the sleet and snow.

"Oh, Estaban, the poor beasts!" she said. "I can't bear it!"

"We won't lose many, Doña Teresa," he said, trying to

comfort her but not believing the lie himself. It was going to be a horrible disaster.

"Oh, get me to the barn!" she whispered. "I want to check on Quapaw."

"He's fine, ma'am," he said cheerily. "I gave him a bucket of oats just before coming for you."

To his amazement the bucket had vanished, and Quapaw eyed him angrily.

"I know I fed him," he insisted and then quickly motioned Teresa to silence. "Well, I'll get another bucket of oats—and here's your basket to fetch the eggs." He stamped his feet as though he were walking away and then halted in place. Teresa was mildly curious as to what he was about.

Estaban listened intently until the sound he thought he had heard came again. Mice and rats nibbled and gnawed, he knew, they didn't grind. Nor were they capable of carrying off an oaken bucket nearly full of oats.

Carefully he started toward the sound, his hands outthrust, searching in the dim barn. They closed over the rough edge of a packing crate. He gave a push and the box turned over, spilling its contents.

From somewhere far below him a small voice shrilled: "Don't you dare touch me, you lousy bastard!"

Estaban didn't heed the warning and hauled the child to its feet. For him it was hard to tell whether it was a boy or girl from the saddle blankets it had wrapped about itself to ward off the cold. It seemed to be about six years old, and it was hammering at his legs and stomach with considerable force.

Estaban paid no attention to the blows but hauled the child out of hiding, with Teresa following at his heels, until they had better light at the open barn doors. The child turned to escape, and Estaban's big hand caught at the knitted skullcap. At once a mass of heavy red hair tumbled down and, matted though it was with dirt and straw and feathers, Teresa knew at once whom she faced. Only one man in her life had she even seen who possessed hair like a summer evening's sunset—the reds and golds and pinks artfully blended to an unnameable hue.

"Oh, Niña," she whispered, kneeling to the child, "how long have you been here?"

The child had recovered somewhat and was staring at them out of round, dark green eyes.

"How long have you been here?" Estaban repeated.

The child shook her head as though she couldn't remember.

"Before the storm," she said calmly. "I was told to stay here until you found me. I did—there." She pointed toward the packing box.

The child studied her with grave eyes.

"I should have known," Teresa whispered. "Well, we better get you into the house."

"You a whore?" she asked simply.

Estaban gasped and almost cuffed the girl alongside her head for such insolence.

"No, honey," Teresa said gently, "but I'm well aware why you would ask the question. You were afraid that was the only place your mother would take you, wasn't it?"

"That was the threat my grandmother always used to make if I wasn't good." She shrugged indifferently. "If I was very bad, she said she'd give me to five soldiers at the same time without charging a peso."

Estaban Duran stood gaping, his eyes mooned. From a staunch Catholic family, he had yet to know his first woman at age twenty. To hear such things from the mouth of a mere baby gave him more embarrassment for Teresa than himself.

"It's a long story," Teresa grinned at him foolishly. "Let's see to food and bath for her first."

In the main house the child looked about wonderingly. Clearly she had never seen such comfort before in her life.

"Estaban," Teresa said, "there's some soup in the kitchen that Don Felix was not awake to eat. Heat it up, will you, while I give her a bath?"

"Sure," Estaban grinned. "I'd like to see what she looks like under all of those saddle blankets."

"Thank God for them," she shuddered, "or we might have found her out there frozen to death like the poor cattle."

She was remarkably clean under the filthy saddle blankets. Her hair had suffered the most and took four complete rinsings before it was soft and shining. Instantly Teresa was aware of what her hair brought back to mind—the gypsum rose she had received from Santa Anna. It was a prism holding all the hues of the desert. And the child who came from the bath was a creature of bewitching beauty. She was rosy, slender gaminelike. On her face was a starry field of multihued freckles.

While Teresa ladled up a bowl of soup, Estaban put a big finger under the child's chin and lifted her little face.

"What's your name?" he asked.

"Niña," she answered promptly.

"That's what you are, not who you are," he retorted, not understanding.

"Exactly," Teresa said, putting the bowl down in front of her, "and it's going to stop right now. I think I have a name for you."

The child could care less. They stood, fascinated, and watched her noisily devour the soup as though she had never eaten before.

But Teresa's thought would not go away. She could see that the child would develop into a beauty—a russet, stunning beauty. As beautiful as the desert rose. But like the stone rose itself, it would be a beauty that could not be mastered, a hard, flamelike beauty—utterly provocative.

No man will think himself worthy of loving her, Teresa thought suddenly, but all men will want her.

"Elena," Teresa murmured, but it was not the name she had intended to say.

"Like the one of Troy?" the child asked suddenly, unexpectedly.

"How did you know that?" Teresa gasped.

"You'd be surprised what some of the men knew who came to visit grandma after she retired. One of them said I might someday become like Helen of Troy." Then she shrugged. "It's as good a name as any."

Teresa was slightly amused and Estaban totally chagrined. It was a situation that was to last through the rest of the winter. Teresa ignored Elena's fiendish temper and

Estaban was beside himself at the child's vocabulary—one that would have put a veteran sailor to shame.

When the weather was mild enough for Doña Patricia to pay a visit, Teresa was quite candid with her old friend.

"I think I've made a grave mistake in keeping her," she said despairingly. "She's so unusual, Tía. She can't seem to bear being loved. And now, with the doctors saying that Felix could slip away at any minute, I so desperately need something to cling to and hope for."

"There, there," the kind old doña soothed, "give her time. She'll change."

The change was twofold and unexpected. Because Elena had been denied entrance to Felix's room, she cunningly plotted until she was able to find out what was being denied her behind those closed bedroom doors. The first look had stunned and frightened her. Then she had kicked and screamed until someone would tell her exactly what had happened to the man.

Her second secret visit to the room, when she knew the nurse would be gone for a while, was born out of curiosity. But when she reached the side of the bed and saw the questioning wonderment in Felix's eyes, she became demurely quiet. In almost a single gasp she told him who she was and why she was there. His eyes stilled and softened. Automatically she took one of his hands and swore ever after that she felt the slightest amount of pressure. It had a startling effect on her, and she became after that almost a model child; meanwhile her dark, mysterious little mind was constantly busy trying to fathom the real message in Felix's eyes.

Because her simple, undemanding presence seemed to make him forget his own pain, Elena was allowed to spend more and more time with him. An inquisitive child, she also attached herself to Estaban Duran and marveled at all the ranch scenes he showed her. Bubbling with enthusiasm, she would relate each new experience to Felix and thus became his window of assurance that the land he so dearly loved was in capable hands.

On the day before Christmas a brightly painted sleigh brought Emilia and her sons across the frozen river.

"I couldn't let Christmas go by without a visit," Emilia said timidly, almost apologetically. "We have some things in the sleigh for you."

"Come in," Teresa said. "Come in, all of you! Oh, Em, I'm so glad to see you!"

They hugged and brushed each other's cheek with a kiss.

"Auntie Esa! Auntie Esa!" Raoul shrieked for attention, tugging at her skirt. He had never been able to pronounce her full name, and the nickname had stuck.

"Hello, my dumpling," she cried, scooping him up into her arms and being rewarded with a bear hug around her neck. She reached out to capture Ramon with her other arm, but he timidly sidestepped the embrace and hid behind his mother's wide skirt. Estavar marched past her as arrogantly as his father might have.

Big John brushed the snowflakes off his greatcoat and came in with a basket filled to overflowing with colorful *piñatas*, brightly wrapped packages, and tins of special foods Maritza had been preparing for weeks.

"Where is Marta?" Teresa asked, putting Raoul down.

"Sick again," Emilia said sadly. "That child seems to go from cold to cold without a break in between."

"Poor child. For her sake I hope we have an early spring."

"So do I," Emilia said fervently, "and to think that last summer I was praying for a piece of ice like we used to have at Beauwood. After this winter I don't care if I ever see ice again."

Teresa noticed that they were still standing in the foyer, Big John awkwardly holding the basket in his arms.

"Let's go into the parlor," she said. "I'm afraid I've done next to nothing about Christmas this year, Em. I suppose I should have for Elena's sake."

"That's why I brought over a couple of *piñatas*. Miguel came back from Mexico City with enough for a hundred children. He spoils them enough as it is."

"I was unaware he was back," Teresa said dryly.

"Oh?" Emilia exclaimed with a note of surprise. "I thought sure Maritza would have mentioned it. She keeps me fully informed on events over here after her weekly visit to Felix. That's one reason I came today. I was hoping to see him and wish him a *Felice Navidad*."

"He would enjoy that, I'm sure. Why don't you go on up, and I'll make some chocolate for the children and tea for us. You'll find Elena with him. Send her down to meet the boys."

It wasn't until Emilia started to ascend the stairs that Teresa became aware of the fact that it was not Emilia's dress that was bulky, but the woman herself. She had grown to be almost as wide as the stair passage.

Emilia sailed into the room, casually dropping her fur wrap on a chair, and coming to kiss Felix on each cheek.

"Merry Christmas!" she cried, her eyes brimming with tears. "And a Merry Christmas to you, Elena. I'm your Aunt Emilia from across the river."

Elena studied Emilia Escovarro closely. She was still magnificently beautiful, with her shimmering hair and snapping eyes. She looked like a Wagnerian heroine—and had the voice to match her appearance. It was as though she thought Felix deaf instead of speechless. Elena was developing a dual impression of the woman. Her clothing, and the fact that she lived in the large pink villa, made her appear enormously rich to the girl who had known near poverty living with Carmen Morales. Her other impression came from Felix's eyes. They had lightened with joy at her exuberant entrance and had almost instantly dulled with a heartbreaking look of sadness. Elena could not understand why he would feel sad for someone who seemed to have so much.

"Teresa is fixing hot chocolate," Emilia rushed right on, not lowering the pitch of her voice. "She would like you to come downstairs and meet my sons. Would you like that?"

She seems, Elena thought, incapable of speaking quietly. In a way the woman cowed her, and she looked at Felix for instruction. He blinked at her, and she almost detected a trace of a smile upon his lips. She gave him a rewarding smile.

As she passed the chair, she let her arm trail, and the barest touch of her fingertips played over the luxuriant fur.

It sent such a sensuous thrill up her spine that she shuddered and turned quickly to see if she had been caught. Emilia was lowering her bulk into the chair that Elena had just vacated and Felix momentarily had his eyes closed.

Elena ran from the room, her heart pounding. Some day, she promised herself, she would have a coat like that and would never take it off. Never . . . never . . . never . . .

She stopped short and her joy faded when she came to the parlor door. Three boys sat stiffly on the hearth bench sipping at steaming mugs. They appeared to her as about the same ages as Anna-Maria's boys and her heart hardened toward them at once. Her half brothers had been the only boys she had ever known at close hand, and she automatically assumed that all boys would be as cruel and mean and selfish as that trio.

"There you are," Teresa said warmly; coming from the kitchen with the tea tray. "Come and meet your cousins. Raoul and Ramon are the twins, and their brother Estavar. Boys, this is Elena."

Raoul promptly jumped down and came curiously forward. Ramon tried to hide his shyness in the chocolate mug, and Estavar just eyed her indifferently.

"How old are you?" Raoul demanded bluntly.

Elena took it as some sort of challenge, something she would never let the Perez boys get away with.

"Ten," she barked and eyed him coldly.

Raoul giggled. "I'm just five and nearly as big as you."

For that she had no rejoinder, for he was nearly up to her height, so she had to use a different attack.

"It still makes me twice as old as you," she simpered.

"Really," Teresa laughed, "what is all this silly talk about age and size?"

"It is hardly silly, Auntie Esa," he chirped maturely. "Someday I'll be bigger than she is and perhaps just as old."

And sometimes, Teresa thought, your five-year-old mind utterly amazes me, Raoul Escovarro. What with the stately stature of his mother and father he would definitely outgrow the elfin Elena.

Teresa laughed again. "You have that partially right. Now go and finish your drink while it is still hot. I have a mug for you on the tea tray, Elena."

As children will most commonly do, they like or dislike instantly. Raoul took Elena's hand and started to tug her toward the hearth bench.

"Only if Elena sits with us," he said.

"That's entirely up to her."

Elena nodded and didn't pull her hand away. It was a new experience being with a boy who could be friendly. Just then Big John came in with an armload of wood for the fireplace. Raoul dropped her hand and ran to the man gleefully.

"Big John," he demanded, "tell Auntie Esa that I'm right."

The big man blinked foolishly and looked to Teresa for help.

"You know," the boy prompted before Teresa could speak, "what Mama Maritza told me. That you are ten years older than she is, but now that you are both old, it doesn't matter."

Big John flung back his massive head and roared with laughter. "Miz Teresa," he chuckled, "dat boy am somethin' else. He sure am." He ruffled Raoul's golden head playfully, and the boy marched back to his newfound friend triumphantly gloating.

"He's also a big showoff," Estavar shrilled meanly.

"Am not!" Raoul growled.

"Are so!" Estavar snapped right back.

"*Stop!*" Big John boomed, glaring savagely at Estavar. "Ah declare you heathens ain't got no company manners. Massa Raoul, you come 'n' sit ober here. *You* stay put! One more word and I'll be borrowin' Miz Teresa's woodshed."

"Lay a hand on me," Estavar hissed under his breath, "and I'll tell Papa."

Ramon looked up shyly and saw that the outburst had not seemed to phase Elena in the least.

"Don't mind him," he whispered, his voice thin and shaky. "He's Papa's pet."

306

Estavar glared at him with murderous rage. He stuck out his tongue and spat: "At least I don't wet the bed."

Ramon turned instantly scarlet and tried to shrink down inside the collar of his coat. Elena's heart cried out with pity for him. He was suffering what she had suffered so many times at the hands of the Perez boys. She sat down on the bench so that her back was purposely to Estavar.

"Your mother," she said quietly, "told Felix that she had brought a Christmas basket. Would you show it to me?"

Now the blush of a different type of embarrassment stole up his neck, but he nodded sheepishly. Anything would be better than having to stay close to Estavar. He almost raced across the room to where Big John had set the basket down.

Seeing what was afoot, Raoul started to rise and go to his twin brother and Elena.

"Sit!" Big John warned as he took a cup of tea from Teresa.

"But I only want to show Elena—"

"Sit!" Big John cut him short.

Raoul glowered, but it was directed more toward his stammering brother and the wide-eyed Elena. He didn't want to share his newfound friend.

After they had left, Teresa stood looking about the room and mentally kicking herself for her selfish lack of Christmas spirit.

"Darling," she said to Elena, who was stacking the mugs on the tea tray. "Put on your coat and go find Estaban for me, please."

The girl went so quickly and quietly to the foyer that it puzzled Teresa and made her instantly follow. She had noticed that Elena had been unusually quiet since going to fetch Emilia for tea.

"Let me help you," she said so that she could turn her about and study her face. It was pinched into a sullen knot. But something else drew Teresa's attention away.

"Oh dear," she said sadly, "these elbows are near threadbare. I'm going to have to see if I can't cut one of my coats down to fit you."

"Doesn't matter," Elena said sharply. "Not as long as I'm going away."

Teresa quickly knelt down and took her by the shoulders. "Whatever gave you such an idea?"

Elena hung her head. "That woman," she said weakly, near to tears. "I heard her ask Felix if you were going to keep me."

It was a decision that Teresa had not tried to face. Her immediate intention, after finding her in the barn, was to return her to Anna-Maria as soon as the weather permitted. She had kept telling herself that the weather hadn't permitted it so far. But had this day taken the decision right out of her hands, she thought. How easy it had been for her to tell Elena to come and meet her cousins. Now she wondered why she had used the word unless she had meant it to be a permanent relationship.

"I think," she said slowly, raising Elena's chin so that she could look into her eyes, which were like liquid emeralds, "that the question should be reversed. Do you want us to keep you?"

"I think Felix wants to keep me," she answered shrewdly.

Teresa drew her quickly into her arms, hugging her tenderly. "Well, he gets pretty much what he wants around here, you know. But, my darling, I want you to stay as well. Now go get me Estaban, before I start blubbering like a fool."

A new thought sent Elena winging on her way. Anyone could have a new fur coat, but not everybody could have a *new* momma and poppa.

Elena was barely out of the front door when Estaban came in from the back of the house.

"I just sent Elena for you," Teresa said. "Let me catch her."

"Wait!" he cried.

He came quickly down the hall, a bundle under his arm. He was blue with cold, and his handsome young patrician face was bleak. But when he saw the Christmas basket, some of his gloom left him.

"*Piñatas!*" he cried. "I thought she wasn't going to have a Christmas."

"That's why I sent her for you," Teresa said gently. "It is not too late for us to gather some boughs and holly berry for this room. We'll need a *piñata* stick, of course. This year we'll just have to do without the customary—"

She stopped short as Estaban sheepishly unrolled his parcel on the lamp table. Teresa's hand trembled as she picked up the crib and noted the exquisite carving of the baby lying in its vee.

"They're beautiful," she gasped.

Estaban blushed proudly. "I carved them, and my sister Estella painted them. My mother made the robe for the Madonna and the cape for Saint José. It is the gift from our house to your house."

"And what is this?" she cried, holding up the object the figures had been wrapped in.

"My rabbit traps have been most successful," he said modestly. "I have had pelts drying and curing since September. I had little use for them until I began to fear for the *niña* in her thin coat. It didn't take many pelts for my mother to make this coat for her."

"Oh, Estaban, she will love it—and love you for it."

"No, no!" he gasped. "It is not how Estaban wishes it, Doña Teresa. The child speaks all the time of no one but Don Felix. Knowing he is unable to get her something by himself, I wish for her to think that he had Estaban do the trapping and Estaban's mother do the sewing at his request. Our hearts will be filled if she thinks this thing!"

Teresa could hardly speak, the tears were so heavy in her throat. "Thank you," she croaked. "Now go find her before she barges in and spoils the surprise."

All the way up the stairs she prayed that Elena would not spoil the simple, loving ruse. The child, better than anyone, knew that Felix was quite incapable of making such a request.

She laid the white coat on the bed and began explaining Estaban's desires for its presentation while she rummaged through a trunk in search of a New Orleans dress box that wouldn't look too worn or travel crushed.

"I think this one will do," she said, rising and starting back toward the bed. "I think it is one of the most unselfish, beautiful things I have ever—"

Her jaw flew open, and she could only stare in stunned disbelief. Felix had somehow pulled the coat under his right hand and was gently stroking it with a single finger, quite similar to the way Elena had stroked Emilia's coat.

For Felix the coat was a God-given miracle. He had watched the child pass the coat and had sensed her desire as clearly as if she had spoken. He had quickly closed his eyes, feeling immediate remorse that he was incapable of answering her youthful prayer. His hatred for his brother had never been stronger than at that moment.

At first that had been the only thing that made him cling to life, the memory of the man who had betrayed him and brought about his suffering. But he was incapable of telling anyone the truth, and no one seemed capable of reading it in his inflamed eyes.

He had hardly paid any attention to Teresa when she first told him about the child. He had hardly paid any attention to the child when she had first barged into his sickroom. Then, as Elena's visits became more frequent, he came to look upon her as someone Teresa would be able to cling to when he died; for he knew he wanted to die rather than suffer so—but only after he made someone understand about Miguel's treachery.

Then, as a close, almost mystic bond developed between the man and child, he began to cling more to thoughts of living than to self-destruction. His thoughts were less and less of Miguel and more and more of what tale Elena would tell him about the ranch that day. God had given them a child to see to each of their needs. And now that God had given him this unexpected miracle, he prayed to be forgiven for his thoughts against Miguel earlier in the day. He would leave whatever wrath and punishment awaited Miguel in the hands of God. A warm contentment spread over him.

He could actually feel Teresa's tender lips and burning tears of joy upon his hand. He strained mightily to raise his hand and turn her face toward his eyes.

"Oh, my darling," she sobbed. "This is the only Christmas present I prayed for."

His eyes were smiling so brightly that she blinked away her own tears and stared.

"Yes," she said slowly, "I think I understand. You wish this good news to be your Christmas present to Elena."

He closed his eyes slowly, as though to underscore that that was his heartfelt desire.

Teresa refrained from telling him that she had decided to keep Elena. She could see that Felix had long since made that decision for both of them.

For the first time in months she had a real desire to live, to plan, to dream. If Elena had been capable, as a child, of restoring his desire to live, then she was capable of giving that child a glowing future.

After she had packed the coat away in the dress box and hid it in the trunk, she went into the alcove and opened her father's desk. She opened the inkwell and selected the sharpest quill from the tray of turkey feathers. From a pigeonhole she took a fresh sheet of paper and went to work. Her pen raced. She amazed herself at how accurate her memory was, and the drawings and figures seemed to appear on the paper as though by magic.

"You probably wonder what I'm about," she laughed over her shoulder to her bedridden husband. "Emilia gave me the idea today, when she mentioned the summer ice we had at Beauwood. Why can't we have the same? We have fresh-water ponds that are frozen over. I remember what their ice saw looked like and have just drawn one. I think I have the size of the blocks correct as well. My figures on the size of the building may be off, but Estaban can figure that out." She paused. "Damn! The pen dripped and when I went to reach for a blotter it slipped under the back panel. I'll try to get it out with the letter opener before it ruins the whole page with a big blotch."

Teresa had developed the habit of constantly chattering while in Felix's presence. At first it had annoyed him, and he had closed his mind to the sound of her voice. Then he had come to realize that she was attempting to hold up both ends of a conversation, and that had amused him and made him love her all the more.

Now she was silent for so long that he rolled his eyes far to the right to get a view of her. She was intently studying a parchment scroll.

"I had totally forgotten," she said numbly, rising and coming to sit next to him. "While I was prying to get the blotter out, I must have touched a hidden spring, for the whole panel popped open. This letter from King Joseph was inside. Remember, I once told you I was presented at his court as a child of six. You'll get a laugh out of this. It seems that he was so taken in by my gracious charms that he bestowed on me a land grant, to become effective upon my reaching the age of thirty and nontransferable to any other claimant. How odd," she mused. "First, for his having picked such an age and for the reason that I shall turn thirty this spring."

Then she laughed. "You see, my darling, you married well after all."

Well indeed, Felix thought. Very well indeed.

Teresa heard the merry sounds of the returning Estaban and Elena rise from the floor below. She replaced the document in its secret niche and forgot about it, but she did not forget to take her plans for an icehouse down to Estaban.

Because the joy of a *piñata* would have been wasted on a single child, Estaban had fashioned a dozen *piñata* sticks and early the morning of Christmas supplied an equal number of well-scrubbed and excited younger sisters, brothers, and nieces and nephews to take their turns at being blindfolded and given the opportunity to swing at the suspended clay pots.

Although the odds were highly against it, Elena was successful in cracking open the pot that had been decorated to look like a chicken; totally destroyed the pot resembling a fat hog, and took the crown off the pot that was supposed to be an inverted *sombrero* with a single swing of the stick.

That she was a three-time winner mattered not to the other children, for they all shared equally in the cascade of candy and small gifts that rained down from the broken vessels.

"Now, Estaban, now!" Tina Duran shrieked, jumping up and down and pointing at Elena. As a ten-year-old equal, she had already received her customary Christmas gift. It had been placed gently upon her straw pallet before she had awakened, and now she could hardly contain herself for Elena to receive hers.

"Tina!" Estaban scolded and shrugged at Teresa. "Señora, in a family the size of my own, a secret is something that is unknown. You had best do it quickly, before one of these blabbermouths unloads her face of candy."

Elena stood silent and respectful as Teresa phrased her words exactly as Estaban had wished them. Then, as though the box might harbor snakes, the slender girl carefully lifted the lid and peered inside.

Her face became like a burst of sunrise out of the east. She didn't speak, but the looks she cast upon Estaban and Teresa were poetic. In a single movement she flung from the room and was thrusting her arms into the coat as her feet made the stairs three at a time.

"Poppa Felix," she cried, flinging herself across his chest. "It's beautiful, Poppa Felix! I love it! I love you!"

At first she was unsure what she felt drop upon her head. And when she was sure that it was his fingers stroking her russet tresses, she hugged him all the harder. Then she reared back and read his eyes.

She laughed gaily.

"It's gone! The hate in your eyes, like the hate I saw in my grandmother's eyes, is gone! Now nothing can stop us from making you well! Teresa says I can stay. I'll help you from ever hating your brother again."

Teresa, who had felt she had a right to share in that joyous moment had waited a few moments and then come upstairs. She had arrived in time to hear Elena's final words and had quickly stepped back around the open doorway, feeling oddly like an intruder. She was amazed that Elena was aware of any ill feelings between Felix and Miguel, unless she had gained the information from Estaban. But she felt that this could hardly be the case, because the young Spaniard had always seemed quite reluctant to even discuss the matter with her.

Elena might be quite willing to help Felix forget his troubles with Miguel, but Teresa wasn't quite sure that she would be so forgiving. Quietly she went back downstairs and prepared their Christmas breakfast.

When they were nearly finished eating, Teresa opened the inquiry quite calmly:

"How were you aware there was trouble between Felix and his brother?"

"You heard?"

"Yes. I didn't mean to eavesdrop."

"It's all right. It's like I said. I saw it in his eyes."

"His eyes?"

"Sure. Every time someone would mention his brother—Maritza, Estaban, or that woman, Emilia—I could see the hate in his eyes."

Teresa sighed. "That goes back a long way, Elena."

"Not really," she said sagely. "This is new. But it's over now. I don't believe he wants to think of it ever again."

The statement stunned Teresa into momentary silence. "Yes," she said slowly, "I suppose he doesn't want it on his mind ever again."

But that would not prevent her from ever discussing it again. She masked her true emotion from the child that she was beginning to see as remarkably perceptive, chiding herself for not having been more perceptive herself in the grim months past.

CHAPTER SEVENTEEN

The muddy waters broke the unbreakable rip of ice. The chockcherry bushes shed their canopies of frozen crystal; a million anemones burst the steaming peat and thrust tulip-like faces toward the sky. Everywhere summer grass unfolded delicate green tongues of bountiful promise. The cows walked awkwardly, their bellies drum-taut with life, and the chicks pecked playfully during their first adventure outside of the coop. The world was a welter of color and a madness of song. Not for another twelve months would it be as promising, as beautiful, as richly alive.

And in the midst of this land where every square inch of the earth was celebrating the end of winter, an island of winter bleakness survived. Around the Escovarro ranch Christmas had lasted but a single day. The morning after such happiness Felix awoke with a burning fever. An undiscovered slug had been festering in his right calf, its damage so far advanced that the leg had to be removed below the knee. Weak from the operation, his liver and kidneys refused to function properly, and yellow jaundice set in. The pall of his continuing illness hung over the ranch like a madness that was never going to go away.

It was hardest, perhaps, on Elena. In the weeks before Felix's leg was removed, something had happened to her. She had been touched, if only briefly, by something she had never known—a sense of belonging. She had become accustomed to their daily visits and sharing of ranch news. When he was denied all visitors after the operation, she fully understood, but she did not understand the change in Felix when he began recovering from the jaundice attack.

Felix kept telling himself it didn't matter that he had lost a leg, but his appearance belied his thoughts. There was no flesh left on his face, just skin and bones and a tight grim line around his mouth. Outwardly he would try to make his eyes speak of hope for Teresa and Elena, but inwardly the hard shell of determination to rise and walk again had been totally shattered. Now, with the thought of forever being a cripple, there was no retreat from despair.

It was doubly frustrating for Teresa because his attitude left her helpless to help him. There was no way to strike back against such depression. Every gesture she made to bring him back to the point he was at during Christmas went unnoticed or made him worse. When she spoke about anything that had to do with the future, her words were greeted with tightly closed eyes. The only person who seemed to reach him was Elena and that was becoming rarer and rarer.

Teresa had so looked forward to spring and a renewal of time spent with Quapaw, but Felix's attitude seemed to sap even that desire. The most she could bring herself to do was curry and comb the big beast. Standing in the warm spring sun, turning his winter coat to a shimmering summer gloss, gave her solace. Quapaw also couldn't speak, but at least had the decency to return her silent love. If the bed had become Felix's prison, then loneliness was surely Teresa's dungeon.

"Hello."

Turning from Quapaw, she had to shield her eyes to see who had spoken to her from atop the horse. Teresa caught her breath.

"Fine-looking animal," Miguel Escovarro said as though nine months had not passed since their last meeting.

She swallowed the lump in her throat and tried to make her voice sound normal. "Hello, Miguel."

He came off his horse in a single liquid motion. The weight he had lost while suffering with the mumps had not returned. As though he had made a pact with the devil over his sexless state, he had been given back a certain youthful quality and bounce. His hair had come back in rich tight golden curls, exactly as Felix's had been before it started to dull and gray.

Teresa bit her lip, trying to keep herself under control. He had looked so much like Felix when she had squinted up at him that it had given her a horrible fright.

"You look a mess," he said, with his usual ruthless candor.

Teresa felt her temper flaring. With an effort she forced herself to say nothing. The man, she saw, was as insensitive as ever. How would he understand that nine months of hell had corroded her nerves and left her sleepless and always exhausted?

As if he had read her thoughts, Miguel chuckled. "I always seem to say the wrong thing at the wrong time. Maritza keeps us well informed, and we know how rough it has been on you. Is he getting any better?"

Teresa swallowed painfully. "It's taken you a long time to come and ask that question."

There was a long pause. Then, like an errant child, Miguel drew a circle in the dust with the toe of his boot and shook his head, refusing to look at her.

"It's been hard on me, too," he said tonelessly.

Teresa exploded. "*On you*! Are you paralyzed and without a leg?"

He raised his head but didn't speak. Instantly Teresa felt such revulsion that she made a lunge to get by him and to the house. Miguel's big hand flicked out, snapping her to a halt.

"Don't you think that guilt is just as horrible a wound to suffer?"

Teresa shook the restraining hand off angrily, because there had not been the least hint of guilt in his voice.

"Tell me about it," she said icily.

Again Miguel's hand bit into her arm hard. "For the love of mercy, woman *let it rest*! I'm hated by three fourths of the people in this area because they somehow think I am responsible."

With unusual calm she removed his hand and almost whispered: "Can you tell me that you are not?"

Miguel snorted. "How was I to know that Henderson was on to our trap? How was I to know that Felix's men would flee after he fell and not give battle. Those escaping soldiers could have come at my force or Major Cuesta's force just as well. No one takes into account that we suffered only one wounded man in capturing the entire Henderson command."

"Who just happens to be your brother."

Miguel shook his head miserably.

"I didn't know his true condition until I got back from Mexico City. I had been told that he had been killed, but I had an obligation to get the prisoners to Santa Anna."

"That obligation was fulfilled months ago," she said dryly.

Miguel hung his head again. "Would he have seen me if I had come? You know the answer to that, as well as I. I thought it best to give him time to recover and get back on his feet. Was that wrong of me?"

"No, Miguel, I guess . . ." She stopped, torn between the truth and the thought that he could have at least shown her some sympathy and understanding. "You did as you thought best. So, what brings you here today?"

"Ranch problems. We are still a family, you know."

Teresa forced a smile she was far from feeling. "I was unaware that you had ranch problems, Miguel."

"We both have. Don't you have the figures yet on what cattle you lost in the blizzard and afterward?"

"I'm not sure. I'll have to ask Estaban."

Miguel snorted. "The boy is a good farmer, Teresa, but hardly a cattleman. It's imperative that we learn the figures quickly. Guido tells me that on our range we've lost over two thousand head, with several hundred more lamed by frostbite."

Teresa's jaw dropped in astonishment. "That's almost half your herd."

"The serious matter, Teresa, is that it seemed to kill off more bulls than cows. If the same is true over here, it will take us four to five years to build back."

"I—I—honestly, Miguel, I haven't talked with our vaqueros since Christmas."

318

"Then I think it's time for you to saddle that horse of yours, so that we can go learn what's going on around here."

Teresa was seriously flustered. Her mind had been so bogged down with worry over Felix that she had just let the ranch run itself, willy-nilly. She had probably done Felix a bigger injustice by neglecting the ranch to fuss over the invalid.

"I think you're right," she stammered. "If you'll ask one of the men in the barn to saddle Quapaw, I'll go to the house and change." She took a few steps away and turned back on a thought. "You'd best tell them to put Felix's saddle on him. That terrain is a little rough for sidesaddle."

Miguel shook his head in agreement. This was going far better than he had expected. He had anticipated, on his return from Mexico, to create one big ranch again. That Felix was still alive had greatly shaken him, until he learned that his brother was unable to speak. He had waited, week by week, for Maritza's prediction that Felix would die to come true. He thought sure it would happen after the leg operation, was astounded when the severe jaundice attack didn't do him in. Then the blizzard's effect spun the arrow of fate back in his direction. The two ranches could not successfully survive unless the herds were combined once again. He felt very confident that he could convince Teresa of such a necessity. Once he controlled the cattle, he in fact controlled both ranches. He no longer cared if Felix lived or died. He would still accomplish his aim.

Teresa felt a little foolish in a pair of Felix's trousers that nearly wrapped around her twice and vowed to have Señora Duran sew her up a better riding costume.

"What is that?" Miguel asked as they crowned the hill of the last farm and started down toward the duck pond and the vaqueros' adobe village.

Teresa looked at the new structure built into the side of the hill and laughed helplessly. "Oh, Miguel, I had forgotten all about it! It was a project I started to keep my mind occupied and the farmhands must have completed it. Come, let me show you."

They rode up the track to where the back of the building was on a level with the top of the hill. But even when Teresa had thrown open the leather-hinged door, Miguel was still confused as to what he was seeing.

"Wood chips and sawdust," he said with little interest.

"But," she cried triumphantly, dusting off a layer of the covering, "look at the ice cakes it is protecting from the heat. I had the men cut them out of the duck pond and haul them up here by wagon. Those chutes over there were used to lower them to the floor and make it easier to build up the supply layer by layer. This summer the cakes can be easily taken out from the lower side of the building. Just like at Beauwood we should be able to keep food from spoiling so fast in the summer heat."

He looked at her with newfound admiration and suspicion. Perhaps it was not going to be as easy to fool her as he had anticipated.

The cattle on the north ranch had fared much better, protected by the hilly terrain and timberlands. The spring roundup count showed that fewer than five hundred head had perished. Unlike the south ranch, bulls were a problem of a different sort.

"Too many born last spring, Señor Escovarro," the foreman told Miguel respectfully. "They'll be the first into the slaughter pens."

"How do you think they'll be for mating?"

The old man gave him a toothless grin. "Same as any other young critter. Just show them the way."

Miguel turned to Teresa, ready to start closing his trap. "The rangeland to the south and east is going to be quite bountiful this year. If we combined the herds, we might suffer no loss at all."

There was a long silence while Teresa considered the offer. "It doesn't seem wise. If they mate now, they will be birthing in December or January. What if we have another hard winter? Still what if we don't. Why don't you take fifty bulls now, another fifty next month, and fifty again in June. The rest, and the cows, we'll keep here on the hills, which also seem to be bountiful this year."

He had no other choice but to say: "Sounds reasonable."

"Of course," she went on softly, "there will be a stud fee. Shall we say ten percent of the calves born from the union."

"Jesus!" he exploded. "Where did you learn to be so hard-nosed?"

"In Mexico," she laughed, "and the hard way."

For the moment Miguel had a strong need for the bulls and so he agreed. He had plenty of time to wait for the rest of the herd.

He was unaware that he had opened for Teresa a long-closed door. Once before she had been frightened of an almost insurmountable challenge forced upon her and had risen to meet it. Then she had been forced to run the Casa del Sol ranch for a man she had thought to be her husband. Now the challenge was more personal; she felt duty bound to run this ranch for the sake of her real husband, herself, and Elena.

She became a tireless taskmaster of everything that transpired on the farms and ranchlands. She left the care of Felix to the nursing women, and Elena and was almost constantly in the saddle or holding intense discussion with Esteban or the vaquero foreman. The regular hours, the sun, the fresh air revitalized her in spirit and complexion. If Miguel's newfound youthful looks came from a pact with the devil, hers was derived from a pact with nature.

Outwardly she showed the ranch people a laughing, happy, exuberant face, even though inwardly she was growing lonelier and more afraid with each passing day. The harder she tried to make the ranch successful, the more it seemed to grate upon Felix's male vanity and turn him against her.

Miguel became a quite frequent visitor to everywhere but the main house. Elena, innocently, reported the fact to Felix and saw the old hatred burn anew in his eyes. Although the girl had met the man but once, she determined to hate him just as equally and try to make Teresa do the same.

"Look, Elena," Teresa said when the subject was broached, "the Lord only knows that I am well aware of the bad blood between them. But I am also aware that

Miguel has been a great help to me on several matters this summer. I wish Felix could understand that, and I hope that you can."

"Are you falling in love with him?"

Teresa blinked in total dismay. "Hardly. What makes you ask such a foolish question?"

Elena shrugged. "You always seem to be with him and never around here."

Teresa sighed. "I don't think Felix listened to me about the matter either. The reason, Elena, that we have been together so much lately is because of a notion of mine. We have been having the men, from both ranches, dam up a portion of the river and build a waterwheel and gristmill. By harvest time we will be able to grind all of our own corn. That hardly seems like a romantic adventure to me."

Elena started to rise and walk away.

"And where are you going?" Teresa asked.

"To tell Poppa Felix what you just said."

Teresa felt annoyed. "Am I to understand that he, in some way, got you to probe me with the last series of questions?"

"He knows that I won't lie to him and that you won't lie to me," she answered with brutal honesty and left the room.

Teresa sat stunned and utterly dejected. Whenever she tried to please Felix, he was able to whiplash back and make her feel the guilty party. She buried her face in her hands, but the tears had long since been used up.

The artistry for the gristmill floor was left in the capable hands of José Cordova. It had to be watertight against the river's dampness, of a wood hard enough to discourage rats from gnawing through it, and smoothly laid so that fallen meal could be recovered. It was a job José would not entrust to any other man, and he declined Teresa's offer to assign him helpers. He could not, however, refuse another who took a great deal of interest in the project.

Daily Miguel would ride over and silently watch the master woodworker plane and shape the basswood planks, paint their bottoms with creosote, and set them to dry in the exact position they would take once laid within the building. It was like watching a huge rectangular jigsaw puzzle take form. When the day came to start laying the prepared wood on the subflooring, Miguel arrived at the site almost at the same moment as José. Without being asked, Miguel began to help carry the planks into the adobe mill.

They finished the work along about late afternoon and José, grateful for the assistance in a job which was backbreaking for one man but relatively easy for two, opened a jug that he had been saving to celebrate the moment. A half hour later neither of them was fully sober. José had always had a secret and somewhat guilty admiration for Miguel because the man was everything that he himself was not. José was a small man, Miguel was a giant. José lived in a one-room adobe house, Miguel had his towering villa. José's past had been bland and uneventful, Miguel's had been adventuresome and filled with travel and excitement. José's only travel had been from the old ranch to the new ranch.

As a boy and young man on the old ranch he had always envied Miguel his daring. He still recalled with a chuckle the time Miguel had brought the striking prostitute to the old ranch and nearly sent Señora Escovarro into a fit of apoplexy. He had spent his life with a plain, simple ranch girl while Miguel had ended up marrying his gorgeous prostitute. José had always wondered how a prostitute made love and what she said to her man when they were in bed together. On the old ranch when he was making love to Juanita regularly and listening to her girlish squeals of ecstasy, he would try to imagine what Miguel's new bride would be like if she were flexing her loins beneath him— what lewd, lascivious things she might be whispering in his ear. What tricks to excite a man did she know that would horrify Juanita if they were ever suggested to her? Standing next to a man who knew the answers to all these questions gave José a peculiar feeling of pride and envy. He felt expansive and convivial. They were standing on the new planking of the mill, leaning against the base that would house the grist stone. Above the low-lying hill the top of

Teresa and Quapaw's heads popped into view. José took a long pull at the half-empty jug and handed it to Miguel. "Seems like someone else is anxious to see our finished work." Miguel grunted and tipped the jug to his lips.

"She is quite a lady."

Miguel wiped his mouth with the back of his hand and passed the jug back. "Yes, I suppose so."

"But you have quite a lady yourself."

Miguel only grunted. Teresa was now in full view, framed in the mill door as she rode down the path. It was Sunday and she let Quapaw pick his way along at a leisurely pace. Any other day of the week she would have been urging him to carry her quickly from one chore to the next, jumping in and out of the saddle with the agility of the best vaquero on the ranch, her newly made riding pants giving her freedom of movement. But Sunday was a day she would revert to type and ride about sidesaddle like a proper lady.

José took a deep breath, but he didn't have the nerve to keep Emilia in the conversation. He had a suspicion Miguel wouldn't tell him anything anyway. He said instead, "She's quite a horsewoman, Doña Teresa. Prettier now than I can remember. Always figured she'd never make a ranch wife. We all thought she'd move into Santa Fe after Don Felix was paralyzed, but we figured wrong."

"I guess we all did."

"Nice of you to help the way you do, Don Miguel."

"That's what families are for."

"It's still nice. She must be real lonely."

"Lonely?"

"Must be hard on a woman who has a husband who can't be a man to her any longer."

There was a long silence while Miguel considered this remark. It never once crossed his mind that Emilia was in the same boat as Teresa. He had learned to so condition his mind not to think of anything sexual that the statement began to irritate him. After awhile he said, "Better stop discussing her, José. She's almost within earshot."

Teresa stayed but a few minutes, delighted with the

progress of the work. She began to think of other projects for José's talented hands.

"José, give me a hand back up," she requested, "I'm riding out to the vaqueros' village. Señora Cardenas gave birth last night, and I want to check on her." Once settled, she turned to Miguel. "I'll meet you all in about an hour."

Miguel's head snapped up. A puzzled look came into his eyes.

"Meet who, where?"

"Maritza sent over some watermelons from her patch. I put them in the icehouse. Emilia is bringing the children over about five o'clock for a picnic supper by the duck pond."

Miguel pursed his lips. He thought about the fight he had had a few days before with Emilia over his demand that he didn't want his children associating with Elena, and he said, "Seems to have slipped my mind."

Teresa laughed as she rode away. "Stay out of that jug or it'll slip your mind again."

Miguel spun back into the mill and deliberately took the jug in hand. He took an enormous pull and savagely thrust it at José.

"Goddamn that woman and her sly tricks," he roared.

José was unsure of what to say and said nothing. The statement so confused him that he handed the jug back without taking a sip.

"Do you let your woman get away with going against your word?" Miguel demanded harshly.

"I try not to," José said quickly. "Leastways, I used to, but you know women, señor. Let them get three or more kids and they think they can start ruling by cutting off what a man wants most from them. They ain't trained to know how to do it without getting another child. But, of course, you don't have that problem."

Miguel's face went tight. His eyes smoldered. He knew how the ranch people gossiped. Again he was unaware that José was talking about Emilia's past. He read into it only that José had some knowledge of his condition. If their tongues were wagging about his sexless life, he'd make them sorry for it. He reached out and gripped José's arm with a force that made José wince. He said slowly, "You tell me the truth. Are people talking about my problem?"

José turned a trifle white, realizing he'd gone too far. "Well, some I guess, nothing serious, mind, but they figure . . . since you've had no more children and all . . ."

Miguel released José abruptly and turned to stare stonily out over the river. José rubbed his bruised arm and wet his lips. Despite his concern at the way the conversation had gone, he felt a little sorry for the big man. It just proved to him that having a prostitute for a wife was no different than having a regular one. They could cut a man off just the same and make his life miserable. He took a long swig from the bottle and the added warmth gave him courage. He said, "Listen, it is probably not my place, Don Miguel, but sometimes a little nip of the juniper-berry drink the Indians make will get a woman to wanting it again."

Miguel's angry face furrowed now into a look of acute bewilderment. He stood for so long without moving that José began to feel uncomfortable; then without a word Miguel turned on his heel, crossed to the door, and swung around the corner out of sight. A minute later he urged his mare up the hill track and went over the crest without looking back.

Halfway to the duck pond, he pulled the mare off the track and let her crop the grass while he sat the saddle nervously twisting and untwisting the end of the reins. He was there for a full hour debating whether José had lied to him or not. He would have felt debased if the lowly peons were snickering behind his back. He felt no debasement if they were snickering about Emilia treating him like they had been treated, from time to time, by their own wives. He started to laugh, realizing that was all it was. It was quite common knowledge among the household staff that he and Emilia had not shared the same bedroom since he had had the mumps. He again pulled the horse onto the track and headed for the pond.

When he arrived, he avoided rekindling the argument with Emilia because of the presence of Elena. There was something about the way that the young girl looked at him that spooked him and made him wary of her. She was polite but aloof in his company, although she appeared quite comfortable with Emilia.

He sat with his back against a tree trunk, watching the children play at the water's edge, amazed and amused at their reaction to Elena. His amazement centered on Ramon and Marta. The girl seemed capable of forcing Ramon to shed his sensitive outer shell and laugh and play quite normally. Marta, who at three, already seemed to sense that she was less than pretty and would befriend no one, not even Maritza, followed Elena about like she was a chick to Elena's mother-hen strut.

He was amused that Raoul seemed overly jealous of the attention Ramon was giving the girl; but his true amusement and pride centered, as usual, in Estavar. The boy's looks, poise, and attitude toward the girl suggested that she was so far below him that it would take her forever to just climb as high as his bootstraps.

Teresa had not yet arrived by the time Emilia called him for the picnic supper; then he sat on the blanket without taking his eyes from the plate. When he had finished, he suggested that he had better go in search of Teresa.

No one had seen Teresa at the vaqueros' village that day, so Miguel began to backtrack toward the mill. Off the path, in a small clearing atop a hill that overlooked the river, Miguel spotted her horse.

Quapaw was at the far side of the clearing, his reins trailing, grazing casually at the soft rich grass which covered most of the tiny meadow. Miguel rode up to him and dismounted, then caught at his reins. He tied both horses to sturdy saplings, then looked for Teresa. She wasn't in sight.

He crossed the meadow to the break in the trees where he figured she must have entered. There she lay, in the soft turf behind a juniper seedling. She was on her back, arms stretched out from her shoulders, with one leg flat on the ground, the other drawn up with her knee in the air, and her bootheel almost in contact with the creamy flesh of her buttock.

The velvet skirt was tentpoled by her knee, and the absence of any underclothing revealed the glorious treasure of her lovely furry reddish triangle.

Miguel was frozen in fear and awe—fear lest she had been killed by the fall and awe of her utter beauty. Then he felt cheated. The sight of such truly beautiful feminine sexuality should have been an enormous stimulus to his male juices but did not affect him.

He kneeled beside her and felt her wrist, scarcely noting what he took to be a scratch partly hidden by her sleeve. The pulse was reassuring. She was unconscious but not in shock. He checked her head, and there seemed to be no evidence of injury there. He was fairly sure that she had just had the wind knocked out of her and had fainted.

He was going to gently shake her to wakefulness and suddenly stopped himself. He leaned back on his heels and stared at the superb beauty of her dimpled knees, gleaming satin thighs, and the bright chestnut triangle of curls which formed a cleft hill at the base of her glorious belly. Deeming it would be his only opportunity to view her thus, he savored every moment.

On a mad impulse he leaned over her and kissed the dimple of her raised knee. Its amazingly soft warmth made him trail his lips and tongue down the slanted thigh, and catch the ghost of her delicate cologne in his nostrils.

Then his cheek touched the feathery curls, and he turned to bring his lips in contact with their delightfully magnetic tendrils. A faintly musky scent surrounded them, as it mixed with the cologne, and he was drawn more magnetically toward the source of the compelling odor.

Forgetting that he could not finish what he started, he began tasting the heat and moisture of her female flesh. Teresa began to moan faintly, but he could tell she was still not conscious—although he didn't think he could have stopped what he was doing even if she had awakened. But unconsciously she was participating, for the fleshy lips of her femininity were swollen, and the moisture she exuded was almost a steady flow.

As Miguel gulped hungrily, thrilling deep within himself at her utter femaleness and her vulnerable helplessness, he felt a wild gathering of his soul in the depths of his loins, and for the first time since his illness the strain of his erected manhood pressed against the taut material of his trousers. Without even thinking, he opened his fly and released it to the summer air. Then its true meaning hit his mind sharply, and he sat back and stared at his engorgement with almost boyish awe that such a change had taken place in his member.

"Ohhh," Teresa moaned from the depths of the dream world he had created in her mind. "Don't stop, Em . . . don't stop . . ."

It sobered Miguel quickly, and he stared at her as though he had heard wrong. Suddenly he slammed his fists together.

Goddamn, Emilia! . . . *Goddamn her for being a whore and a lesbian!*

At first he was so puzzled by the discovery that he couldn't move or think. Then he tried to determine the implications. When had it happened and was it still happening? He suddenly saw the whole thing as a damnable affront to himself. Just as that thought crossed his mind, Teresa moaned loudly and gasped for air.

He whirled to look at her. Her eyes were still closed, and there was a look of extreme discomfort, but not of pain, on her lovely face. It told him that she needed something from him that Emilia would be incapable of giving. Quickly he pushed her skirt up to her belly. Then he moved to kneel between her legs.

It had been so long since he had entered anyone that he was almost timid and gentle. His thrusts were so mildly implanted that it aroused Teresa only momentarily.

She was unaware of where she was. The sunset filtering through the quaking aspen leaves helped to retain the dreamlike quality of her mind. She felt the man upon her, but his movements were so slow and prolonged that it seemed hardly a sexual encounter at all. She turned her head and saw the mass of golden curls. Her mind went back into limbo, knowing it had to be a dream, because Felix would be incapable of such an act other than in a dream.

Miguel's long dormant passions rose and burst quickly.

329

Within seconds of entering her, he was pulling out, tugging down her skirt as he went. He was rather unsteady on his feet for a moment, and then he thought he should do something to bring Teresa around before someone else came looking for them.

"Teresa," he called, gently shaking her shoulder.

Her eyes opened, and after fluttering a bit, remained open. She continued to gulp in air, and he slipped his hands under her, raising up her rib cage to help stimulate a return to normal breathing.

"You had the wind knocked out of you," he told her, and her slow nod confirmed it. Then she tried to sit up, and it made her gasp more loudly for a few seconds. Finally she could speak.

"Thank you, Miguel. A blue jay must have thought I was too near her nest. She kept diving down at me, and I took a swing at her. She pecked me on the wrist, and I lost my balance. Wouldn't have happened if I hadn't been on that damn silly sidesaddle."

Miguel smiled to himself, thinking that what happened would not have happened if she had been in her riding pants.

She started to rise and noticed for the first time the sunset through the trees. She turned very pale as she let her eyes rove up to Miguel's curly golden locks. She was miserable in the knowledge that it had not been a dream.

She studied Miguel for a moment before she spoke, and when she did, she leaned forward and grasped her knees, hugging them toward her, almost in a gesture of locking the barn door after the cows have gotten out.

"For your sake—for both of us—you must forget everything about this afternoon except that you found me knocked out. And I will forget everything also—including what you did while I was unconscious!"

There was a small triumph in her eyes as she noted his reaction to that. For once in his life Miguel blushed heavily.

"But . . . how could you know, if you were . . ."

". . . unconscious?" She had a strange smile on her face. "My dear Miguel, contrary to what you might have read or heard, when a woman has been treated in such a manner, even in her sleep, she knows about it when she awakens."

That she was taking it so calmly brought his arrogance surging back.

"Then the next time I'll make sure that you are not asleep."

"There will be no next time," she corrected him automatically and sternly.

"Oh, Teresa! You know how badly you needed it!"

She grinned slyly as she seemed to be thinking of some secret thing, then she looked directly at him with cold, hard eyes.

"Yes, I guess I did, and that's why I'm not making a big fuss about it. The next time I will, if you try. Now you'd best help me up. I can hear the carriage coming down the track."

There are times when the honest truth appears as an overly varnished lie to others. Emilia listened to the reason for Teresa's absence from the picnic with an emotionless face. She kept her mind just as emotionless until the children were all in bed and she and Miguel were alone in the parlor.

She moistened her lips and tried to keep her voice easy. "When did you learn that you were capable of being a man again?"

There was a lengthy pause and then he said, "Who says I've learned?"

She laughed coldly. "You forget my background. I can smell the musky odor of finished sex on a woman a mile off."

He said nothing, but she sensed the struggle in him. There was a fluttering now in the pit of her stomach, and her palms were moist. It was ridiculous of her to carry on like this, and still she couldn't help it. She didn't want him again, but she didn't want Teresa to have him either.

"Well?" she said.

This time he found his voice. "I suppose you're right."

"There is no supposing about it. You are capable again, then?"

"Yes."

"Today was the first?"

"Right again."

The next was hard, very hard, but she got it out in a rush. "I suppose it was an act of frustration on Teresa's part, and I'll forgive her because this has been the only time."

Miguel's blood began to boil. Without saying it, she was crucifying him without considering his own frustration, yet was willing to quickly forgive Teresa.

"Why not forgive her," he sneered, "considering what you have been to each other in the past."

Emilia took a gasping breath. She sensed what was coming, and she was desperately trying to marshal her defenses.

Miguel waited for a reply, and when none came, he braced himself and in a burst of desire to hurt the woman drastically, hurled the vicious lie at her. "She told me all about your lesbian affair!"

The words tore through Emilia's heart. It had been so long ago, almost a forgotten thing in her mind. She opened her mouth to rebut it, and the words would not come. She stood up. She realized that for some unfathomable and stupid reason she hated Miguel more for having learned of the event than of Teresa for having told him.

"Now whose turn is it to do the forgiving?" he demanded meanly. "Tonight you will open your bed to me, woman!"

"I can't!" she gasped. She turned and ran up the stairs to her room. The click of the lock was audible.

Miguel stood up, the dreadful finality of the words hammering in his brain. *She had refused him*! He turned and strode into the dining room, his face black, his pulses pounding. *She had refused him*! She could forgive Teresa, but she couldn't forgive him. He yanked the top off a whiskey decanter and held it to his lips till it was more than half empty. The hot liquid burned his throat and stomach. He felt like he wanted to kill somebody. His eyes were wild as he tilted the bottle again, emptied it, and then with one violent movement hurled it at the mirror over the fireplace. The sound of shattering glass exploded into the silence of the house. He stood stock-still, looking at the spider web remains, a little trickle of liquor running down his mouth, and then he flung himself toward the stairs.

The raw liquor seared his stomach and made his head swim. The drunker he got on his climb, the clearer his hatred grew. She had refused him for the last time! He tried the door to her room and found it locked. With a sudden release of pent-up viciousness, he slammed his huge fist through the panel. It splintered into a thousand pieces. The blood ran off his torn knuckles. He looked at them unseeingly and then smashed his hand again and again into the panel until only the splintered framework remained. He flung open the door, cursing and ripping at Emilia's nightgown, paying no attention to her screams and threats.

"Get hold of yourself," she pleaded. "Act like a normal human being."

There was such a long pause that Emilia wondered if he had heard. Then without saying anything, he tore off his own clothing and pulled her roughly down onto the bed and into his embrace; for a brief second before his mouth crushed down on hers, she caught the acrid odor of the liquor. She was suddenly aware that his whole body was trembling.

For the sake of the children, she told herself. For their sake alone I shall be quiet and not fight him back. But this shall be the last time ever he enters my bed. And to keep her mind from even trying to enjoy the act, she began to build a hatred for Teresa in her heart.

Miguel was trembling out of fear. Nothing was happening. He was not being stimulated. The more he tried to force his mind to think upon what he desired, the more flaccid he became. Then he thought of the meadow and the manner in which he had found Teresa lying. Arousal came almost at once. To keep it thus, he transplanted the two women in his mind and was as gentle with Emilia as he had been a few hours earlier with Teresa.

Having always been a brutal lovemaker, it made Emilia instantly suspicious and increased her black thoughts against Teresa.

The noise had aroused the children, except for Marta

who still slept in the third-floor nursery. Peering from their doorway, Ramon's face was ashen with fright and Raoul's a gloating mask of superior knowledge.

"What is it?" Estavar hissed from across the hall, his face as emotionless as ever.

"They're making love," Raoul giggled.

"How do you know?" Estavar demanded sternly.

"Because I'm six and a half and know things that you don't know."

Estavar looked totally shocked and disgusted. "Do you mean like the bulls and cows."

"Naturally, stupid!"

"Ugh!" Estavar grimaced and quickly closed his door.

Ramon looked at his twin brother with eyes big with respect. "How do you know about it?"

Raoul put his finger to his lips and spun Ramon about so he could close the door.

"Do you promise to tear your heart out if you ever reveal my secret?"

Ramon nodded openmouthed, while crossing his heart with his finger.

"Then let's get under the covers so I can tell you all that I've learned. Old big-ears Estavar is probably listening at the keyhole."

Although nothing sexual had ever been mentioned between them, Raoul gave full credit for his knowledge to Elena so that he could prove once and for all that she cared more for him than Ramon. Ramon was heartbroken with the news.

CHAPTER EIGHTEEN

Teresa Escovarro found her fierce resolution to blot the incident from her mind a difficult one to keep. The first few weeks were not so hard. Every instinct of her womanhood had cried out against what had happened. But a forbidden fruit once tasted leaves its mark.

The prurient memory which stung deepest was the terror she had felt upon reliving those moments in her dreams. She would awaken in the dead of night, her body enflamed by the passion of her dreams. She would spend the rest of the night walking the floor in a rage and dropping at last exhausted enough to sleep without dreaming:

"I will not do it again!"

When four weeks passed without a further attempt on Miguel's part, the first skirmish between desire and pride began. There was something perverse in her somewhere, she began to think. Perhaps they did need each other. She was without a husband for all practical purposes, and for two years Emilia had made no bones about her locked bedroom door. And had Emilia lied to her? She had seen no evidence to indicate Miguel impotent as was reported by Emilia. Perhaps . . . ?

Again she resolved for the hundredth time to banish the last thought of desire for him. If Emilia did not wish him sexually, then that was their affair; she could live without sex just as she had been doing.

During the harvest and the inauguration of the gristmill they were forced into almost daily contact, Teresa always finding an excuse to have Elena or Estaban Duran present. She loathed herself for such deceit.

Then Miguel was called into Santa Fe to help Doña Patricia on a project she was attempting to put together. Teresa didn't see him for two months, for when he did come home on an occasional weekend, Emilia found a thousand excuses to keep him from crossing the river.

When Miguel casually let word drop that he had purchased a house in town, Emilia was canny enough to surmise that it also had a mistress hidden within one of its bedrooms. This time she felt no jealousy or anger. She would much rather have Miguel's mistress in Santa Fe than right across the river. Besides she was pregnant again and had a perfect reason to refuse him without locking the door against him.

The harvest and fall roundup had made it impossible for Teresa to visit the villa, and she'd accepted without question Emilia's excuses of not visiting on account of illness. But when the news of Emilia's pregnancy reached her, it was like being shocked with an unexpected bucket of ice-cold water.

For an odd little moment she felt as though she had been betrayed, as though she were the wife and Emilia the intruder.

"I . . ." Teresa gasped for the right words. "She's . . . she's always told me first, Maritza."

For a long time the black woman searched Teresa's face for something she could not find.

"I suggest, Doña Teresa, that instead of worrying about her reasons of late, you concern yourself with your own health."

"My health?" Teresa repeated softly. "That's a funny thing to say. My health has never been better."

Maritza shook her head sadly. "Call me, child, when you have need of me."

It was several days before Teresa came to know what Maritza had suspected and she had been too blind to realize. There had been no morning sickness, no warning, and no appreciable abdominal swelling, even though she had to be three months along.

It was only when her riding pants began to fit too snugly that she began to fear and examine herself more closely. Her mind became rattled trying to recall the missed periods, which she had discounted at the time as being late because of the excessive amount of riding she had been doing at the time. Now the memory of them brought terror.

She suffered silently for another month until Miguel made his next visit out from Santa Fe and then sent word that he had to meet her over a problem at the gristmill. When Estaban Duran brought back word that Miguel could not possibly see her this visit, she sent him to find José.

"I'm aware," she told the carpenter, after outlining her plan, "that it will take some little time. How much, however, do you think you can accomplish in four to five months?"

José shrugged. The project greatly intrigued him, but he was reticent to be away from his family for so great a length of time.

"Of course," Teresa went on smoothly, reading his thoughts, "you will be able to take your family and all necessary provisions and equipment with you. Also, because winter is coming, take whatever workers you may deem necessary."

José beamed. "In four or five months I can work miracles."

But five days after José's little cavalcade departed the ranch, she no longer needed a miracle. By a vaquero she had never seen before, Miguel sent word that he would meet her at sundown at the gristmill.

Teresa had been prepared to berate him at once, but one look at him stilled the words in her throat.

"You wished to see me, Teresa?" His face was bloated and blotched from his return to an almost constant drunken and lascivious life-style. He had regained nearly sixty pounds, and the majority of it seemed concentrated about his middle. His clothing was far too grand and ruffled for simple ranch living.

"Miguel," Teresa said pathetically. "Come in. There is a problem that has come up which we both must face."

Miguel stood rigid, as though waiting for something terrible to happen. Once, twice, he took deep breaths. Then he focused a murderous gaze on her stomach.

"Speak!"

Teresa, her face immobile, her body trembling, blinked once and gave Miguel a quiet solemn reply. "There is no longer any doubt of the facts. I am going to have your child."

It was said so simply, so matter-of-factly, without malice or anger, that Miguel was caught completely off guard.

He reached out and slapped Teresa with a quick, stinging blow. Teresa blinked, not fully aware of what had happened. Then it hit her with almost as much impact as the blow itself. She was alone with the man, and no one was aware of it.

"You're lying," he yelled.

"I have no reason to lie about such a thing," she stammered.

"Shut up! Now you listen! I don't give a good goddamn whether you are or not. But if so, you'd best shag your ass into Santa Fe and find a midwife who will abort it for you."

"What are you saying?" she gasped. "It's a living being. That would be murder!"

"I could hardly care less. You've already got one bastard-born child on the ranch so why bother yourself with a second one."

"I can't do it," she said weakly. "You're going to have to claim it so that it has some future."

"Future?" he roared. "To hell with its future. I am more concerned with my own."

"I should have known that would be your answer," she said softly. "Well, forget it. I'll handle the situation on my own."

Miguel started to rage but knew that she was adamant. He could not, he would not allow her to contaminate his children with yet another bastard among them.

His fist caught Teresa high on the head. She went down on her knees, shook her head savagely to clear it, then came up slowly, covering her stomach with one hand, grasping for the grist stone with the other. Miguel struck again, sending her flying the length of the mill floor. Teresa rose, supporting herself on the sill of the open window that overlooked the mill pond. She turned, stunned, and opened her mouth to plead. Miguel shuffled in front of her, set his weight properly, raised his left boot, and planted it firmly into her stomach.

Teresa spun backward, somersaulted through the air, and landed flat on her back in the water. Stunned and not quite sure what had happened, the current rolled Teresa slowly over and began pulling her toward the churning waterwheel. Her last conscious thought, if it really was a thought, was that she had been here before and this time the paddle wheels of the *Yellow Stone* would surely crush her.

A million years seemed to pass before Miguel saw the waterwheel snatch at her body and begin lifting it. He watched in dreamlike fantasy as it carried her to the top of its curve and then toppled her unmoving form down into the foaming water. He found himself wondering how quickly he could get a court order pronouncing Felix incapable of handling his own affairs. Then he cautioned himself to act with judicial calm. No one was aware he had ridden down that day from Santa Fe. No one was aware he had hired a vaquero from a distant ranch to bring her the message. He had not been seen and was fairly sure that Teresa had told no one of their meeting. He would just quietly ride back to Santa Fe and await word to come home for the tearful funeral of his sister-in-law. Then, and only then, would he feel compelled to take the burden off of Felix's shoulders and make the ranch as one.

Elena sat tensely beside Felix as he stubbornly refused to take the mouthfuls of supper she was trying to force upon him. She knew that it was not unusual for Teresa to be detained on some errand or other after dark, but never before had he acted in this manner. Slowly, over the months, she had wormed her way back into his confidence. He had regained, again, slight use of his right hand, and she had devised a way whereby they could communicate by the tapping of his forefinger to simple questions.

"Now eat your dinner," she scolded. "She'll be along any minute now."

He turned, and the fright that she saw in his eyes stunned her.

"Do you want me to go in search of her?"

He tapped his finger once for an emphatic "yes."

"I know it's silly, but I'll do it, although I'm not quite sure where to look first."

Felix strained until he was able to stretch out and grasp her hand with his. It brought her eyes immediately to focus upon his. What she saw was an insistence that he was right.

"I'm sorry," she said dully. "It's not silly and I'll go at once."

Felix had been frightened before but never like this. He felt remiss in having to send the twelve-year-old girl on an errand that might turn out to be folly and his urging nothing more than something bad he ate for lunch. Still his stomach was a mass of crawling worms, and he could almost feel his whole body tingle and tremble.

There was a breath of frost in the air. The leaves of all but the evergreens had long since been splashed with great masses of flaming color and were now gone. The juniper bushes were bright with scarlet berries, and the ground was beginning to lose its soft springiness. After having been to the barn and two nearest farms, Elena began to regret that she had not put on her fur coat.

"She wasn't going out to the vaqueros' village today," she learned from Estaban Duran as he rubbed the stubble of his chin thoughtfully. "Last I saw her she was talking to a vaquero."

"Which one?"

"Not one of ours or theirs. Stranger. Then she rode off toward the river. I thought it was kind of funny at the time."

"Why funny?" she demanded a little angrily, wanting to quickly get on with the search.

"She had a dress on and had to bunch it up in the middle to get into the saddle."

"Then she probably went to the gristmill," she said on a note of hope. "I'll go on down there."

"There's a wind rising. I think I better go with you before it blows up nasty."

The storm broke before they were halfway to the river. The first blast of wind struck with such force it nearly knocked them from the path. It tore the breath from their mouths and left them gasping. And with the wind came a swirling, menacing vortex of flying snow. Taking her hand, they ran the rest of the way to the mill.

Elena's heart began to sink when she saw no sign of Quapaw. That terrible sense of futility which affects anyone who doesn't quite know where to search next began to gnaw at her. Estaban had to shout to make himself heard over the shrieking of the wind.

"Elena, we'd better wait for a while in the mill."

Elena nodded. At first it appeared that it would give them little respite from the storm. The wind and snow drove right through the open windows and door of the structure without mercy. Estaban signaled for Elena to help him start closing the wooden shutters. It took both of them to swing the northern window shutters into place and bar them across securely. But once those passages had been sealed off, the noise dropped a few pitches.

"Hope the river doesn't start freezing tonight," he said as he began working at the south window. "It could do a lot of damage to that waterwheel and then . . ."

His words trailed off so oddly that it made Elena turn quickly. "What is it?"

Estaban looked troubled. "I thought I saw something on the wheel, just as it was entering the water. Wait."

Elena, watching tensely for what he had seen, saw the knots of hard muscle leap into prominence on his jaw. His customarily dark face got darker. "Look, it's part of the dress she was wearing! You stay here! I'll start searching downstream."

Elena's eyes were as big as saucers. "No, I'm coming too."

Estaban didn't want to waste time arguing and quickly relented.

Again they had to fight against the storm, slipping awkwardly on the riverbank rocks and trying to stay out of the water itself. Elena suddenly grabbed Estaban's arm, and he automatically reacted to keep her from falling. But she was not falling, she was pointing frantically downstream. Even through the vortex there was no mistaking the massive frame of Quapaw.

Estaban took one look at the scene and could see that the horse had pulled Teresa's limp body from the water and had been valiantly dragging it to higher ground. The horse was still trembling from fright and cold. It was abruptly apparent to Estaban that Teresa was badly hurt and required immediate attention.

He put his mouth close to Elena's ear and shouted over the wild moaning of the wind. "I want you to get on Quapaw and go across the river for Maritza. I'll start carrying Doña Teresa back to the ranch."

But Quapaw balked and shied away from Elena. He was not about to leave his mistress.

"I'll go for Maritza," she shouted. "You take her back on Quapaw."

Estaban shook his head in refusal. "You'd never get across the river." The wind made his shout sound almost like a whisper.

She set her jaw and shouted back. "I know the shallow place, where I wade across to play with Raoul and Ramon."

She was up and running before he could call her back. Only then did he notice that she was wearing nothing but a cotton dress.

Elena bit her lip and ran a hand over her face, into which the biting granules of snow were driving with painful force. Her head ached from the intense cold pressing against her temples. Her nose was running, and there was excruciating pain now in her wet feet. The hem of her long skirt was starting to freeze and stiffen. She tried to put all of this out of her mind, because the candlelit windows of the pink villa glowed invitingly just before her.

Her fingers were so numb that she felt no sensation of touch as she knocked at the oaken door. Now that she was motionless, she began to tremble from fright and cold. It seemed forever before the door came flying open.

Emilia stood looking down at her, a trace of wonderment and curiosity on her face.

"Well?" she said tonelessly but did not move aside for Elena to enter.

"It's Doña Teresa," Elena gasped. "She's hurt bad."

Emilia said, with typical curtness, "And what am I supposed to do about it?"

Elena began to shiver and stutter. "S-s-send Maritza!"

Emilia's face became cunningly arrogant. "Impossible!"

Elena stumbled on awkwardly. "S-s-she must have been c-c-caught in the waterwheel and a-a-almost drowned."

Emilia's reply was cold, disinterested. "Maritza is far too busy caring for Marta's head cold. Now you better go back."

Before Elena could raise her next argument, she found herself staring at the closed door. She stood, abashed. Unaware of the problem that had arisen between Teresa and Emilia, she was stunned by the change in the woman she had always gotten along so well with. She began to blame herself for not making the urgency of the matter better understood and began to pound on the door again. It was not reopened and so she continued to pound.

"What is all the commotion?" Maritza asked, coming out of the kitchen hall with a tray of steaming soup.

"Nothing that concerns you," Emilia snapped. "Take Marta up her soup."

Maritza scowled. "I've felt trouble coming all day long. Who is out there?"

Emilia looked at her, with all her cold naked fury in her eyes. "The bastard girl from across the river. I sent her packing."

Maritza was silent a moment, then she said steadfastly: "Don't sound like she did it. She better come in out of this storm so we can find out what she wants."

"No," said Emilia with low bitterness and hatred, "she will *never* set foot in my house, and I am well aware of her mission. Teresa has cooked up some scheme to get you to come running over there. I forbid it as long as Marta is so sick."

Maritza looked at her fixedly and set the tray down on

the hall table. "No one sends a child out on a night like this unless it's right important."

"Don't open that door," Emilia spat with icy passion.

Maritza ignored her and was stunned by what her eyes beheld. She quickly tugged the shawl from her shoulders and thrust it out to the shivering girl. "Run around to the kitchen porch," she ordered, after hearing Elena's quaking request for her aid. "Maritza will be there in a moment."

She turned slowly, as if shaken to her very depths, and regarded Emilia with dark and accusing eyes. "I thought you were a woman, Emilia. Knowing the circumstances of your life, I thought you never could be that cruel. That child is near frozen, and you were going to just leave her out there. See to your own child. I'm going to see about Doña Teresa."

As if she had said something heinous, something intolerably insulting to her, something most contemptible and indecent, Emilia regarded her with a stern expression, even an outraged one:

"You are a fool, Maritza! I overlook your insults because you are a free woman. But don't forget that you are still nothing more than a servant here. If you leave this property tonight, you'd best not plan on coming back!"

The black woman looked at her with sudden warning sharpness. "Then you'd best start learning how to care for your own children."

She spun and marched down the corridor to the kitchen. When she had gone, Emilia stood with her head high and stiff. But if her attitude was indomitable, it was also unbearably desolate. She would not admit to a living soul how lonely the rift with Miguel had made her. She had trapped herself in a folly. She had become an arrogant, dominant woman, who loved the power of being the mistress of a grand house and ranch. She could not bring herself to be friendly with the ranch women and so was friendless and lonely.

Suddenly she laughed. Her whole mood was ridiculous. She had been a loner all of her life and had never felt this depressed. It was the baby causing it, she determined. She was having just as much trouble with this child as her first and her added weight was not helping matters. Still she would not listen to Maritza and eat more sparingly. She wanted everything in sight, like a starving child. She had very little else to do, and so she ate. She could concentrate on the taste of the food and not have to think about anything else. But she did set aside time to think about one thing—the baby.

With all her heart she wanted this child to be a girl. She wanted her to be a beautiful girl and hers alone. The twins belonged to each other; Estavar was his father's, and Marta was a mystery to everyone. This would be her child. She wouldn't even let Maritza have a hand in raising it.

Suddenly a sound brought her out of her reverie. Big John! Who else was allowed to drive the enclosed hansom carriage but Big John? It infuriated her anew. Now Maritza was affronting her by getting *her* servant man to take her across the river. She was out the door before the carriage could round the house and depart.

She waved frantically, but the canvas covers were rolled down against the storm. She waddled to the end of the veranda so they could not help but see her as they passed. Here she was not as fully protected, and abruptly the full force of the storm caught at her skirts, nearly dragging her from the porch. She clutched at the porch railing and screamed, "Big John! Big John!" The words were drowned out by the roar of the wind, and the carriage rolled hurriedly on.

"Damn nigger!" she snarled. "I'll kick him off, too!"

She turned in her fury, bracing against the wind, and as she did so, there was a slight pain somewhere. Her legs felt hot and wet. She raised her skirt and looked down at the snow-covered porch. Where she stood, the whiteness was slowly melting away to scarlet. The color began to drain from her face. She stared at it unbelievingly. "Oh, no! Oh, not that! Not *my* baby!"

Then she felt the strength rushing out of her. She struggled to get back to the main door and sank down just short of it. "Alone! They've deserted me!" She felt consciousness leaving her. She opened her mouth for air, and the snow drove in, choking her. I'm dying, she thought. I'm alone and I'm dying here in my own blood, and I've lost my baby! What more do you want, Teresa? You tried to take away my husband; you took Maritza and Big John away when they could have been here to prevent this. I *did* want this baby! I did! I did! I'll never have another, and it will all be your fault.

Big John felt the blast of cold air on his feet when he came back to the kitchen from hitching up the hansom for Maritza. The wind had blown open the hall passage door and he snorted. "Wouldja look at dat. Some fool done 'n' left the front door wide open. Hard enuff ta keep this ole barn warm widout such foolishness."

He almost closed the front door without looking out, but a movement on the snow-covered porch caught his eye and puzzled him! Like a snaking river a finger of red was inching its way along. Cautiously he came out to see its cause, and his mind went cold sober. He lurched to where Emilia lay and knelt down. She was still conscious.

"Big John? You didn't leave?"

"No, ma'am. Maritza took the hansom. How'd you get hurt?"

"The baby! I've lost my baby!" Her voice was weak, only half audible over the flooding noise of the snow and wind.

He stared numbly, then swept her up in his huge arms. In spite of his strength he staggered with the bulk that she had become. There was a wild churning in his head to run out and bring Maritza right back. He set her down on the parlor couch. His arm and the right side of his sodden shirt was red. The red ran off her skirts with the snow water, staining the couch. He shook his massive head helplessly. "Wat'll I do?"

She bit her lip. She couldn't faint now, not now that she was no longer alone. She and Big John had been through many things together in life, and together they could weather this storm. She said, "Stop bleeding . . . snow . . . get snow . . . pack me with it."

The nearest thing at hand was a cut-glass fruit bowl. He raced into the yard and packed it tight with snow. He took the hem of her skirt and tore it open to the waist. Her underthings were a sodden mass of blood. He thrust the ball of snow against her groin and in a second it was beet red.

"No . . . time for modesty," she whispered.

Her words gave a fragment of control over his wildly racing mind, and he set his jaw and ripped her underthings away. For an hour he raced back and forth until the parlor floor was a pool of red water and the snow pack no longer discolored on her groin.

"Children . . ." she breathed heavily. "Don't . . . let them see . . . please."

He closed the parlor doors behind him before going upstairs. He gave Raoul the responsibility of seeing that everyone got ready for bed, after explaining that their mother was sick and Maritza was away.

"Bet she had a miscarriage," Raoul said sagely.

Big John frowned. "Boy, where y'all hear such a word?"

Raoul smirked. "I hear that Auntie Esa has them all the time, so I figured Mama must have one once in a while too."

Big John shook his head in bewilderment. The boy was a perplexity to his simple mind. "You jest ne'ber mind about dat stuff, boy. Jest get 'em all ta bed so dey don't disturb your mama."

"What about Marta? She's sick."

Big John smiled wickedly. "Dat chile's on de tird floor, Massa Raoul. Ain't gonna hurt 'er skinny throat none ta bawl itself ta sleep fur change, and none of us am goin' ta hear a thing."

Raoul giggled with delicious delight, happy to see that he was not the only person who considered Marta overly coddled and her constant illnesses a mere ruse for more attention.

Big John's presence of mind was now fully restored. He stopped in Emilia's bedroom and gathered up fresh clothing. There was no longer any reason to keep Emilia packed in snow, so he brought hot water and towels from the kitchen to bathe her and help her redress. Fearing that

347

she would start bleeding again, he refused to let her walk up the stairs and laboriously carried her up to her own bedroom.

After swabbing up the mess on the parlor floor, he found the untouched soup for Marta on the hall table and re-heated it for Emilia.

"Do you remember Paris?" Emilia asked as she spooned the broth up to her ashen lips.

"Yes'um," he answered, tucking a napkin higher up on her neck.

"I think I'd like to see it again, Big John. Now that I don't have this new child to think about, I think I'd like to get away. It will be far easier than the last time, because we will have more money. We can leave the children in Marit-za's good care and not have a worry in the world."

For the moment he overlooked the popish "we!" He cleared his throat. "I thought you told her not to return?"

Emilia nodded gravely. "I can see now that she felt she had an obligation to Teresa. This night will settle that matter once and for all. Remind me tomorrow to send a note up to Don Miguel in Santa Fe about our trip."

Big John shook his head doggedly. "Ain't wintah comin' there, same as here?".

"Naturally," she said smoothly, "that's why I'm thinking more in the realm of the south of Spain for now and Paris in time for spring."

"Dat long?" he gasped.

Emilia looked down into the bowl of broth as though it held all the answers. "The longer the better," she said dully.

She sat silent for so long that Big John quietly left the room and stood for a long time in the hall with his own thoughts.

There was no woman in the world he respected more than Emilia; there was no woman he loved more in the world than Maritza. He could not bring himself to even think about such a long separation from his wife but was dumbfounded over how he would be able to say "no" to Emilia. With all his heart he wished that night had never come about.

* * *

His wife was mirroring his thoughts across the river. She sat exhausted at the kitchen table sipping a cup of tea and forlornly watching the ashen face of Elena. When they had arrived, she had barely given the child a chance to change into dry clothing before she had to press her into service as her assistant. The fetus was dead in Teresa's womb and had to be removed before it killed her as well. Maritza feared that she could not wait long enough for Estaban to go through the storm for one of the other ranch women. He was assigned the task of keeping the fires high, the water pan boiling, and staying out of the way.

In spite of her birth and rearing around Carmen Morales, Elena was still little-girl naïve. But in a single night a child was forged into a woman.

While the operation was taking place, her young mind ceased to function, and she became a robot extension of Maritza's hands. Now the tensions flowed out of her muscles and left her with a single thought.

"Will she live?"

Maritza nodded gently.

Elena closed her eyes. A tremor ran over her face. "A baby. I didn't even know she was going to have a baby. I wonder if that means she wasn't going to keep me after it came."

Maritza felt a surge of loving sympathy. She said quietly, "I doubt that very much—and she's going to need you now more than ever, child. Teresa is not going to be able to have any more children."

"I don't think Poppa Felix should be told that," she said sagely.

Maritza looked quickly down at her teacup. There was anguish and desolation written in her face. It was now blatantly obvious to her why there was coolness between Emilia and Teresa. She said emptily, "I don't think anyone need be told, child."

"It's going to be hard enough for Poppa Felix to understand how she fell into the pond in the first place. She's lucky that nothing was broken, and she was only severely bruised."

There was a sharp snap from Maritza's fingers. She

looked down. She'd pressed so hard on the teacup that it cracked. She took the pieces to the garbage basket and flung them in irritably. She paced over to the window and looked out at the swirling storm. It was as wild as her own mind at that moment. Keep your mouth shut, she told herself. The child's right. The whole thing will be hard to understand—except for three people. She too might have accepted the fact that the bruises and abrasions had been caused by the waterwheel paddles and river rocks if it hadn't been for the distinctive marking on the pit of Teresa's stomach. The blue-black imprint of a bootheel and sole were as clear as though they had been made in wet sand. She was well aware of who it was that wore heavy knobby-headed brass studs in the heels of his boots—the floors of the pink villa were pitted from their tread. It was an unholy mess, an unholy night.

Teresa opened her eyes and stared at the kitchen ceiling. Her head ached. Every muscle in her body was stiff and sore. She tried to reason out why she was lying on a cot in the kitchen. She turned her head. All she could see was Elena sitting at the kitchen table.

The slight movement was like a bugle call to the girl, and she was to the cot in almost a single bound.

"It's all right, Momma Teresa, *it's all right!*"

Then Teresa saw Maritza hover into view. She stared, frowned, and then remembrance flowed through her. A tremor shook her whole body.

"Just lie still," Maritza soothed. "You're going to be just fine. And, Elena, I think you can take yourself to bed now. I'll sit with her through the night."

Elena did not protest, she was wrung out emotionally and physically. She kissed Teresa gently on the forehead and smiled her good night to Maritza.

"Again?" Teresa asked when they were alone.

Maritza nodded, knowing exactly what she meant.

Teresa sighed, but there was no bitterness in her voice when she spoke—only a kind of hollow finality. "Perhaps," she said, "he did us all a favor."

CHAPTER NINETEEN

The maturation of her mind was soon running a footrace with Elena's body. In the next two years the elfin lines began to reform into a budding woman's body. Almost overnight, it seemed, she was at eye-level height with Teresa and almost on an equal par with her breast, waist, and hip measurements. The pinched, freckled quality to her face vanished, as did the flame tones in her hair. Nature repainted her with deep-curling rosy auburn hair, lips wine red and a trifle full, her eyes emerald-smoldering beneath a heavy curve of brows, and her complexion as smooth and soft as eiderdown.

At fourteen there was no question that she would be beautiful—flaming, stunningly beautiful . . . utterly provocative. And there was no question that she would possess a mind to equal her body. Teresa had trouble keeping her in reading material and the subject matter was far ranging. She would read and reread anything she could get her hands upon. Nor was it knowledge that filtered in one ear and out the other. From a Spanish translation of a Charles Dickens tale she gained a good enough description of a wheelchair to have one fashioned for Felix—and found the grit to force him to begin to use it.

Nor was all of her education purely from books. A colt sired by Quapaw became her thirteenth birthday present. It was her responsibility to raise and train the mare, and the mare in turn was helping to teach her how to become an exceptional horsewoman. She soon began to ride with Teresa and came to know every square inch of the ranch and the functions of every farmer, vaquero, and beast.

For Elena the two years seemed to melt together as

though a single blissful day—except for one minor dark cloud.

Emilia had done better than her word. She had left the ranch in time to arrive at Valencia for Christmas. But when Big John flatly refused to budge without Maritza, she accepted her defeat. She was worn out with fighting Miguel, tired of endlessly resisting his attempts to get back into her bed. Her surrender meant that she had to take the children, as well as Big John and Maritza, to Europe with her.

As her stay lengthened, so did Miguel's in Santa Fe. It became almost a natural thing to see the pink villa constantly dark.

The lengthened stay also gave Teresa hope that time and distance would heal the wound between herself and Emilia. Her heart was thankful that Guido Herrera was running the south ranch, and that she had not been forced to see or do business with Miguel since their last fateful meeting.

For Teresa, Elena eased the pain of realizing she would be unable to have a child—by any man. She devoted herself to Elena, Felix, and the ranch. Except for a few troublesome clouds, her days were almost blissful.

Constant rumors of war brought drifters and adventure seekers down the Santa Fe Trail so that they could slip into west Texas by the back door. Usually arriving at Santa Fe with little or nothing, they thought it their God-given right to live off other peoples' land as they headed south. For a single meal they would slaughter a steer, cut out just enough to spit over their campfire, and leave the rest, when they rode out, for the buzzards to feast upon. Some of the more daring would rustle several head of cattle to give them a better beginning in Texas.

The north ranch, with only ten vaqueros, was too vast and hilly to totally prevent the losses. Guido Herrera, with ten times the manpower, was far more successful, and there were many dark rumors abroad in the land of midnight "neck-tie parties."

For the spring roundup of 1846, Elena was given the honor of keeping the tally sheets. When she had the totals well in hand, she frowned thoughtfully and went to find

Teresa, who was discussing a farm problem with Estaban.

"Even if you subtract some for the wolves and coyotes," she explained, "five percent lost seems an awfully high amount for a few Anglo stomachs and rustlers."

"Doesn't sound high to me," Estaban said.

"Oh, Estaban," Elena scolded. "That's over a hundred and fifty head of cattle that have been slaughtered or stolen."

His black eyes popped with disbelief.

"I know, darling," Teresa sighed, "but it would cost far more to establish more vaqueros on the ranch than the losses total."

"Well," Elena snapped, her green eyes turning almost black, "it seems like we should be able to do something. How about the farmers riding the herds at night, just as the vaqueros help them with the harvest?"

Teresa laughed. "The vaqueros work the harvest," she explained tenderly, "because their chores are fewest at that time of the year. I'm afraid after a spring day in the field the farmers would just fall asleep in the saddle."

Estaban was frowning as though on a deep thought.

"Doña Teresa," he said very soberly, "let Estaban think on this matter for a few days."

She nodded, although she was aware that all the thinking in the world would not solve the problem.

That night Estaban slipped across the river to the south ranch and did not return until near dawn. His brothers and sisters snickered that he must have finally taken an interest in a girl. Señora Duran frowned darkly at her husband and indicated with her head that a lecture was in order, even though Estaban was a fully grown young man. She would not condone such goings-on in her strict Catholic home. But after the father and son were together in whispered debate for some little time, it was the older man who came away with a gleam of respect in his eyes. But knowing the wag of his wife's tongue, he held his silence.

Three mornings later Estaban stopped short coming out of the door of his parents' adobe house. On the step were a pair of straw-filled shoes. He wisked them up quickly and hid them under his wide *camisa*. His heart singing, he contemplated the safest place of hiding them until the time for their proper presentation.

That night he slipped away again, but this time was not home by dawn or breakfast or even supper. Señora Duran fretted and worried; Señor Duran fretted and pretended not to worry. He knew that the next week would be extremely hard on his wife, her eldest son going unheard from, but he kept his own proud heart masked behind his stern weather-beaten face. What was happening, he understood, was God's will.

It was a puzzlement to Teresa. The more questions she asked about Estaban's mysterious disappearance, the fewer answers she got. She had had people run away before, but never of the quality of family background of Estaban.

During that hour between night and dawn, when the blackness makes men wonder if a new day will really come, a shoeless Estaban stumbled painfully up the path to his home, each step leaving a bloody imprint of his advance.

As though by magic the leather-hinged door silently opened, and a grateful father, who had anticipated this seventh-morning arrival, helped his son on the last few steps of his arduous journey.

As Señor Duran gently eased his son down onto a stool, Estaban whispered faintly into his ear.

With a slight chuckle the beefy farmer lighted a single candle and indicated with a nod of his head that he had long since smelled out the hiding place of the shoes. With pride he handed them to Estaban. Estaban returned that pride by noting, in the candle shine, that his father had expertly prepared everything else that would be necessary.

Carefully tiptoeing around the other sleeping children, the farmer went to the curtained-off portion of the room that he shared with his wife.

"Woman," he whispered, "you must come awake."

"Who is asleep?" she growled. "Who has slept for six nights?"

"The Penitente is home," he said softly and went back out of the curtain to begin quietly waking his other children.

At first Señora Duran thought that she had heard wrong, then the tears of realization welled into her eyes. It was a reason for his absence that had never crossed her mind, and the import of its meaning overwhelmed her. Numbly she rolled her rotund frame off the straw matting and rose on trembling legs. She gave no thought to putting on a bathrobe and went through the curtain in her nightdress, her unbraided hair cascading down her wide back to her buttocks.

By custom of the secret religious society, she avoided looking upon the face of her son or any of her other children. She kept her eyes downcast until they came in view of the dirty, bloodstained feet and the earthen basin of water.

With loving tenderness she bathed each cut and swollen foot and dried them carefully with her own hair, until its natural oils made the skin soft and clean to the touch. Then she reached up, still without looking, and accepted the shoes from her son's hands.

From each she extracted the straw and placed them in two little mounds on the dirt floor. Estaban's feet were then placed down upon them and she leaned forward to kiss each instep. He was now united with the Beginning—the straw from the Bethlehem manger. Next she took the shoes and slipped them onto his bare feet, symbolizing the travels he must face in life to protect all that was good and righteous.

Then, for a brief second, her heart faltered. She become, in that instant, another mother of long ago who also had felt her heart falter before feeling the steel flow back into her indomitable spirit and give her courage to look upward. Marta Duran could almost hear the voice that had spoken to the other Marta: "Mother, look upon thy son!"

One after the other she took Estaban's hands, palm up, and examined the week-old wounds left by the hammer-driven nail spikes. She kissed each crucifixion mark, her tears forming tiny pools in the cup of his hands.

Only then did she know it was proper to raise her eyes all the way to her son's face. It was so radiant in tenderness that she knew ever afterward that she had been blessed to look upon the face of God.

Estaban's brothers and sisters had viewed it all in mind-boggling awe. They were well aware that a new dimension had come into their family life. It was a matter to be kept secret, sealed away in the secret reaches of their hearts. There was now a Penitente among them—a chosen one—a special personage. Outwardly they must treat him little differently than they always had, for to expose him would bring about their own ruination. Inwardly, in spite of their awe, they felt little different than normally toward him—deep love and respect and admiration for an elder brother.

Rafael Duran's awe and pride in his son were deep. He was old enough to know that the secret religious society, although none would admit it, was composed exclusively of the wealthiest dons and a few of their more outstanding vaqueros. That his son had not only been selected but chosen to be one of the crucified, was something he did not want to ponder or even question. His mind was basic enough to accept what was God's will, and not *why* it was God's will.

Estaban Duran greeted Doña Teresa that morning as though he had just seen her the previous day, although artfully keeping his hands hidden from her view.

She was so momentarily shocked at his sudden reappearance that she never gathered together the proper words to question why the absence had taken place or the reasons behind it.

By the time spring slipped into the humid days of summer, the slaughtering and apparent rustling was on the decline. The vaqueros could give Teresa no reason to account for it and shrugged it off as good fortune. Teresa wasn't convinced. She knew that the spring and summer months were the busiest for the Santa Fe Trail—a time when the long wagon trains could come through Raton Pass without the danger of blizzards and sleet and the dreaded avalanche of snow and rocks burying hundreds at a time.

In July a long-delayed post for Elena took Teresa's mind off everything else. In a boyish scrawl Raoul had written to say that the family would be coming home overland, via New York, by the middle of August.

After two years of near freedom Teresa suddenly felt like the warden was coming back to take up residence across the river. She hated herself for feeling guilt but knew how it would sound to protest her innocence to Emilia. She hated Miguel for having let Emilia know about the incident in the first place and was still disbelieving his words that Emilia had known at once. If that were true, she pondered, why then try to kill her and actually kill the baby.

More and more she found her mind reaching backward for answers that would really solve nothing. To try and push them from her mind, she developed the habit of riding alone with Quapaw each summer evening when the Rockies and Sangre ranges sent down their cooling breezes. At such times there was no past, present, or future, but just the moment at hand. Her eyes would absorb the sky, the mountains, the mesa in a thankful prayer.

"Damn! Your earthly servants are stupid asses!" she cried out so suddenly one day that it made Quapaw start and her voice echo and reecho throughout the hills.

It was a Sunday evening, and she was uncommonly upset. During the spring and summer months, ever since their arrival, a friar from the mission in Santa Fe had ridden out once a month on his donkey to celebrate mass for the people of both ranches. For a year Teresa's request for the baptism of Elena had fallen on a deaf and uninterested ear, but that day a new priest had arrived, and she felt tempted to try again.

The Father was freshly arrived from Spain and had already set his heart upon being slain by the Indian "savages" and going to beatification and sainthood as a true martyr. That Santa Fe was so tame and urban left him callous and bitter.

"Really," the priest had said cruelly, "the church could hardly give instruction and communion to such as she."

"Oh!" Teresa had faltered, but for a moment. Then she had returned to the attack. "Precisely what do you mean?" she had demanded.

"Precisely what I say," he repeated. "That the child

comes from an unholy union in the eyes of the Mother Church and is beyond grace."

"Oh, damn the church's grace anyhow!" Teresa had exploded. "How does the church's grace handle the bastards that pop from you priests and nuns?"

The priest quickly bent his head, as though in prayer, his face white and still.

"I see," he murmured. "You have been too long among the savages. I shall pray for your eternal soul."

"You had best pray for your own," she said calmly, "because if you are not off this property in five minutes, I may just turn all of my people into Lutherans and baptize Elena myself."

He fled as though she had just sprouted horns and would deprive him forevermore of his rightful place in church history.

She was unaware how long she had been staring at the finger of smoke rising into the sky. Her mind had been solely on how she could next try to get Elena into the church. She followed the curling spiral down to the ground and the campfire. In the gathering gloom she could make out six horses, but not bunched as her vaqueros would leave them. She squinted at the distance to see if she could spot their owners. It wasn't difficult. A short distance away five bearded men held a calf to the ground, while a fifth slashed at its neck with a knife.

Anger boiled into her mouth, but before her voice could scream out and her heels spur Quapaw into a gallop, another sound echoed through the hills and stopped her short.

Swooping down on the slaughterers, from two sides, four riders charged, their throats full throttle in a banshee wail and their guns firing in staccato bursts. Two of the would-be Texans never left New Mexican soil and the other four probably rode their horses until they collapsed from exhaustion and fright.

The second band of intruders were a real curiosity to Teresa. Once they had the cowboys on the run, they came back, swooped up the slain calf, and disappeared into the hills. That their heads were covered in black hoods gave her reason to believe that they were simply another brand of pirate who stole from their own ilk. She sat for a long time waiting to see the direction of their own camp smoke so she could warn her vaqueros, but no smoke came.

A golden summer dusk had settled by the time she was back to put Quapaw into the barn, a time she thoroughly enjoyed. The stable hands would normally be home for summer supper, and she could curry and groom Quapaw at her leisure. But the moment they entered the barn door Quapaw warned her that this would not be a normal evening by his pettish snort.

At the far end of the barn, where it normally was not done, Estaban was dressing out a calf.

Puzzled, she put Quapaw into his stall and went to Estaban.

He was well aware of her entrance, although he had not expected it. Still he greeted her respectfully.

"You will have fresh veal for your supper tonight, señora," he grinned.

"I was unaware of ordering such," she replied coolly.

He shrugged. "Some vaqueros came riding in and said they had found it nearly slaughtered. It is already bled dry."

"Our vaqueros?" she said dryly, moving forward.

"Not exactly," he stammered, unused to lying in any form.

Teresa said nothing. She was staring at something that she had never seen before. The manner in which Estaban had been cutting away the hide, and pulling it from the flesh, left his hands exposed to her full view.

"How did that happen?" she asked with a frown. "Those wounds to your hands."

She sensed, rather than saw, the change that overcame him. The jolly, kidding boy was instantly replaced by a sober-faced but oddly tender adult male.

"Señora," he said quite calmly, "it is a matter quite out of your realm. Please do not ask again."

His words and calm manner rankled Teresa rather than soothed her. "Don't ask," she snapped. "Oh, no! I overlooked your week's absence without question. A moment ago I almost let you get away without telling me what vaqueros brought you this calf. But I think you'd best know, before you answer my next question, that I was up on the north forty this evening and saw a calf slaughtered and then stolen away by some men in black masks. Now would you know anything about that?"

"Everything," he said just as calmly as he had said before. "But in spite of that I have only one question for you."

"Well?" she demanded, hotly.

He looked at her and smiled on a slow grin.

"Do you wish veal chops, veal steaks, or cutlets?"

"Estaban!" she stormed, but the stern reproach on his face kept her from raving on.

"Doña Teresa," he said heavily, "please do not intrude into this matter. You are an admired and remarkable woman for what you have accomplished here. Some things require a stronger hand. I can tell you no more, so please don't try and force me. Just be content that you will eat the veal and not the Anglos and vultures. Can you promise me this?"

He had opened her mind to many other questions, but she silently nodded her consent and let them go unspoken.

As she returned to unsaddle and curry Quapaw, she recalled the conversation in which Estaban had asked for time to think of something to solve the problem. She was not quite sure if she approved of the solution he was attempting, or what problems it would pose for her in the future. But for the moment, she realized, it must be the reason for the drastic reduction in slaughtered and rustled cattle.

It was not unusual for the United States military to supply escort service to the Santa Fe Overland Express Company out of Independence, Missouri. Not unusual, because it had the power and the wealth to demand such service from a "foreign" nation. In 1846, the firm alone would have three thousand wagons, four thousand men, twenty-five thousand oxen, and one thousand mules on the Trail, over which it would haul fourteen million pounds of goods.

The escort for the wagon train that arrived on August 18, 1846, was uncommonly large. Many thought that it was due in part to the large, ornately decorated European-type carriage included in the train. The advance riders had set the town abuzz with the news of the impending arrival of its occupant. The count of Medina, Don Carrillo del Campo, was a distant cousin of Queen Isabella II. With a Mexican war crowding the horizon—and England had pressed hard to keep the Texas lands independent and out of the hands of the United States—it was important that nothing unforeseen happen to the Spanish visitor. Texas had been admitted to the Union in December, forcing England to throw its weight behind Santa Anna to recapture the land he had lost a decade before. President Polk didn't mind fighting Mexico, but wanted Spain to be kept as neutral as possible. But he had a far more important mission for the military escort than the mere protection of Don Carrillo.

"Poppa!" Estavar shrieked, clamoring out of the carriage before it was fully halted. "Poppa! Poppa!"

"My boy!" Miguel cried, scooping the running lad up into his arms. "Good God, how you've grown! You weigh a ton!"

"That's because I'm almost ten, Poppa."

"Stand down and let's have a look at you."

Miguel's eyes misted at the sight. It was truly like looking into an old mirror and seeing himself at that age. Estavar was the only one he had missed in all that time.

Emilia came out of the carriage with the regal grace of a reigning queen. She had lost a great deal of her excess weight and now wore clothing that enhanced her full figure and made it appear again alluring and provocative.

A tall, lean middle-aged man stepped down behind her and then turned to lift Marta from the carriage. His long-jawed face might have been plain if it were not for his elegant attire and bearing. The flamboyant dress seemed responsible for toning his face and giving it a touch of life. Otherwise he would have appeared as totally bored and indifferently aloof.

"Hello, Miguel," Emilia said without enthusiasm and bent her head so that he was offered only her cheek to kiss. Then she half turned, smiling.

"Let me present our guest," she said grandly. "The count of Medina, Don Carrillo del Campo. Carrie, my husband, Don Miguel."

The two men bowed stiffly, without shaking hands.

"This whole trip is the count's doing," Emilia bubbled right on. "He wanted to see America and he's seen it. Ghastly long way to come. Horrible food and miserable lodgings. We do live at the uncivilized end of the earth. Marta!" she snapped suddenly. "Will you stop dragging on my skirt and greet your father!"

Without lifting her head, Marta mumbled tonelessly and moved farther behind the full hoop of the skirt.

Miguel nodded without answering, his mind on a different matter.

"Don Carrillo is to be our guest, you say?" he said. "Then you'll want to leave for the ranch right away."

"We can hardly stand another mile of travel today, Miguel. I anticipated staying in town for a few days."

Miguel hesitated. "My house is really not very large and grand," he demured. "Perhaps we can impose upon Doña Patricia to play hostess."

He still has a mistress, Emilia thought bitterly. Strange that it still bothers me. It shouldn't; not now, not any more.

"Very well," she said coolly. "I thought you would have the room because we are two less."

Miguel's head whipped from side to side, searching.

"Where in hell are the twins?" he roared.

"I thought it best to leave them in Spain for proper schooling. Carrie was a dear and helped me get them into an academy which accepts only the children of the nobility and the well placed. It's time they learned to become gentlemen and not little ruffians."

Miguel pursed his lips. "A good thought and it does alter the picture. The house is ready to receive you, if you want to come along now."

Emilia looked at Miguel with grim amusement. It appeared he did have the common decency to hide away his mistress for her arrival.

"In a moment," she murmured. "I wish first to say good-bye to this gentleman. He has been most gracious."

A tall officer, with graying russet hair and a face of chiseled granite, had come riding up, his hat already off in salute to Emilia and the count.

"General," she said with a winning smile, "I wish to thank you for our safe arrival and present my husband, Don Miguel."

He doffed his kepi and saluted smartly. "Steve Kearny at your service, sir. I was hoping to meet you and seek a favor."

The words filled Miguel up with pride.

"Then I am at your service, señor."

General Kearny came off his horse with military stiffness. "I know it's right improper of me to take you from your family so quickly," he drawled, the New Jersey twang quite evident in his voice, "but I wish to pay my respects to the governor-general.

"I've sent an officer on ahead to ask for an audience but thought it might be more proper if I had a *don* of your caliber to introduce me."

Miguel beamed with importance. He saw that the request had also made an impression upon the count, and that pleased him all the more.

"Gladly," he exalted. "The palace is but a short distance. Emilia, will you excuse me? Big John should still remember how to get to the house. The housekeeper's name is Carmen, and she has food and drink and rooms ready for you. I won't be long."

It was far longer than Miguel anticipated and more unusual than he could have possibly dreamed. They were ushered into the inner office immediately upon arrival. An officer stood with his back to them, staring out the window at the square. Don Pedro fluttered importantly behind his desk. But before Miguel could open his mouth, the general took command.

"Governor," he growled, "I am Brigadier General Stephen Watts Kearny, commander of the United States

Western Force and a personal representative of President James K. Polk. It is my duty to inform you that war was declared on Mexico in May. You may therefore consider yourself and your city under capture. My force is quite large, so resistance would be futile."

Miguel collapsed into a chair, his mouth agape.

"Capture?" Don Pedro spluttered. "But you . . ."

"Can't?" Kearny roared. "Sir, by God I have! You may now leave *my* office and consider yourself under house arrest. My troops are already deployed throughout the city and should have your small force well in hand."

Don Pedro slunk away, his mind still stunned by the suddenness of Kearny's announcement.

Miguel came out of his stupor quickly.

"Why," he demanded sharply, "the ruse of bringing me along?"

Kearny smiled pityingly, as one smiles at a man in his dotage.

"I learned much about you on this trip, señor," he said gently. "Minor tidbits from your wife but mainly from your boastful son. Normally a man in my position would not put much stock in information gained from a child. But, Señor Escovarro, the lad is unusually bright and not given to lying. Good head on his shoulders, I'd say."

"That's gratifying," he said bitterly, "but answers me nothing."

Kearny sat in Don Pedro's chair and tried it for size, rubbing his thin fingers together.

"Ah, Señor Escovarro," he grinned, "the meaning is simple. You are a conquered people. To date this has been a bloodless victory, and with your help I intend to keep it as such. As one of the largest landholders I shall look to you to help persuade the other landholders to surrender peacefully."

"Surrender?" he asked dully. "Is this Texas all over again?"

"And why not?" the officer at the window bellowed and spun about.

Miguel's eyes flared. "Bowditch!" he choked.

"*Colonel* Bowditch," he sneered.

Miguel spun his head back to Kearny. "I congratulate you on the caliber of your ranking officers, General," he rasped. "You have here a fine example of cheat, thief, and would-be kidnapper."

"You lying son of a bitch!" Bowditch bellowed and started toward Miguel. "You're the one who stole my land and ruined it!"

Miguel looked at him aghast. "I beg your pardon!"

"Stop!" Kearny commanded sternly. "I don't give a good goddamn about Texas and the past. I've told you that right along, Bowditch."

"But I am!" Miguel sneered dangerously. He saw that he had to discredit the man or stand to lose to him all over again. "If you want my help, it will be settled."

"We don't need his damned help!" Bowditch demanded.

Black rage mounted in Kearny's face. He wanted to be quickly done with this godforsaken country and strike quickly at the true prize—California. A West Point man, he was resentful that Bowditch had been able to purchase a rank it had taken him years to obtain. That the man had bribed his way into being named "temporary military governor" after the conquest had not bothered Kearny at the time. In fact it meant that he would be well rid of the arrogant, uncouth man after the Santa Fe expedition. But upon leaving Independence, the man had been spotted by Señora Escovarro and his past revealed. Loath to lose the element of surprise, he had kept Bowditch well away from Emilia during the trip down the Trail.

"I," Kearny said icily, "and only I will determine that, *Colonel*. Sit!"

Vince Bowditch, at that moment, was beyond speech. He knew that Kearny had the power to change his orders, and he slumped into a chair and scowled.

"I am aware," Kearny went on in a chilly monotone, "of a certain New Orleans incident from Señora Escovarro. It has nothing to do with me, so the matter is closed. I also have information, true or false, that you were approached by an agent for a General Green for the purchase of that land."

Miguel laughed, to stall the man and get in a point against Bowditch.

"As you say," he explained, "my brother and I were approached with a letter signed by Sam Houston which was going to all but force us off land held by my family for three hundred years. We balked, of course, and the agent—I believe his name was Thackery—seemed well aware that we might balk. He was then willing to offer a purchase price for the land, and we sent him back to General Green for the money."

"Was Bowditch mentioned," Kearny inquired.

"His name was listed on the letter as an agent," Miguel answered smoothly, "but this Thackery informed us that he had returned to his family and farm in Virginia, I believe it was."

"Then what happened?"

Miguel tensed internally but kept his face emotionless. This was the crucial moment. That Bowditch had mentioned that the land was ruined meant that he had seen it. When?

"We prepared to leave the land and move up here," he said slowly. He left the door open for Bowditch to supply him with further information. Bowditch stepped into the trap feeling he held all of the trump cards.

"But the question," he said grimly, "is how did you leave the land and Thackery."

Miguel blinked foolishly, internally knowing he had just hit pay dirt. "Leave," he stammered. "Why I left with the main vanguard of our people and never saw Thackery again. My brother, Felix, stayed with the vaqueros who were returning to Spain to run the ranch and collect the money from Thackery."

Bowditch bristled, thinking he had sprung a trap of his own. "And how much did you receive from your brother on the purchase price?" he demanded fiercely.

Miguel frowned. "General Kearny," he said stiffly, "at any other time I would consider that information none of his damn business, but I shall answer it for your benefit alone. When my brother Felix arrived in Santa Fe, he presented me with over ten thousand in gold coin."

Bowditch immediately demanded shrilly: "And you know damn well how he came by it! I arrived to find the land in ruins: fields salted, orchards chopped down, buildings razed to the ground, and the slain body of Samuel Thackery!"

Miguel gasped in horror-stricken surprise. But calmly he thought: you stupid unseeing bastard! You have just given me the only missing piece to the puzzle. You killed Thackery and took the money he was bringing. Now let's see who wins the next round. I now hold all the trump cards.

"Oh, no!" Miguel moaned and pressed his face into his hands. "I cannot believe this! Felix would not do such a thing to our parents' land! Felix would have no reason to rob and kill for such a petty amount!"

Bowditch was angry. With a muffled "damn!" he rose from the chair and stalked to the window, his face heavy with frowning. He had guessed wrong again. The moment he had heard Miguel Escovarro's voice he had felt he had the man trapped. He had never suspected the mild-mannered Felix Escovarro of such a horrible trick.

"This has suddenly become," Kearny said mildly, "a rather serious matter and charge." But a matter and charge that was swinging to his liking.

"Charge?" Miguel echoed blankly. "Why?"

"Murder has been suggested."

"Yes," Miguel whispered, "so it has." Then he gulped. "It is hard to admit that you have been duped by your own kin. I believed Felix when he told me how drastically they had reduced the purchase price, and now it will all happen again. Anglos will come in and offer us pennies for what we've spent hundreds on to build up."

"It need not be that way," Kearny said patiently. "Cooperation has always been a great equalizer."

"And while I cooperate," Miguel spat savagely, playing his part to the hilt, "Anglos will come in and devour land and cattle and businesses such as the Santa Fe Overland, and I'll be branded the traitorous blackguard."

Kearny laughed mirthfully. "Land and cattle, perhaps," he chuckled. "But enterprises such as the Overland are automatically protected."

Miguel frowned, puzzled. "Why?"

"Because of the citizenship of their owners."

Miguel sat back and suddenly roared with uncontrolled laughter. "This is horribly priceless," he chuckled. "My family can reside upon this land for three centuries, and it can suddenly be taken from them by an upstart nation that is barely seventy years old. A woman of nearly that age can come to your shores from Ireland, be recorded as a citizen, require a business in these parts, and thus not be touched by the sword of your conquest. It is madness!"

"Poppycock!" Kearny snorted.

"Is it?" Miguel challenged. "Then tell me of your plans for the Santa Fe Overland Express."

"Plans?" Kearny said warily. "There are no plans. It is an essential economic lifeline that has to be maintained and kept fully operational."

"Even though it is owned exclusively by my aunt, Doña Patricia de Escovarro?"

"My God!" Kearny gasped; his granite face lighted up with respect.

"That's right," Miguel chortled. "She is Irish by birth, American for a few months of citizenship, and fully Spanish by long heritage and virtue. It was I who suggested that she establish the business under her maiden name."

"What interest, if any, does she have in your ranch?"

It was a question that surprised Miguel and at the last second his mind stopped him from answering, none.

"I do believe," he said thankfully, "that she holds a longstanding note on the majority of the equipment."

Damn it all! Kearny thought morosely. Bowditch was going to have a hell of a time getting the man to play traitor without a single carrot to dangle in front of him. Well, it would just have to be Bowditch's problem.

"I wish to be on the march within forty-eight hours, Señor Escovarro. Colonel Bowditch will contact you when he wishes to continue this conversation."

Miguel shrugged indifferently, but his mind was a beehive of plans for that conversation.

* * *

With the city humbled so abjectly, any thought of revolt melted away, and the vaqueros were kept on the ranches and saw to their chores. Don Pedro disappeared; the true supporters of Santa Anna disappeared. General Kearny departed for California. Everyone went back to their normal routine. The wagon trains rolled on the Santa Fe Trail.

One aspect of Santa Fe life did alter greatly during that first week of American military rule: the dinner parties increased enormously. Everyone who was anyone wanted Don Carrillo seated at their table; or plotted to get an invitation to the table at which he would be a guest. Colonel Vince Bowditch was not so lucky.

Miguel stiffened suddenly, hearing the tread of Emilia's feet in the hall and the tired quaver of Big John's voice telling her he was in the library.

He sat very still and waited.

Emilia came into the room and stood there looking at him, her lovely face as cold and still as death.

"How dare you?" she said.

"It is my house . . ." he mumbled.

"Granted. But it's madness to invite that man to dinner. Have you forgotten what he did to me in New Orleans?"

"Hardly. But you are forgetting that he is the military governor and everyone is purposely snubbing him. You know how dangerous a man he can be, and I think he's about ready to start striking back."

"That is your concern. I will not be humiliated . . . and I will not let Carrie be humiliated," she added coolly.

"So—" Miguel said heavily, "you *have* been carrying on with him."

"Yes, Miguel," Emilia said. "I have. For over a year. What else could you expect?"

"Nothing, I guess. I asked for it. At least I had the decency to remove my mistress before you returned. I think that deserves a favor in return. Could you reconsider on Bowditch coming . . ."

"No," Emilia said. "I couldn't."

"Dear God, Em! The man has the power to . . ."

Emilia bent forward a little, her soft lips smiling.

"That is precisely what I want, Miguel Escovarro! You see, I've come to a lot of truths while I've been away. You made me and too many others suffer too long and hurt all of us far too much. I never realized how evil you were until General Kearny asked me if I knew how the old ranch came to such ruination. No wonder you were so nasty about sharing the sale price with Felix. You and Bowditch should team up. You're both gifted at coveting what you don't own."

Miguel looked at her and smiled with grim mockery.

"It's a very good suggestion," he said.

"No, it really wasn't," Emilia said clearly, "and don't try it or I might be forced to reveal much more about you."

"What?" Miguel roared, half rising from his chair. "What the devil do you think you could reveal, Emilia?"

"Precisely everything." She leaned forward, looking into his face. "Oh, you great selfish ass!" she said bitingly. "How often did I look the other way when your greed got in the way of everything else. I was just as bad, because I wanted you to build up something grand for the children. But when I realized what you had done to the old ranch, it came to me that you would also be capable of doing that to people. Say to your own brother? That made me question if I had misjudged Teresa. I forced the true story out of Maritza last night."

Miguel sank back into the chair, his face ashen, his mouth working, shaping words that never came out.

"She lies!" Miguel finally bellowed, then his big voice broke. "You can't prove it, Emilia," he got out.

"Rumors never need proof—but are just as ruinous!" Emilia said cruelly. Then she turned from the desk and walked toward the door. In the doorway she turned.

"We are leaving for the ranch within the hour," she said. "I hope you have an enjoyable dinner with the colonel!"

Miguel slumped in his chair. The truth he could twist to appear like a lie—but the damage of a rumor could only be overcome if a person were strong enough and powerful enough to ignore it and outwait its effect. He reasoned that he would just have to become that strong and powerful.

* * *

Miguel had purposely made Vince Bowditch's invitation for a half hour after the other expected guests. When no one arrived by six forty-five, he surmised that the news had been spread that the count would not be attending. He had the housekeeper close the dining room doors and set a table for two in the library alcove. It amused him, in a way. He was quite accustomed to having intimate dinners in that nook. But this dinner would be of a very different intimate nature.

Surprisingly it was exactly what Vince Bowditch had expected. He had come for business and not pleasure. Still he enjoyed the excellent food and didn't push beyond the realm of small talk until they had been served brandy, coffee, and cigars. Once the housekeeper had been wished a good night, Bowditch saw the advantage of having their conversation here rather than in his palace office.

He swirled the contents about in his glass, took a neat swig, pursed up his lips, and shook his head seriously.

"Never could get used to this stuff, Señor Escovarro."

"Isn't it about time we returned to a first-name basis?"

Bowditch grinned. "Like when we were on the boat with your brother?"

At the mention of his brother, Miguel's face saddened, became gloomy.

Bowditch stared. His face reflected a genuine if puzzled delight.

"Worried about that murder he committed?" His face became even more genial, if slyly arched. "There are always ways of keeping a thing like that away from the ears of the authorities. As far as we know, I was the only person to stumble upon the body."

Miguel's expression darkened into complete somberness. But he was thinking of how quickly Bowditch had reentered the trap. "Possibly," he answered shortly, "but there is also a point of danger in that. We can never let him become aware of our knowledge."

How well aware I am of that, Bowditch reflected. He leaned forward and scrutinized Miguel with unusual intensity. Again he found himself on the short end of the money flow. Nearly all he had stolen was gone, and only a cunning ploy would get him reestablished in New Mexico. He spoke in a soft and confidential voice, molding his hairy hands about the brandy snifter.

"Now, let's set him aside for the moment. I've already learned that your two ranches are separate, so you're safe there. You're aware, also, that I'm not a rich man. Damn near took everything I had to get this commission and position. But with me running the government and you doing as I say . . . I can become rich and you a hell of a lot richer."

Miguel said nothing. But his dark eyes narrowed and glinted with greed as they fixed themselves intently on Bowditch.

Bowditch saw that look and was content. He proceeded with more confidence, his head on one side, his glassy hazel eyes noting every expression on the other's face as a physician watches every faint shadow of pain which might give him a clue:

"The Mexican peso ain't going to be worth shit when this war is over. You'd best start changing yours for hard coin or American dollars. You have a way of doing that quite quietly through your aunt's business. Don't leave too much in the bank, because I'm going to order them closed for a few days. It will force people to dig out their secret hoards."

"What will they need the money for?"

Bowditch leaned even closer and reduced his gruff voice to an even more confidential whisper:

"Wars cost money to run, and the losers usually have to shell out their portion. I've already made out a list of what land-war tax I'll have the soldiers start collecting from the big ranchers. Your job will be to convince them that they should pay. Now I purposely left this tax quite low so we don't start a revolution. But it will bring some of them pretty low on their cash reserve. Then, when the fall roundup count is complete, we slap them with a dollar a head cattle tax—to be paid in American money or cattle."

Miguel's eyes quickened. "That's all well and good for the government coffers," he said disdainfully. "But it sounds like I'll be paying the same land and head tax."

Vince Bowditch burst into rolling mirth. He sat back and slapped his thighs over and over.

"Of course you will be paying it." His voice came, muffled and stifled with his mirth. "But you will be getting your money right back—and more. I've already got the lads picked out who'll do the deed for their share. One is a right smart bookkeeper who will see that the government will get enough to keep them from asking any questions. Besides it will be six months before Washington gets a civilian administrator out here and maybe longer if Old Zack Taylor is wrong about being in Mexico City for his Thanksgiving dinner. In six months, man, we can be buying up land for a song. Of course, I'd advise you to secretly buy it in your aunt's name."

Miguel had listened with absorbed attention, his expression becoming more and more inscrutable. He saw that the plan was quite feasible because of the power Bowditch could wield. But would the people go for it? Bowditch had been left with only an occupation force of a hundred men. He could match that in vaqueros alone. The other ranchers combined . . .

"You have, of course, a small force," he said, putting his thought into words, "and the ranchers could far outnumber you if they banded together. What if they resist?"

Bowditch stared at him in tender affront. "It is going to be your job to see that they don't. But a couple of good examples at the first should keep them all at bay, my friend. I have standing military orders that any person caught or *suspected* of being a spy for Santa Anna or the Mexican army is to be imprisoned and their land and property immediately confiscated. Do you happen to know of any such spies lurking about?"

Miguel grinned. "I'll give it some very serious thought."

Bowditch burst into wild laughter, shaking his head, knowing that a union had just been formed.

"However," Miguel said so slowly and significantly that the smile faded instantly from Bowditch's face, "so that we don't leave any loose ends that one or the other might feel they could use to incriminate or to blackmail, I think we'd best discuss once again the infamous Sam Houston letter and my former Texas land."

Bowditch looked up quickly, scowling.

Miguel nodded knowingly. "I think it's only fair to warn you that it was I, and not my brother, who stayed behind with the vaqueros. I never saw Thackery, because I did not want to see Thackery. I did not want their blood money for my land. Now do we understand each other exactly and perfectly?"

He stood and held out his hand. Bowditch, remaining on his chair, looked at the hand in stunned befuddlement, then slowly took it. He did not release it. His cold dank fingers closed strongly about the other fingers. He felt their hatred, harsh and strong and unshaken. They were wedded, as surely as two pirates designing to join for the plundering of the seas.

CHAPTER TWENTY

Ever since man first learned to hoe his first row and barter away his excess crops, other men quickly acquired the art of turning that profit to their advantage. Soon they had the knowledge of power. Other men, subjected to that power, learned only to grumble against them but were powerless to strike back. Ruefully they learned that power breeds absolute power.

In the near decade that Miguel Escovarro had been on the land, he had become a man of power. Behind his back he was likened to a vulture—a strange beast of prey that allows others to do its killing and then swoops in to fend off the killer and feast on the carcass of the victim.

"He's become worse than a vulture," Jimmy Yerby growled at Don Eduardo Bellam. "I've avoided his water holes; I've made my own cattle drives; for the sake of my wife I avoid even thinking about what he did to her family. But for him to sit there, with those damn soldiers, and tell me the land tax is fair and just, makes me want to puke. And how are we to pay within a week with the banks closed?"

Don Eduardo, old and fat, was one of the richest and most envied grandees of New Mexico. His richness was unique: he trusted the coin of no man or government and put his money immediately back into land and livestock. Jimmy Yerby was the tenth man to come to him that week. His sage advice had been the same to each of them.

"The man has done me several harms in the past as well," he said slowly. "For the present I shall pay their troublesome tax in cattle. I advise others to do the same. In time the Anglo soldiers will be forced to become vaqueros to look after the new government's herd and will be useless as a military unit." He paused, smiled. "Or we might begin to see our cattle spring up on the Escovarro lands and will then know the price that Don Miguel has set for being a traitor."

During her walk to Sunday mass Doña Patricia caught the words of a couple of tipsy army revelers. They paid no attention to the black-shawled old woman. "Why do we have to tend those goddamn smelly cows?" one asked.

The other, whose whiskey had made him philosophical, replied, "Because these stupid Mexes think more of them than they do their kids or land. He'll drain 'em dry when we start taxing the cattle. Then they split." He began to cheer wildly. "Viva la vamoose! Viva . . ."

Doña Patricia passed by.

That night she asked, "Miguel, what does everyone know that I do not know?"

"I do not understand, Tía."

She had been busy asking all manner of questions throughout the day but had received nothing in return but evasions and embarrassed looks.

"Do you understand why everyone else seems to be taxed and I am just hearing of it?"

Miguel shrugged. "You're exempt."

She smiled slyly. "Then you do understand. Are you exempt, as well?"

"Hardly," he scoffed. "They stuck me with a bill for over five thousand dollars."

"Dollars?" she mused. "Not cattle?"

His face darkened. "Yes," he said. His voice was so low Doña Patricia could hardly hear. "I was smart enough to get my money out of the bank before it was closed."

"And convert it to American coin through my company treasury?"

"Ye-es."

"Thank you, at least, for not lying," she said stonily. "However your greed has placed me in a very dangerous financial position."

Miguel rubbed his chin reflectively. "I hardly see how.

Your bankers in Independence will still honor the Mexican peso."

"They didn't!" she snapped. "The train that arrived yesterday had to nearly deplete my accounts in Independence to pay for the supplies that had been ordered for the return trip. It didn't worry me, yesterday, because I thought the office safe contained ample American currency for several more trips. Before mass this morning I heard several things that disturbed me. You can then imagine my shock upon going to the office and finding nothing but Mexican pesos. Tomas is going to have some tall explaining to do come tomorrow."

"He had nothing to do with it," he blurted out. "I told him I was doing it on your authority."

He *was* being honest, she thought.

"Well," she sighed, "perhaps we're still not in too bad a shape. You'll just have to buy a majority of those pesos back so I can keep the trains operational, war or no."

He winced and dropped his eyes. "That's not going to be completely possible, Tía. I've already purchased most of the cattle they have been collecting for taxes. I couldn't afford to let such an opportunity pass by."

She eyed him shrewdly. "An odd time to be buying cattle, Miguel, don't you think? Won't they get them right back when they start taxing the cattle per head?"

Miguel paled and gasped. "How in the hell did you know that?"

"I might ask the same question," she said emphatically, "but you have just given me the answer. I couldn't believe my ears today when several people suggested that you were in league with Colonel Bowditch. Without saying so, you have just confirmed it. Have you made a deal? Will you be exempt from the cattle-head tax?"

"Yes," he said sourly, "but only on the cattle just purchased. I'll need the rest of the dollars to pay the tax on the existing ranch herd. That's the only way I came to learn about the tax, believe me."

He sounded sincere to her. His once handsome face was pale and in deadly earnest.

"Tell me honestly," she said quietly, "have you any influence with Colonel Bowditch, whatsoever?"

He looked at her searchingly. "Perhaps. For what purpose?"

"To reopen the banks." Doña Patricia laughed.

"Hardly," he scoffed. "He's already furious that these idiots are paying in cattle and not in their hidden gold treasure. He won't accept their Mexican pesos even if the banks were opened."

"But what if some of them were able to pay in hard currency?"

His eyebrows arched. "Who for instance and how?"

"It would be a respectable list—including Felix and Teresa." Then she laughed. "It might have included you, as well. Were you given only Mexican pesos when you withdrew your funds from the Bank of New Spain?"

"Naturally," he said shortly, "what else?"

She laughed again as though it were a wry joke. "At least they held firm on my standard policy."

"*Your policy?*"

She eyed him narrowly. "It's apparent you did not acquire any of your uncle's nose for business. How did you think I was able to build my company so rapidly? I was moderately rich, but not that rich. Being the 'ears' in the governor's palace gave me certain advantages. A few years ago I learned that Don Victor had made some very foolish investments with the bank's money. I was able to use my assets to forestall the scandal and secretly win control of the bank. You and Don Victor are the only two other people who know that fact. You see, my boy, I was not about to charge myself the same loan interest rates as I would others."

Miguel eyed her with new respect. "Interesting," he said slowly, "but how would opening the bank help?"

She sighed as though he were a dull-witted student. "It was quite common knowledge in the palace that we would have war, sooner or later. Right from the first I established a policy of having the bank's solid assets converted immediately into gold or hard American coin. Our fluid assets were always in Mexican pesos. So, at the first opening of the doors, my bank could operate in the coin the occupation army demanded."

"But for how long?" he sneered.

"For about six million dollars worth," she answered evenly. Then she added slyly: "There is no possible way there could be a run on the bank, Miguel, if that is your worry. Less than half of it is depositors' money."

His jaw hung loosely, his mind awhirl. In spite of what he had just heard, he thought her a little stupid. He began to laugh foolishly.

"And you were worried about money for your wagon trains," he chortled. "All you have to do is take the Mexican pesos from your office safe and exchange them for gold in the bank vault."

"Idiot!" she barked. "If it wasn't for Guido Herrera running your ranch affairs, you'd probably end up penniless. The bank doors are sealed and guarded, *if* you haven't noticed. There is no way I can touch those funds until the government order is lifted."

By a curious mental armor he had developed, Miguel did not feel chastised. He was thinking instead of how little was the world he had been attempting to create, while his aunt had quietly spun together a much greater world. He had never before given a single thought to who would win control of her world when the childless widow died. It suddenly became a very important question in his mind. But he kept his face void of such a thought.

"I see," he said as though he had just been scolded. "I could talk to Colonel Bowditch, of course. But what of the other two banks? Are they going to be able to pay out in the same manner?"

Doña Patricia closed her eyes as though thoroughly exasperated. "Miguel," she said softly, "do you worry yourself over the affairs of your competitors? I hardly think so, unless it is to get a step ahead of them. If they take a loss on the falling Mexican peso, it will only make my bank that much stronger for the future."

"I'm sorry," he said, a deep note of apology in his voice. "I really was acting quite selfishly. I should have discussed the matter with you before I acted."

"I didn't scold you, Miguel."

That wasn't enough; he wished she would. He wanted to worm his way into her affection. "It would be easier if you did."

"It is not in my nature. I am Irish, to be sure, but I don't cry over spilt milk or carry a pinch of salt in my pocket to ward off the fairies and evil spirits."

"Then I am forgiven?"

Her eyebrows mentally arched. Was this Miguel? Or did he just want his ego *te absolvo*, neatly, so that his conscience might be purged and he might win favor in her eyes?

"Naturally," she smiled. "Besides it won't just be for me. I had a note from Teresa this afternoon. She has very little ready cash and hates to pay the tax in cattle. She wanted to make a loan."

"How much is their tax," he asked as though he had not helped Bowditch set the figure for his brother's land.

"The same as yours," she said sadly, "which seems horribly unfair. Poor child! She has so many burdens on her shoulders already. I had so hoped that he would regain his sense of speech, now that they have him in a wheelchair and he has the use of his arms back. Then, at least, I could have moved them into town, and he could have become a useful person again."

"In what way?"

"In a most important way to me. That wheelchair doesn't stop his sharp brain from operating. By running my businesses for me, he would have been assured of a future."

Miguel swallowed the bitter gall that had instantly risen in his throat. I should have known, he thought bitterly. The old crone had always been more partial to Felix. His hatred for her suddenly equaled that he held for his brother. But outwardly he showed her a very sympathetic face.

"Don't give up hope," he soothed, "and on my sacred honor, Tía Patricia, I'll get Bowditch to open your bank."

But first he had to turn it to his advantage.

"You must give me more time," Teresa said.

Sergeant Dunraven ran a hand through his moustache,

giving it a shaggy and unkempt look. It made his face much fiercer.

"I said," Teresa began again, "that—"

"I heard you!" Dunraven snarled. "Now you're getting tiresome. I hear the same damn excuse a dozen times a day."

"I am hardly a liar!" Teresa said flatly. "My aunt said that the moment the bank opened, she would send the money out by messenger."

"And who might she be?" he asked as though it really didn't matter. He was getting fed up with doing all of the dirty work of forcing the tax money out of the ranchers and getting only the leavings. This case angered him more than any of the others. He could be mean and fierce with the other ranchers because they were men, and he normally had Miguel Escovarro with him to soft-soap them and counterbalance his roughness. But he found it hard, and a little embarrassing, to be rough and hard and businesslike with such a dainty and beautiful woman. This was his third trip to the ranch, and he resented the fact that Miguel Escovarro had come up with an excuse not to ride with him each time.

"To prove that I'm not lying," Teresa said, "you may check with her on your return to Santa Fe. She is Doña Patricia Escovarro."

Dunraven looked at her a little stupidly. "But she is also Miguel Escovarro's—"

"Aunt," Teresa supplied. "Exactly whose ranch did you think you were on, Sergeant?"

He shrugged sheepishly. "I am not much one for the written words, ma'am. I just know this as the northern section of the Ranch of the Two Brothers."

"The description is quite accurate," she said coolly. "Over there, where you see the pink villa, is the ranch of Miguel Escovarro. This is the ranch of his brother Felix."

Because Dunraven had heard that the owner of this ranch was an invalid, he had tried to be more lenient. This news took some more of the anger out of his big frame. There wasn't a man in Bowditch's troop who wasn't aware that Miguel Escovarro had been buying the cattle with hard currency—of which he would share. And there wasn't a person in Santa Fe that wasn't aware that the banks were reopening that day—and that one of them was rumored to be backing their depositors with gold and American coin. He relaxed, feeling she had been quite truthful with him. After all, wasn't she related to two of the richest people in Santa Fe?

He touched his hat brim smartly, with a single-finger salute.

"All right," he said quietly. "I'm sorry to have been a bother, ma'am. By the time I'm over this way next, your messenger should have arrived."

It was very still in the barnyard after he and his two companions had gone. Teresa turned, putting her arms upon the corral gate and looked over the land.

Why do I hold on to it? she thought. What on earth will I do if another emergency should arise? This tax payment will all but wipe out what we've been able to save in the bank. She had been so proud of the little over five thousand she had been able to save, at Doña Patricia's insistence. She blamed herself that it was not more. Had she been foolish in supplying more and more money to José Cordova for her secret project? Every few months he was back with his hand outstretched and his eyes gleaming. She didn't have the heart to stop him from continuing. But she knew now that she coudn't keep it up—not if they were to survive. No ranch could. The rustling was beginning to take on a frightful total. Many ranchers had paid so heavily with cattle to cover their tax that they were now unsure if they would be able to send a fall cattle drive north along the Santa Fe Trail. She was well aware that she could not mount such a drive on her own.

She put her face down upon her arms, but she did not weep. The matter now was past the help of tears. She needed the advice of a strong male voice, but Felix's voice was lost to her forever.

Two miles down the road to Santa Fe, Sergeant Dunraven saw the fat little Mexican, his sombrero far down over his sleeping face, ambling along on his lazy burro.

"Stupid greaser," one of his soldiers chortled. "He ain't got sense enough to lift his goddamn legs. Lookit 'em drag in the dirt."

Dunraven was looking at and thinking of something else. Across the rump of the donkey rested a rather new saddlebag. Not something a peon of that dress would rightfully own unless he was . . . carrying something of value to the Ranch of the Two Brothers.

Greed is an insidious reptile that can strike quickly and leave its victim unaware of the overpowering influence on his mind. Dunraven was unsure when the thought occurred to him, but he was very much aware of the amount of money the sleeping man was carrying. It was ten times as much as Bowditch had offered him for the entire tax-collection fraud, and he now reasoned that the Escovarro brothers were quite capable of standing any unforeseen loss.

His problems he saw as twofold: first convincing the man that he was the tax collector who had been waiting for the money, and then figuring out how to outsmart his dull-witted soldier companions.

The messenger was initially frightened at being so rudely awakened and then grateful to have such a horrible burden taken from his shoulders. But upon passing his heavy saddlebag up to the soldier, his mind froze again with fear as he saw the man's other hand slowly move toward his holster.

"Whatcha doin'?" one of the soldiers demanded.

"Shut up!" Dunraven barked. "A dead greaser don't tell no tales."

"Count me out," the other soldier croaked.

"I intend to!" Dunraven snarled, whipping his pistol upward and firing in a single motion. His smoking barrel was instantly turned on the other soldier. "It means a thousand for you if you stick with me, three cents worth of lead if you don't."

The young soldier could barely get the words past his lips. "I—I'll—stay with you, Sarge."

They were the last words he ever spoke. Riflemen, well aware of the arriving money, had seen the encounter and judged the situation correctly. Before their rifles had stopped barking, only the cowering messenger remained alive. Then the black masks of the new arrivals frightened him even more than the would-be soldier-robbers.

"Is your name Tomas?" one of the hooded men asked him so calmly that it frightened him all the more in being recognized.

"Yes," he quavered.

"And," Estaban Duran went on calmly, "you work for Doña Patricia Escovarro."

The tears of fright were in his brown eyes now. Miserably Tomas shook his head.

"Then you will return to town with this tale. You were robbed of the money charged to you by this man, who is known as Sergeant Dunraven. You will tell whomever you wish that your miserable life was spared because hooded men, such as we are, came and drove off the robbers just as they were about to kill you. You will continue to say that the robbers made a safe escape with the hooded men in pursuit."

"But the—the—"

"Bodies," Estaban supplied. "They will never be seen again. Now get back to Santa Fe."

Vince Bowditch was furious. "Damn it all to hell," he shrieked. "I trusted Dunraven completely! Cheap, common thief! And who in the hell are these masked riders who went after him and the soldiers?"

Miguel cautioned him to silence. "Thank you, Tomas," he said quietly. "You have done well and may go now."

"Well?" Bowditch hissed when he was gone.

"Penitentes," he answered testily.

"And who in the hell are they?" Bowditch said with stubborn insistence.

Miguel was dumbfounded that he was unaware of the "guerrilla"-type operation that was afoot in the territory he claimed to control. He saw at once an opportunity to turn misinformation to his pure advantage.

"Really," he said suddenly, "you have a most inadequate intelligence staff. Do you mean to tell me that you are unaware that these hooded men are the agents of Santa Anna."

The color slowly left Bowditch's cheeks, so that the crease lines stood out like vivid canyons against his pale skin. At the corners of his mouth a little tremble started. Then all at once he was beside Miguel, clutching at his coat lapels.

"Why," he snarled. "Why are you only telling me this now."

Miguel brushed him off as though he were a troublesome gnat.

"Bowditch," he said gently, "I was unaware that you didn't know. You assured me that this Sergeant Dunraven would be quite capable of smelling out any of Santa Anna's agents."

"I urgently request," he said suddenly, fiercely, "never to hear that bastard's name again."

"Just as you wish."

But Bowditch swung back toward him wildly. "Wait a minute," he whispered, savagely. "Masked men? On your brother's ranch? Mexican agents?" He stood quite still, smiling down at Miguel with murderous contempt. "Come, Miguel—how about a little bit of truth on your brother."

"No, Bowditch," Miguel said wildly and sped through the door, slamming it behind him. But he walked away slow enough for Bowditch to come to his senses and come and fling the door open.

"Wait, Miguel—" he began.

He turned slowly, studying the man's face to see how he should react and respond.

"She," Bowditch said at last, the single syllable shuddering up from his throat. When Miguel hesitated, he screamed it at him:

"She! Your brother's wife! I just remembered the rumor that she had once been Santa Anna's wife. What better spy to have up here? Who would ever suspect?"

Miguel did not answer.

"But you suspected," Bowditch said accusingly.

Gloomily Miguel shook his head. "But I doubt that she is in it alone," he said wearily. "My brother served with Santa Anna for many years, remember."

"But he is a cripple," Bowditch protested.

Miguel smiled knowingly. "I have suspected for some time that that was nothing more than a charade. Why else would he refuse to see me for these past several years?"

Bowditch stiffened suddenly. "You put me in a very embarrassing position, señor. What do I do now?"

"Be patient," Miguel answered quietly. "When the time comes for you to be a hero, I shall quietly step aside. In the meantime let them stew over the 'stolen' tax money and why it is not demanded anew. Then they will fret over the cattle-head tax demands. We will sit back and see how desperate their masked hooligans become."

Bowditch eyed him narrowly. "Why? Why side with me against your own kind?"

Miguel shriveled him with a single look, having misunderstood. "I was never aware we were of a kind, Bowditch. That is obvious in the fact that you think in thousands, while I think in millions. When it comes to sides, I am on my own side. Cross me and you will find it the wrong side to be upon."

Bowditch was not about to cross him. He had doubted his word about the capital worth of his aunt's bank, but upon personally checking had been stunned. His mind couldn't even start to calculate such vast amounts. He was incapable of planning how to get control of it on his own but judged that Miguel Escovarro already had a plan or else he wouldn't have asked him to lift the restriction. He would just have to be patient on other matters, as Miguel asked. But in his heart he was beginning to fear that he was losing power to the man.

Teresa had no reason to question Estaban Duran's word that he had met the bank messenger and brought the money on to her. The absence of Sergeant Dunraven during the next several days gave her a glimmer of hope that he might overlook collecting the tax.

Across the river nothing changed, and the nobel guest was constantly entertained, though summer wore into autumn, the flowers faded, the golden fruits dropped to the ground, and the year went into its colorless winter rest.

Men of New Mexico talked of many things in the fall of

1846. They whispered bitterly of Miguel Escovarro and his ability to buy up the government cattle. When the cattle-head tax was imposed, they rumbled angrily that they had paid a dollar-a-head tax, and he was able to buy their cattle back from Colonel Bowditch for only twice that amount.

The peso fell to three cents, and a month after reopening their doors, the other two banks in Santa Fe were forced to permanently close their doors. The fiscal policy of Doña Patricia's bank became highly conservative in its acceptance of pesos from other than regular bank customers. It was making so many enemies for Don Victor that he publicly proclaimed the name of the true owner of the bank and told the people to take their woes to her.

Oddly enough it was not Doña Patricia who took the brunt of the blame for the bank's policy. The name Escovarro was all many needed to hear to link it immediately with Miguel and determine in their minds how he was able to have so much ready gold to purchase so many head of cattle.

In California and Mexico men went on dying in senseless battles, and Santa Anna wrote long, impassioned letters to the dons of New Mexico crying for them to rise up against their occupation and bring their vaqueros south to his aid. His letters went unanswered due to many of the messengers getting caught and a fear by those dons who did support him that any uprising was doomed before it could get started because Miguel Escovarro would probably side with Colonel Bowditch. Bowditch would read the intercepted letters and put them aside, angry that they were never addressed to any given person. He did not strike out against anyone as a "traitor" because he wanted that singular honor to fall on Felix and Teresa. Besides he was much too busy with other things: piling up his mountain of gold, basking in the tender glow of his dreams, and awaiting the first rancher to break and sell off his land.

He lay, one cool night in mid-September, by a young Mexican girl's side and tried to fall asleep. But the bitter events of the day tugged at his mind. He had been rousted from bed early by a screaming and ranting Miguel Escovarro. During the night a large number of hooded men in black dress had raided the south ranch and driven off over eight thousand head of cattle—nearly the total amount that Miguel had been purchasing. Four of the Escovarro vaqueros had been wounded but not seriously.

"What the devil—" Bowditch had begun.

"I hold you responsible," Miguel stormed. "You are the law and order! Start cracking down on these crazy hooded men! I'm going out to my ranch to personally take charge of trying to find my cattle. You better start getting busy finding out who was responsible for the raid!"

Damn it all! Bowditch thought morosely. There's no understanding this man! Bowditch was sure in his mind that the hooded men were the same who were receiving messages from Santa Anna. Always before Miguel had advised him to ignore the matter. He was really quite unsure of where to start looking for faceless ghosts that seemed to come and go at will.

Early that afternoon the arrival of two gentlemen from Washington added to his misery. Samuel Cory Peevy had been appointed by the president as the "occupation governor"; and with him was Nathan Bergman as Indian agent.

The vastness of the West utterly confused Peevy. A small, frail man, his face white and frightened, bedewed with a fine tracery of travel sweat, he could only stare and blink and be quite content to leave the affairs of the government in Bowditch's hands until he was given a few days to rest up.

Nathan Bergman was a far different sort. Bony and raw faced, he had been an Indian scout and felt that the only "good Indian was a dead Indian." Next to Indians, his personal hatred centered on army officers.

"I can't help your problems, Colonel," he sneered. "My orders are to do an immediate census of the Indian tribes so that we know how many savages we are facing. I'll expect to have thirty men mounted and ready to ride out with me in the morning. I think you'll find that Governor Peevy will back me up in that demand."

Time was running out for Vince Bowditch. He was considering how long it would take Peevy to uncover his scheme when he was interrupted by a dusty outrider. The soldier had come across a dead Mexican near the Rio Grande. It appeared the man had been waylaid by bandits, for he had been stripped of everything but a letter pouch. Most of the letters were the same as those Bowditch had seen before. But one made his heart quicken and his hands begin to tremble. It was addressed to Teresa Escovarro. It made so little sense that Bowditch puzzled over it again and again.

> Señora:
>
> I have been remiss, but believe me my heart was heavy with the news. My anger lay with the messenger who informed me of the event and should not have been directed toward you. Just remember that the "desert rose" means that you can return home at any time and find protection under the badge of my office.
>
> Antonio L. de S.A.

And as Bowditch lay awake pondering the words, he considered that there had to be a hidden coded message within the text. His mind was incapable of sorting it out, but he felt sure he knew someone who could do it for him.

When Teresa saw Miguel standing in the doorway of her home, she did not say a word. Instead she stood quite still and looked at him while the silence between them stretched out to the boundaries of their mutual hate.

Then, slowly, she brushed past the two soldiers guarding her and started to walk toward him, her footsteps echoing hollowly in the funereal silence that had surrounded the house for the past half hour or so. Miguel watched her come, holding his breath hard in his throat. He was unsure of what Bowditch was up to but had come the moment Estaban Duran had come across the river for him.

"Teresa," he murmured, "what is this all about?"

She stared at him, her eyes very wide and dark.

"I—I don't know," she said slowly. "That man Bowditch came here with soldiers about a half hour ago. He demanded that I explain to him a letter sent to me by Santa Anna. I hardly understand it myself."

"Where is he?"

"Upstairs," she groaned. "The man is mad. He doesn't believe that Felix is a cripple, and he's taken the letter and two soldiers up to prove his point. Two other soldiers have Elena in the parlor. She's frightened to death, Miguel."

"Just be calm," Miguel urged. "I'll go up and find out what this is all about."

But before he reached the bottom of the stairs, Bowditch appeared at the top of the stairs. Next to him, being pushed by one of the soldiers, Felix sat bewildered and confused in his wheelchair.

Miguel could not help but look upon his brother. The sight so shocked him that he had to quickly avert his eyes to Bowditch. Felix was only thirty-seven and looked to be near sixty.

"What are you up to?" Miguel croaked.

Bowditch gloated, but did not speak. He handed one of the soldiers a piece of paper and indicated he was to take it down to Miguel.

Miguel read the short note and understood at once, although he kept his face impassive. It was obvious to him that Santa Anna had not learned that Felix had not been killed. That last part of the letter he didn't understand, and it helped him to lie more effectively.

"I—I don't understand it," he exclaimed.

"One of these two people do!" Bowditch said suddenly, fiercely. "There is some kind of message in those words. Now, damn it, I want to know what it is, and I want to know right now!"

"I have been telling you," Teresa begged, "if there is a message there I, and my husband, are not aware of it. Miguel, make him see reason and stop—" But it was she who stopped suddenly on a thought. "Miguel, when you went to Mexico, you thought Felix was dead. Is that what you told Santa Anna? Is that what this is all about?"

"I don't see how," he answered calmly and evenly. "The man refused to see me after I turned the prisoners over to him."

It was truth in part, because Santa Anna had refused to see him after their one stormy meeting. But his words did not fool Felix. Since boyhood he had always been able to see into Miguel's innermost thoughts. The letter made a great deal of sense to him, but it was beyond his realm to explain it. He had heard from Esteban the manner in which the prisoners had been marched away. In spite of everything else he knew of the man, Felix looked upon Santa Anna as a soldier who would have cringed at such treatment, and the "messenger" mentioned in the letter had to be his brother.

Felix also wished he could make Teresa remember the piece of gypsum rock Santa Anna had given her at San Jacinto. She had been very honest telling him the whole tale at the time and now seemed to have totally forgotten it. He would never want his wife under "the badge of Santa Anna's office" but thought the gesture was a courtly one.

"Stop all this bullshit!" Bowditch said fiercely. "We've got ourselves a new governor in town, Don Miguel. We've also got ourselves a very live-wire Indian agent. They're not going to like what's been going on around here. Let them get one whiff of all these attacks by these hooded Santa Anna agents, and someone's tit is going to get caught in the wringer."

Miguel was suddenly apprehensive that Bowditch was going to go too far. He shook his head, his big face tightening. He opened his mouth to sternly roar at the man and still the words in his throat.

Felix had seen Elena come to the foyer arch and started to raise his right arm to warn her back. Bowditch saw the movement and fully believed what Miguel had told him about Felix not being as crippled as reported.

"Look out!" he bellowed and dived for the rising arm. The soldier spun into Bowditch and they collided into the back of the wheelchair. Bowditch was able to grasp Felix's skinny wrist just before the front wheels touched the lip of the top step. It was an awkward grasp and he had to strain to keep the heavy chair and man from tumbling. Below he could see the horrified expressions that had sprung to Teresa and Elena's faces, and it gave him an added sense of power.

"All right!" he bellowed anew. "Tell me what I want to know!"

A few simple, logical words from Miguel could have ended the matter right there and then. Teresa, knowing that nothing she could say would convince the man, pleaded desperately with her eyes toward Miguel.

Wryly he shook his head. Was he denying Teresa's plea? She thought so, and her heart and mind froze in stunned disbelief. Was he denying Bowditch's demand? The man thought so, and it flared his quick temper to the flash point. He released his grip of Felix's wrist and kicked viciously at the back of the wheelchair with his foot.

No one who witnessed it would ever be able to forget. No one who heard the long, piercing screams that erupted from the throats of Teresa and Elena would ever be able to drown the sound out of their memory.

It was a scene that seemed to take forever to reach a conclusion. Felix seemed to float out of the wheelchair, his arms slowly rising as though to greet someone he had been expecting for a long, long time. His useless leg-and-a-half weighted his body down so that the forward momentum was of torso and head. Never once did a look of fear or dread cross his face. His eyes seemed to be riveted on a spot in the foyer—the spot where Miguel stood icy and intent.

And even after the wheelchair had rolled over him and he lay motionless on the bottom stair, his eyes burned into Miguel with damaging accusation.

Miguel was indifferent to the whole scene. He had somehow divorced himself from what had transpired as though he were not even there. He was not aware of Teresa and Elena's rush to get to Felix. He didn't see the stupefied expressions on the faces of the suddenly unnerved soldiers. There was no awareness that Bowditch slunk down the stairway like a child afraid of the ghosts he was going to meet in the dark.

Miguel turned, as though he had just entered a party that was not to his liking, and brushed by a grief-stricken

Estaban Duran in the doorway as though he were not even there. And later, as though he were discussing a chore he wished the man to perform, he would quietly tell Guido Herrera: "My brother just died!"

Colonel Vince Bowditch rode back to Santa Fe not fully sure of what he had just brought about. Over and over again he told himself that he had been protecting his own life against an agent of Santa Anna. The six soldiers who had ridden with him that morning to the Ranch of the Two Brothers were well aware of what they had seen and heard. Once their colonel had departed from them for the governor's palace, they kept riding, without consulting each other, until their horses were on the Santa Fe Trail and a return to the world of sanity and their homes.

Maritza came across the river as soon as she heard the news from Guido. There was none the equal of the black woman for taking charge at such a time, and she asked no help in bathing and shaving and dressing the corpse for the rosary. Only when it was time did she ask Estaban and his father to place the quickly built pine coffin on four chairs in the parlor and help her place Felix therein.

To the people of the north ranch, seeing him by the light of the four candles at head and foot, he was a remembrance of times past. His face was peaceful and handsomely youthful.

The artful forming of pillows, overlaid by a satin cloth, made them forget his crippled state . . . and remember the pleasant things, such as the man as a vibrant youth, riding the old ranch like a whirlwind . . . Remember him as a grandee soldier, or the thrill at the memory of his preparing them expertly to travel north to a new land. Remember the spirit he had given them to build farms and a ranch out of land that had at first seemed hopeless.

They came—man, woman, and child—full of the story they had heard from Estaban's on-the-scene description of the event, but their faces showed none of the trouble and misery they felt in their hearts. They smiled down upon him with a feeling of great loss and a message of heartfelt love that he had touched their lives.

To Spaniards, who love the ritual of reverence for their

dead, there was solemn acknowledgment that the focal point of attention conducted herself with regal dignity. In a simple black dress, her hair braided and twisted into a crown, Teresa greeted every person at the door.

"I'm sorry for your loss, Doña."

"It is a loss for all of us."

"Is there something we can do for you?"

"You have already done it by coming to be with me," Teresa managed.

They would move on to the parlor, kneel while making the sign of the cross, intone a prayer, and then bunch into little knots about the room trying to learn more of what actually happened.

"How can you do it?" Elena asked sadly. "You haven't shed one single tear for him."

Gently Teresa put her arm about Elena's slender waist and drew her close. "The only time I ever let him see me cry, my darling, was when they were tears of joy. Any tears shed now would only be for myself and the desolation of knowing that I will never see him again."

Her arm stiffened so quickly that it made Elena start. Big John was bringing the landau to a silent halt outside the open doorway.

Emilia knew it was not the wisest thing to do. It could conceivably open new wounds between them; but she had to come. This much she owed Felix—this much she owed the respect she bore him.

Teresa stood still, watching Emilia alight and come across the porch. For a moment her mind played a fanciful trick on her, and she could almost hear Sam Houston expressing his wish to see what manner of beauty Emilia would be when she was nearing forty. He would have been as amazed as Teresa. Her beauty had become queenly and poised. Having regained her self-assertive nature, it showed in the positive carriage of her tall frame and the proud tilt to her head.

Then Teresa whispered: "Come in."

Emilia slipped into the foyer, and Teresa guided her into the parlor. Emilia stood there looking down at Felix, holding tight reins on the grief that tore her. But her grief was not solely for Felix.

"Damn!" Emilia said, suddenly, harshly. "Why must he be the way he is?"

Teresa turned and looked at Emilia, seeing with surprise that the haughty poise of her face was ravaged by grief, the hurt rising unbearably in her eyes.

"I don't have an answer for you, Em," she whispered.

"No one has," Emilia said sadly. "He refused to let me bring the children. I can't stay with him, Teresa. Not after this. I'm going back to Spain as soon as possible."

As though they had conjured him up by not mentioning his name, Elena came running into the parlor and whispered darkly: "He's here."

Miguel came into the room, walking with the calm assurance that he had every right in the world to be there. And in his face the image of Felix stood out like a damning cry.

Silently he crossed over to Felix's bier and glanced down. Then he turned toward Emilia and Teresa, his face turning hard and cold. He drew back his hand suddenly and slapped Emilia across the mouth.

"Get out of my house, whore!" he growled. "And don't forget to take your royal playmate with you."

Oh, my God! Teresa thought, close to tears, You might have spared me this . . .

But before she could order him from her home, he marched off like a victor; but Emilia still remained there, the prints of his fingers vivid against her golden skin.

There was nothing else for Teresa to do, so she put out her arms. It was her day to be comforted, but Emilia needed the comforting more.

Estaban shook his head heavily, as if to clear it of misery. He approached Don Diego and Don Carlos as though they were his comtemporaries, although they were each well past middle age.

"I think Easter will come early this year," he said quietly.

Don Diego nodded sagely, but Don Carlos's black eyes were enraged with dire hatred.

"Yes," he snarled, "but this year let it be Barabbas!"

Don Diego nodded again. "Tomorrow night, after we have said our farewell to Don Felix?"

Estaban and Don Carlos silently agreed.

Near sundown Doña Patricia arrived from Santa Fe with a priest. Teresa went out to greet them and was mildly surprised. The priest was a new face to her—a small man with iron-gray hair and definitely, not Spanish. He was stooped, and his hands trembled. There was, Teresa saw, something else in his face. And, after a moment, she recognized it for what it was. Frustration peered out of Timothy O'Neil's tired eyes. He isn't comfortable here, Teresa thought. Then she heard the soothing music of Doña Patricia's voice making the introductions, and a great weight seemed to lift from Teresa's shoulders. The old woman was the rock she could hold onto and keep from drowning.

"Our new padre," Doña Patricia was saying, "Father Timothy O'Neil."

Because the introduction had been made in English, Teresa answered in kind and thanked him for coming.

"Child," he wheezed, "would you be having a wee dram in the house?"

"Of course, Father. You look like you could use it."

"That I could," he readily agreed. "My new parishioners don't take kindly to it on my Boston breath, however. But unable to understand their mumbling, I just ignore it."

"You don't speak Spanish at all?"

"No," Father Tim said, "but my Latin is good enough to make them respond during mass."

Felix had been moved to the living room and the chairs arranged for the services the next morning. Father Tim went to him at once and performed the last rites. Afterward he joined them in the parlor and sipped the fiery Mexican whiskey. He could feel the slow warmth it brought curling down to the tips of his toes. Teresa sat there with a cup of tea and looked at him with her soft brown eyes as though she were studying an unusual problem.

"Father," she said at last, "I don't mean to sound rude,

but how do you account for being sent to an all-Spanish parish?"

Timothy O'Neil considered the question.

"Well," he said, "the powers that be had to fill the slots when the bishop of Tampico was ordered to call his friars home. I am not the only priest being sent to this country and into Texas and California."

"But why?"

He smiled thinly. "We have a new Pope this year, lass. 'Tis a man with little love for the Spanish cardinals and their refusal to give more than a mere trickle of colonial monies to the Papal treasury. Pope Pius IX must feel the trickle will become a stream if the churches come under the stern eye of American bishops."

Teresa's head jerked upright.

"You mean," she got out, "money is more important than the good of the people?"

Father Tim looked at her, his gray eyes hard.

"Hasn't it always been thus," Doña Patricia said, stepping into the conversation. "I can remember as a child in Ireland that the priests always wanted the church built larger, even though the congregation grew smaller and poorer."

Father Tim smiled knowingly. "And 'twill be the same here, dear lady. One of my first duties is to see to the building of a school so that teaching nuns can be sent from Saint Louis."

"Fiddlesticks," Doña Patricia scoffed. "There is already a fine school in Santa Fe."

"*Jesuit* run," he scoffed. "We need to educate the children in the English language as soon as possible. How else am I going to be able to be a good shepherd to them."

"By learning Spanish," Teresa said coolly and evenly.

He turned to her, anger mottling his cheeks.

"I am a little too old to be learning new tricks," he said firmly.

And so are the people who will need you most, she thought sadly. Would they still enter the confessional box, knowing their words would fall on all but deaf ears? Would his English-spoken homily fall on all but deaf ears? First the new government and now the church wanted to chip away at their heritage and customs.

"Tell me, Father," she said suddenly, to see if his apparent liberalism could be turned to her advantage, "what is your feeling on the baptism of children?"

He looked at her as though he hadn't heard correctly. "All babies," he stammered, "should be baptized. It is God's grace to protect them from Adam's original sin."

"But," she went on smoothly, "what if one or the other of the parents are outside of the church?"

"God does not make little babies suffer for the sins of the parents," he said loftily. "It's a matter of the priest getting the errant parent to take instructions in the faith and promising that the child will be reared Catholic."

"But what if that is impossible? Can't an adopted parent make the church that same promise?"

"Perhaps," he said slowly. "But, lass, you're asking disturbing questions without giving me the full facts to judge them by."

Teresa's brown eyes were filled with mischief.

"All right," she laughed, "full facts you'll get. The child is fourteen. She was born in a brothel and as far as I know the mother was never baptized. The father was a patrician and died before he could claim the child, which was his intention. She has been in my care for four years, and the former priests refused to baptize her. I would say that she has been made to suffer for the sins of her parents, wouldn't you?"

Father O'Neil frowned, looking down into his empty glass. He opened his mouth, then closed it again, grimly.

"I'm sorry," Teresa said. "Perhaps tonight was not the right time to bring up such a subject."

"To be sure," he said quickly, "to be sure. Let us consider the matter again tomorrow after we have seen to the main purpose of this visit. Perhaps I might now be shown to my room."

Nor, to Father O'Neil's great relief, did the topic surface again the next morning after the service and burial. To make sure that it did not, he hurried Doña Patricia along for a swift and speedy departure.

As a priest, Timothy O'Neil had never matured into being a full man. At fifty-five he was still as indecisive as he had been as a seminary student. This flaw in his character had prevented him from rising in the church. In thirty-five years he had served in an equal number of parishes. It was not that he was disliked as an individual, for he was hardworking and pious. But never once in his thirty-five-year priesthood had he made a decision on his very own. In each parish, therefore, he quickly would become more of a troublesome burden than an asset. When the archdiocese of Boston received their quota for the Western expansion, they filled it rapidly with the Timothy O'Neil types—and breathed a sigh of relief.

Father Tim had no way of knowing that Teresa had no intention of opening the subject of Elena's baptism with him. He had said enough to convince her that he was just as uncaring as the Spanish priests had been. But it no longer mattered to Teresa. The man had mysteriously opened up a long forgotten memory for her.

When everyone was making their farewells, Teresa grabbed Maritza's arm.

"Could you stay with Elena and me for just a little while longer?"

"Gladly," she breathed. "That house over there is the one that seems like it was conducting a funeral today. He threatened to kill her if she came over for the funeral this morning. He's got Estavar locked in his room so that she can't take him back to Spain with her."

"Please," Teresa begged, "no more about them. Another word about what he might or might not do could just make me decide to do something foolish. Come. I have something prepared in the parlor and asked Elena to meet us there."

After they were seated, Teresa faltered.

"I—I think, Elena," she stammered, "you will recall my once telling you that baptism was an absolute prerequisite to heaven."

"Of course," Elena laughed lightly, "because I had to ask you what prerequisite meant."

"At that time," she went on more evenly, "I had forgotten my own first baptism. Naturally I would have because I was just a few hours old, and they feared that I might die. My father baptized me, because a priest was not readily available. The fact was overlooked until I was six and ready to leave for Spain with my father. Because of the dangers of travel, father wanted me rebaptized by a priest. The man, to waylay my fears, was careful to explain that I was validly baptized, because *anybody* may baptize if no priest is available. I asked Maritza to stay behind to act as your godparent, although she is just now learning of my reason. Elena, after what has happened to Felix, I don't want another moment to pass without you being baptized. Do you wish it as well?"

Tears brimmed in Elena's eyes. She had felt so lost during the mass for Felix—almost like an intruder into something she did not understand. In a single movement she was on her feet and then down on her knees beside Teresa.

After so much anguish in her heart, Teresa thought, how simple it all now seemed. Maritza came to hold back and cradle Elena's head in her cupped hands as Teresa took up the little silver bowl of water she had already prepared.

There was no reason on her part to ask the young girl if she believed in God, the Father; Jesus Christ, His Only Son; the Holy Ghost, the Holy Catholic Church, the communion of saints, the forgiveness of sins, the resurrection of the body, and life everlasting. She knew *her* daughter well enough to know the answers already.

Pouring the water slowly over her forehead, she intoned with loving feeling:

"Elena Escovarro, I baptize thee in the name of the Father, and the Son, and of the Holy Spirit. Amen."

Elena rose silently, while the water dribbled down her face. Teresa became conscious that she was gazing down at her with wonder in her eyes.

"You . . ." she smiled. "You called me Elena Escovarro!"

"I think that is exactly as Felix would have wanted me to call you."

Her youthful emotions, held so long in check to ape Teresa, gushed to the surface and could not be quelled. Sobbing deeply, she had to turn and flee to a place of solitary grief.

"Let her go," Maritza whispered. "In the years before her, when she recalls this day—and she will recall it often—she will remember that it ended on a note of love and not bitterness."

And in the years before her, when Teresa would recall that day—and she would recall it often—she would only remember the bitter oddity of its ending.

When at last alone, Teresa could not stand the loneliness that seemed to drop over the house like a shroud. She curled up in the wing-back chair before the parlor fire and didn't move. She could not bring herself to rise and go to her room. It would mean passing Felix's room, and she feared the thought of gazing upon his vacant bed. It would make it all so final—so shattering. Here she could be content and almost pretended that he was upstairs.

The knocking at the front door was incessant, but it took her mind several moments to register the sound and react.

"Señor Duran," she gasped, peering out of the opening crack and then flinging the door wide. "What is the matter? Please enter. You are pale as a ghost."

"Excuse, señora," he jabbered, bowing his way into the foyer, "I am aware that the hour is near midnight, but only now have I heard of this thing from my wife. My Estaban is not home, you see. What I say may mean my life, but tonight I am unsure if the Penitentes do right or wrong."

"The who?"

Duran's eyes fell. "The hooded ones. They normally do good, but tonight I question their motive."

Teresa was amazed. "Estaban is one of them?"

He nodded.

"What are they up to?"

"They have Miguel."

Teresa's first thought was that she could care less, but her second thought centered on the father's deep concern for his son.

"What do they intend upon doing with him?"

Slowly, sadly, Duran shook his head.

"I may not say, señora," he said. "That I have said this much could mean my life. But they need not know. There is not a man among them that does not know you. There is not a man among them that respects your word more than my Estaban. Please, I beg of you, go to where they are and make them see that they should not do this thing."

The urgency in his voice was such that it made her respond at once.

"See to the saddling of Quapaw for me, Señor Duran. I'll go and change."

The fall night was clear and crisp, the velvet blanket of night sky bejeweled by uncountable star diamonds. Had it not been for Elena asleep back at the ranch, she might have been very tempted to ride away from the mountains and to her second dream near the banks of the Rio Grande. But she relentlessly kept Quapaw on the paths that Señor Duran had indicated that she should take. He seemed fretful, as though aware this was a journey that they should not be taking.

It was nearly two in the morning when she saw a faint glow beyond one of the foothills and veered Quapaw in its direction. She was seen and recognized before she reached the clearing in the small dale. Estaban Duran wanted to head her off and force her to return to the ranch. The other Penitentes overcame his objections, and they melted into the forest to await her arrival.

Ever after, Teresa was unsure of her true feelings at the first viewing of the scene. On a bare knoll stood three crosses made of pine logs. The first was ablaze with licking orange flames; the second rather symbolically bare and rather lonesome. The third had been inverted to show the true disgust the Penitentes felt for the figure securely nailed to its crosspieces.

For Teresa there was no mistaking the golden curls that hung limply down from his head. But his eyes, which would have been normally rolled upward to heaven, were fiercely glued backward to glower down at the ground and whatever satanic kingdom resided deep within its molten center.

Perhaps that's what she thought: he was beseeching the devil to come and take the soul that he had so cheaply sold and gained so little profit for.

Perhaps she thought of all of the reasons why it seemed so fitting, that the punishment was justly deserved in view of his many crimes.

Perhaps she thought of how horrible this would be for Emilia and his children to face.

But actually Teresa was not thinking at that moment at all. Her eyes and mind had frozen upon the scene and had ceased to function.

"Hold it right there, mistah," the order was barked. "We've got you covered."

Cautiously the army patrol came into the clearing, disbelieving what they were seeing.

"Turn about," the sergeant in charge commanded.

Teresa did so, without full awareness of what she was doing.

"*Gee-sus!*" he exclaimed. "It's a gal and I know who in the hell she is. Git him off'n tha damn contraption and onta a pack mule. We gotta shag ass back to Colonel Bowditch!"

Feeling that a power struggle was close at hand, certain members of the patrol "shagged ass" to Governor Peevy and Agent Bergman as well. They viewed the corpse, the still stunned prisoner, and Bowditch with almost the same look: questioning disbelief.

Bowditch said reassuringly, "You gentlemen are new to some of the problems we have been facing during this occupation and should be glad of it. Take her away, Sergeant. Time enough to question her in the morning."

Bergman smiled knowingly.

Peevy was totally confused.

"That's all right, Governor," Bowditch went on, "we've been rounding up these hooded devils for months, but haven't been able to capture Santa Anna's ringleader until tonight. There she goes. I'll be turning over a quite safe territory to you when you are ready."

"Oh my, yes!" Peevy said, and his beady eyes filled with

so much joy that Bowditch turned his face away in disgust. The new governor went scurrying back to his bedroom.

Bergman saw the look. He was nobody's fool. He waited until everyone was out of earshot and he was alone with Bowditch and the corpse.

"What is it, Bowditch?" he said. "You're troubled. Do you want to tell me about it?"

"No!"

"I see. Bowditch—is it that woman? She's some looker."

"Damn it all, Bergman!" Bowditch burst out. "Who in the hell is going to believe that she could have done this thing alone. *Or at all?* That man was her brother-in-law, although it could be proven that she did have motive for wishing him dead."

"Were you involved with him . . . financially?"

Bowditch hesitated. He looked down at Miguel and knew that the goose who had laid his golden egg was dead.

"Your silence condemns you," Bergman said gruffly. Then he changed his attack so artfully that Bowditch was caught off guard. "What were you before you became a soldier?"

"Farmer," Bowditch stammered. "Cotton farmer."

"Aha!" Bergman chortled. "A business that requires a certain amount of slave labor, shall we say. And I presume your interest is still in that field?"

"Hell yes," Bowditch said earnestly.

Bergman eyed him coldly. "I did not come all this way west to merely collect a government salary, Bowditch. I think we see things eye to eye. If you can supply the money, I can easily supply the land and labor that you will require."

"Where? How?" Bowditch enthused.

Bergman grinned. "There are thousands of acres out there under Indian control and thousands of Indians who will soon be under my control. Why buy slaves when I can supply them for free."

Bowditch was suddenly suspicious. It all sounded too good. "What's the catch?"

"No catch," Bergman said earnestly. "You resign your army commission and go back east to get the seedling crops you'll need. By the time you get back, I'll have the land and the Indians in control."

Bowditch frowned thoughtfully.

"What about this mess?" he asked. "Peevy won't let me leave with it still hanging fire. She'll have to be tried or something."

"Aha," Bergman said expansively, "perhaps there was a catch after all. If the rumors in this town are correct, she is a rather recent widow. I wish her to be a *free* widow. Leave Peevy to me and what explanations are due. Either she becomes mine, and without force, or you can kiss your cotton fields good-bye."

He uttered the threat so seriously and with so much force that Bowditch was stunned to momentary silence.

He had the money and lacked only land and slave labor. His golden goose had just been reborn and laid a double egg for him.

"Done!" he said merrily. "I'll prepare to leave tomorrow!"

Bergman bowed his head and nodded scoldingly.

"After you've seen to her release," he whispered. Then he shouted: "And mind you not to mention my name! I intend to meet her on an equal social plane and not as one of her former captors. Am I understood?"

Vince Bowditch's cowardice in the face of superior people surfaced quickly. He nodded and raced off to find where they were holding Teresa prisoner.

His search was short-lived. He found the sergeant and two of his soldiers sitting on the ground no less than a hundred yards from where he had left them. They were stunned and rubbing large knots on the backs of their skulls. Doña Teresa was gone.

Sternly he ordered them back to their barracks and forbade them to discuss the events of the night or the woman's escape ever again. He waited an hour before he reported back to Nathan Bergman to inform him that the woman had been allowed to escape. To his surprise Bergman asked no questions, and Bowditch went back to his room to write his letter of resignation from the army.

CHAPTER TWENTY-ONE

Teresa was unsure of what had actually transpired. In her dazed state of confusion she had not seen the shadowy figures silently fell her guards. So quiet had the attack been that she had continued to walk forward. Another shadow loomed up before her and Quapaw's reins were thrust urgently into her hands. No word was spoken; no word needed to be spoken. She sensed that she was being commanded to ride away quickly. As she swung into the saddle, she saw two figures throw Miguel's body over the back of a horse and vanish with it into a dark street.

It never occurred to Teresa to seek refuge at Doña Patricia's house. Her head ached dully, and her mind worked slowly, painfully, and centered on the single desire to just get home and pray that she would wake up in her bed and find that it had all been a nightmare.

She settled back tiredly in the saddle and gave Quapaw his head. The darkness was all around her like a living thing—around her and within, filling up the vast and echoing emptiness of her heart.

For a couple of hours she actually slept in the saddle. It was the first deep and refreshing rest she had had in two days.

In the hour before dawn she began to sort things out in her mind. She had not seen who had assaulted Miguel; she had not seen who was responsible for her release. As she rode along, she deeply sensed that she was not alone, that she was being secretly guarded against an attempt to recapture her. She also felt assured that Estaban Duran would be among that number.

She saw with a sense of frustration that she could not

openly accuse him of anything. She had only the word of his father that that was where he *might* be. Could she condemn him without having seen him at the site . . .

The thought struck her that the Penitentes were the only law-and-order body seeing to the needs of the Spanish people. But did that give them the power of punishment?

Long lines of pink fire ran level with the eastern horizon, which appeared to recede as day brightened. A bank of thin, fleecy clouds was turning rose. To the south and west the sky was dark; but every moment it changed, the blue turning bluer. The eastern sky was opalescent. Then in one place gathered a golden light and slowly concentrated till it was like fire. The rosy bank of cloud turned to silver and pearl, and behind it shot up a great circle of gold. It widened swiftly, blazing out the darkness between the ridges, and giving color and distance to the sweep of land.

From the ridge Teresa was able to look down and watch the sun bring life to the Ranch of the Two Brothers—but not for the brothers themselves. She smiled a little wryly to note that there was a horse tethered outside the Duran house. But the activity in the stable yard behind the pink villa held her attention for many long moments.

"It looks like the horse dragged Miguel home by the stirrup," she said to herself.

Slowly the enormity of her simple statement sank into her neat and orderly mind. Was it the Penitentes' intention for it to look like this was the cause of his death or was it the wry quirk of a vengeful God who was well aware of Miguel's many guilts and black and unholy soul?

Utterly astonished by the sudden departure of Bowditch, Samuel Peevy had no recourse but to assume the duties of his appointed office. It didn't take long for him to become well aware of the deplorable manner in which Bowditch had run the military government.

"My God!" he gasped at Bergman, "the scoundrel has made off with thousands upon thousands. I will begin an immediate investigation to learn who else was a party to this fraud."

Bergman shook his head. "I'd let it lie if I were you,

Peevy. I've been doing some checking myself this morning, and it's not all good."

"Well? Well?" he snapped impatiently.

"Seems like," drawled Bergman and stretched out his legs as though it were going to be a long tale, "the man Bowditch was dealing with was the same man we saw dead last night. Also seems like Bowditch was responsible for the death of the woman he was trying to make out to be a spy."

"Your point eludes me, Bergman," he roared.

"Won't for long," he went on calmly. "Seems all we have is the word of Bowditch and the soldiers that the woman was responsible for the man's death. Now it strikes me right funny that those same soldiers also acted as Bowditch's tax collectors. It also strikes me funny that those soldiers don't seem to be around this morning. They're gone. Bowditch is gone. The woman is gone."

"She's what?"

Bergman smiled wryly. "The story the soldiers left behind was that they were waylaid and she was spirited away. I find that a little suspicious. I suggest that it might just be that Bowditch and his men got just a little too greedy, did in their Mex partner, and saw a neat way of getting rid of the woman. Who would have believed her against such strong eyewitnesses?"

Peevy frowned. "Then there were no hooded men?"

"At other times, probably, but I doubt it last night. Why else would Bowditch resign and leave so quickly unless he was sure you were going to tip over his can of worms?"

"Valid!" Peevy snorted. "What about the woman? Do you think they killed her as well?"

Bergman scoffed. "Not likely. That would have really pointed the finger of guilt at them. You saw her. You saw her stupefied fright. I'll lay you money that she is back on her ranch quaking with fear that someone is going to come and rearrest her. I think we can use her fear to learn a great deal more."

"Hm-m. Are you asking for the assignment?"

"It didn't dawn on me." He was all smiles. "I am leaving tomorrow with a troop to check out the Santo Domingo Indians. I'll pass right through the Escovarro land."

"And we say nothing about the man's death?"

"What man's death?"

"I see," Peevy reflected. "We know nothing of it until the family sets up a howl for us to investigate."

"Very good," Bergman laughed. "I think you might make a very clever governor after all."

He scowled. "Even though Bowditch has taken all the riches out of the reward."

"From the greasers, yes, but the Indians are still untouched."

He saw Bergman was serious. "We must talk on that point someday," he said with a sly smile.

They gave Miguel Escovarro a funeral that would have done credit to an ancient grandee. The pine coffin remained closed because of the condition of the body. Dons and their families came from fifty-seven surrounding ranches to pay their respect to Emilia and belatedly to Teresa. Their farewell to Miguel was like one long sigh of relief. There was no man present who had not at one time or another been lied to, cheated, or defrauded by the corpse. It was equally true of at least three of the women present for the ceremonies. Emilia could feel no present grief, only grief for the man who had died in her heart years before. It had taken every ounce of stamina for Teresa to attend at all. She felt the hypocrite. But sitting in the grand salon, dry eyed, she reflected on the words of Don Diego as he had pulled her aside before entering the villa.

"A man confesses many sins before he dies, señora," he whispered softly. "There are those who wish you to know that you will never be alone again."

She had been granted something rare and utterly unusual. The Penitentes were all but confessing to her that the punishment had fit the crime, and they were locking her lips with the secret.

Someone else was locking their lips with a secret. Doña Patricia had been waiting for Miguel to come back to town so she could confront him with the letters of credit he had so skillfully forged her name upon. Upon hearing of his

death, she had burned them. There was already enough ill
will and scandal over the manner in which he had obtained
the cattle without making the matter worse. To her way of
thinking, the stolen money was a family matter and
wouldn't even be discussed with the family. She hated herself for thinking the thought, but she was actually very glad
that he was dead.

Of the ceremonies, Father Tim had not been advised
what to say about the man and so said nothing. Miguel
Escovarro de Sanchez's name was never mentioned once
throughout the service. It was as though it had already
been erased from the Book of Life and it would have been
blasphemy to utter it.

Of the over five hundred dons, vaqueros, farmers, wives,
and children within and without the villa there was only
one heart that was filled with genuine grief.

Estavar Escovarro gazed quietly at his mother, sitting
there beside him . . . He was not going to let you take me
back to Spain, Mother. He told me all about you, you
know? I can never understand how he loved you in the first
place. I can understand his hate, because you must have
been just as cold and loveless toward him as you are
toward me. But his hate is now my hate, Mother. He
wanted me to be the Escovarro don and *I shall be!* Get in
my way and I will destroy you just like you destroyed
him!"

And like his father Estavar didn't wait for fate to show
him the future; he manipulated it to his own choosing.
After the service, and throughout the burial in the little
used cemetery, he paid cavalierly attention to his *grande
tía.* And, like his father, he stood a little in awe of the
shrewd woman. But not so much in awe that he was afraid
to let her know his hatred for returning to Spain.

It was a matter that came up when Emilia and Doña
Patricia were at last alone.

"The finances of the ranch are a little rocky right now
for you to be leaving," the older woman said accusingly.

Gloomily Emilia shook her head.

"It's my own money that I shall use to return to Spain

411

and live upon," she replied. "Carrie saw to it that I made some very sound investments in olive groves. Their oil is becoming quite an import item in the eastern United States."

"What of the ranch?"

"It will continue as it always has, under the capable hands of Guido. Without Miguel's greedy interference I'm sure he'll have it set right in no time. It won't be long before the boys can take over from him."

"Will they want it?"

Emilia ran her tongue over her lips before she could answer.

"The twins, yes," she mumbled. "They were mad as hell being left at school in Spain, as it was."

"And Estavar?"

Lying was no good now.

"He always was Miguel's child," Emilia said wearily. "I can feel his hatred toward me like it was a living, breathing thing. It's something I'll just have to learn to live with and cope with."

"Perhaps," Doña Patricia said dryly. "Unless you would consider leaving him with me."

"You mean it," Emilia said huskily, "you—you really mean it?"

Slowly she nodded. "I suddenly feel the need for someone of my own. Besides, I think Estavar's temperament will be better suited for the world of finance, and I can more than supply that world for him."

Emilia's sigh was gusty with relief.

. They had told her that she would never be alone, but Teresa felt helplessly alone when news was brought to her that upward of thirty soldiers were riding toward the ranch house. The day was gloomy and wet, with a soft rain that threatened to turn into snow before nightfall. The day suddenly fit her mood. There was no place to run, and she knew that she would not run and leave the consequences on the shoulders of her people.

The main force of the soldiers were left in the barnyard

dell, and only a single figure waded through the slush and mud up to the door and jangled the cowbells. She opened it at once to admit a tall, muscular man with a worried expression.

"I'm Bergman," he growled to intimidate her at once, "the Indian agent. You're Teresa Escovarro?"

"I am," she said evenly. "What may I do for an Indian agent?"

Bergman faltered. Without fright she was even lovelier than he had remembered. He gazed down ruefully at his mud-caked boots. Teresa saw the glance.

"Come in," she said. "We're quite used to mud at this time of the year."

She led him through the foyer and paused at the parlor archway.

"Elena," she called, "we have a guest! Would you bring him something warm to drink?" Then, turning to him, she explained, "My daughter—Elena."

Elena came down the stairway at once. She was wearing a simple cotton dress that molded to her body with every step and fit snugly about her firm young breasts. Bergman stared in open lust. He had come to set the stage for the quiet wooing of a woman he had considered could be a smoldering flame under her aloof patrician exterior, but he was now confronted with a creature that reminded him of red hot searing fire. If he could not possess the one, he would possess the other—or perhaps both.

Teresa saw his look and it put her instantly on guard. The man was hardly what she would pick for herself or for Elena. He appeared rather uncouth in his buckskins and untrimmed hair and moustache. His rawboned face and lascivious eyes reminded her so much of some of the drunken riverboatmen on the streets of Natchez-Under-the-Hill that she almost shuddered.

"What is it I can do for you, Mr. Bergman," she asked calmly.

"First, thank you for speaking English," he grinned broadly, revealing his yellowed teeth. "The Indian jargon I can get, but not this Mex stuff."

She didn't comment, so he went right on:

"Governor Peevy asked me to stop by on my way to see some Indians. He was worried about what happened to you the other night."

Here it comes, Teresa thought. She indicated a chair for him and still did not comment.

"When Colonel Bowditch left the territory," he continued as though he had memorized the speech, "we began to check into a few matters. One of them, of course, was your disappearance. Weren't a soldier left the next morning that could tell us anything about that night. The governor is well aware of your fright, ma'am, and you could be of great help to us."

"How?" she asked, her guard wavering.

"We're under the impression that Bowditch wouldn't have run unless he had something to do with the murder of your brother-in-law. I hate to be the bearer of bad tales, but they were connected in some illegal tax collecting and cattle-sale schemes. We've also gained knowledge as to Bowditch's involvement in your own husband's death. Were you forced to be with them the other night?"

"No," Teresa said heavily.

"Don't say anything more," Bergman put in suddenly. "The governor already holds you blameless for whatever might have happened. Bowditch tried to claim it was some hooded men who did the deed, but that's rather farfetched."

Bergman studied her curiously to note her reaction to a lie that he was almost beginning to believe himself. When she remained impassive, he tried another approach.

"We have reason to believe," he said softly, "that the man will return. We would appreciate learning all we can about the man before that time comes."

Teresa sighed. To think of all she knew about the man was as bitter as wormwood. Bergman had calmed her fears that he was there to arrest her, and she saw little reason not to tell him about Bowditch. Even she was amazed that the tale took so long and she had so much to relate: their meeting on the *Yellow Stone*, his involvement in the kidnapping; the Sam Houston letter and the attack on the Escovarro ranch; and the final confrontation and murder of Felix.

Bergman was sure that there had to be more—much more that the woman was unaware of—but the men who could supply him with the information were both dead.

He went away satisfied and sad. Satisfied that he had gained enough personal information on Vince Bowditch to make the man dance to his tune upon his return but sad in the knowledge that he had made no great impression upon either the woman or her comely daughter.

He had never had trouble with women before—his cut of women. But these two were like nothing he had ever encountered before. He had left Teresa with a feeling that was unknown to him and made him uncomfortable—respect for her womanhood and courage. They would never change, he was damn sure. Then he had to change, he saw clearly. He had to gain money and power and poise, so that neither one of them would look at him like a savage beast right out of the jungle.

Teresa had not been as satisfied as Bergman. She still feared that she had not heard the last of Miguel's death and continued to sleep curled in the wing-back chair in the parlor, much to the chagrin of Elena. It also saddened Teresa to think that the pink villa was soon to be dark again. Then she would be alone, except for Elena. In Spain Emilia would be just as dead to her as Felix and Miguel in the ground. She wondered, morosely, if she would not have been better off dying during one of her miscarriages.

It was the slightest of noises, but it brought her instantly erect in the chair.

Inside the room it was dark, but Teresa was aware of the room as though it were a living thing. Every one of its still shadows had become a part of her in their shared sorrow, and she was aware which ones were alien and moving. When it was close enough, she put out her hands and caught the figure. Its instant fear gave it strength enough to pull her upward. They swayed back and forth, knocking the wing-back chair over until Teresa was aware suddenly of other hands tugging feebly at her dress. She released the first and turned her attention to the new opponent. Her hands encircled a thin throat and squeezed hard, but a woman's voice shrieked:

"They're my sons! Don't kill them, they're my sons!"

Teresa turned the boy loose, and at that moment Elena came bounding into the room. Unknown to Teresa, she had taken up the habit of sleeping on the living room davenport to be close at hand. There was the scrape of a brimstone match, and a lamp spread its smoky glow about the room.

The boy Teresa had been choking was no more than ten; his face caked with dirt and his eyes filled with hatred. Wordlessly her first attacker walked over to where he lay whimpering on the floor ànd helped him to his feet. He was near the same age, but tall and stringy.

Teresa felt a slow sickness spreading through her middle as she saw the woman who had screamed at her in the dark. Anna-Maria stood gazing at Elena with nodding approval.

"Hey!" Anna-Maria chirped. "She's all right! Can't you say hello to me, Niña?"

"My name is Elena," she said darkly, well aware of who she faced.

"Pretty," Anna-Maria sneered, then turned abruptly to Teresa. "Sorry to barge in, but it's been a damn rough trip. You have some food for my boys? No one will give anything to anyone on the road. They are too filled with people fleeing Mexico."

"Fleeing?" Teresa asked numbly.

"From the Americans. They are winning everywhere."

"Oh—I—Elena, take them to the kitchen. There is plenty left from supper. Anna-Maria?"

"No," she said sourly. "We'll stay and talk."

Teresa went and rekindled a fire in the hearth and looked at Anna-Maria. The woman lounged upon a chair, smoking a cigarette, a habit she had given up upon marrying Pedro.

"I though you had given that up?"

She turned slowly, trailing twin streamers of smoke through her nostrils.

"I've given up so much lately that I started taking up some of the things I like."

"Oh!" Teresa had faltered but for a moment. Then she had remembered that she was not the intruder. "Precisely what have you given up?" she demanded.

"Precisely," she intoned very matter-of-factly, "a husband killed in the war and a son trampled to death in the frantic retreat of the army. Minor, wouldn't you say?"

"Oh, no!" Teresa murmured. "I—I'm so—"

"Don't give me that sympathy crap," Anna-Maria exploded. "That's not what I want."

Looking at her now, Teresa was suddenly terrified to ask what it was that she did want. The quiet mother who had sat in that room almost four years before had reverted to something hard and provocative. That's lip rouge on her mouth, Teresa realized. It is! And her cheeks are painted too!

Anna-Maria laughed throatily. "Your face gives you away, Teresa, it always did. Well, let's not mince words. I've come to take my daughter back!"

"You can't!" Teresa gasped.

"Can't I?" Anna-Maria echoed in near reverse. "Do you have some way of stopping me?"

"But why?" Teresa demanded shrilly. "It's quite obvious that you are not even able to care and feed the two children that you do have left."

"Exactly," Anna-Maria sneered, "my very point. I am not able to demand the prices that I did before I married Pedro, but at that time I was under my mother's tutelage. As I provided for my mother, it is now Niña's obligation to provide for me. The boys do not bring enough money, and besides I've never thought much about boys being with men in the first place."

"My God!" Teresa whispered. "You can't do this! She has a good life here!"

"She can have better!" she declared. "That body was not made for her to become a wife, but to make money."

"I—I—no!" But Teresa could not discount the fact. There was nothing about Elena that suggested domesticity.

"Aha!" Anna-Maria chortled as a graven-faced Elena

ushered the two boys back into the room. "They look contented in the belly for a change. You got beds for us for tonight?"

"Yes," Teresa said weakly. "Elena, put the boys in the back bedroom. Anna-Maria can have my room. That way they won't be disturbed when the soldiers return in the morning."

"Soldiers?" Anna-Maria asked on a rising note of interest.

"Yes," Teresa said sadly, warning Elena to silence with her eyes, "we have been forced to quarter them here during their occupation. This is their one night out of the week that they are allowed to go into town. They return quite rowdy. As you will be leaving tomorrow, you probably won't be seeing them."

"Boys!" she barked. "To bed! Perhaps we won't be starting the long trip back to Saltillo as soon as I anticipated. Niña," she added sweetly to Elena, "you may show me to a room as well. And remind Doña Teresa that I love to sleep late."

Teresa opened her mouth to hold Anna-Maria back and then thought differently on the matter. She had come very near to offering Anna-Maria money for Elena but saw at once it would become a thing of constant demand. She pondered how sensible was the plan that had sprung into her mind until Elena returned.

The girl's face was sad and troubled.

"She told you?"

"Yes," Elena said miserably, "and I don't want to do it."

"That's all I needed to know," Teresa said clearly. "I think we'd best get busy making some plans."

Elena looked at her gravely. "Does the plan have something to do with the lie about the soldiers?"

"It wasn't at the time. It was just one way of making sure that she would not want to leave with you at the crack of dawn and to give me more time to think this thing out more clearly." She looked at Elena, and a hard glint appeared in her eyes. "We had better stop thinking and start acting. Get a couple of saddlebags out of the tack room, Elena. In spite of the hour I'll have to go give Estaban some instructions. Pack just enough for a few days, without letting anyone hear you. I'll saddle Quapaw and Pawpaw on my way back from Estaban's. I want to be into Santa Fe by first thing in the morning."

Elena made a sour face.

"Oh," Teresa said, startled, "is something not to your liking?"

She shrugged. "If it means that we will be staying with Tía Patricia, then I'll have to put up with that nasty Estavar."

"I think," Teresa said clearly, "it will be easier to put up with Estavar for a few days than your mother for a lifetime."

At once Elena was abject. "I'm sorry," she whispered.

"I'm not," Teresa said. "It shows me that you really don't want to go with her. I want to make sure that she can never ask for you back again. I want you to be 'Elena Escovarro,' not 'niña puta' in the back of some filthy Mexican saloon. Now, let's get cracking."

It was an hour before she had finished talking with Estaban—a session that turned into a family council before it was over. The suggestions put forth by Estaban's parents startled, amused, and amazed her.

She saw the merit in their suggestion that she hide and lock away the silverware and other things of value; equally important to use this opportunity to return the five thousand in gold to the bank. She was unsure that she wanted to take along a rifle, but due to the fact that the suggestion had come from Señora Duran, she followed the woman's advice and selected a light weapon and tin of ammunition. Their other suggestions were things they would accomplish after she had departed.

The next morning Teresa returned to Doña Patricia's house, her face gray with misery. The old woman took one look at her and jumped to her feet.

"Don't tell me he refused!" she roared.

"Flat out," Teresa whispered. "The governor claims he could do little about such a quick adoption at this time."

"Then in what devil's time can he do it?"

419

Teresa sank down dejected. "He mumbled something about when the war was over and we were recognized as a territory." She sighed deeply. "But not even that is going to help. He looks upon Elena as a Mexican-born citizen. As she isn't a true orphan, I can do nothing without a written release from Anna-Maria. I was a damn fool to think I could thwart her with a quick adoption."

"Jehosaphat!" Doña Patricia exploded. "I'd make her an orphan right quick if I could get my hands on that snippy Anna-Maria for two minutes!"

"You may get your chance," Teresa said grimly. "I'm sure she'll make a beeline right for here after Estaban gets finished with her."

Doña Patricia pursed her thin lips. "Then I think you'd best go right on with your plans, my dear. Leave this old war-horse to handle her."

When Anna-Maria walked into the parlor near noon, Estaban stood up and faced her soberly.

"Who in the hell are you?" she growled.

"Estaban Duran, the manager of the ranch."

"Where's Teresa?"

"Señora Escovarro," he intoned with deep respect, "departed quite early this morning with her daughter."

Her face paled, then red came back, deeper than ever.

"All right, *macho*," she snarled. "I want some answers. Are they across the river with that whore Emilia?"

"They have departed for Spain."

It was really not a lie. He had just failed to clarify who the "they" were.

Anna-Maria stepped forward slowly, her breath making a loud rustle in the room.

"I want three fast horses," she said quietly, "and I want them within five minutes. You can keep my three donkeys in exchange."

Teresa had given up so much lately that she stubbornly refused to give up the last happiness in the little world of her heart. She, above all, knew that happiness was an elusive possession. It had a tendency to slip away like quicksilver unless one were vigilant. She knew that she was doing little more than buying time, and she wondered if it would not have been just as smart to buy off Anna-Maria.

"There's a jack!" Elena cried suddenly.

Teresa paid scant attention to the jackrabbit. It was as large as a dog, and its ears were enormous. It appeared to be impudently tame, and the horses kicked dust over it as they trotted by. From then on Elena tried to call Teresa's attention to everything on the trail to pull her out of her deep-seated mood of gloom. Coyotes stealing away into the brush; buzzards flapping over the carcass of a cow that had been mired in a wash; queer little lizards running swiftly across their path; cattle grazing in the hollows (which probably were part of the successfully scattered eight thousand head rustled by the Penitentes); adobe huts of Mexican farmers; wild, shaggy horses, with heads high, watching from the gray ridges—all these things Teresa glanced at, indifferently at first, because they were not a part of the past or future, and then with an interest that gradually grew as she rode on. It grew until sight of a little ragged Spanish boy astride the most diminutive burro she had ever seen awakened her to the truth. She became conscious of faint, unmistakable awakening of long-dead feelings— enthusiasm and delight.

"Hello!" she cried. "Are you not the grandson of José Cordova?"

The cherubic face was all a smile. "Welcome, Doña Teresa," he chirped happily. "The vaquero has brought your message from Señor Duran. My *abuelo* has sent me to show you the southern boundary of your land. Welcome to Ranchero de la Blanca Rosa."

Teresa had not instructed José to name her secret project, but the title made it sound like home. When she realized that, she breathed deep of the cold, sharp September air and experienced an inward joy. And she divined then, though she did not know why, that henceforth there was to be something new in her life, something she had never felt before, something good for her soul in this land. Now she looked at every square inch with a possessive intent. She recalled having looked at the Escovarro land in nearly the same way. But that had been different. She had looked at that land as though through the eyes of her husband. She looked at this land through her own eyes.

From the top of a ridge Teresa saw down in the valley the muddy sweep of the Rio Grande and a land brown with the dead leaves and grasses of winter. But to her it was green and summer heavy with leaf and waving grange grass. Her eyes misted and she had to bite her lower lip to keep it from trembling.

"Momma!" Elena gasped. "I've never seen a house like that in my life!"

Teresa was too thrilled to comment. She just wanted to soak it all in with her eyes and her heart. José had picked an ideal location to erect the three-storied replica of Beauwood. It seemed to rise right out of the gently sloping knoll as though grown there by nature. To others it might have seemed strange and out of place to have a white-columned, wrought-iron-balconied, antebellum plantation manor smack in the middle of adobe country, but for Teresa it was the most gorgeous sight she had ever beheld.

Thank you, my darling Felix, she thought deep in her heart. Without your love I never would have had the plans. Thank you, my loving darling, and good-bye. You will always live in my heart, but I can't take you with me into this house. It must become a happy place for Elena.

"That is my unconditional offer," exclaimed Doña Patricia, businesslike and crisp.

Anna-Maria's mind was all in a blaze, and every muscle and nerve of her body tingled and quivered. Her hands, as she endeavored to put up the loosened strands of hair, trembled and failed of their accustomed dexterity. Then she faced about and looked at her ragtag sons.

Her laugh was shrill. "If I could sell them for the same money, I'd be quite a rich woman."

"This is not a slave auction," Doña Patricia growled. "The five thousand pesos I offered has nothing to do with Elena as such. Let us say that it is your *salary* for writing out the paper that will give me full authority to adopt her. Because you have no record of her birth or baptism, I want it airtight and ironclad."

A faint dark smile touched Anna-Maria's lips for a moment, but she made no comment. Then from the depths of her cloth bag she brought out a crumpled envelope and tossed it to Doña Patricia. "My Pedro was a stickler about paperwork. The army didn't pay a man quarters and rations unless he could prove his woman was his wife and his brats his own. How much are you willing to pay for these pieces of paper?"

Doña Patricia opened it hesitantly, after a long and furtive study of Anna-Maria's somber features. Then she read, her thin lips moving silently over the words on the often folded documents.

"Very odd," Doña Patricia mused. "These read: 'Niño Perez, August 10, 1836—Niño Perez, June 8, 1837—Niño Perez, April 14, 1838.' Why no names?"

"I let Pedro decide about that when they were baptized," she answered indifferently.

How easy, Doña Patricia thought, the three documents would make it for her. She suddenly saw the whole thing as rather amusing. A month before she had been a barren and lonely woman who had stilled her needs by making her business ventures her main interests and children. Then she had brought Estavar home with her and taken an immediate if distant liking to him. She saw that his cool and arrogant approach to life would make him a remarkable businessman but wondered if any woman would ever be able to get near to his cold and loveless heart. And now she was seriously contemplating Anna-Maria's flippant offer.

"Come here," she said to the seated boys.

As though it were their soldier father who had barked the command, they sprung up and marched to the front of her desk.

"Have you names?" she asked softly.

"I am Pedro, after my father," the taller one snapped as though answering roll call, "and he is my brother Gordo."

"Do you understand anything of what has been said here?"

"Most everything," young Pedro said thoughtfully. "You wish to buy us like the man in Saltillo did last month."

Doña Patricia's violent reaction to this was even more pleasing to Anna-Maria than she had hoped. She had feared that Pedro's ability to be nothing but honest had cost her the five thousand pesos for Elena. She expected to be ejected from the woman's business office posthaste. Doña Patricia rose as though she were a spring suddenly unwinding. Her old face turned ghastly. She could not speak. She looked down at the boys with a truly terrible expression of misery. Anna-Maria nodded dolorously.

"He shouldn't have told you that, señora. It happened after my Pedro and youngest son were killed. We had to eat. Would have been better if I'd had the girl with me."

Doña Patricia slowly reseated herself. Her face pinched into total disgust. Anna-Maria saw this, but she did not see the expression in the eyes of her sons. Nor could she know of the pain in their hearts over what she had forced them to do.

Doña Patricia saw it and thought to herself: I don't care a damn what she does with her body and her useless life. It's hers. But I can't stand by and let her pervert children—her own children.

"I am not sure if you were jesting," Doña Patricia said dryly, "but if you were serious, I accept the offer."

But she did not catch Anna-Maria unprepared, for that brothel-educated feline, knowing an easy target, had already formulated the answer to just such an eventuality some minutes before. So she gazed at Doña Patricia with a countenance which she allowed to assume slowly an expression of reserved sadness, and she shook her head, turning away at last and sighing.

"I'm not one who has had many wishes in life, señora. Pedro was one that was granted, but he's gone now. I had the kids because they made him happy." She sighed again. "Funny, isn't it, how you can hate someone and yet envy them what they have. That's the way I felt toward Emilia. It would be nice to have clothes and a house like she had in San Antonio."

"Fifteen thousand pesos can get you a great deal of that." Doña Patricia had barely breathed out the words.

"Very generous of you, I daresay," said Anna-Maria with a cynical half smile. "I was thinking of a figure about double that amount."

Slowly, with deliberate calm, Doña Patricia placed a fresh piece of paper upon her desk and shoved the inkwell and quill holder toward Anna-Maria. Then she swung her swivel chair about so rapidly that it made Anna-Maria start. She had never seen such a chair before in her life. It so mystified Pedro and Gordo that they began to giggle.

"Shut your traps!" she barked. Then she stared at the blank sheet of paper as though it were as startling as the revolving chair. She was still staring at it when Doña Patricia swung back from the open safe with three bound stacks of Mexican peso notes.

"I—I—don't know how to put the words down," she said shortly. "You'll have to do it for me."

"As you wish," remarked Doña Patricia soothingly. "You may count your money as I write."

At this mention of money, Anna-Maria glanced behind the woman to the open safe. It was crammed full of stacked and bound peso notes. Her face became dark and closed. "I've counted," she replied, in a dull voice. "You must not have understood. I meant double that amount for each of the children."

Doña Patricia ignored her for a moment. "You are a very artless businesswoman, my dear," she said snidely, continuing to write. "Do you continue to change the prices on your customers after you have them in bed? Don't answer, for I really don't care to know. Now, be quiet and let me finish this, or I may just call the whole deal off at once."

The room became like a cemetery at midnight, with the rapidly scratching pen the only break in the silence. At first Doña Patricia's face was sullen over the words she penned, and then it relaxed into a cunning grin. She wrote:

"Don Quixote tilted at windmills because he thought they were dragon monsters. This foolish woman tilts at windmills because she feels motherhood is a burden and not a blessing. She should be locked up as surely as was the errant knight. But like the windmills, why should her children be made to suffer or be damaged by stupid thrusts. She wants ninety thousand—I'll give ninety thousand. Poor Don Quixote! Poor Anna-Maria!"

She blotted the sheet carefully, turned back to the safe, and added six more stacks to the three on the desk. She could have added twenty more stacks without feeling a twinge. The money was totally worthless to her and to her bank. The Mexican economy was near collapse. A pound of cornmeal, if it could be found in Mexico City, was selling for five thousand pesos. Doña Patricia felt she was getting quite a bargain. At the current rate of exchange she was getting each child for about nine cents each.

"Do you wish me to read the document to you before you make your mark?" She paused and waited for Anna-Maria's protestations, which came with gratifying promptness.

"I don't know if I should be doing this, even for money. It seems a lot, but . . ."

Doña Patricia picked up the sheet as though immediately prepared to rip it to pieces.

Anna-Maria waved her hand and laughed. It was a reluctant laugh, as if natural merriment had rusted sadly in her. She knew she could not gain another peso out of the old woman.

"I know what my own name looks like," she sighed. "Point it out to me, and I'll make my mark."

Doña Patricia had been shrewd enough to anticipate her knowledge and pointed to the words: "Poor Anna-Maria."

Anna-Maria hastily made an "X" over the spot, gathering the stacks of pesos into her cloth bag, and turned without an after look at her children.

Doña Patricia was pulling on her bell cord before the woman was half turned. Pablo Cruiz nearly collided with the woman in the doorway in his quickness to answer his employer's page.

Doña Patricia drew a deep breath, for unaccustomed

emotion choked her. Estavar was hers only on loan, Pedro and Gordo were going to become hers forever. She was just sad that it was happening so late in her life.

"What are you staring at, Pablo?" She drew up haughtily. "*My* boys have had a rough trip and are a little travel worn. You will take them to the emporium and have Señor Diaz measure them for proper clothing. Then take them to my house and tell the housekeeper to see that they are given proper baths." Then she smiled. "You might also tell her that there will be four of us for dinner tonight. One more thing, before you go. How near is the next train to leave for Independence?"

"Within the hour, Señora Escovarro."

"Tell the wagon master to wait. I have an important letter to send. Tell him he might be a man short coming back because I want this letter to get quickly to the attorney in Salem who fought us on that case before the Eighth Judicial Court last year."

For an instant an inscrutable look passed over Pablo's features. "Señora, beg your pardon, but that man beat us."

"Damn right he did," she snorted. "Now I want him to beat someone else for me. I'm going to write him right now. Do you recall his name?"

Pablo closed his eyes for a minute. His brain was capable of remembering every pound of freight that was shipped north or south and who it was assigned for. He smiled. "Seems to me, señora, that it was Lincoln. Abraham Lincoln."

She pursed her lips and waved him and the boys from her office. Because she dealt in intracountry traffic, she had made it a policy to keep abreast of the news on the northern end of the Santa Fe Trail. She was aware that Mr. Lincoln had gone to the Congress of the United States and had been a strong voice against the Mexican war and President Polk's declaring it. Delightedly she knew she had picked the right man for the job and pulled fresh paper toward her.

"And therefore," she wrote, after a very lengthy two-paragraph recap of who she was, "you, more than any other man, will understand my personal feeling toward this war and why I have taken these children under my roof. You fought me before, sir, on the grounds that I had been without the United States for too long to claim full rights as a citizen. You won. Can you overlook that win in favor of these children? I enclose their records of birth, and pray you do not lose them—although one is in error. They are not three boys, but two boys and a girl. On a separate sheet I list their names and vital information. As Mexican children I cannot adopt them because of the war, because I am considered Spanish because of my marriage. As an American citizen, you could act on my behalf to have them adopted at once through the Eighth Judicial Court. Have you children, sir? I have not and long for them."

CHAPTER TWENTY-TWO

By the time Lawyer Lincoln was able to act favorably on Doña Patricia's petition, the war with Mexico was over. Santa Anna signed the Treaty of Guadaloupe, ceding claims to Texas, California, New Mexico, Nevada, Utah, and part of Colorado. Rather than find themselves embroiled in lengthy court battles, the treaty upheld long-standing land grants and the United States paid three million dollars in claims and an additional fifteen million dollars to Mexico for the vast lands. The people of New Mexico braced themselves for those who would heed the headline advice of Horace Greely's Eastern newspaper: "Go West, Young Man!"

A dramatic event that year saved New Mexico from the land-hungry throngs. The wagon trains pushed right on past in their fevered state to reach California and its newly found gold. New Mexico was all but forgotten by the pioneering farmers. It was not forgotten by others.

In the first part of April, 1848, Vince Bowditch returned, via Texas, with a ten-wagon train, twenty black slaves, and an authorization from the United States government to conduct a most unusual experiment. Bergman had no choice but to agree and kept the news from Peevy.

In the last part of April, 1848, Big John and Maritza returned from Spain, via Veracruz, with gifts for everyone sent by Emilia. Before their departure Emilia had become the countess of Medina, and the black couple began longing for home. One look at the plantation manor, and they knew that it would be their home forever.

In the late spring of 1848, another breed of man made his appearance on the scene—the ex-soldiers of Santa Anna now formed into roving, murderous, thieving guerrilla bands. They would come up out of Chihuahua, using the banks of the Rio Grande as though it were a highway for their private use. Their main objective was guns and ammunition, which had been taken from them at war's end; but they would loot and steal anything within sight. Their favorite targets were the more remote ranches.

Between Teresa's ranch and the little hamlet of Chimayo there were two other ranches, the farthest being as well established and run operation as the Escovarro family had had in Texas. It had been in the Clava family since the early 1700s.

Bordering the Ranch of the White Rose was a vast farm that was almost the black rose in comparison. Upon her arrival José had advised her that it would be a waste of her time to pay a courtesy call. The grandee was an absent landowner, residing in Mexico City splendor and using Mexican laborers as though they were slaves. With war's end came a deep depression, and he returned to the only thing he had left. José still protested that it was no time to pay the man a call. But Teresa insisted, and it required only a few words and a persuasive smile to get Elena to ride along.

From the rise the cluster of adobe houses added a picturesque touch of color and contrast to the waste of gray valley. Near at hand they proved the enchantment lent by distance. They were old, crumbling, broken down, squalid. A few goats climbed around upon them; a few mangy dogs barked to announce their arrival; and then a troop of half-naked, dirty, ragged children ran out. They were very shy, and at first retreated in fright.

With a kind word and smile Teresa made known her reason for being there. They began to follow her in a body, gathering a quota of new children at each house.

A feeling of sickness grew within Teresa, increasing as she passed by house after house. She had never even seen this type of squalor in old Mexico. The huts reeked with filth; vermin crawled out of the open doorways as though they were the true inhabitants.

There was no evidence that there had been labor in the

fields, although spring was well along. Idle men and women sat in small groups, some silent, others jabbering. They did not resent the visit of the two women, nor did they show hospitality.

The main house was little different. It had been neglected for years and was in odd contrast to the gilded carriage that sat awaiting passengers at the front entrance.

"I'm sorry," Teresa said. shading her eyes with her hand to view the man who had quickly stepped out onto the porch. "Perhaps we've come at a bad time. I am Señora Escovarro, and this is my daughter, Elena."

Don Hernando Santella blinked nervously and swabbed his beefy face with a scented handkerchief. He mumbled his own introduction and bluntly agreed that it was the worst time possible.

"My wife," he confessed, "would kill me if I dared invite you within. It is twenty years since we have visited this place, and you can see that it is . . . ah . . . discouraging."

He was joined by a florid woman with birdlike eyes. One sight of Teresa and Elena in *pants* nearly sent her into vapors. She acknowledged the introductions with cool aloofness.

"Now, it is my turn to further apologize," Don Hernando went on quickly. "I will not subject my dear sensitive wife to one more night of this primitive life. You must forgive our rude departure, but it is a very long trip to Doña Rut's mother's home at Laguna de Santa Maria."

"A long trip indeed," Teresa agreed. And then an idea came into her mind so forceful that she couldn't block it out. "Señor," she began, and paused, strangely aware of a hurried note, a deeper ring to her voice. She strove to attain calmness and not appear overeager. "Don Hernando, could you spare five minutes more to discuss the possible sale of your land?"

He sighed deeply. "Señora, the five minutes could be spared, but to await your husband for such a discussion would be too much for my wife. When the doors of this house are shut, there is no ventilation, and even with the doors open, she feels choked and stifled. Do you smell that

431

powerful penetrating odor pervading from its interior? These peons used *my* home to distill their liquor from the cactus plants. Horrible pigs. As much as I never want to see this land again, I must decline."

A germ of an idea was in Teresa's brain, and she wouldn't let go of it. She turned her full charm on the overdressed, overfed Doña Rut. She sensed the woman was not Spanish or Mexican.

"How heartsick you must feel in finding things in this condition," she said sadly. "May I offer the hospitality of my home, so that you will be afforded a good night's rest before starting your long journey."

Ruth Hurley Santella couldn't help but wonder if she would not do better taking her chances at the first hamlet's inn. She had been born to wealth in England, coming to Mexico as a young woman when her father was named ambassador. A widower, Alexander Hurley married a landed woman after Augustin I became emperor of Mexico and England at first refused to recognize the new government. Childless, Doña Marcia saw to the proper marriage of her step-daughter into the rich and powerful Santella family. As Ruth she had never wanted for anything; as Rut she had known a life in Mexico City that would have put European royalty in the shade—and now it was totally and irrevocably gone.

When she did not answer, Teresa went right on. "It would give me an opportunity to discuss this land with your husband. I have begun to develop the adjoining land that I received as a land grant from King Joseph when I was a child of six."

Although it was said quietly, Teresa was beginning to hate the fact that it had made her boast.

"Your land?" Don Hernando flustered. "But your husband?"

"My husband is dead," she said simply. "He was Felix Escovarro de Sanchez."

"Of the *Tejas* Escovarros?" Doña Rut demanded.

"Why, yes," Teresa said as though surprised anyone would recognize the name and working hard to hide her mirth at the woman's snobbishness. "We came here when things became so difficult in Texas."

Husband and wife considered that the woman's husband must have been a victim of the recent war and thought it best not to delve into that heartbreak too deeply.

"I'm sorry to hear of your loss," Doña Rut said with sickening sweetness. "It's kind of you to put us up for the night, and we would do you an injustice if we did not accept. Hernando, get the horses moving out of this horrible place."

Teresa rode alongside the carriage, making sure she gave out only the information she desired to expose. She saw no harm in letting Don Hernando know that they had land near Santa Fe, but that she had brought only a few of the vaqueros and only three of the farm families onto this land. She thought she would be able to use the Mexicans for such a purpose on both her land and that she wished to purchase.

"Oh my, dear lady," Don Hernando scoffed, "that is a most futile dream. They are lazy and unmanageable and will leave you the moment they learn I have sold the land. Still . . . how much land did you have in mind?"

Teresa didn't bat an eye. "I want to buy your farmlands—and try to engage the Mexicans to stay on. I want to buy your northern graze lands and watershed rights to the extent, say, of fifty thousand acres."

"Señora," he gasped, "perhaps the news has not reached this wilderness, but we no longer belong to Mexico and that country's money is worthless. Your intentions are honorable, I am sure, but the amount of Mexican pesos I would have to ask you for such a purchase would be unbelievable to your ears."

"I do not deal in pesos," she said coolly. "My offer shall be in gold."

Don Hernando's fingers closed so tightly about the reins of the carriage horses that they turned white and began to ache. It had been twelve years since he had seen or felt real gold. He had dealt so long in Santa Anna's phoney paper pesos, that were printed at will, that even the word gold made his heart flutter.

"What," he stammered, "is your offer?"

"Five thousand in American gold coin."

It had been said so softly and so slowly that it seemed to become a part of the endless space of silence that followed. Teresa felt a moment of desolation that he would consider the figure horribly small, but it was all she had on hand—the money she had forgotten to deposit with Doña Patricia after her horrible meeting with Governor Peevy.

The silence that surrounded the husband and wife was born out of shock and total surprise. They could only think in terms of pesos and knew that when they left Mexico City an American gold dollar would bring fifty thousand pesos. This amount, if spent judiciously, would reestablish them in their own society.

Upon seeing the mansion, Don Hernando mentally rebuked himself for having so quickly agreed to her offer.

"Oh, Doña Teresa," his wife gushed, "I can see now why you call it the ranch of the white rose. That house is a perfect flower in your garden. Of course, being a native of England I am partial to the rose and the lovely things made of *madera rosa*."

Rosewood, Teresa mused to herself. I'll think upon that for a name.

Later, when she reached into her strongbox for the bags of gold, her hand came across something warm and velvety to the touch. She experienced a moment of *déjà vu* as she gazed at the long forgotten piece of gypsum stone. It were as though the "desert rose" had been waiting all these years to announce that it was back on the land from which it came and was at peace. She felt as if it was an omen of good fortune on her plans for the new land.

The summer months brought all that Teresa had dreamed of, and so many more changes and improvements and innovations that it was as if a magic touch had transformed the old ranch. Because Teresa did not ask the Mexican laborers to do anything that she would not do herself, they were soon ignited by her spirit and daring. Her tireless efforts divorced them from their laziness, and the bountiful harvests returned their pride. Many was the night that she was too tired to ride back to Rosewood and would collapse in the renovated ranch house.

Such was the case the day she supervised the loading and departure of five wagonloads of produce for Santa Fe. She had promised Elena that she would come home that evening for her birthday dinner, but near sunset she knew that she would have to rest for a while or she would never make it home.

The moment she dismounted, however, Quapaw jumped and trotted off. At the edge of the corral fence, he halted to lift his head and shoot up his ears. Then he let out a piercing whistle. Teresa turned to the sound and saw an unfamiliar company of horsemen rapidly riding down a hollow leading from the foothills. They would not be her vaqueros coming from that direction and Señor Clava's vaqueros had been there that morning to buy several wagonloads of baled alfalfa hay. Fear gripped her like cold hands, and she fled into the house.

Teresa bolted the door, and, flying into the kitchen, she told the servant girls to start shuttering the windows. Then she ran to the rooms she had been using. It was only a matter of a few moments for her to close and bar the heavy shutters, yet even as she was fastening the last one in the room she used as an office a clattering roar of hooves seemed to swell up to the front of the house. She caught a glimpse of wild, shaggy horses and ragged, dusty men. Their uncouth, lean, and savage looks announced them for what they were. A second glimpse assured Teresa that not all of the guerrillas were Mexican.

She hurriedly collected the money she had received from Señor Clava for the hay, ran out, closed and locked the door, crossed the patio to the opposite side of the house, and, entering again, went down a long corridor to the storeroom. Hiding the money in an unused crock, she began to examine the rifle rack to determine which of the long unused pieces would offer her the most protection. And before she made up her mind, a battering on the door in the direction of the kitchen and shrill screams from the servant women made her select quickly.

Swiftly she put extra ammunition in her black pants

pocket and raced down the corridor to a door that would
lead out of doors. Gunshot reports sickened her as to what
might be happening to the Mexican women. She opened
the door cautiously a few inches. She looked out upon a
green slope covered with wild flowers and bunches of sage
and bushes. Neither man nor horse showed in the narrow
field of her vision. The eastern sky was already growing
dusky, so she went around that side of the house to keep
within the shadows. When she got to the south corner, she
was able to view the adobe homes of the laborers, and she
could not believe that so much could have happened in so
short a time. The few men who had not gone into Santa Fe
had put up no resistance and stood huddled with their families while a half-dozen guerrillas ransacked their little huts.
Fear, wrath, and impotence contested for supremacy over
her and drove her to desperation. She was alone here, and
she must rely on herself to protect her property.

She began to fire at the men but aimed over their heads.
It brought a moment of startled confusion. The guerillas
scattered for cover, and the Mexican farmers dashed their
families back within the huts. The outlaws did not determine where the fire was coming from and started shooting
wildly. Teresa stopped firing. The outlaws were scaring
each other with the sound of their guns, making it seem as
though a dozen men were hidden on the ranch shooting
back at them.

A shrill yell, followed by the running and mounting of
the guerrillas, roused her hope that the ruse had worked.
Rapid thumping of boots on the porch told of men hurrying from the house. Several horses dashed past her, not ten
feet distant. One rider saw her, for he turned to shout back
and drew a bead on her with his pistol. This drove Teresa
into a panic. Hardly knowing what she did, she raised the
rifle waist-high and fired all in the same motion. The outlaw was lifted sharply out of the saddle and thrown to the
ground.

The fright of one of the kitchen girls kept Teresa from
being detected again. The girl tried to make a desperate
dash to get to the protection of her family. Horses with
shouting riders streaked past the girl, taunting her with vile

suggestions. Then a powerful guerrilla clasped her about the waist and swung her aloft. Her kicking and screaming lasted but a second before he cuffed her hard behind the ear, and she went limp across the saddle.

They were gone so quickly that Teresa had been unable to react. Then she became nothing but movement. The house was a shambles and one of the kitchen women had been badly pistol-whipped. Teresa barked orders for someone to see after the woman and for one of the men to get to Rosewood for help from the vaqueros. No one questioned what she was about, it just seemed quite obvious and natural that she was going to track the outlaws until the vaqueros could catch up to her and secure the girl's release. She didn't even think what she was about as she jerked into a coat, tied a bandanna about her neck, and secured the caballero hat strings under her chin. Quapaw sensed what she was about more than she did, for he was never fleeter of foot.

Night brought with it a sharp rise in the wind and a dust storm out of the east. Teresa had to tie the bandanna about her nose and mouth to keep from choking to death, and with her eyes tightly shut against the stinging pellets of grit left the tracking to the keen senses of Quapaw. They began to rise off the plain and foothills into the mountains and forests. Here the bite of the storm was not as harsh. After what seemed a thousand weary hours Quapaw stopped abruptly. She smelled wood smoke and opened her eyes quickly. Quapaw had stopped at the edge of a sparse grove of firs. Not fifty feet away, in the clearing, a group of men stood and sat round a campfire, eating like wolves. Mostly they were thin-bodied, thin-bearded Mexicans, black and haggard and starved. Whatever they might be, they surely were hunger-stricken and squalid. Not one had a coat, although the night at this elevation was turning bitter. A few had scarfs. Some wore belts in which were scattered cartridges. Only a few had guns, indicating the reason why they had departed the ranch so quickly. It also appeared that the main intent of their raid had been for food. For the moment it appeared that the Mexican girl had gone untouched for them first to satisfy their ravenous appetites.

The girl sat next to the fire, her arms huddled about her knees and her head bowed. It amazed Teresa that they showed no signs of anxiety in being pursued. She was about to turn Quapaw back into the shadows of the grove and go in search of the vaqueros when the high-risen dust cloud seemed to melt away and a full moon began to illuminate the scene.

A low exclamation and a sweep of arm from one of the guerrillas caused the whole band to wheel and concentrate their attention on the edge of the grove and up beyond it. Grimy hands sought weapons, and then every man stiffened. Teresa had almost forgot that she sat with the rifle at the ready and now saw what hunted men looked like at the moment of discovery; the sight was terrible. She was only one and fearful of the moment when their guns would leap out.

There were muttered curses, a short period of silence followed by whisperings, and then a clear voice rang out, "Penitentes!"

A strong shock vibrated through Teresa and made her realize she still wore the black bandanna about her nose and mouth. They had not only taken her for a Penitente, but for a man. Then she realized the man had shouted the word as plural, as though she had not come alone. She had to keep them thinking that, to get the girl away, but she dared not speak and lose part of her advantage. She motioned with her rifle toward the girl and then flicked the rifle upward.

One of the men nearest her kicked her and growled out an order. The girl started running toward Teresa and then stopped short. Instantly she was more fearful of the masked rider than of the outlaws. Teresa feared the rescue attempt was going to fail right then and there.

"Keep coming, Carmaleta," a bass voice boomed. Teresa heard the slow, heavy thump of hooves. Soon into the narrow aisles between the trees moved men on horseback, with rifles at the ready. Then Teresa saw the first man, and she recognized Estaban Duran, the last person in the world she expected to see.

He rode up close, his face grinning. "I heard them

shout," he whispered, greatly amused. "Are you trying to steal a chapter out of my book?"

Teresa couldn't speak, feeling a suffocating sense of gladness and relief and wonder.

"Elena is waiting for you back on the ridge," he said. "Start for home and we will see to the girl and this motley crew."

The guerrillas stood with their weapons undrawn. The man from the farm, who had called out the girl's name, helped her up to the extra horse they had brought along. And as she rode away, tugging the kerchief off her face, Teresa could hear Estaban shout out:

"You have strayed into dangerous country, señors. You have seen that we are capable of defending our own. You might pass the word along that there are Penitentes in this area. Now, finish your supper. We will be near at hand awaiting your departure within the hour. If you wish to stay longer, I would advise you consult the man who recognized the black rider as to what would next happen."

The event had greatly disturbed Elena. Still confused and fearful, she was silent for a long time on the ride back. Then, striving for a newfound conviction, and succeeding only in making her voice uneven and breathless, she said: "I want to learn how to shoot a rifle!"

Teresa answered, with firmness and calmness: "I killed a man with a rifle today. Once before I felt I was responsible for killing a man about to kill me, and I felt great guilt. I have always loathed violence. But I can't tell you what I felt today, because I can't remember. I'm unsure of what I feel right now, Elena. I still loathe violence, but if beasts like this are allowed to roam our supposedly civilized world, then I suppose the lioness has every right in the world to protect her cubs. Yesterday I might have forbidden your request. Tonight? No amount of words from Estaban is going to warn them all off, Elena. These were but a handful, and there must be hundreds more like them out there robbing and looting. A few rustlers now and then was one thing, but these demons have formed into packs just like wolves and coyotes." She sighed sadly. "The war isn't really over; it has just changed battle dress."

"Enough of such talk on your birthday," Elena scolded. "To make you forget tonight, I think I'll spring Estaban's surprise right now."

Teresa laughed thinly. "Seeing him ride into the clearing was surprise enough. Why is he here?"

Elena frowned. "It was really supposed to be Tía Patricia who was to bring you the surprise, but she wasn't well enough to make the trip and so sent Estaban in her place." Then she brightened. "She's been able to adopt me and my two twerpy little half brothers. Isn't it a laugh? The likes of we three become the first American citizens here because of the adoption."

Teresa smiled a little, subtly, with a cold hurt that paled and molded the lines of her mouth. Doña Patricia had been able to do what she had not, and although it legally made Elena an Escovarro, it was not as though Teresa had been able to grant the gift herself. She knew that Doña Patricia's intent had not been to hurt, but it still hurt.

As Teresa foresaw, the war only changed battle dress and took on a different face. For the next seven years the dictatorial insanity by which Santa Anna would rule a lessened Mexico and keep the people near starvation only tended to increase the number of sizes of the guerrilla bands. The stern Indian policy of the Pierce and Buchanan administrations forced the outbreak of a hundred wars, little in size but monumental in the human lives taken and the Indian lands stolen away.

Men also fought personal wars in this new land. With names like Goodnight, Chisum, and Lawless they sought to carve out cattle empires to break the dons' hold on the land. Such men were furious when California was quickly granted statehood without slavery and the power of the old Spanish families was somehow heard in Washington, and New Mexico was granted nothing more than territorial rights. But in losing that battle, they won a more important one. The question of slavery was left hanging in the balance because of the Indian situation.

*   *   *

"Two more were found in the fields," Elena announced one chilly fall day when Teresa returned from the farmlands.

"Where are they?" she asked sadly.

"Big John took them directly into Santa Fe so that Tía Patricia could quickly send them north." Then she added quickly, "And it wasn't but a couple of hours later before that overseer showed up."

"Damn that man Bowditch," she said bitterly. "He doesn't dare come and face me directly but is sure in his black heart that I am the one responsible for his slaves constantly running away."

Elena smiled slyly. "They do seem to find their way here quite quickly. How do you account for that?"

"It could be that they have an expert guide," she answered wryly. "I may learn more about it tomorrow."

"Tomorrow?"

"I'm unhappy with the strain of corn we produced this winter. I thought of riding down to Santo Domingo to purchase next year's seed crop."

"When do we leave?"

She gazed at Elena tenderly. They were now nearly inseparable, and it warmed her that Elena had automatically included herself in on the trip.

The warmth in Teresa's heart turned steadily colder as they rode into the pueblo village. It was almost like a ghost town with only a few old squaws sitting about. The pottery wheels were unattended and looked as though they had not spun in months. Santo Domingo should have been alive with Indians and Spaniards bartering and trading for seed corn, grain, and pottery goods. Only the yapping of the dogs brought someone out to see to the noise and greet them.

Elena sat looking at the man, her jaw dropping foolishly. "What a man!" she whispered.

"I agree," Teresa said. "I had forgotten how long it has been since I have seen him."

Teresa slowly dismounted as Ta-Tak-To came to her all smiles.

"Doña Teresa!" he began. "I mean——Señora Escovarro . . ."

"Mother, dear," Elena said admiringly, "introduce me, won't you? He's much too young for you . . ."

"My daughter, Elena," Teresa said, "for whose horrible manners I freely apologize. Ta-Tak-To, I'm awfully glad to see you. You look fine . . . just as young as the day we first met."

"My own thoughts," Ta-Tak-To murmured. "I—I never thought to see you in my humble village."

The pain of love flowed back into his heart so quickly that it seemed like only moments before that he had vowed never to see her again. So many times he had wanted to come to her after she had become a widow, but his strong moral code had kept him faithful to his wife, children, and people.

"I have come on business," Teresa said. "I need advice on the purchase of a good corn seed for next year."

Ta-Tak-To glanced at her uneasily. "I think you must come into the pueblo and greet my father. As chief he will discuss the matter with you."

"Don't include me," Elena said. "I'd rather have a look around while Mother has her talk."

He frowned darkly. "As you wish, but stay within the village."

Po-Nee-Chee, a little wiry man with a dry face like a sharp ferret, was surprised to at last see the woman who had given his son's heart so much trouble. He could see that she was beautiful by white man's standards but not by his own.

"We welcome you, señora," he said, briskly squatting down on the floor of the dim room that smelled of smoke and old hides and ancient adobe mustiness. He eyed Teresa curiously as she went directly to the reason for her visit.

The old man cleared his throat and spoke quietly: "I wish it were possible for me to grant your request." He paused and studied Teresa apprehensively. It was not his custom to discuss business or tribal matters with a woman. They were too emotional and did not see matters clearly.

"In the past few years we have been barely able to grow enough corn to feed our people through each winter."

"How can that be? I have had bountiful crops, although the quality is poor."

Po-Nee-Chee allowed a grave expression to come over his face. He suddenly wanted to test this woman's emotions. He nodded somberly. "Such would also be our case. Our best lands have been taken over by a man with a paper from the chief in Washington. It says that our lands may be used by him and that we must help him or be sent off our lands."

There was a sudden silence in the room. Then, stiffly, as if a broom handle had been forced down her shirt, Teresa sat up rigid.

"You mean," she said very quietly, "that this is the land Vince Bowditch is using to grow his cotton?"

"Yes," said Po-Nee-Chee in a sepulchral voice. "He is the man with the paper."

After a long pause Teresa spoke tonelessly: "I had heard that he had land near Santo Domingo but not Santo Domingo itself. We have been getting quite a few of his runaway slaves on our land."

"That would be the work of my son," he said proudly, relieved that the woman was quite easy to talk to. "It is a matter of concern to us." And now Po-Nee-Chee betrayed some embarrassment. "Bowditch brought only black men with him. Our people do not want the mixture of that blood any more than we will allow the mixture of white or Spanish bloods. But it has happened several times, mostly by force, and the man thinks it is quite amusing and will do nothing. We can do nothing but help those men escape and then punish the girl by our tribal code.

Teresa said nothing. She felt nothing in herself but desolation.

The high, piercing scream momentarily chilled them and then electrified them into instant action. Almost as one they bounded into the pueblo yard in time to see Elena kick and claw her way loose from the powerful arms of a scarfaced big black man. She came at them on the run, her blouse shredded. At the same instant Ta-Tak-To filled the air with a horrible curse and started to run after the man. But just as the man raced around the corner of the last pueblo building, a horseman came charging around the same corner and cut Ta-Tak-To off.

"Leave him be," Bowditch growled, cracking his whip into the dirt just before Ta-Tak-To to make his point. "Come, I got words for your father."

Bowditch then became aware of who stood next to the old chief, and a tighter look appeared on his face.

"Come to bring me back some of my blacks?" he said coldly.

But Teresa no longer lived in abject terror of him. All the memory of years of humiliation and suffering stood in her calm brown eyes. She inclined her head. "If I had my way, I would set them all free," she said in a voice as cold as Bowditch's.

Bowditch gave her a long look of bitter contempt. He had never forgiven her for the part he assumed she played in Miguel's death and the fact that it had kept him from becoming a very rich man. Nor was he becoming richer with his present project. Year after year one thing or another went wrong with the cotton crop. That year he had anticipated his first profit, but an unusually early frost was already killing off the plants. That thought took his mind away from Teresa and his purpose for being there.

"Ta-Tak-To," he barked. "Tell your old man that I'm sick of his games. If your people do not start picking that cotton faster, I'll let the overseers use the whips on them just as quick as they use them on the blacks. Next! For every black who escapes from now on, I'm going to chain one of the young squaws into their compound with them. Last! And mainly for the benefit of Señora Escovarro, it is illegal to help a slave escape. Let me find one of my blacks on your land, lady, and I'll fight with my last dollar to see you in prison."

He sat his horse, scowling down at them, but Ta-Tak-To stubbornly refused to translate. It had not been necessary, Po-Nee-Chee had understood every word, but part of their stalling tactics over the years was to force Bowditch to come through Ta-Tak-To for everything he wanted from the chief.

Angrily Bowditch snapped his whip back and brought it forward to slice into Ta-Tak-To's cheek and open a deep wound. The Indian did not flinch or cry out or move a single muscle in his body.

"That does it," Bowditch stormed. "I don't need you damned savages. I'm enforcing the terms of my contract. Get your people ready to move. I'll have troops here from Fort Sumner in two days time."

The old man did not unmask himself by replying to the threat. He was not intimidated. He looked steadfastly at Bowditch with his grave gray eyes with such loathing that Bowditch was forced to turn and spur his horse away.

"He can't do it, of course," said Teresa in a soft, shocked tone. "The territorial treaty says they can't take away granted lands."

Ta-Tak-To put his hand to his cheek to stop the blood flow and scoffed. "It does not apply to Indians. His paper says he can take the land just as they have taken it from our brothers in the east and south."

"My son speaks the truth," Po-Nee-Chee murmured in distress.

"Then perhaps it's time to lie, just as he must have lied to get that paper," she said soundly, a germ of an idea popping into her head.

"I could not think of such a thing," he said flatly.

"No," she said contemptuously, "but when it comes to that man, I can easily stretch a point. Ta-Tak-To, are those cattle I saw grazing offspring of the original gift from my husband." He nodded, unsure of her point. She smiled gently and looked upon Po-Nee-Chee reassuringly. "A gift cannot be accepted without giving in return. Would it be wrong to write a paper saying the Santo Domingo lands were such a gift in return?"

Po-Nee-Chee, that astute analyzer of character, knew now what had attracted his son to this woman. She had the face and body of a woman, but she had the heart and the spirit of a mountain lion. Crafty, alert, untrappable, and emotionless in the face of danger. He nodded his agreement.

"We have some business at the old ranch," Teresa said, which made Elena look at her oddly. "We will be back for the paper before the troops arrive."

"Why did you tell them that?" Elena asked as they rode away from the village.

Teresa avoided the question. She asked instead: "Did you bring in your saddlebag what I requested?"

"Of course."

"Then you'd best change shirts. You're flapping in the breeze."

Looking down at her nearly exposed condition, she began to giggle. She had not been aware of it until that moment.

Bowditch's overseer had been giggling to himself since he left the man to deliver a letter to the commander at Fort Sumner. He could tolerate the blacks but could not stomach the smell of the Indians. He would be well glad to be rid of them.

After crossing a shallow ford in the Rio Grande, the giggle dried in his throat. The trail was blocked by two masked figures in black with drawn pistols. He nervously dismounted and held his silence while one of the duo rifled through his saddlebag. He was totally confused that they took no more from him than the Bowditch letter and then tersely wrote in the riverbank sand: "Go south! Don't come back!"

He did go south but recrossed the river and headed back to report to Bowditch. It was just after dark when he came up on the far side of the black compound and saw the same two masked men releasing some wide-eyed and frightened slaves. The night guard laid sprawled on the ground. He was about to pull his pistol and capture the outlaws when he felt the cold circle of a rifle touch his neck. He had not even heard the man approach and from the corner of his eye could see that he was similarly masked.

"You were told to ride south," a voice whispered in English with a strong Spanish accent. "I suggest you do it, if you want to keep living."

The overseer did not turn back again.

The fear that was instilled in the remaining slaves angered Bowditch more than the suspicion in his mind that Teresa Escovarro had something to do with the Penitente raid. Good to his promise, he had ten young Indian squaws chained within the black compound. The next morning they were released unmolested, but ten more of his bucks had vanished during the night. And by noon the guard who had been caught unawares two nights in a row also vanished.

That night twenty squaws were chained in the compound, and Bowditch and his remaining two white overseers stood a constant vigil throughout the night. It was an eerie night: the black men intoning ancient jungle prayers against the powers of the black masked capturers and the Indian girls chanting prayers to protect their virginity.

By dawn Bowditch's ears could stand no more of the babble. He stormed back to his adobe cabin and began to drink savagely. The overseer's nerves were equally shot.

"You thinkin' what I'm thinkin', Barney?"

"Maybe, Lem," he drawled. "Ain't had no trouble with the Indians so far, but how far is far? Ain't going to give up my scalp for the lousy wage he's been a payin', no sir."

A half hour after they left, the three masked men spirited away the twenty-five remaining black slaves. It was quietly observed by Ta-Tak-To. It was his moment to act, as he knew he should have acted from the first day Bowditch had brought the paper to his father. His brothers, getting old and fat waiting for the chief to die, had been as old-womanish as had been his father. For too long the Santo Domingo people had been docile, unwarring traders. He went to those he could trust and spoke quietly. Within the hour a strange sight appeared on the Rio Grande. Hundreds of bales of cotton floated along with the current like a huge armada of rectangular ships. While this was being accomplished, silent hands pulled the remaining cotton plants up by the roots and left them to wither.

Ta-Tak-To sensed who was responsible for the rebirth of

his courage and manhood. He saw her coming alone, fording the river and rode out to meet her.

He felt, all through him, the old sickness and desire and passion, the old love. This was Teresa, her flesh, her presence, her faint fresh scent, her beloved brown eyes and calm beautiful face. All at once he wanted to forsake everything just for her.

Teresa had to take but one look at his face to know his thoughts and that he could not be lied to. Others might be fooled by the black attire and mask, but she had been aware for years that he knew every line of her body and that was why he stayed away from her. She had deeply respected him for it while Felix had been alive but suddenly wondered what it would really be like to be locked within his powerful bronze arms and feel the touch of his lips upon hers.

He looked down at her as their horses sat abreast, and he thought: I can't endure this. I must have her! I will renounce my squaw and children and ask to be called Santo Domingo no more!

The brown eyes, fixed so urgently upon him, saw all his thoughts. They softened. They filled with tears. She turned aside her head, and he saw her profile, delicate and beautiful, but inexpressibly moved and shaken.

"Ta," she whispered. The frail muscles of her white throat stood out above the black bandanna and trembled.

"Teresa," he said. Involuntarily his hand reached out and seized her crushingly.

She struggled with her wants and her desires. Was she being faithless to Felix's memory in wanting to love and be loved again by a man? She could share many things with Elena, but not the thoughts and words and dreams that only a man and woman could hold as special little moments in time. The tears were so thick in her eyes that she had to distend her lids to hold them, sternly. She swallowed. After a moment she knew exactly what she must do.

"Later," she said tonelessly. "Right now I must see your father, alone."

She felt the grip on her hand loosen, slacken, fall away. The ride to the pueblo was pervaded by a deathly coldness.

The wiry old man stood outside his pueblo door, his face an immobile mask. He accepted the fact that she wanted to see him alone without question and motioned for her to enter.

"And now?" he said almost inaudibly. "And now what is it you wish of me, Señora Escovarro?"

"Our lie about the land would be useless. Yesterday I learned that there are new men in Santa Fe who are questioning even the Spaniards' right to keep their land. It seems that it shall be up to each of us to fight for our lands as we see fit."

"Can you fight for your land without a man to protect you?"

"That seems to have been my fate of late. Can you fight for your land?"

"We have never been a warring tribe," he said bitterly. "We were always able to be the diplomats and traders among the tribes. We thought to handle the white men in the same manner we handled you Spaniards. We have been proven wrong, and I am too old to retrain my thoughts to lead my people differently. My sons who wait to replace me are equally as wrong and weak."

She was silent a moment. Her eyes did not leave his, though their sternness increased. She said unemotionally: "Then perhaps you should look to the one son who does have the strength."

"Are you mistaking strength for the love he carries for you in his heart? Among my people are no secrets between father and son. I have seen his attitude alter since your return. I watched you two meet together on horseback. I felt at that moment I had lost my son forever. Is there a reason you did not kiss-him in your fashion?"

"Yes," she said in a tone as measured and controlled as always, "there was a very good reason. Once he wanted me, and I was married and unattainable. He is not unattainable for me. His people and family need him more than I."

He stammered, out of the welter of his emotions. "You shame me for the dark thoughts I have been harboring. My other sons must never hear these words I speak to you, but you seem to sense that he is most special to me. Perhaps I was wrong to force him to take a squaw when his heart was full of you. You would have made a most powerful daughter-in-law."

She said, still with firmness and calmness: "You must make him instead a powerful son. When I leave, I will send him to you immediately. Do not let him follow or I might weaken."

"No, my daughter," he said, his heart incredibly soft and tremulous, "you are not made of a material that weakens. In my heart you are from this day Te-Chee-La: One-who-lasts-as-long-as-the-great-mountains. Go with Manitou!"

The power of daily tribal authority was quickly passed, although Po-Nee-Chee would still hold supreme authority until his death. His word was not questioned, because his was the voice that went unquestioned. The elder brothers of Ta-Tak-To could do little but return to their pueblos and sulk. The hearts of the young Santo Domingo braves were rekindled as they had not been in years.

A drunken Vince Bowditch came roaringly awake to find himself bound and hoisted into a saddle, where he was securely tied to the pommel to keep him from falling off. His possessions had been packed onto a trailing mule, and he was sent on his way bellowing out his vile curses against Indians, cotton, and mainly Teresa Escovarro.

He was found some fifty miles later by an army patrol, still ranting and cursing his lot. The mild-mannered officer, in charge of the patrol, listened to his accusations with amusement.

"I would think, sir," he drawled slowly, "that it's about time for you to think about heading back home. We don't say it out loud, except to a fine gentleman like yourself, because we wear army uniforms, but the day is coming soon when we are going to war over this question of slavery. Forget this horrible dry western land. The money in slavery will be made when we win that war and take over this country. I can put you in touch with some of my friends, if you've a mind."

"What's your name, Major?"

"Beauregard, sir. Major Pierre Beauregard."

Five years later General Pierre Beauregard would demand and receive the surrender of Fort Sumter, North Carolina, after heavy bombardment. It would launch a war bearing many emotional titles: the War Between the States, the Civil War, the War for Human Determination, the War of Freedom and Equality.

But when Bowditch was rescued by the major, he was unaware that he would be able to give his own emotional name to the national conflict: the War of Revenge.

When the messenger brought the news from Santa Fe, Teresa stood stunned and dazed, not wanting to believe his words. It was odd that she had never once thought of the possibility of Patricia Escovarro dying. The woman had been indestructible in her mind. Why she could only have been . . . Teresa's mind boggled. For too long she had used only Elena as her measuring stick of time, and that was an error. At twenty-six Elena was still as youthful and vibrant and provocative as she had been at sixteen. She was the passionate desire of every man in the Chimayo area of any age, but none had dared approach her. It wasn't Elena they feared as much as Teresa. Among the Spanish people she had gained the reputation of having the "Midas touch"—nothing she attempted failed. She had even been able to bring Basques back from Spain and her sheep herds now nearly totaled those of the cattle. How could anyone approach the daughter of such a person without immediately arousing suspicion that he was greedy and power hungry.

It all had a tendency to greatly amuse Elena. She enjoyed the company of the young men at the various parties and balls, but when they attempted to get amorous, she grew stiff and cold and unapproachable. She knew that somewhere, sometime, she would experience a love such as Teresa had felt for Felix, and she didn't mind waiting for it to materialize naturally and not be forced by a stupid sexual encounter.

For reasons unexplained to Teresa they brought Doña Patricia to the Ranch of the Two Brothers for services and burial. It made many people travel out from Santa Fe unnecessarily, including the bishop of Santa Fe who had clashed with Teresa and Doña Patricia on several points since his elevation. An Irish Catholic, he was soundly determined that the new parochial schools would be taught in English. Without students the nuns could teach nothing, while the Jesuit school became overflowing. Only when he needed funds for a new church roof did he cave in and meet their demands.

"Well, Father," she said, purposely not giving him the respect of his full title, "I assume you had good reason for setting the services out here."

"It was all this young gentleman's doing," the bishop murmured, flushing scarlet.

"Hello, Auntie Esa."

Teresa turned and stared. She had been prepared to accept Estavar as the young gentleman mentioned, but not this young prince. He reminded Teresa suddenly of Felix in his youth, though the face was not quite correct.

Raoul wore a Napoleon—the emperor's styles were all the rage of Europe—and his fawn-colored gloves flapped gracefully between his slender fingers. His clothes were perfect, avoiding excesses of either fashion or conservatism, Teresa decided, and turned once more to his undeniably compelling good looks. There was an exotic quality about them—Spanish without a fault, a young grandee. The regalness of his bearing seemed to emphasize that in his body, but the haughtiness of his face and black eyes were pure Aztec, although the proud arch of his Roman nose was pure Escovarro.

"Oh, Raoul," she cried, throwing her arms wide. "Oh, what a surprise. It's been so long."

"Eleven years," Raoul said, kissing her sweetly on each cheek.

"That long?" Teresa mused. "Is your mother with you? Where is Ramon?"

His laugh was deep and booming and was one more reminder of Felix. "The countess, as we are instructed to call her these days, is still in Spain. Since the death of the count she has taken her position quite seriously and has become quite the favorite of Queen Isabella. My little brother

452

should be around here someplace. Oh, here he comes now."

To Teresa it was as though Ramon had never grown up, although nearly of the same height as his twin brother. He was thin and reedy, giving his shy movements a shadowy quality. The whiteness of his skin accented the raven hue of his hair and the soft doelike quality of his eyes. There was the patrician Escovarro handsomeness to his face, but it was more like they had been done in pastel chalks rather than chiseled out of stone.

He was as timid and shy in his greeting of Teresa as ever and just as he had finished merely pecking at her cheek, Elena ran into the room.

"Mother!" she began, then she saw them. She stood quite still, her green eyes becoming round and enormous.

"Raoul? Ramon?" she stammered. "I didn't know . . ."

"Elena?" Raoul murmured smoothly and reached out to take her hand. She stood wordless, but there were great pink roses, suddenly blooming, in her cheeks.

Caramba, Raoul thought, what a beauty she has become! Too bad she's older than . . . Then he suddenly remembered.

"Do you recall when we were children, and I said someday I would catch up with you?" he laughed gently. "Twenty-one doesn't sound too far away from twenty-six, does it?"

Elena recovered, taking her hand away. "You're not supposed to remind a lady of her age," she laughed. She turned to Ramon.

"It's so good to see you, Ramon. Do you have any *piñatas* to show me?"

"No," he said softly, flushing red. Then: "I did bring you a present."

"Wonderful! I just love presents!"

"I brought gifts also," Raoul said gruffly.

Nothing ever changes, Teresa thought. They are still vying for the full attention of Elena. But now they are at an age when they can vie for her affection. She was surprised at how much she suddenly opposed such a thought.

* * *

No less than an hour after the burial of Doña Patricia they were gathered together in the drawing room of the pink villa. Estavar Escovarro surveyed them with his pale brown and watchful eyes. He sat in stiff dignity behind his father's old desk, his delicate hand lying importantly on a sealed envelope.

He had absolutely no aversions or likings for a single person in the room, for he had become a young man of no strong emotions at all. He was only a piece of machinery; competent, keen minded, and as carefully balanced as the debit and credit columns in the bank.

"I have been named executor of the estate," he intoned without preamble, "and saw the wisdom of handling the matter of the will while we were all together today."

He had little trouble reading and understanding the terms of the will, for he had been present when it had been drafted. The minor bequeaths were handled rapidly: adequate sums for Doña Patricia's household staff and certain older employees of the bank and express company. For his past services and friendship, a handsome sum for Big John. A grand sum for the erection of a convent for the training of Spanish-speaking nuns. And minor sums to a few old friends and charities.

The Santa Fe house, possessions, and the woman's personal jewelry were left to Teresa.

The one hundred and fifteen thousand acres which had been purchased in her name by Miguel were to be divided between Raoul and Ramon, with the proviso that they had to take an active interest in the running of the land to obtain it.

The bulk of the estate centered around four people: the presidency and controlling interest in the bank went to Estavar. Pedro and Gordo Perez Escovarro were named as equal partners in the ownership of the express company. Besides a large endowment, to serve as her wedding dowry, Elena was given a directorship and stock in both the bank and express company.

"Hey, that's going to make you quite some catch," Raoul laughed mirthfully.

"Not really," Elena answered soberly. "At twenty-six I really haven't had a desire to wed. The dowry isn't going to change that feeling."

"Someday a man will come to change your mind."

"And perhaps not," she said without emotion.

He looked down at her as she sat beside him, and he thought: perhaps I am that man.

Elena averted her head and leaned back against the tree trunk. The day was hot and humid and the horizon seemed to shimmer and dance.

"What do you plan on doing with the land?" she asked, aware that they could be just as comfortable and straightforward with each other in spite of the years of separation.

"Develop it, I guess. That's why I came home, to run the ranch. I hated Spain and the silly useless life I was leading. Everything there came too easily for me, without any challenge. I had to but snap my fingers, and I could have any girl I wanted."

Elena gave him a sour, mocking look. "You haven't changed a bit, have you, Raoul?"

He frowned. "How's that?"

"Still the little boy," she laughed, "always slyly moving the conversation onto a sexual theme. You got me into hot water with your mother doing that once too often."

"I did? When?"

"When blabbermouth Estavar overheard you tell Ramon that you knew someone who told you all about sex. Considering my background at the time, Emilia thought for sure I was the culprit, and she and Teresa had quite a to-do over it."

Raoul flung back his head and roared. "That was the Ruiz girl. I was ten and she was about fourteen. She always wanted to play 'show me.' I didn't have much to show at the time and neither did she. I was always tempted to play 'show me' with you, but it's best I waited. You certainly have much more to show me now than you did then."

The hand stung his face with all her strength of fury.

He looked at her haughtily contemptuous face. The lines of her mouth were hard; the exquisite distended nostrils seemed carved from marble. It was a mouth that needed kissing to softness; a nose that must smell the scent of love.

He caught her in his arms and pressed his mouth hard upon hers. She melted against him. He felt the wild and tumultuous beating of her heart against his chest. A wild rapture swept over him. His large hands pressed her demanding body, hot and seeking, and her firm flesh softened and yielded under them.

They were aware of nothing but their turbulent coming together, satisfying their desperate outer hunger.

Then he felt a power in her, impassive, immovable.

"No, Raoul," she said with firmness and calmness.

"I turned into a little boy again," he said, his heart plunging.

"It has nothing to do with that. I cannot deny that I have always found you . . . appealing . . . interesting. I still have the single letter you wrote to me from Spain. I was crushed when you didn't come home that time." Then striving for the old relationship between them and succeeding only in making her voice uneven and breathless, she said: "Teresa has given me a different life. I hated my beginning. Detested it. It was repugnant to me to know my mother had been a whore. I always felt dirty in knowing that my grandmother had a man in her bed. And now? I tolerate the restrictions imposed by the narrow ranch life. I have found that I have nothing in common with the eligible men I have met." She paused, and now her voice was stern: "You are eligible, and we do have a lot in common, Raoul. But, as yet, it's not love. I don't intend to ape my mother in learning about love."

A return to Rosewood helped her momentarily to blot Raoul from her mind. But the fall roundup and a major decision on the part of Teresa brought them back. At first it seemed quite a common thing to live within the ranch house and see the pink villa ablaze across the river. The twins were back and forth daily, and Elena couldn't outright avoid Raoul. Each sighting of him would make her remember his arms about her crushing with cruel force, his hot lips on hers in mad, unasked kisses. The heat would rise in her face, and she would have to turn away. She would not let herself get caught alone with Raoul but thought nothing of riding the range with Ramon.

"Mother has studied your plan of combining the herds, Ramon. She likes it. It will release her vaqueros to move to Rosewood."

"It will be more economical" was his laconic response. "I don't mean to talk against the man, but Guido Herrera is a bit old-fashioned when it comes to getting the right amount of work out of the men. Raoul, I'm afraid, will be about the same."

Elena couldn't help but laugh. "Ramon Escovarro, those are the most words I've heard you string together in your whole life."

He looked at her steadily with no shyness. "I finally have found something to talk about. I used to sit in school and daydream about two things. One was of the day I could get out from behind Raoul's shadow, become my own man, and run this ranch as I know it should be run. I visited Scotland on the way home, while Raoul partied in London. I saw something there that really excited me, Elena. They have a breed of cattle called the Black Angus. If we could crossbreed it with the Brahma strain, it would produce a cow two to three hundred pounds heavier than what we have now. I used every last cent of my own money to buy four bulls and have them shipped over. I'm going down to Corpus Christi to get them in a couple of weeks."

Elena looked at him through different eyes. He literally glowed with inner excitement. Once before she had seen this look on his quietly handsome face, on the first day they had become friends. His excitement was transferred to her.

"It sounds marvelous," she enthused. "And what was the second thing you daydreamed about."

Ramon flushed, but he didn't avert his eyes. "My gift should have given you a clue."

"No clue," she said truthfully, "but I have been remiss in thanking you for it. The lace is like nothing I have ever seen before."

"Perhaps," he said softly, "I was in Spain too long and

got carried away by their old customs. A young man does not give a young lady such a mantilla unless he has deep and serious thoughts about her in his heart."

Elena stopped Pawpaw short. Her heart was fluttering like butterfly wings. "Thank you, Ramon," she whispered. "That is the most beautiful thing anyone has ever said to me." Then she did an impulsive thing. She leaned across from her saddle and kissed him tenderly on the lips. He returned the kiss without touching her with his hands. When they broke away, they searched each other's eyes for many long silent moments. He gently took her hand and clucked the horses forward. They each needed that quiet moment for their personal thoughts.

For Ramon a wellspring had erupted in his heart like a geyser. His daydream of love had bloomed into a reality with a single kiss. If put to the test, he would have been able to recite every word Elena had ever spoken to him since the day he shyly showed her the *piñatas*.

For Elena it was a moment of profound confusion. Was this love? Her heart felt the same as it had the day she rushed at Felix with her new rabbit-fur coat. Her body tingled and she suddenly never wanted to release the warm, reassuring grasp of his hand. But was it love or the enchantment of being wooed in a gentlemanly old-fashioned way?

Her newfound relationship with Ramon altered her attitude toward Raoul. Again she could feel comfortable around him, could kid and joke and laugh. She knew that she could control his amorous nature by holding him at arm's length with just a dash of teasing. And when he kissed her again, as she knew was bound to happen, he was not harsh and brusque but gentle and compelling. When she tried to compare the brothers, she found that she could not. She had fallen in love with a part of each, but not the whole of either one.

". . . and that's the size of it, Mother," she finished after baring the whole thing to Teresa.

She sat very still, looking tiny and frail in her customary work shirt and pants, and absurdly young for all her forty-four years. And she had listened quietly while Elena poured out her divided heart. Now she stood up calmly.

"And you don't seem to love one any stronger than the other?" she demanded.

"Yes and no. That's why I want you to make up my mind for me."

Teresa wasn't sure she wanted to make up her mind in either direction. It wasn't that she did not love the boys equally herself. She was just remembering the horrible mistake she had almost made in life by allowing her mother to make the arrangements with her union with Fernando Martin Flores.

"I appreciate you coming to me with this, Elena," she said. "You know my feelings about the old ways and customs, but you have caught me in one that I don't think I really believe in any longer. My parents' marriage was miserable because it was planned for them, as it nearly was for me. I could stand here and give you the good points and bad points of each of them, but that would only be my feelings. I could stand here and give you one name or the other, but it may not be the one you really wish to hear. I can only say give it time for your heart to make the final answer."

Teresa had really a single name on her mind that she might have been tempted to utter. She had come to regard Ramon's ability quite highly. He was becoming the type of man she could turn over the management of the ranch to without a qualm. Raoul? For all her love for her nephew, she could see so much of his father in him that it frightened her. Elena's life would be hell with him, because he would start bed-hopping the moment she became pregnant. She would not press, one way or the other, but she silently prayed for it to be Ramon.

The matter smoldered on for a year. The track between the ranch and Rosewood became deep rooted with the frequent trips made by each of the twins.

And when Elena made her final decision, she also prayed that it was the correct one.

She and Ramon stood hesitantly before Teresa after they had made the announcement, studying her quiet face apprehensively.

Although the choice was to her liking, it was a moment Teresa had been dreading. She was going to lose Elena—not wholly, but in part. She doubted that her mother had felt the same way, because they had never been as close as she had been with Elena. *Elena, my little daughter!* . . . Then she straightened up and beamed at them.

"When do we start planning for this wedding?"

Ramon started speaking at once, as though he had never suffered a shy moment before the woman in his life. "That's just the point, Auntie Esa. We are just getting into summer and the busy time of the year. We thought late fall—"

"*You* thought late fall," Elena interrupted.

"*I* thought late fall," he amended himself, "but for sound reasons. We can then take a winter honeymoon in Spain when we are needed here the least. It would also save Mother the trip here, because we could then see her there."

Practical Ramon, Teresa thought. Practical to the point of taking everything and everyone into consideration. She rose and kissed each warmly on the cheek and left them to be alone.

Ramon drew Elena immediately to him. His kiss was like none he had ever given her before. It left her a little stunned and mystified. It was a little like Raoul's kisses—endlessly promising, hinting of unequaled delights.

"Are you staying the weekend?" she whispered as she stood in his embrace.

Ramon frowned. "No," he said shortly, "I must get back tonight. There's something I have to do . . ."

"What is it, Ramon?" Elena demanded.

"Nothing that concerns—us."

"Secrets?"

"Hardly. Jealous?"

"Not unless you've got some little Mexican girl hidden away somewhere."

He blushed deeply. "I have known no woman in my life."

"Nor have I known a man."

I hope not, he thought, as he left Rosewood. He was hardly a fool when it came to knowing his twin brother like an open book. He had been well aware of the dividing of Elena's time between himself and Raoul. And throughout that time there had been no doubt as to what Raoul's true motives might have been. He had been unable to shake himself free of the exasperating, maddening thoughts that Raoul might have tried to use Elena in the same way he had seen him use girl after girl in Spain. He prayed that Elena had not lied to him. He wanted her. God, how he wanted her forever! But he had sense enough to realize Raoul's desire of her as well. They had been born a duo but could not continue sharing the same woman as a trio. So he had to break up the triangle now. At once . . .

Ramon had purposely timed the three-hour ride back so that only the drawing room window of the pink villa would be aglow with lights. He knew his brother's habits as well as he knew his own. This was the quiet hour before midnight that Raoul could secretly fortify himself with several drinks before going out to seek other forms of amusement.

Raoul sprawled out in a wing-back chair and stretched his drinking arm to Ramon.

"Little brother," he shouted, "I expected you to stay the weekend. Come join me in one . . ."

But Ramon remained standing, shaking his head.

"Raoul," he said hoarsely, "I—I came to tell you—"

"Yes, Ramon? Tell me what?"

"About Elena," he blurted.

"Elena? What about her?"

"It's—it's just that Elena and I are going to get married next fall."

It was out now. He had never thought he would be able to say it.

Raoul didn't answer him. He sat very still in the chair and his mouth tightened slowly into a hard line. Ramon realized that he was not going to fight him—that there would not be any scene. But the silence was infinitely worse.

Then, ever so slowly, Raoul stood up. With deliberate purpose he reached down and picked up the liquor decanter. Then he stood and emptied a quarter of it down his throat.

"Preparing yourself for Marta Ruiz?" Ramon asked sarcastically.

"I have no need for a whore tonight," Raoul said simply. "I am going to Rosewood."

"You don't understand," Ramon said. "Tía Esa's already given her consent."

"How nice," he sneered. "I'm going to discuss the matter with Elena." He turned and looked his twin brother full in the face. "*While* we're in bed," he added softly.

Ramon stood there foolishly questioning whether Elena had lied to him. The crash of the door, as Raoul slammed it, awakened him from his reverie. Then he turned and went up to his bedroom, fully content in his heart that Elena was as virginal as himself.

It was almost morning before Raoul came in sight of Rosewood and realized that this was not the way to handle the situation. But once the idea of how to handle it most effectively came to him, he acted immediately. He turned about and went right back to the ranch, writing the letter he had been drafting in his mind during the long ride as soon as he arrived.

It took two months for the letter to be delivered and another two months for the reply to come back. It was unfortunate that Teresa was the one to receive the reply and in person.

The Independence stagecoach had broken down so many times during its trip that a graying dawn was breaking over Santa Fe before it arrived. There was no one to greet it, and the passengers were left to fend for themselves. A tall and stately woman pushed the annoyance from her mind, walked the few blocks familiar to her, and climbed the stairs to the gothiclike mansion. Her intent on her mission was so fierce that she paid no heed to the fine tracery of travel dirt upon her face.

She recognized the face of the woman who opened the door to her but could not recall her name.

"I'd appreciate it," she said, "if you'd awaken my son for me. "I am the countess of Medina."

"I am aware," Carmen said coolly, remembering the woman's last visit. "But I am afraid your son is off on a business trip."

"Then who else is here?" she demanded shrilly. "The house is ablaze with lights for this ungodly hour."

"Yes, madame," Carmen replied aloofly. "Doña Teresa is here. And I don't think I have to awaken her. She's in the study. Truth to tell, she hasn't been to bed, and it's had me most worried."

"Why in the world would she be here in the first place?" Emilia wondered aloud, more to herself than to the old Mexican housekeeper.

Carmen snorted. "House is hers. She lets Don Estavar live here because she don't have no use for it."

Teresa was sitting in a big chair before a dying fire. Her hair was disarrayed, and she had loosened the top few buttons of her high-collared dress.

"Em," she gasped, "wherever in the world did you pop in from?"

"What is going on?" Emilia snapped.

Teresa's jaw dropped a little. "Going on? What the devil do you mean?"

"This marriage," Emilia said grimly. "I'm here to stop it."

"There may not be a marriage," Teresa said calmly. "Your trip may have been in vain."

"Don't lie to me! Raoul wrote me about everything! I've forgiven you for the past, Teresa Escovarro; but I will not let you get your hands on one of my sons to marry to that whore-bred daughter of yours!"

"Forgiven me!" Teresa roared, rising in one motion. "Thank you, Emilia. Thank you for forgiving me for the time your husband tried to rape me in Beauwood. Thank you for forgiving me for the time he raped me here and made me pregnant. Thank you for forgiving me the time he kicked the hell out of me and left me to drown in the river.

Thank you for forgiving me the fact that he could have saved his brother's life and stood silent and let him be killed. And thank you for reminding me of something far more important. I may just be tempted to send an affixture to their wedding banns attesting to the fact that Elena not only was born to a whore, but unwittingly acquired one as a mother-in-law."

Emilia sank into a chair, feeling the stiffness in her limbs. Yet for some reason she felt as though she would never move again. She had heard too much, too soon, and every word of it had rung with the truth she had feared for years but had never had the real courage to admit and face up to.

"I'm—I'm so ashamed," Emilia whispered. "Please forgive me. I never knew what Miguel put you through."

"Because you loved him," Teresa said simply, "and you were a loyal wife, Em. There's nothing on earth blinder than that. But as far as Elena and Ramon are concerned, it has been taken out of our hands for the moment."

"Oh?"

"That's why my sleepless night," Teresa said grimly. "I came into Santa Fe this morning to begin making preparations with Bishop O'Dair for the service. The arrogant old codger refuses to perform the service because he does not recognize Elena as having been properly baptized. Tell me something, Em. Were any of your children ever baptized in any way whatsoever?"

"Of course," she said gruffly, her throat suddenly tight on the apparent lie.

Teresa laughed. "That was the stumbling block he threw at me time and time again today. Well, it's no longer a stumbling block. There are other ways for them to get married."

"Dear God, Teresa! I'll be finished in Spain if it is . . ."

Teresa bent forward a little, her soft lips smiling.

"It has nothing to do with our lives, Em! You see, we've lived pretty full ones to date. You were made to suffer because you wanted to marry Miguel. How can you, of all people, deprive these children of that same desire?"

Emilia looked at her and smiled with grim mockery.

"I was not then who I am now," she said. "I have no other choice but to fight this marriage every step of the way."

"Señora," Teresa said clearly, "I must then ask you to leave my house."

"What?" Emilia roared, half rising from her chair. "At this devilish hour of the morning. Where do you expect me to go?"

"Your husband's former house is still occupied by his mistress. There you will at least have something in common with the lady of the house."

Emilia rose as though she were Queen Isabella herself and glowered down at Teresa.

"Poor Teresa," she sneered. "I'm afraid you've grown quite unworldly. Just sit back and watch the power that I can command to break you and avert this foolish marriage."

Teresa only smiled and began to put a new plan to work in her agile mind.

"You're what?" Emilia bellowed a few days later at her son.

"Must I repeat myself, Mother," Estavar sighed. "I said I have no other choice than to attend the wedding."

"I flatly refuse to let you go," she declared stoutly. "I can just as easily disinherit you as I did Ramon this morning, remember that."

Estavar grinned wickedly. "Which means I would lose nothing that I didn't want in the first place."

"Don't be snide!"

"Just practical, Mother. Auntie Esa is the biggest depositor in the bank and Elena is the next important director on the board to myself. I can't afford to snub this wedding."

Emilia scoffed. "Rubbish! You talk of mere peanuts!"

"Don't be common, Mother. I am well aware of international affairs and more aware of local affairs. If she wished, Auntie Esa could probably buy the entire country of Spain twice over at the present time. Isabella isn't exactly the best administrator in the world."

"Don't be a damn fool!" she said bitingly. "You could

become the count of Medina upon my death, in case you are interested."

"Mother," he said softly, a look of profound pity in his eyes. "That is your world, not mine. Throughout my younger years Father tried to make his world mine and that didn't work either. All of this pulling and tugging left me rather a cold, callous, insensitive person." He laughed derisively. "Odd that Doña Patricia saw that those were the exact qualities needed to be a successful banker. You offer me the chance at a royal title. Napoleon and his Empress Eugénie are selling such a prize on the open market to finance their Franco-Prussian war. By the time I reach your age, there are going to be more and more democracies like America and fewer and fewer monarchies. The former are founded upon finance and industry. You are overlooking the fact that at twenty-one years of age I am probably the youngest bank president in this vast new American giant. Between my bank, the Santa Fe Overland Express, and the farm and ranch holdings of the various other members of the family, we can have our own empire."

"Which forces you to work with people you've looked down upon your whole life!" Emilia said cruelly.

"I no longer see them as people," he said indifferently. "They are just so many dollar-and-cent figures that flow in and out of my bank." Then he got up from the chair and walked toward the door. In the doorway he turned.

"Go back to Spain," he said. "Go back to Marta—make her the object of your royal title. Who knows, you may be able to marry her off to someone higher than a count."

Even though Judge Hardy Simmons nervously conducted the service in a language he was finding very difficult to learn, Teresa thought the day developed quite beautifully.

It was not as lavish as her own wedding, although Rosewood made a spectacular setting for such an event. It was all for naught, because Elena stole the show. Walking slowly down the curve of the stairway, with a stateliness totally unlike the elfin dance of her usual gait, she was like a red rose wrapped in satin and lace. Elena, at twenty-seven, still kittenish, still a darer, was mercurial and virginal, as wild as a forest creature within, as tame as a house cat without. And watching her, Teresa suspended judgment on what manner of mother she would become, while what was left of her own youth looked upon her daughter with joy.

The fiesta was small, because the main celebration was to come after the honeymoon . . .

"Scotland," Estaban Duran said thoughtfully. "Why Scotland?"

Teresa laughed. "Why to see the castles and the heather and the fox hunts."

"A fox, all right—crazy like a fox," Estaban said. "He's going to buy more of those Black Angus cattle, isn't he?"

Teresa shrugged as though she knew nothing. "I'm giving them title to Felix's ranch."

Estaban frowned. "Right across the river from Raoul?"

"He will get over his hurt feelings," she said soundly. "I think he even would have attended today if Emilia hadn't turned churlish and decided to stay with him for a few days at the pink villa. But enough of them. I wish to discuss you. Now that you have also decided to marry, I want you to come and manage the Mexican farms for me. You can have the big farmhouse for your bride."

Estaban was stunned and he could only think aloud: "What of my family and the old farms?"

"I'm going to give each farmer title to the plots they farm. Elena and Ramon can buy directly from them. You may move your parents here if you wish; that is entirely up to you."

"It will be entirely up to my mother," he grinned. "Because it will be the first time in their lives they have owned anything, she will say stay."

"There is another matter," she said heavily. "I can't get out of my head reading of those debates between Mr. Douglas and Mr. Lincoln. Passions are getting to the fever pitch over this slavery question. Mr. Lincoln is right when he says that a house divided against itself cannot stand. If he gets elected this coming fall, it will mean war. There is no doubt in my mind that Texas will side with the proslavery forces. That will put the war right close to home, Estaban. We will probably have to protect ourselves more then than we do now. I wish you upon this land because I will not have Elena here to ride with me, if I make myself clear."

Estaban's face at that moment was a study in heroine-worship. Teresa found the look embarrassing.

"On that same note," she said quickly, "I am going to say something that you are to forget I ever said . . . or even suggested. Not only the territorial government, but now the Roman Catholic Church has outlawed a certain religious society that I will not call by name. Although this Chimayo area is developing quite rapidly, I think you will find yourself quite alone when you move here. I don't think you should be alone by the time war comes."

"I understand," he said simply. "I will make sure that I am moved here within the month, Doña Teresa."

"Raoul!"

Elena gasped out the name and stared.

"Hello, Elena," he grinned as though he had seen her but the day before.

"Dear me, Raoul! I declare I'll be a week recovering from the start you've given me! We were talking about you only at breakfast. We were both absolutely certain you were going to stay in Spain forever."

"Am I to be invited in?"

"Of course. Ramon's up in the nursery." He made such a startled expression that she laughed. "You have a nephew—Rolando—who is almost three months old. You had better go get acquainted."

Raoul took the center hall steps three at a time and walked into the first open door. Ramon stood by a crib, pale and wide-eyed. "It is, by God! It *is* you. Nobody else gallops stairs like that."

Raoul approached him, stretched out a hand uncertainly, and then put out both arms. They locked in a back-slapping *abrazzo*. Raoul backed off awkwardly and abruptly. "I owe you an apology. I was feeling hurt that you won Elena and stupidly let Mother talk me into escorting her back to Spain. I'm sorry." He walked away from him and went to stare down into the crib. "Well, you finally have evidence that you learned how to use the thing. I had forgotten that little babies look like nothing but little babies." As though he had returned from an errand in town, he chattered right on. "You didn't miss much by not attending Marta's wedding. The Marques de Cadiz is almost as attractive as poor Marta is unattractive, plus Mother almost went livid when she found out he is near penniless . . ."

That was how the matter was left. Raoul went back to the pink villa, and within a few days the old routines were restored. It was as though Emilia had never disinherited Ramon, as though Raoul had never been away for fifteen months. Raoul saw to the general running of the south ranch but left the cattle for both ranches under Ramon's guidance.

The return was hardest on Elena. She had had fifteen months to banish all thoughts of comparison but was again faced with it daily. Marriage was not what she had anticipated, although she was gleefully happy with her child. She had become so used to being a daily part of the bustle of Rosewood and a sounding board for Teresa that she suddenly felt rather useless in doing nothing more than running the house and seeing to Rolando.

It was such an unusually mild winter that the Santa Fe River hadn't frozen over by late February. One night at dinner Ramon hardly spoke, ate less than usual, and helped himself to two glasses of wine. In that household, where things were so monotonously the same day after day, night after night, the first glass startled Elena, the second totally shocked her. Finally she said, "Ramon, what was the visit from Estavar about today?"

Ramon came out of an abstracted stare with a little headshake. "Texas has left the Union and become a Confederate state."

"Even before Mr. Lincoln is inaugurated next month?" Elena said.

"That's the odd part. They seem to be cutting off their

noses to spite their faces. Estavar has learned that because of the antislavery raids in Kansas last year, the shippers in Dodge City grew frightened and refused to accept any of the Texan herds this fall. It's caused the price of beef to soar, and the supply is short."

"Can't they quietly get the Texas cattle back?"

"Not really," he laughed. "It seems the American cowboy is not like our vaquero. After such a long drive to Kansas he expects to be paid. He can't be paid unless the cattle are sold, and it seems they grew fearful that they would not be paid in returning them. They just vanished and now the plains east of us must be teeming with unattended cattle."

"And you want to get your hands on them?"

Ramon sighed and laid his napkin on the table. "Estavar thinks that would take too long, and they might be too travel worn to bring a good price. Although I wanted to let the Angus breed have this winter to graze, he thinks I should cull out at least a half a thousand and take them north. They're paying a dollar a pound on the hoof. With their added weight it would be like taking fifteen hundred of the Texas cattle."

Elena smiled. "Then if you are leaving tomorrow, why drink so much wine tonight?" Then she added, "You had made up your mind, hadn't you?"

"Yes," he sighed. "I just didn't want to leave you alone."

"Nonsense! I would go with you if I didn't have Rolando to look after."

It never dawned on her that Raoul would not go along. It never dawned on her that Raoul would show up for his customary Sunday dinner with them, even though Ramon was away. Nor could she have foreseen the fact that a killing sleet storm would swoosh into the valley so suddenly that they just had time to bring Raoul's horse onto the kitchen porch before he was drenched and frozen in his tracks.

Sudden gloom surrounded Elena. She had made sure that Ramon was present whenever Raoul was around so that she would not be drawn too far into the conversation.

"Stir the fire, Raoul. I'm cold. Maria's brought in green wood, as usual."

As he made the fire blaze, she curled into a wing-back chair and thought it best to keep the conversation about anything but themselves. She launched into a lengthy discourse of what had been happening during his absence—although he had been back for almost three months.

Raoul was bored by every word, yet he was fascinated and grateful for what it was bringing about. She was unwittingly taking him back into her life. These words, which were not personal, were ending the long tension between them.

Elena was the one person he had ever met who meant as much to him as his brother did. In the same way, almost, he hungered for the old relationship with Ramon. Each had felt that it was not the same, as it had not been the same with Elena.

Something in her tone brought him back to concentrate more intently on her words.

". . . and then after Rolando was born, it was almost as if I became more fragile in his eyes. I really wanted another child right away, but Ramon seems hesitant."

"Well, it took him a long time to figure out how to make the first one. Perhaps he thinks it has to be different each time."

"That's hardly amusing, although it sounds exactly like the claptrap you planted in his mind for so many years. He didn't, and still doesn't like a lot of fussing and petting. He was more unsure than I what we were supposed to do. He can't seem to fathom it yet."

Raoul wondered if he had missed something early on in her irritable garrulity. She was gesturing broadly, talking breathlessly, and her eyes were wild. "And then you had to complicate matters."

"Me?"

She stared at him. "Don't you know what you do to me?"

He said or rather stammered, because the sudden penetrating sexuality in her glance altered their normal positions. "I don't think I do."

"All right then, I'll tell you. When I am with Ramon, it is like being with a young boy who so excites himself over the thought of what he is about to do that the fewest strokes possible leave him limp and quivering and completed." She peered at him, her eyes shining and enormous. "I cannot help but wonder what it is like to be with a man!"

Very hoarsely he said, "Do you really want to know?"

He got out of his chair and went to her. She jumped up and they embraced. "Oh, yes," she said, clinging to him, and she kissed him and kissed him. "Yes," she muttered. She thrust her hands in his hair, she caressed his face. "Yes . . . yes . . . yes!"

Hardly a slugabed, Elena forced herself to be one the next morning. She lay tense until she heard Raoul stir in the next room, Maria come to see to the wet-nursing of Rolando, then the house was silent. She rose in a daze, overwhelmed by her emotions. She could still taste his lips, the feel of his body in every fiber of her. She wanted more than anything in the world to feel guilt. She could only feel the fulfillment of her womanhood for the first time.

Foolishly she thought that she would not feel the guilt until someone else was aware of her crime. The roads were much too slick for Pawpaw, and so she had a sleigh and horse harnessed. She pushed aside Maria's warning that the baby should never be out in such icy weather and left for Rosewood.

Teresa's delight at seeing her grandson was overshadowed by her innate ability to sniff out that the trip had another motive as well. She held her silence, knowing Elena could not keep a secret from her very long. It took three days.

"Was Felix a good lover?" Elena popped out at breakfast one morning.

Teresa had to carefully chew the bite of food she had just taken to keep from choking on it. "Yes," she was finally able to say.

"I mean, Mother, when you were first married. Who knew more, you or Felix?"

"If memory serves me correct," she said on a sigh, "he was very shy and conservative and timid. Ramon reminds me a great deal of him."

Elena said with an abashed grin, "If you only knew. Did you ever think what it would be like with another man because he was that way?"

For a moment Teresa sat pondering, holding her hands in her lap, as she saw everything quite clearly. "I only thought how I could make him into the man that I wanted without comparing him. I think that's what you should do as well. If you have come here to bare a guilty conscience, I really don't care to hear the details. I've lived with enough of those in life to know they can't be shared to make them go away."

"Mother, whatever are you talking about? I've done nothing to feel guilty about."

It was the first lie ever between them—Elena wasn't sure why she had even uttered it—and this breaking of their long, tacit truthful relationship gave her an awkward, unpleasant sensation. Here was her guilt, but not in the form she had been expecting.

Teresa was also aware, forcing her into a certain aloofness toward Elena, and bringing a horrible dread into her heart.

Elena had gone to Teresa to rid herself of one form of guilt and took to Ramon's bed on the first night of his return to rid herself of another form of guilt.

"Oh, Jesus Christ," Ramon growled, angrily pushing her writhing body flat, "can't you lie still!"

"I was only trying to help get some feeling into it."

"Well stop," he snapped. "You're not some whore in a brothel that has to do it that way. You're just a wife. Now lie quiet and let me do what I'm supposed to do."

Her body went rigid, almost unyielding. He took it as little more than a command to his order.

Elena walked through the next weeks in a fog of shocked grief. This was all her love life was ever to be. She was not even going to be able to remake Ramon, as Teresa had done with Felix. Each day she began to see more and more of what Raoul had sensed and protected for years. Ramon's shyness had made him very self-centered and self-interested. In obtaining Elena, he had achieved a minor goal; a first in outdoing his brother. He had looked upon Rolando with the same curious interest he had gazed upon the first calf brought about by his inbreeding process. To him it was a marvel that he had achieved both purposes. But like the mother of the calf Elena was just another cow to give forth with another child. The bull showed no emotion on his part of the process, and Ramon saw little reason why he should show emotion either.

In his ears he could still hear the horrible sounds of human sexual emotion at its worst. Born on a ranch, and with a great clutter of misinformation from Raoul, he had concluded that the tirade mating of his mother and father had produced an inferior product—a stillborn child hardly developed. Quietly he began to study the bulls and the cows—and make rather odd comparisons with his own family. The normal bull would work himself into a feverish lather, charge the docile cow, penetrate for a quick few thrusts, and retreat snorting of his superiority. The calf produced from such a union was normally healthy and vigorous. He concluded that Raoul and Estavar must have come from such a human union.

But there were other bulls, he knew, that could not contain their passion. They would hump the cow at once, their eyes wild with desire. They would communicate their fright to the cow, make her dance and fight to get away. She would freeze on him, locking him firmly within her. The pain of the narrowing tissue about his pulsing length would drive him near to insanity. He would low and pound and fight until he could force her to relax for his release or they fell sideways, breaking his length in the fall and requiring his destruction. And for reasons unknown to Ramon such unions usually brought about a sickly, skittish calf that never really amounted to anything. He saw Marta as such an offspring.

And of himself? Because of the vast rarity of twin births in cattle, he had no personal comparison to go by. He was a shadow. If Raoul was to do a thing, it was automatically expected of him. Their names were always connected as though they had come from a single umbilical cord. If love were given, he was left to take Raoul's leavings.

His first original thought had come when he began to daydream in Spain. He saw that he could break from the shadow and succeed on his own as a rancher with a plan for the future. It seemed futile to him to embarrass his shyness any further in attempting to gain a wife when it seemed quite reasonable that Elena was there and available. Because of her *background* he never dreamed his brother would be interested, except for the reason that Raoul was always interested in girls of that class. It had rather excited him to take Elena away from Raoul. He had felt like a bull fighting off the other bulls for an unusual cow in the pasture. And that was his only intent. He was very sure, in his daydream state, that the two of them could produce a better breed of children than his parents had brought forth.

When Elena was fully sure she was with child, she was also fully sure who had fathered it. Now comes my guilt, she thought. I have been so careful to keep Raoul out of my mind and my life since that one time. But now comes my guilt. Thank God I took Ramon to bed on his first night home. Please let him suspect nothing.

"Damn you, woman!" he screamed at her only moments after she had miscarried in her seventh month. "It is your fault for trying to be too amorous that night. You did not take the seed right. I know these things because I have studied them in cows. A waste! A waste! Disaster on disaster around me. The South is going to win this damn war because that idiot Lincoln is trying to be his own general. Bah! Why do I even waste my breath on you, when you're not even capable of carrying the normal length of time!"

Elena closed her eyes so that the midwife could not see the truth that was in them. His words had burned the agonies of guilt right out of her soul. He is mad, she thought, and I must be strong to spring back and protect him. I'm sorry, Raoul. You have tried to warn me for several months of his growing strange behavior, but I thought it was a trick on your part. Now he may be unreachable by love or regret.

It was a shock for Teresa to hear of the change in Ramon. The cruel nature of Miguel she might have expected to show up in Estavar or Raoul, but never in Ramon. She was proud, and yet unhappy, that Elena had not mentioned her troubles while they had been at Rosewood for Christmas. Teresa had seen little difference in Ramon, mainly because he had talked nothing but cattle with her during the visit. It wasn't till mid-March, and a troubled visit from Raoul, that she had learned the truth.

Working to free a frozen pump gear on one of the windmills, Teresa cursed the stubborn gear and her own stubborn nature. As much love as she had for Elena, she did not want to start becoming like her own mother and meddle in a husband-and-wife relationship. She, like Elena, also had to weigh how much of Raoul's story was repeated out of jealousy.

"Excuse me, sir. Might I get water from the trough."

She spun, startled at the English words. Her mind had been so preoccupied that she had not heard the approach. Pushing back the brim of her old work hat, she looked directly into a perplexed, greatly freckled young American face. The gray of his uniform put her instantly on guard.

"Water's brackish!" she snapped in Spanish.

The boy's blue eyes flared. "Sorry, ma'am, I thought you were a man. I don't speak Spanish."

He looked so young that her guard came down. "Gear's stuck," she said in English. "Mill won't pump."

"May I try?" he stammered. "My paw is a miller and taught me some." The boy accurately pointed out the problem, with great relish for his own expertise. "Now a few dabs of that axle grease should set it right. All a body has to do is keep it greased—which this hasn't—and the rigging wrong! It's too bad how people slop their work, given half a chance. Well, there comes the water."

"Let it overflow before you let your horse drink," Teresa warned. "Why, he's lamed."

"Yes'm, he is. Happened a few miles back and I've been out of his saddle since. Didn't seem bad enough to shoot him."

Teresa stooped and examined the fetlock. "You may know windmills, boy," she said sourly, "but don't know horses. It's badly broken."

"I feared," he said, his eyes welling with tears. "My paw gave him to me to go to war. I ain't got the heart to shoot him."

"How old are you, boy?" she asked soothingly.

"Sixteen, April comin', ma'am."

So young, Teresa thought sadly. Why do they always send the very young off to fight the wars?

"If you leave him here," she said softly, "he'll fall prey to the coyotes and buzzards. I suppose it could be splinted, but he'd never be able to carry a full weight again."

"What a time for it to happen," the boy replied nasally, with a none too kind look at the horse. "I was carrying a message for the general. He'll be that furious with me for taking so long to get to Glorietta." He gulped. "Is it much farther to walk?"

"I'm afraid so," she said, masking her immediate interest in his words. "Where did you start from?"

"Santa Fe, ma'am."

"But Glorietta is southeast of Santa Fe," she blurted. "You're far to the northwest."

"Oh no, ma'am," he declared, pulling a wrinkled map from one pocket and thrusting it forward. "The sergeant gave me this."

Teresa took a quick look and laughed. "What were you saying about people who slop their work, son. Whoever drew this map did it upside down. It is hardly your fault."

The boy turned ashen. "You try telling that to General Bowditch, ma'am. He's the meanest s.o.b. in the whole Confederate Army."

Teresa gave him a quizzical little glance. "Would that be Vince Bowditch, by any chance?"

"It sure would," he said gravely. "General Vincent Bartwaller Bowditch."

Teresa burst out laughing. "*Bartwaller?* That has to be something new to go with his rank."

"Do you know him," he gasped, "personally?"

"Too personally," she smiled at her own quick grim joke. "What is your name?"

"Fitzgerald, ma'am. Gerald Fitzgerald of Arch Creek, Arkansas."

"Well, Gerald Fitzgerald of Arch Creek, Arkan*saw*," she mimicked, "this old lady doesn't like the looks of those storm clouds. You tie your horse to the back of the buckboard, and we'll take him back to the ranch. I'll have one of the vaqueros splint him and saddle one of our horses so that you can be on about your general's business."

"I'm sure the Confederate States of America will see to the repayment for the horse," he said seriously if naïvely.

"I'm sure," she answered sourly.

The conversation died there in a sudden cold quiet. There were questions Teresa wanted to ask but did not want to tip her hand too soon. When they were in sight of Rosewood, Fitzgerald shyly stammered: "Who lives there?"

"I may not look the part in my work clothes," she laughed, "but that is my home."

"Golllly," he wheezed. "Down home, people who live like that have niggers to do their work."

Teresa looked at him for an uncomfortable five or ten seconds. "We don't have slaves here, Gerald. We don't believe in it."

He interjected in a sharp serious tone, "We've been told the Mexicans are your slaves."

"By Bowditch, I suppose," she snapped angrily. "Oh, how that insufferable man can twist events to his own purpose. If that were the case, why then did he bring blacks here a few years ago as slaves and then try to enslave an Indian tribe. I'm sorry. You would know nothing of that. I'm just surprised the man has returned here after the beating he took the last time. I will never be able to understand how people can buy and sell one another into slavery."

Gerald's mobile pink face turned grave, and he coughed, glancing at the woman. "Ain't got the answer myself, ma'am. We ain't got no slaves. Paw don't believe in them. He's got sons and sons-in-law to do the work."

"Then why did he send you to fight this war *for* slavery?"

A peculiar flash, not wholly pleasant, came and went in his troubled blue eyes. "My paw's biggest client at the mill didn't have no son of his own. He talked Paw into letting me go as more or less his son."

"Talked, my foot!" Teresa scoffed. "Outright blackmail!"

"That's what my maw said," he said timidly, "but Paw told her to keep quiet 'cause things were bad enough as it is."

"Well, her mind can be a little at ease, you being out here where there's not going to be any fighting."

"There will be tomorrow," he said dully. "That's why I have to get the message to the forces at Glorietta. The Union patrol is coming back from Fort Sumner tomorrow morning, and they don't know we've taken Santa Fe."

Teresa ignored him as though he had not even spoken, although she had come very near to the information she really desired. Expertly she drew the buckboard to a stop and began issuing curt orders.

"Pedro, take the lame horse to your father and see if he can be saved. Fernando, saddle a horse for this soldier, make sure it will be a surefooted one for our terrain. That's some storm coming. Gustavo, ride over to the farm and tell Estaban I want to see him as soon as possible. And now, Gerald Fitzgerald, why don't you come into the house and have a bite to eat while they get a new horse for you."

Teresa agilely jumped from the seat, whipping off her work hat and shaking out her hair. She turned back and nodded for him to comply with a broad smile.

The boy came off the buckboard in a stumbling, stupefied awe. Because of the heavy shadow cast by the wide brim of her work hat and the loose fit of her masculine-type clothing, he had assumed he had been talking to a *very* old lady. She was energetic enough to make them contemporaries: an imposing, rather Dresden-doll beautiful woman of middle age with fine skin, a wealth of soft chestnut hair, and a smile that was gentle and sweet. She firmly took his hand, surveying how she could use that admiring glint in his eye to her advantage.

"I have been most remiss," she said with a soft feminine purr. "I am Doña Teresa Escovarro."

He pulled his hand away as though it had been suddenly stung by a bee. "You got relatives in Santa Fe?"

"Yes. Some nephews. Is something the matter?"

"It's very bad, ma'am. If they have anything to do with the bank and the freight company, then they are in jail and everything they own confiscated by the general."

During all this Teresa was training her eyebrows like weapons at the boy. Bowditch had come back for personal revenge and had struck quickly.

"When," she asked calmly, "did this all happen?"

"When we got to Santa Fe three days ago. We knew the Union patrol was out of the city, and no one expected to see Confederates ride in. The governor gave up at once, and an hour later the general started having certain people arrested."

Teresa took awhile to answer. "Well, Gerald, I guess that I shall just have to ride into Santa Fe and have a talk with my old friend General Vincent Bartwaller Bowditch about the release of my nephews."

His eyes widened. "That would be a waste of your time, ma'am. That's why he wanted the rest of the force to wait for him at Glorietta. He's riding out with the Santa Fe troops to meet them and crush the Union troops."

Teresa grinned and headed him toward the house. Over her face came the look of complacent, devilish slyness. "Then I'll just have to await his return to Santa Fe."

A crashing thunderstorm, with thick rain hissing down from skies black as night, did not stop the young soldier from accepting new directions and going about his mission. Teresa waited for Estaban in the breezeway where a cool damp wind brought in a smell of rainy grass and the promise of a very early spring.

She didn't even greet him but launched immediately into what she had learned.

Estaban made a skeptical face. "What can we do?"

"If the Confederate troops are on their way to Glorietta

in the morning, I anticipated that you and some of your *friends* could successfully raid the jail."

"And you?"

She frowned. "I'm not fully sure of the size of the Confederate force. I can ride to the ranch tonight and get Raoul and Ramon to roust out their vaqueros. No one would question their movements because the new grazeland almost touches the Mexican village."

"I agree."

After another silence Teresa said, "Other riders would be helpful."

Estaban gave her a stare and then smiled. Teresa remained impassive. "You must handle the message very carefully, Doña Teresa," he said. "Many were unhappy with Don Diego when he revealed himself to you. But when he died, they no longer worried about you." He hesitated. "They are unaware of our relationship, you know. I have never told the Penitentes that I helped you at the Santo Domingo village or here on the ranch. This was for your protection."

"Time is wasting," she said shortly.

Estaban's answer was as sharp and short as his former speech had been wordy. "Say: 'The love for Jesus and Spain must never die,' is all."

Teresa said rapidly: "To whom?"

"Guido Herrera!"

Teresa found it surprisingly easy to accept the fact that the old foreman of the vaqueros could be the exalted ruler of a clandestine group of men that most considered composed mainly of the rich dons. He had always been the quiet force behind the successful operation of the south ranch. What troubled her was that it was almost contemptuous the way Estaban had spat out the name. Not contempt for Guido, but toward her. As though Estaban had been forced into the admission because of who he was and who she was.

"Thank you," she said slowly and carefully, "but I was thinking of something else when you said the name, Estaban, and didn't hear it. It's all right! Please, don't repeat it. Perhaps tomorrow is a time for vaqueros and dons to ride as themselves to keep this from becoming a slave state and territory. I shall ask for help in that way, starting with the foreman of the Ranches of the Two Brothers."

Like a grandee he quickly took her hand and touched it lightly to his lips, and then spun and fled on a deep blush, his eyes streaming with tears.

CHAPTER TWENTY-THREE

"Damn!" Teresa snapped.

"You're certainly cursing a lot, Mother," Elena chided.

"You're just lucky I'm not saying what is really on my mind, young lady. What a stupid time for Ramon and Guido to say they're going to be someplace and are not. Did Ramon say why they were taking so many vaqueros with them?"

Elena shrugged with an innocent smile. "Ramon tell me anything? I had to learn from Maria that he left yesterday."

"If Raoul doesn't find them soon, we'll have to do what we can with the twenty vaqueros we have."

Elena's smile went away. "You mean it, Mother?"

The words were bitter in her mouth. "I'd rather die than let that slave monger get a toehold again."

Elena nodded. She hadn't heard her mother speak like that in years. It made her as cold on the inside as the outside. They had been riding for hours in winter blackness and in deadly silence. They had left the ranch as a party of thirty-three, with Teresa's spirits fearless. She became vulnerable to a tinge of doubt when they came upon the grazeland camp and found it deserted. Not even the old Mexican cook was with the chuck wagon. It would not have been unusual to find the base camp thus during spring roundup—small bands of vaqueros being gone for days to search out the cattle on the one hundred and fifteen thousand acres. But it was only March 26, nearly two weeks before the roundup would normally start. It puzzled Teresa. She sent Raoul and ten of the vaqueros off on a frantic search while she kept the others moving steadily toward the foothills and Glorietta.

The graying dawn seemed to make the air chillier. The low-hanging clouds would keep the mountains from view, and the rising sun would offer a dismal light and no promise of warmth.

"My God!" said Elena. "There they are! There they come! Where on earth are the vaqueros?"

They sat in a pine grove, staring down at a camp awakening for the day. Barely visible up the valley came a long stream of horsemen, riding two abreast, their gray uniforms almost a part of the day.

"I don't even think they would help." Elena's voice shook.

The mass of soldiers were coming out of tents like ants from a disturbed hill, filling the air with the sounds of their awakening. She estimated them at over two hundred, with another hundred approaching under Bowditch's command.

Without warning, from the hills behind the camp, the pop and thump of scattered rifle fire seemed pitifully sporadic at first. One "V" wave of vaqueros rode out of a ravine; in the gray distance several more appeared, swelling to unbelievable numbers as they descended upon the surprised camp.

Elena said, "Looks like every vaquero within a hundred miles."

So it seemed, in their first view of this all-out Valhalla attack. So it seemed too in the Confederate camp, where men were falling before they could reach their stacked weapons. But after the first assault they were able to marshal their forces and return the fire. The smell of gunpowder grew stronger; flickering red and yellow flashes gave the camp a fiesta look of exploding firecrackers. The Confederates began to take their toll of the vaqueros.

Elena looked up the valley. What had been a caterpillar column was now slithering like a snake. "They will alter the surprise attack," she said.

Teresa said coldly and abruptly, "Get down the road and find the Union troop from Fort Sumner. Every man is important now."

"What are you going to do?"

"Stall Bowditch as long as I can." Teresa suddenly

looked about as ugly as she could: a grim, nasty face with hate scored on it by the set of her mouth.

She rode the vaqueros along the crest of the hill, keeping within the shadow cover of the trees. When the column had passed by and was within a half mile of the action, she gave the signal to ride. They came from behind, firing at will and then charging up the opposite hill and back into the woods. The column was unsure whether to go on or prepare for another rear-guard attack. The hesitation gave Teresa time to get the vaqueros abreast of the middle of the column. Again they rode from cover, slicing through the cavalry, turning abruptly and slicing through again. It became an effort to push through the second time, because the Confederates had broken rank and were riding in every which direction, firing at long range and using their rifles as clubs at short range.

A shrill rebel yell, followed by a sharp blow to the shoulder, sent Teresa tumbling to the ground. She rolled and came to an upright sitting position. Several horses dashed past her, inches away. Hardly knowing what she did, she began to crawl toward her fallen rifle. Her body seemed leaden. She felt the same horrible powerlessness that sometimes came over her when she dreamed of being pursued. Horses with shouting riders streaked past her in the sagebrush. There was a thunder of hooves behind her. She rolled aside, but the thundering grew nearer. She was being run down. The rifle was almost within her grasp.

His face a contorted grimace, Vince Bowditch aimed and kept firing his pistol until the wooden stock of Teresa's rifle was shattered

Teresa rose on a note of panic, staggering, was about to fall, when he viciously rode past and cuffed her alongside her head. A sudden blighting pain made sight and feeling fade from her.

But she did not become unconscious to the extent that she lost the sense of hearing the pounding hooves and his satanic laughter. She fought to keep the violent black waves from overcoming her. For a few moments she could not determine where he was. The sounds of this battle seemed to be fading rapidly into the distance. Somehow she stayed on her feet. Soon she fought off the red darkness from veiling her eyes, although her head swam, and she felt pain only dully.

Then she saw that she was facing Bowditch on his horse, and he was calmly reloading his pistol. She could not move a hand; she could not tell if her hands were still attached to her body. Then she heard the report of the pistol. A spray of dirt shot up at her feet like a stone hitting water. The second shot nearly ate through the toe of her boot. The look on Bowditch's face made Teresa close her eyes and quietly prepare to die. She was fearful of the moment when the gun would bark again, but she would not give Bowditch the satisfaction of seeing her cringe or beg for her life.

There was a muttered curse, a short period of silence followed by guttural whisperings, and then a clear voice rang out: "No, General, no!"

A strong shock vibrated through Teresa, and her eyelids swept open. Instantly she associated the voice with Gerald Fitzgerald and experienced a sensation of strange regret. It was not her own death she thought of then, but the boy's. For his interference he would surely be killed by Bowditch, for he had his pistol leveled right at the boy's heart.

"Soldier," Bowditch growled savagely, "ride away and do not mess into matters that do not concern you."

Fitzgerald turned his horse, as though to comply, and then suddenly swung back, bringing the stock of his rifle around in an arc, its molded edge catching Bowditch square upon his Adam's apple. Without moving from his saddle, he seemed to leap, as if a powerful current had shocked him. He dropped the pistol and his hands swept up in a gesture of surprise and pain. An odd little smile froze on his lips. His eyes rolled upward and the broken neck could no longer support his head, and it tilted queerly to the side. The horse, smelling death, reared and tried to be free of its rider. It could not do so and raced wildly away until it stepped into a gopher hole, and horse and rider went tumbling.

Only then did Teresa's limbs give way, and she crumpled as though she had just been unstarched. She was only partially aware that another Confederate soldier came galloping up, shouting at Fitzgerald for the whereabouts of the general. He went off in the direction of Fitzgerald's pointed finger. For no apparent reason her eyes went in the same direction. She saw the fallen horse and the motionless rider, and she knew she was not the one who was supposed to die that day. When doubt was no longer possible, she felt a suffocating sense of gladness and fear and wonder.

"Geesus!" the soldier called, riding back. "Horse threw the general and broke the bastard's neck. I'm getting the hell out of here. The Blues have joined up with the greasers and nearly have the camp wiped out. I ain't going to be no prisoner of war out in this godforsaken country."

It seemed to Teresa only seconds later that Fitzgerald strode to her side, leading the roan. Quapaw reared and snorted when he saw his mistress prostrate. Fitzgerald knelt, still holding the bridle.

"Are you all right?" he asked.

"I think so," she replied, essaying a laugh that was rather a failure. "I thought I was dead for sure."

Dark blood covered his face, and lightning hatred for what he had almost witnessed shot from his eyes. Without a word he lifted her upright and then upon Quapaw. Teresa reeled a little in the saddle, and she had to hold hard to the pommel with both hands.

She saw him gaze furtively into the hills on both sides of the valley. And it surprised her to see the Confederates riding away in panic.

"You—go," she said a little unsteadily. "I'll—get back to Glorietta on my own."

"No, ma'am," he said hoarsely, "I can't. He was going to kill you! Not because of the war, but because he wanted to. I've never killed before, except wild animals. I figure that's all I killed—a wild animal. I don't want to kill no man. You understand? I don't want this war."

Teresa gazed at him, astounded more by his speech than his excessive emotion.

"My dear boy!" she exclaimed. And then she paused. The dark blue uniforms of the scouting patrol were evident even at a distance.

"That is one of my vaqueros lying over there, son," she

said quite calmly. "I think it best that you exchange clothing with him before that Union patrol arrives."

With the patrol was an anxious Guido Herrera. Dust streamed from his sombrero as he doffed it. His dark face seemed to melt as he straightened weary shoulders.

"Bless the Mother of Jesus, you are alive!"

"Thanks to this young vaquero," she said, "and your ability to hold the main force in check."

"It was but one of many," he replied.

She leaned close and whispered. "It takes one to make sure that there are many."

His body went rigid. It was not fear nor embarrassment nor awkwardness. And it was only momentary. In that instant, as her keen gaze searched his dust-caked face, she met the full, free look of his eyes. Her own gaze did not waver, and they glowed with genuine pride. The moment was ruined by the approach of a young Union captain.

"Here comes trouble," Guido hissed.

Indeed he bore some faint resemblance to a thundercloud as he approached. He was a short, powerfully built man, so broad across the chest and shoulders that he seemed almost square.

"Señora Escovarro?" he said quietly.

"Yes. What is it you want?"

"Your cooperation," Captain Webb explained simply. "I wish prisoners and have but fifty men. Your cowboys want to let the rebels escape without running them down. It is your duty to the Union to order them to cooperate."

"Look around," Teresa said heavily. "I can hardly order dead men to rise. These were the vaqueros from my ranch and the only men I could order about. The others belong to my nephews and the other ranchers. There will be much grief without adding to it."

"Then you should see my point," Webb said. "If they escape, that leaves them to come back and fight again."

Teresa smiled a slow, quiet smile.

"I seriously doubt that, Captain."

Webb studied her curiously.

"I think I can change your mind," he said. "At Fort Sumner we have felt all along that your people would side

488

with the Confederates. The Union has the power and the right to declare martial law and confiscate all weapons owned by territorial citizens."

"Really?" Teresa gripped the pommel so hard her knuckles turned white. "I suddenly see that the only difference between the Union and the Confederacy is the color of their uniforms. The one side wishes us to have slaves and the other side to make slaves out of us. We did not battle today, sir, for the Union. We fought for our land, our heritage, our freedom. You will have a hard time imposing your will with fifty men—five hundred men—fifty times that number. Come, Guido! Come, Gerald!"

"Wait," Webb said shortly. "I think the scene at Glorietta will make you change your mind."

It only made Teresa's resolve more absolute. The anger and disgust inside her at such human waste were bitter as wormwood. And because Captain Webb knew that she would be personally touched by tragedy and said nothing, she felt betrayed and shamed that one of the main purposes of the day had been to save himself and his troop from ambush.

The vaqueros lashed their fallen comrades to their horses under the leaden sky. The wind whipped down in gusts, driving the snow before it. They left for their respective ranches in small silent groups, until all that was left were the people from the Ranch of the Two Brothers.

Teresa walked tiredly to where Raoul had knelt on one knee for the longest of times, put her hand on his head, and stroked it like she had done when he was a boy.

Raoul looked up, his face colorless and still, his eyelids moving rapidly in an effort to blink back his tears.

"Auntie Esa," he whispered, "do you know what he kept asking me before he died?"

Wildly Teresa shook her head.

"His cows," he said, his voice clear and toneless. "He asked me to look out for his cows. Not his wife! Not his son! Just his damn stupid cows."

"Come," Teresa whispered, spacing the words one after the other with great pauses in between, "it's time to take him home."

He rose mechanically, no longer fighting Guido's attempts to get Ramon's body onto a horse; then he looked back at Elena's still face.

"You know," he said flatly, "that he was probably thinking of you, too."

"Don't lie!" Elena's voice had the first thin note of hysteria in it. "It is long past the time for lying. At least he had something that he loved. Why not his cows? There was no love for him in his home, with a wife who had turned his marriage into a thing of hatred."

"That responsibility is mine," Raoul whispered. "I never should have come between you."

Teresa put up a tired hand and pushed back an auburn lock from Elena's brow. With an effort she managed a smile.

"This is not the time to look backward," she said, "for any of us, or we'll blame ourselves right into a grave with Ramon. I want to get home. I want to start thinking about tomorrow. We are the only three Escovarros left who have a love for the land. That is our bond—our only bond."

Afterward, when she was in her grandmother's bed in the house that Felix had built for her across the river from the pink villa, Teresa loosed the tears that had to be shed for so many old friends she had lost that day. They were better out of her. Out, they broke another link with the past.

She allowed herself a few moments luxury of remembering her love for Felix. then she devoted her full attention to the future.

Elena would be all right, she knew. In time—respectful time—she anticipated that Elena would marry Raoul. She would not fight it. In time—a very short time—Raoul would have to learn to see after Ramon's cows. That was important to her future dreams. She felt the time to plan for the war's end was while it was still raging in the southeast. She could see in her mind's eye the large herds of stray cattle roaming the western plains of Texas. They were there for the asking if someone had the foresight and manpower to round them up. It was a task that appealed to her sense of conquest of the impossible.

And as a new day was breaking, she rose and went to look out across the fields left covered by the fluffy spring snow. The sky was cloudless, and she knew that the snow would be melted and gone by midday.

That is how they all think of us, she thought. That we will melt and be assimilated into the ground and their way of thinking and their way of life. That would be her biggest job in the years to come, she saw clearly. She would use every bit of her power, her money, her strength, to preserve and protect their Spanish heritage, customs, and language.

Yes, she thought. Yes, my beloved land and people, we will fight to keep you as you have always been. . . .

EPILOGUE

The procession out of Santa Fe was in no way distinguished; a flatbed wagon and a couple dozen silent riders. They made a strange tattoo in the early morning dawn, almost funereal, so quietly did the hooves beat upon the bricked street. The horses' nostrils ejected a ghostly gray mist, a sharp contrast to the somber black ponchos and hats of the participants, their heads huddled deep into their necks to ward off the crisp January morn.

Only the occupants of the wagon seemed alert and immune to the cold. The driver, a handsome youth of sixteen, his dark eyes glistening with the honor which had befallen him, handled the two black bays with the confidence of maturity. He emulated the rider beside him, even down to the starched back and staunch set of the jaw. Manuel loved his great-grandmother with a reverence that knew no bounds. Even though she had forbidden it, he had secreted a six-shooter under the wagon seat, fearing for her safety on this strangest day of his life.

Elena Escovarro did not fear; it was a word she had eliminated from her vocabulary decades before. At eighty she didn't even fear death and some days actually prayed for it when her "ailment" kept her old bones from hardly moving. This day she was determined to make all of her bones work for her. This was the day which had kept her alive.

"*Abuela*," Manuel said softly, reining the horses to a stop beside a long adobe building with squarely arched colonnades. "You wished a stop here."

Señora Escovarro did not answer but climbed from the wagon with the agility of youth. A slight breeze caught at

493

the yards of black lace flowing down from the bone comb perched on her snow-white hair, billowing the mantilla out like a bride's train. The height of the comb seemed to mask how much she had shrunk with age. Taking short, purposeful steps, she went directly to a plaque on the low adobe wall. She had never read the words before; the plaque was only two years old. Now she studied it intently, weighing each "Anglo" word against her Spanish translation:

El Palacio Real
Fortress and Castle Built By Order Of The
Spanish Crown, 1610–1612
Seat of Government Under Three Flags
Spanish, Mexican, and American
From 1610 to 1910
The Residence of Over 100 Governors and Captains General
The Oldest Public Building in the United States

It was not as obnoxious to her as she had anticipated. From the folds of her skirt she extracted an object and placed it at the base of the plaque.

At first it appeared to be nothing more than a common stone. Closer examination showed it to be a rare "desert rose," a piece of gypsum carved by the winds of time into a perfect brownish-red rose.

"Well, Mother," she said, almost as if in prayer, "after three hundred years it comes to this. Now we will see how important this journey is for the future of our people. As you once asked of me, I leave the desert rose to the Anglos to remind them of the land."

Once across the Santa Fe River the procession made its way through a countryside swarming with "native" partisans. The Anglos, territory people of North American stock, rarely ventured into this farming and cattle country. The small communities along the way were Spanish, cohesive, proud, and wary. Some even traced their roots to the days of Francisco Vásquez de Coronado.

The farms were set apart by weathered mesquite wood fences; and the land upon which they sat had once been

494

owned by various members of the great Escovarro family but were now privately owned little farms.

By design the procession avoided the larger communities and traveled by unfrequented circuitous farm roads, a factor which would keep them from their destination until sunset. But had Elena Escovarro been careless and unlucky, had her people been arrested and the wagon searched and her true mission uncovered, her delay would have been longer, perhaps permanent. After her fight to have the new state constitution ratified in both English and Spanish, the authorities were in no mood to allow her further power.

It was not until they were in higher, ruggeder, more dramatic country that Manuel became alarmed.

"Who are they, *Abuela*? And where do they come from?"

Elena, who had been napping with her chin on her chest, turned and surveyed the road behind her family riders. The deep creases of her face smoothed into a knowing grin at the increase in the procession. A hundred or so natives, Spanish and Mexican, had fallen to the rank, some on burros, but mostly afoot.

"They are our people," she sighed, gently patting him on the leg as she turned forward. "They had sensed my purpose and have come out of respect."

"Excuse me if I sound insolent, Great-grandmother," he said with caution, "but what is our purpose? Tonight there shall be a great celebration in Santa Fe to honor our becoming a state today. Shall we miss it?"

Elena laughed, a high dry cackle. "Oh, *niño*, will you never learn not to ask so many questions at once. And as usual I shall answer you backward. No, we shall not get back to Santa Fe this day, and perhaps never for me. Let the Anglos have Santa Fe, we shall do our celebrating at the ranch near Chimayo. That should please you, you haven't seen your cousins in a couple of years."

Manuel's mind was instantly averted from such a pleasant thought. A group of seven men stood to the side of the road a few yards ahead, their faces totally shadowed by the wide brims of their gaily decorated black sombreros. But it was their hands that kept Manuel's eyes and mind alert. Each possessed a lethal-looking knotted whip of black cowhide.

Before Manuel could speak, Elena had raised her hand and arm in greeting, almost with the same quiet dignity a Pope would bless the masses in the square below him. And the acknowledgment was just as regal, each señor doffing his sombrero and arching it down as though dusting his boots. They kept their heads bowed until Señora Escovarro had passed them by and then they joined the procession. Moments later discordant music from reed pipes erupted here and there among the marchers.

"Fools," Elena said proudly. "Their arrogance could cost them their lives."

Manuel's heart was aquiver. He had just viewed some of his heroes without realizing it—and the reed pipes suggested there were scores more such men in the growing throng. But that his great-grandmother would know of the Penitentes and openly salute them amazed him.

"You know such men?" he asked respectfully.

"One does not ask such a question," she said reproachfully, "or the very fiber of their secret religious society would be put in jeopardy."

"But you have always been so against them in public."

"Just as in public I am against children being insolent to their elders, but I seem to let you get away with it in private."

Manuel laughed; it made his dark eyes dance and his smooth golden face glow. "You always said that was because I was so much like your mother."

"Yes, yes," Elena sighed. "And the reason you drive me today, *niño mío*. This is really her day, you know, and I wish you to learn more of her."

Manuel's smile broadened further. "Then I have guessed correctly. On this wagon we carry a headstone for her grave, *sí*?"

"*Sí*, you little snoop," she chuckled.

"But I have yet to learn what is in all the boxes," he queried tauntingly.

"And that you will only learn when the time is ripe for their discovery. They are also for her."

Manuel was content to wait, as long as he now knew that the journey and the mysterious boxes had something to do with a woman he had never met but whose history he knew as well as his own.

He always regretted the fact that he had been born on the same day Teresa Maria de Alarcon Rosa Escovarro had passed away in her sleep. His mother and father never spoke of the woman, due mainly to the fact that his father's mother had detested the woman. It was not until he was old enough to come off the ranch and gain some education in Santa Fe that he came under his great-grandmother's gaze and began to learn of his heritage. Ever since he had clung with rapt attention to each and every word mentioned about her, knowing in his heart that she had to be just as strong and powerful a creature as Doña Elena.

"Do you feel that, Manuel?" she asked, her voice rising with excitement.

He could feel the change, and it amazed him. They were coming out of a bleak and desolate region and mesquite and piñon pine forest and descending into the fertile valley of the Rio Grande. Here the fierce cutting winds of the cruel Sangre de Cristo range lost much of the January chill. No Spaniard, bred in the frigid winters and scorching summers of Santa Fe, could ever pass into Chimayo without sniffing the breeze of wonderment, convinced in his heart that the breed of men in this region was of pure Spanish blood: amiable, seductive, sensuous, close-knit, and peaceable. This was the true land of his heritage, the earth on which Doña Teresa trod during her last days. They were in friendly territory now; he no longer feared for Doña Elena and beheld the land as though seeing it for the first time.

"Look at it good, son," she said. "There are those, even among our own people, who will try to change it and steal it away."

"It is so large."

"Large," she laughed. "That is what really frightened the Anglos in their Washington City, Manuel. Until yesterday we were five hundred miles wide, stretching all the way to the Colorado River and the boundary of California. To the north only the Great Canyon and Raton Pass separated us from the Mormons' Utah and the Colorado state. We were so mighty they are making two states out of us, although there seems to be some delay about Arizona.

"Large," she repeated. "Oh, my boy, it wasn't just land size that frightened them; we are still larger than the state of New York. It was our size combined with the Indians that they still fear. They do not understand how we can get along; that the Indians find us more sympathetic, all in all, than they do the Anglos. They forget that our association with all of these tribes is over three centuries old and that we have had the Anglos among us for just a half century. I'm sure that if they had had their way, we, too, would be on reservations without the right to vote or leave that boundary line."

"I hate them," he snarled.

"Hate is a strong word," she counseled. "Not even Doña Teresa hated that strong. You cannot hate an entire people because of the brazen, arrogant, foolish ways of a few. Those were the ones she fought, the 'robber barons' she called them; greedy, self-seeking men who used graft and cunning to gain what was not rightfully theirs. She fought them until her dying day and then left others to fight in her place. But she also had great compassion for the little man, the emigrant who wished no more than a homestead to build upon and raise his family."

"Like the Fitzgeralds," he enthused.

Doña Elena only nodded, not wishing to delve into that subject matter. Her mother had considered it a debt of honor to allow the young confederate soldier to homestead a piece of their Glorietta land after the war; seeing as how he was instrumental in saving Teresa's life from the Confederate General Bowditch. But now Gerald Fitzgerald's children and grandchildren were as scattered as the Escovarro clan, having grown more powerful during the Lincoln County cattle war, while the Escovarros had suffered the most. But their growing power was not what stayed her tongue at this moment. Even in her adobe-walled Santa Fe hacienda, where men of politics and wealth came to pay her court, she had heard the snickering rumors about the "budding" romance between Manuel Escovarro and Linda Fitzgerald. With matriarchal speed she ordered Manuel in from the ranch for further schooling. Lesser members of the family could see to the daily running of the ranches and the farms, only one could someday replace her and Teresa as the business head of the family. She had decided upon Manuel before he had even reached his teens, and she would not condone a "mixed" marriage in the family, and especially between Manuel and a Fitzgerald.

The church of the village of Chimayo sat like a great adobe and wood rock on the plateau above the old village, "old" because it was little different than a remote clutter of buildings in Castile. None but the native born could love its windswept, sun-scorched vastness. Elena, like her mother before her, loved it intensely, with a fierce Spanish love. They loved as well the green trees in the river valley, the grass on the steppelike plain for cattle to graze that produced some of the finest beef in the nation, bringing prosperity to cities like Albuquerque; and the stubborn earth could be made fruitful by the industry of peons as hardy and stubborn as the earth itself.

But here on the plateau Elena's love was for the two massive cottonwood trees which provided a natural gateway to the *santuario*, and the walled garden that imposed the scene with a sad tranquility. As Elena alighted from the wagon, a different sadness overcame her. She had wished all of her family to be around her this day, but her daughter, Manuel's grandmother, had stubbornly refused to make the long journey into Santa Fe and then this even longer journey to Chimayo. And because she ruled her family with as strong an iron grip as Elena ruled the "entire" clan, Manuel's father and mother were not in attendance either.

"Rolando," she barked at her son as though he were a child and not a man in his fifties. "Get your sons to unload the crates, while I go in to pray. Then the women can begin the distribution, and you go with Manuel to place the stone on your grandmother's grave."

He leaped down from his saddle, opening his mouth to speak, but she interceded.

"And mind you, Rolando, the canvas covering will stay intact until I have arrived."

"That was not my question, *mamacita*," he faltered. "I think we underestimated."

Elena blinked, shielded her eyes from the setting sun, and stood transfixed. The end of the procession had not as yet cleared the piñon pine forest, and that was three miles back. Tears of happiness sprang to her eyes, and her throat turned dry.

"Do the best you can," she rasped and turned quickly to enter the old sanctuary.

Word of the procession had preceded its arrival. Women were kneeling everywhere, surrounded by praying children. They hushed as Elena made her way down the clay floor center aisle, past the religious ornaments, both fantastically primitive and fantastically ornate. Along the walls of adobe stood the crutches of the maimed—those who had been cured by the healing sands dug from a pit that is supposed to never fill up. To Elena's one side was a Mexican flag, behind lace curtains; to her other side heavy pearls looped around the neck of Christ. But an obstacle loomed before her, cutting off her advance to the altar rail.

The priest was a large man and glared down at her like an errant child. She was not intimidated.

"If you move, *Padre*," she said icily, "I would kneel in prayer."

"You are flying in the face of the church," he answered just as coldly. "Our homilies for weeks have ordered that this be a peaceful day."

"Praying is not peaceful?" she asked sarcastically.

"I speak of the rabble you have stirred up to follow you. What is their purpose?"

Doña Elena shrugged. "I am unsure, but I gather the same as my own. We are here to do honor to my mother and place her headstone."

The cleric scoffed. "Sixteen years after her death and on this day of days."

Elena smiled sheepishly. "Well, *Padre*, it does seem long,

but we had to find a special marble to our liking and have it brought from Italy."

The priest was furious. "You mock this holy place, woman. Just as you mocked it by burying her within inches of consecrated ground. You are just as much an outlaw of the church as she was. Out with you! Out with you all," he bellowed. "The church is closing for the night! The church is closing!"

Elena did not budge. Instead she knelt directly in front of the man's legs and began to pray. The red flush deepened on his Irish neck until it was crimson and his mind refused to translate the words he wished to utter into proper Spanish. For the first time he resented the power the church had to place men such as himself in embarrassing political situations to the advantage of only the church. For too long the money from these Southwestern Catholic churches had been drained down through the bishops in Mexico. Now, with full admission to the United States, the money would flow through New York and Boston to Rome. This he could understand; he would never understand the people he had been sent to shepherd.

The Spanish-American rich were far too rich and seldom, if ever, supported the church in the manner it demanded. The Spanish-American poor were far too poor and could not, even when they wanted to, support the church in the manner it demanded of them. The Mexicans were considered too poor to even support themselves, let alone the church. Since his arrival, ten years before, he had prayed for a transfer, even to a mission in blackest Africa. Now he was determined that this old woman and her peasant following were not going to put a black mark on his record and ruin his chances forever.

But when he reached down to forcefully bring Elena to her feet, a noise erupted in the chamber that made him jump back in alarm. The women and children were all on their feet, glaring at him with open hatred, a steady, slow hiss escaping from their lips.

"Please," he whispered to Elena's bowed head. "They will wreck this ancient building unless you leave at once."

Elena crossed herself and slowly rose. "I, *Padre*," she

said slowly, "do not seem to be the bone of contention, nor this building. In it we worship our God and not the little men who try to take his place. Outside I have brought you your flock. Will you come and bless them and the stone for my mother's grave?"

It was a trap, he now saw clearly. He could not do the one without doing the other. He would offend his parishioners if he did not acknowledge them; he would offend the church authorities if he kowtowed to the Escovarro family. He firmed up his jaw and looked directly over her head to the back of the church.

"I shall do neither," he said tonelessly. "The sun has set; the church is closed."

Elena turned and majestically marched up the aisle, a smile of triumph beginning to play upon her lips. Silently the other parishioners marched out on her heels.

Father Donovan felt the pangs of defeat grip his heart. He had failed the church and himself as a man.

Elena's spirits soared as she came out between the cottonwoods and espied the arrival of her youngest son and his family. Next to Manuel, Tomas was the light of her life. At forty, he reminded her so much of herself at that age— the reddish-brown hair of the desert rose, eyes more hazel than gray green, a moon face that was etched with a permanent smile at birth. Their warm and demonstrative greeting made Rolando blush. He had never been able to show his mother affection, even in private, and looked down upon his younger half brother for such an unseemly display.

"What are we to do?" Tomas demanded in wide-eyed dismay. "You said plan a fiesta for a hundred or so. *Caramba!* Here must be three hundred."

Patting his cheek playfully, she began to lead him around the church to the graveyard. "We will do what we always do when unexpected company arrives, *niño mío*. We will make them as welcome as the invited, and start cooking anew. *Que sera, sera.*"

What will be, will be, seemed to be Elena's fate that day. She was stopped short of the graveyard by Don Pedro Villena and his wife. Don Pedro, old and fat as the land, was one of the richest and most envied grandees of Chimayo. His power was unique: he occupied the exalted position of keeper of the Sociedad Folklorcia, an association founded in the early days to preserve Spanish culture and history.

"My good wife was in the church, Doña Elena," he said with a sweeping bow. "In my company is a Jesuit monk making a pilgrimage to all of our Spanish missions. Might I prevail upon him to be of assistance to you?"

"I shall leave it in your capable hands, Don Pedro, *mis gracias.*"

It was now nearly dark, although not quite half past the hour of five. Rolando, Tomas, and Manuel stood beside the canvas-draped marker holding aloft pitch-soaked torches. Elena liked the dumpy little monk the moment he was led forward by Don Pedro. Old Spain was etched upon his face, and his sackcloth robe and wood-carved beads were simple symbols for the simple ceremony that she sought.

His voice was warm and mellow, carrying to the far reaches of the crowd. In the faces of the people one could see that he was taken to their hearts at once. Many of the children were hearing the Latin prayers of blessing for the first time, so used to the arcane mumblings of Father Donovan had they become.

Elena shivered as if she were cold. She had known that she would be expected to say a few words, and she had changed her mind a thousand times on exactly how those words should be spoken. Trying to emulate the priest's carrying power, her first words came out sharp and shrill:

"Today, *mis amigos,* President Taft says we are now full citizens of the United States of America."

There was an uneasy stir in the crowd. The hotheads, of course, wanted this great lady to arouse in them the desire to keep fighting the Anglos. Those of sounder reasoning, such as Don Pedro, prayed otherwise; knowing full well that she could be the spark to light the fuse of revolution. Then she softened her tone:

"This President Taft seems to respect our heritage. He has allowed that we may become the first bilingual state in the nation. We may keep our native tongue without having to speak his native tongue. We may keep our native ways and our native heritage. We are today Spanish. We are today American. We are today Spanish-Americans. It is how I think my mother would have wished it to be.

"Tonight, as I uncover her marker, let us commemorate her memory and this day in the traditional manner of our people. Come, let me help light your way to food and drink at the Escovarro hacienda for fiesta. Let us show the Anglos how we can accept the new without giving up a trace of the old."

There were no cheers as she took the canvas covering off the marble marker and accepted a flaming torch from Manuel. Her words had angered some and cheered others, but neither wanted to show their true face to the other. For the majority, however, their silence was due to a show of deep respect for the act they were about to participate in. They also knew there would be plenty of time to cheer when the fireworks erupted at the fiesta. The Escovarro family never did anything halfway.

Now Manuel became aware of what had been contained in the many wooden crates on the back of the wagon. Rolando's two daughters stood by the crates, passing out their contents as the people passed by, and Manuel marveled that Doña Elena would think of such a simple thing as candles.

Every man, woman, and child came forward to Elena and the gravestone. Solemnly, as though she were giving them life to face the newness of tomorrow, they lighted their taper from her torch and gazed at the magnificent slab of black marble, which shone, as though from within, with millions of candle sparkles of its own.

Most crossed themselves and moved on, gasping at the expense the family must have gone to; a few women curtsied, as though at the tomb of a monarch.

It was the faces of the older men who delighted Doña Elena the most. They gazed at the carved image of Doña Teresa on the stone and then their eyes popped in startled surprise. Slowly a grin would crack their lips and they would move on beaming, patting an area under their ponchos, as though in salute, where they had secreted a knotted whip or a reed pipe.

Soon a serpentine of light crawled off the plateau and into the valley. Hesitantly at first, because only the school children knew the difficult words and music, then with growing gusto, the strains of their new national anthem began to fill the night. Although as discordant as the reed pipes had been during the afternoon, and the words being sung in Spanish, it was a symbol of the blending of the old with the new.

At last only two figures stood at the grave, held in the glow of a single torch.

"Burn this night into your memory well," Doña Elena whispered, linking her arm through Manuel's. "It will do much to confuse our enemies. They will think we have given up. But we will fight them by being a small part of them, yet remaining as separate and as united as ever. It is how she would have wished."

"How is it that they remember her, after so many years?"

Elena chuckled. "Nothing is ever by pure accident, my boy. I did happen to mention to a few people where I could be going today. You see how close-knit a family we really are? There were the curious, of course, but I think the older ones came to see how I would reaffirm her place in our history."

"I don't understand, *Abuela*."

"I sent an oil portrait of her to Italy and my demands on how it should be etched. I'm very pleased with their work. Are you not pleased?"

She held the torch closer so that he could examine the relief work closely. Upon a magnificent steed they had placed Teresa in sidesaddle posture; her mantilla flowing down and becoming the interlacing flower pattern among the carved words. The artisan had captured the face expertly; it was patrician and proud.

Elena tilted the torch slightly, and Manuel gasped.

"There's another rider etched behind her, *Abuela*. Who is that?"

"You must figure it out for yourself, Manuel. It is what the older men saw at once and gave them hope for the future."

He stared in bewilderment. The lines were ghostly, as though a part of her and yet separate. The rider wore a flat-brimmed, round hat and the suggestion of a frock coat. The almost indescernible right arm was raised, bearing a knotted whip whose length had been artfully blended into the marble grain so that it evaporated into oblivion.

"Oh, *Santa Maria!*" he gasped. "She was one of the . . ."

The old woman put gentle fingers to his lips.

"She was many things to many people. Tomorrow you will begin to learn all you wish to know, so that you may share her someday with your children and grandchildren. But that is for tomorrow."

But as she climbed up into the wagon, she couldn't help but cry out:

"Oh, Manuel, would you look at that! It's like a swarm of fireflies sweeping across the valley. How she loved candlelight! How she would have loved this night!"